T0284247

LEAVING
INDEPENDENCE

Look for these exciting Western series from bestselling authors
William W. Johnstone and J.A. Johnstone

The Mountain Man

Luke Jensen: Bounty Hunter

Brannigan's Land

The Jensen Brand

Smoke Jensen: The Early Years

Preacher and MacCallister

Fort Misery

The Fighting O'Neils

Perley Gates

MacCoole and Boone

Guns of the Vigilantes

Shotgun Johnny

The Chuckwagon Trail

The Jackals

The Slash and Pecos Westerns

The Texas Moonshiners

Stoneface Finnegan Westerns

Ben Savage: Saloon Ranger

The Buck Trammel Westerns

The Death and Texas Westerns

The Hunter Buchanon Westerns

Will Tanner, Deputy US Marshal

Old Cowboys Never Die

Go West, Young Man

LEAVING INDEPENDENCE

WILLIAM W. JOHNSTONE

AND J.A. JOHNSTONE

KENSINGTON
PUBLISHING CORP.

kensingtonbooks.com

KENSINGTON BOOKS are published by

Kensington Publishing Corp.
900 Third Avenue
New York, NY 10022

Copyright © 2025 by J.A. Johnstone

All rights reserved. No part of this book may be reproduced in any form or by any means without the prior written consent of the Publisher, excepting brief quotes used in reviews.

All Kensington titles, imprints, and distributed lines are available at special quantity discounts for bulk purchases for sales promotion, premiums, fund-raising, educational, or institutional use.

Special book excerpts or customized printings can also be created to fit specific needs. For details, write or phone the office of the Kensington Sales Manager: Kensington Publishing Corp., 900 Third Avenue, New York, NY 10022. Attn. Sales Department. Phone: 1-800-221-2647.

This book is a work of fiction. Names, characters, businesses, organizations, places, events, and incidents either are the product of the author's imagination or are used fictitiously. Any resemblance to actual persons, living or dead, events, or locales is entirely coincidental.

To the extent that the image or images on the cover of this book depict a person or persons, such person or persons are merely models, and are not intended to portray any character or characters featured in the book.

PUBLISHER'S NOTE: Following the death of William W. Johnstone, the Johnstone family is working with a carefully selected writer to organize and complete Mr. Johnstone's outlines and many unfinished manuscripts to create additional novels in all of his series like the Last Gunfighter, Mountain Man, and Eagles, among others. This novel was inspired by Mr. Johnstone's superb storytelling.

The K with book logo Reg. U.S. Pat. & TM Off.

ISBN: 978-0-7860-5088-8 (ebook)

ISBN: 978-1-4967-4613-9

First Kensington Trade Paperback Printing: February 2025

10 9 8 7 6 5 4 3 2 1

Printed in the United States of America

LEAVING INDEPENDENCE

Chapter 1

Wagon master Virgil Grissom was making his final trip around the wagons circled up on the Kansas prairie west of Independence, Missouri. He would be leading them out onto the two-thousand-mile trail to Oregon Territory at seven o'clock the following morning. While he walked the circle, he couldn't help wondering how many more years would see the phenomenon of the wagon train endure. The year was 1865 and the railroad was already plotting its path across the country. Once the railroad was completed, the trip to the West Coast would be a matter of days, instead of months. *Folks would be able to get there a lot quicker,* he thought, *but they wouldn't be able to take a wagonload of their belongings and their horses, too.* "Well, at least it's my last crossing of the country," he muttered to himself. "This time I'm stayin' put in the Willamette Valley while there's still some land left to buy."

The next wagon he came to belonged to a man and his family who sold their farm in a little town in Missouri called Warrensburg. His name was Matt Moran. He looked like a solid, hardworking man, married to a strong woman named Katie, who seemed a cheerful sort. They had three children: Jim, ten; Sarah, eight; and Hannah, five. Matt had a younger brother, who was to be mustered out of the army now that Robert E. Lee had surrendered. "You gonna be ready to roll in the mornin', Mr. Moran?" Grissom called out as he walked up to their cookfire.

"We're as ready as we can be, I reckon," Matt Moran answered. "Least, Mama says we are, and she's the boss."

"I want you to remember you heard him say that," Katie Moran commented.

Grissom laughed. "I'll swear to it, Miz Moran," he replied. Then looking at Matt again, he asked, "No sign of your brother?" Matt's younger brother was supposed to go with them to Oregon, but he had not appeared as yet.

"No," Matt answered, "but in the last letter we got from Clay before we left Warrensburg to come here, he said he most likely wouldn't get here by the tenth of April. The fightin's over and his unit has already been recalled to be mustered out. So he said he was just gonna catch up with us before we got very far ahead of him."

"I expect he's right," Grissom said. "We oughta make about twelve to fifteen miles a day, especially on the first part of the trip, so he should catch us before long, unless he's walkin'. He ain't walkin', is he?"

"Nope," Matt answered, "he's a cavalry officer and they're lettin' him keep a horse."

"How long has it been since you last saw him?"

"It's been about two and a half years," Matt said. "I hope he's wearin' his uniform, so I'll be sure to recognize him," he joked.

"There ain't been no real Indian trouble out that way for a couple of years now," Grissom said, "but it don't never hurt to have a horse soldier along. Mr. Steptoe would probably tell you the same thing," he said, referring to Elmo Steptoe, whose wagon was behind Matt's.

Matt knew why Grissom made the remark. Elmo Steptoe, a bowlegged little man who talked bigger than the shadow he cast, was burdened with the care of three daughters and no sons. His and Cora's last try for a son resulted in a stillbirth, which was a tragic event, especially for Cora, but the baby was another girl, too, which was discouraging for Elmo. He seemed cursed with an inability to produce a male heir. Ike Yocum, Grissom's cook and wagon driver, was convinced it was because Elmo didn't have a hair on his head above his sideburns. Of course Grissom didn't pass that information on to Elmo. To make matters more mystifying, Elmo's eldest, Irene, was fifteen years old and from a kind fluke of nature in the mating of equal parts Elmo and Cora, had turned out to be a decent-looking girl. Behind her, Millie, twelve and Cassie, ten, also looked promising to cause Elmo to eventually lose the hair of his sideburns when they got a little older and the young men discovered them. What seemed the more remarkable to Matt and Katie was the fact that they learned all this on their first night in camp when they met Elmo at the gathering in the center of the circle of wagons.

"Well, I'll see you at four in the mornin'," Grissom said to Matt and Katie. "I'd best go see if Mr. Steptoe and his ladies are ready to go." He continued his inspection of the circle of twenty-four wagons, a smaller number than in his previous trains but enough to discourage any small bands of Indians.

"I'm glad to see we're going to get started in the morning," Katie remarked to her husband when Grissom walked away. They had been parked there since the ninth for the scheduled departure on April tenth, but tomorrow would be the thirteenth of April. "I'm worried that we don't have enough food to get us there as it is," she complained. "I was beginning to believe we were going to eat it all up while we were parked here."

"I know," Matt replied. "Grissom said we would have left on the tenth, if it had been just one wagon that didn't show up, but there were three of 'em. All three showed up; the last one pulled in today. And on the good side, it gave Clay three less days to make up while he's tryin' to catch up with us."

"I suppose that is a good thing," Katie conceded, "if, in fact, he shows up." She remembered a carefree Clay Moran, who was prone to drift with the wind before he left to join the army.

"I expect he will, since he sent us the money to pay for his share of the food," Matt said.

* * *

Matt and Katie both bolted upright the following morning upon hearing the sudden sound of Virgil Grissom's bugle for the first time. Far from an accomplished bugler, Grissom was able to manage a string of unrelated notes sufficiently loud enough to be heard by everyone in the circle of wagons. "Well, sweetheart, he's playin' our song. It's time to go to Oregon," Matt said as ten-year-old Jim stuck his head inside their sleeping tent.

"Does that mean it's time to get up, Pa?" Jim asked.

"That's what it means," Matt answered. "Get that fire started for your mother while I take care of the horses. Are Sarah and Hannah up?"

"I don't know," Jim answered. "I didn't look in their tent." There were two sleeping tents, one for the grown-ups and one for the children. But Jim preferred to sleep in a blanket under the wagon instead of sleeping with the girls.

"Well, tell 'em to get up, so they can help your mother get breakfast," Matt said as he was pulling on his boots. "Then get the fire goin'."

"Yes, sir, but I got to go pee first," Jim said.

"All right, but don't go too far. It's pitch black. Won't nobody see you. I'll be over at the creek with the horses. After you get the fire goin' good, you can go ahead and pack up the girls' tent." Grissom had gotten there early enough to claim a choice camping spot close beside a healthy creek that eventually emptied into the river. The new grass was just beginning to grow, so there was ample grazing for Matt's horses close to the creek.

When he got back to the wagon, the sun was still struggling to get up, but the tents were packed up and breakfast was well on the way. Sarah and Hannah were cheerfully helping with any little job Katie could trust them with. *Just like a great big picnic*, Matt thought. *I wonder how long that's gonna last.*

Katie thought it appropriate to start them off with a good breakfast on this first day of a journey that would change their very lives. When her husband first started thinking about giving up on their modest farm in Missouri and following the confident dreamers to the fertile valleys in the west, she was not enthusiastic about it. But the more depressed Matt became about the potential yield he would be able to get from their small farm, the more Katie knew something had to change. Then Lamar Johnson, who owned the huge farm next to theirs, offered to buy their farm and Matt accepted the offer even before consulting her. Seeing how excited Matt was over it, she chose to embrace his decision enthusiastically.

After breakfast, she and the girls cleaned up the dishes while Matt and Jim packed up the wagon and hitched up the horses. At seven o'clock sharp, Grissom sounded the signal with his bugle, then stepped off the side of his wagon into the saddle on the buckskin gelding he rode. While Ike Yocum started his wagon on the first mile of a journey that would take months to complete, Grissom rode back to make sure all the other wagons kept up. Ike knew the road as well as Grissom, so he needed no guide, but after Grissom was satisfied that all the wagons were keeping pace, he would normally ride on ahead of the train to spot any trouble. The first few days of travel were usually enough to get the folks accustomed to the routine of the wagon train. But soon after that, they would be faced with their first river crossing when they reached the Kansas River. Once they made that crossing, they would feel as if they were seasoned travelers.

Matt and Katie had met the family in the wagon directly in front of them at the social get-together two nights before. Vernon and Molly Tatum were from Iowa and they had a boy Jim's age they called Skeeter. The two boys hit it off right from the start. Skeeter had a little brother, four years old, who would obviously be their designated pest. Vernon played the fiddle, so he was eager to find any other musicians on the wagon train. He asked Matt if he played an instrument and Katie answered for him. "He couldn't carry a tune in a five-gallon bucket."

"I'm more of a foot-tapper," Matt said.

"But not anywhere close to the time of the music," Katie remarked.

"She's awful hard on you, Matt," Vernon japed.

"She's just a little bit jealous because she can't do all the steps I know when we're dancin'," Matt declared.

"Ha!" Katie laughed. "You'll see what I mean if I ever get him to dance. He looks like a grizzly bear stalking a deer."

"I can't wait to see that," Vernon remarked. "We're gonna have to find some more boys with instruments. There's bound to be somebody else. We'll probably find out tonight after supper."

When they started out from the Missouri, Katie sat in the driver's seat beside Matt and the girls rode in the wagon. Jim started out to Oregon on foot, however. The wagon train had not gone a great distance before he had company when his two sisters hopped out of the wagon to join him. They found the bumpy ride in the wagon too uncomfortable to tolerate. The only set of springs on the wagon was under the driver's seat, and after a while, even they were not enough to keep Katie from joining her children on foot. They were not alone. Before long, most of those who could walk, did, so the horses were not alone in appreciation of the noon and five o'clock rests.

Vernon Tatum had to wait no longer than the first night on the journey to find out if there were any other musicians on the train. It turned out that there were quite a few musical instruments among the wagons and several were good enough to perform with others. So a band was quickly created with sometimes as few as three and sometimes as many as six artists, but usually four regulars. It was evident from the start that Vernon was the most talented of the musicians, so he was the leader. The presence of some musical instruments was something Virgil Grissom had been hoping for. It always helped keep up the morale of the travelers to have music at the social hour after supper, especially later on when the going got rough. He got a big fire going in the middle of the wagons to encourage the travelers to come from their wagons to socialize. "Whaddaya think, Mr. Tatum?" Grissom asked. "You boys gonna be able to make a big enough racket to pull some of the folks outta their wagons?"

"Ain't no doubt about it," Vernon replied. "We're about ready to cut loose with one now, just as soon as we get John Henry's banjo in tune with the rest of us."

"You ain't waitin' on me," John Henry Hyde declared, then assaulted the helpless instrument with a vengeance.

An amused spectator, Molly Tatum chuckled at her husband's efforts to put the ensemble together. "I don't know, Mr. Grissom," she remarked, "I believe you're gonna get a racket all right, but it might scare folks away, instead of bringing them out of the wagons."

"They're gonna get it together," Grissom said. "There'll be folks out here dancin' before you know it."

Molly laughed. "There might be folks out here, but if they feel like I do right now they won't be doing much dancing. I need a big bottle of liniment. I ain't walked that far in my life."

"It won't be long before you'll be used to that," Grissom predicted.

Grissom's prediction proved to be true for Katie because she took only a couple of days to adjust to the daily schedule of the wagon train. She even boasted to Matt that she and the children were going to walk all the way to the Willamette Valley while he sat on his behind. They got to know more and more of their fellow travelers, primarily at the social hour after supper every night. It was at one of these social hours that Grissom announced they would be making their first river crossing two mornings from that night. "We'll travel all day tomorrow to get to the Kansas River, camp on the east bank, and cross over the next mornin'." His announcement brought an immediate murmur of concern from the travelers. "I'll be ridin' on up ahead of you to check the condition of the riverbanks and I'll pick the best place to cross. I don't expect any trouble a-tall. I hope you used that wax in the can I gave each one of you to seal up any cracks in your wagon boxes. If you didn't, it'd be a good idea to use it tonight or tomorrow night." The murmuring returned and the topic of conversation was set for the remainder of the night. "Now go on and enjoy the rest of the evenin'," he concluded.

"Do you honestly believe that wagon will float?" Mildred Lewis asked her husband.

"I don't know," Quincy answered, "Grissom seems to think so, and I reckon he ought to know."

"But you told me our wagon, loaded like it is, weighs close to two thousand pounds," Mildred said, "and nothing about that wagon looks like a boat."

Overhearing their conversation, Eleanor, John Henry Hyde's wife, touched Mildred's elbow and said, "I'm like you, honey, I don't see how that wagon can float, either. And look at that big ol' moose I'm married to. It'll surely sink with him driving it."

Mildred chuckled. "Maybe you'd better make him swim across the river and you drive the wagon."

They set out again the next morning, and after the noontime rest for the horses and dinner, Grissom rode on ahead of the wagons on his buckskin gelding to check the condition of the riverbanks. His intention was to select the place that looked to be the easiest crossing, then he would guide Ike to that spot to circle the wagons for the night.

When he arrived at the river, he found evidence of a couple of earlier crossings, and they were both in the section of the river most commonly used in years before. The banks looked solid and in good condition on both sides. At first glance, he could see no reason why the horses would have any difficulty pulling the wagons up the bank on the other side. From memory, he knew the deepest part and the strongest current was closer to the other side. So he started the buckskin across to determine how far he would get before he had to swim. He found that there had not been perceptible changes in the river's channel. The buckskin only had to swim a little over twelve feet before his hooves found the bottom again and he walked on out of the water and up the bank. Grissom decided there should be no trouble as long as the drivers kept their horses moving at a constant pace, all the way across the river. He knew he could count on Ike to do that, but as a precaution, after Ike crossed over, they would unhitch his team of horses. Then if any of the wagons needed help, they could use that extra team to pull them up the bank. Satisfied that it should be a routine crossing, he rode back across the river and went to meet the train.

Chapter 2

As he expected, Grissom met the wagon train about two miles short of the river at five o'clock, according to his pocket watch. He wheeled the buckskin around to come up beside his wagon. "Any trouble?" Ike asked.

"Nope," Grissom answered, "looks the same as the last time I saw it and the river ain't high. Shouldn't be any trouble."

"We'll see, I reckon," Ike remarked. "First river crossin', the first timers usually bring the trouble with 'em. Who you gonna cross behind me?"

"I ain't had much chance to really get to know the folks on this train, but from what talkin' I have done with 'em, I'm thinkin' about Moran. He strikes me as the type that don't get too nervous about anything. Whadda you think?"

"Good a choice as any, I reckon," Ike said. "He looks like the kinda man that don't scare easy."

"When I line 'em up tonight, I'll set him number one behind you," Grissom said. He changed the order of travel every night so nobody had to eat all the dust every day on the trail. So that's what he did when they reached the river, circled the wagons with Matt Moran lined up behind Ike and everybody else behind him. Then, as he did every night, he lined the wagon tongue up with the North Star, so he would know his directions in the morning. There was much discussion that night after supper and many questions regarding the smaller children. Grissom stressed the importance of keeping the small ones inside the wagons and to keep the wagons moving at a steady pace, especially in the deep part. The musicians didn't stay very late that night, since their minds were on the preparation of their wagons for the crossing to come first thing in the morning, too. As a result, very few of the settlers lingered.

In the morning, the wagon train was awake early and anxious with about half the settlers up and about before Grissom's four o'clock bugle sounded. Breakfast was finished and the horses hitched up and ready to start well before seven, so Grissom gave the signal to go ahead and start. Ike gave his horses a yell and a slap with the reins, and they started down the bank toward the water. Ready to follow Ike, Matt started his horses after him with Katie on the seat beside him and the girls sitting right behind them. Grissom, who had been standing beside the wagon, urged him to keep moving once he entered the water. Young Jim Moran and his new friend, Skeeter Tatum, swam across to save the extra weight on their parents' wagons, so they declared. Sarah complained to her parents that Jim was just showing off and was going to drown. "You think we better call him to the wagon?" Katie asked Matt.

"Too late now," Matt answered her. "I ain't worried about him anyway. I know he can swim. He'll be all right. It's the other boy I don't know anything about." He watched the wagon in front of him as the water rose up toward the top of the wheels, trying to see if he could tell when Ike's horses were swimming. He couldn't be sure, but at least the wagon didn't sink. Maybe Grissom knew what he was talking about, he thought. He had said that the deepest part was only a little over twelve feet wide, and the horses would strike solid bottom again by the time the wagon had to float. So they would pull it onto solid bottom just as long as they kept moving. He had no sooner thought that when his horses started swimming, so he immediately encouraged them to swim hard. He glanced at Katie beside him and said, "We're gonna find out if this wagon can float in about two seconds." In a few moments, they felt the whole wagon sway with the current and sink slightly, just enough to make Sarah and Hannah both squeal fearfully. Then the wheels struck solid bottom again and the horses pulled the wagon up the other bank.

Matt drove the wagon up to park it behind Ike's, who had continued quite a way off the bank, to leave room for all the wagons to line up in that day's marching order, Matt assumed. He climbed down from the wagon and helped Katie down and then the girls. "Are we supposed to unhitch the horses?" he asked Ike when he saw him unhitching his.

"No," Ike answered, "Grissom wants me to have a team handy in case somebody needs some extra help."

Matt and Katie took the girls back down to a spot on the riverbank out of the way to watch the wagons coming across. Below them, closer to the water, they saw Jim and Skeeter, safe and sound, although soaking wet. "He could go up to the wagon and put on some dry clothes," Katie commented.

"He'll walk 'em dry by the time we stop for dinner," Matt replied. "Besides that, him and Skeeter are tryin' to show each other who's the toughest."

Listening to her parents' conversation, eight-year-old Sarah offered her opinion. "They're just trying to show who's the dumbest."

They continued to watch the crossing as wagon after wagon came across with no more difficulty than they had experienced. It was not until the fourteenth wagon in line that a mishap occurred. The wagon belonged to Harlan Rice, who had fought a long, losing battle with alcohol before embarking on this journey with his wife, Annie, and his two daughters, Alice, thirteen, and Jenny, ten. Before leaving Missouri to start Harlan's promise of a new life in Oregon, he had hidden four bottles of corn whiskey in a big sack of old blankets and rags. This was in case of a bout of the shakes that he couldn't rid himself of, or a task that he wasn't confident in achieving. Crossing the Kansas River was a task he was not confident in achieving. So to help steady his nerves, he took a couple of belts of corn whiskey while Annie and the girls were at the fire cooking breakfast. He immediately felt a calming effect, so he took the bottle out of its hiding place and placed it in the front corner of the wagon bed at the foot of the driver's seat. He threw his coat over it, so Annie wouldn't see it. He was counting on the fact that Annie and the girls would probably walk along beside the wagon until they got closer to the water before they climbed on. He was right in his assumption. So he took advantage of the opportunity to draw courage from the bottle while he could.

"Best stop for a minute, Mr. Rice, and let your women climb in the wagon," Grissom called out to Harlan as he rode up to the edge of the river. "You need to keep a steady pace once you get in the water."

"Yes, sir, Captain," Harlan called back cheerfully, "I'm gonna keep a steady pace." He pulled his horses to a stop. Annie and the girls climbed aboard quickly and Harlan started his horses again. "Here we go, keepin' a steady pace," he declared.

Alice and Jenny squeezed in the back in any little spaces they could find in the packed wagon box while their mother climbed back in the seat beside their father. "You sound like you're in a silly mood this morning," Annie commented as she sat down in the seat beside Harlan. "I thought you weren't sure our wagon would float."

"Not me," he replied. "Those wagons up ahead of us are all floatin' across, and if they can do it, I damn-sure can do it."

She paused to give him a look. There was something odd about the silly grin on his face. "If I didn't know better, I'd swear you've been drinking again." He just gave her a wide smile. "What the heck is wrong with you?" she asked, still thinking he was acting oddly. Then she knew it. "You've been drinking. Where did you get any whiskey? Oh, Harlan, why? At a time like this, why?"

"I ain't been drinkin'," he insisted. "Why don't you get in the back of the wagon with Alice and Jenny? They might be scared when we get out in the middle of this river."

"The hell you haven't been drinking! I can smell it on you now. We were worried about having enough money to buy our land in Oregon, and you've been throwing it away on whiskey."

"Oh, quit your blubberin'," he said. "I just brought a little bit along to take when my back problem kicks up from drivin' this damn wagon. Whiskey's the only thing that helps."

"You ain't got no back problem," she mocked. "You just ain't got no backbone. Maybe I'll have to raise the money to pay for our land. Can't depend on a drunk. Maybe I can find a whorehouse and get a job." That was always her favorite threat.

"It would have to be a helluva cheap one," he countered.

"As long as they didn't let drunks like you in," she responded to his insult.

In the back of the wagon there was no trouble hearing every word exchanged between their mother and their father, even with their hands clamped tightly over their ears. "Don't pay them no mind," Alice told her younger sister. "It's just words. They're just trying to hurt each other's feelings." Then they heard Grissom's voice close to the wagon and the sound of their horses' hooves striking the water.

"Pick 'em up, Mr. Rice! You're gettin' too big a gap between you and Steptoe."

"Aye, aye, sir, Captain!" Harlan japed. "I'm gettin' ready to set sail." His speech already beginning to show signs of slurring, he flogged his horses with the reins. Annie cringed when she heard his attempt to be clever. Grissom was puzzled by Harlan's strange behavior as well, but since he closed the gap between his and Elmo Steptoe's wagon, Grissom ignored it and continued back along the line of wagons. He only nodded to Bryan Roland, who was driving the wagon behind Harlan's, since Bryan seemed to be having no trouble at all.

"Are you sure you're all right, Harlan?" Annie asked, concerned more about their safety as the shallow water became deeper and deeper, and the horses were obviously working harder. "You know I can drive this wagon if you ain't feeling up to it right now."

"What the hell's the matter with you?" Harlan responded. "'Course I'm all right. That'll be the day, when I have to have you drive the wagon for me. You just be ready to help the girls in case this wagon starts to sink when we hit the deep part." Steptoe's wagon continued along in front of them with no delays, so Harlan did his best to keep the same pace as they approached the deepest part of the river. "They're swimmin'!" Harlan suddenly blurted when the horses reached the channel of the river. "Get ready! They'll pull this wagon off the bottom. Hah, hah, giddy-up," he shouted to the horses. The horses worked hard to obey his commands and pretty soon they found footing and started pulling up the other side. The front of the wagon settled slightly when the front wheels were pulled into the deep water, causing Harlan to fear it was going to sink. His reaction was to flog the horses to pull harder. When the rear wheels reached the deep water and the back of the wagon sank a little like the front had, Harlan was afraid it was going to keep sinking. In a fit of panic, his natural reaction was to haul back on the reins as hard as he could to stop the wagon right there.

"What are you doing?!" Annie screamed. "Don't stop them!"

He looked at her, terrified, unable to speak. The wagon was now fully afloat. The current was not terribly strong, but it was enough to gently turn the wagon downstream. Consequently there was a problem where there had been none before. With the help of the current, there was more than the two-thousand-pound weight of the wagon pulling against the two horses, and was more than they could overcome. Standing in water up to the point of their shoulders, the horses held the wagon where it was half-sunk. But the current caused it to turn a full ninety degrees, and they could not pull it up the slope. When Harlan obviously didn't know what to do, Annie took the reins out of his hands and tried to get the horses to pull on out of the water. But the best they could do was hold it where it was.

"What the hell . . . ?" Ike blurted when he saw what had happened. "They need help! We gotta tie my horses onto 'em!" he shouted out, but Grissom was all the way down at the last wagon on the other side of the river. Ike backed his team of horses down to the water's edge. One of the men already across and now standing on the bank to watch saw what Ike was attempting to do.

"Here!" John Henry Hyde shouted. "Gimme the rope! You hold the horses!" The big man grabbed the rope and plunged into the river. He went under the surface and tied the heavy rope to the wagon. His head popped up above the surface then and he yelled, "Pull 'em on up, Ike!" Ike immediately popped his reins, and together, the four horses pulled Rice's wagon up the slope. Still in the water, John Henry tried to swing the back of the wagon around in an effort to straighten it a little to make it easier to pull.

When the wagon wheels reached solid bottom again and the wagon straightened out as it came out of the water, Annie put the reins back in Harlan's hands. He took them with a sheepish expression, knowing she was giving him an opportunity to save face. Behind them, Bryan Roland could do nothing to help them, so he veered upstream to keep the line behind him going uninterrupted. "What happened?" Ike asked Harlan when he untied his horses from Harlan's wagon.

"It just looked like the wagon was gonna sink for a while," Annie answered him when Harlan couldn't come up with a response right away. "The girls and I got a little nervous and I'm afraid we distracted Harlan."

"Well, looks like there ain't no harm done, thanks to John Henry Hyde," Ike said. "He mighta been due for a bath, anyway. That's the reason Grissom had me unhitch my horses. You go ahead and pull your wagon on up there behind Steptoe's. I expect we'll wait here for a bit before we start out again."

"Yessir," Harlan spoke for the first time since he wound up safely across the river. "We'll do that right now." As soon as Ike moved his horses away, Harlan drove them up to park them in line behind Steptoe's wagon and Annie and the girls promptly got out. Harlan was aware that his wife had made the excuses for him to save him the embarrassment of having almost caused their wagon to sink. He was grateful for that, but he also knew that he badly needed a drink to finally settle his nerves. So as soon as Annie and the girls walked around toward the back of the wagon, he reached down below the wagon seat and retrieved his bottle. He took a couple of shots, corked it, and hid it back under the seat.

When he walked around to join Annie and the girls, he found Alice and Jenny gathering sticks of dead wood for a small fire. "Ike said we'd have time for a small fire for a cup of coffee," Annie said. "We're gonna let the horses rest for a little while before we start out this morning. I figure we could use a cup." The girls came back with some wood and dropped it where Annie pointed. She handed Alice the coffeepot and sent her back down to the river to fill it and told Jenny she needed a little more wood. While Harlan started building the fire, Annie stepped up on the front wheel of the wagon, reached over, and pulled the half-filled bottle of whiskey out from under the seat. She walked back around the wagon then and waited for her husband to look up at her. When he did, she pulled the cork and emptied the contents on the ground. He froze, helpless. "We're making some coffee to help sober you up some. Then maybe we can forget about how you mighta lost everything we have this morning." She stuck the cork back in the bottle. "This is a good bottle. We can probably find a better use for it." He was totally defenseless. Evidently, when she and the girls got out of the wagon, she had looked back and saw him reach for his bottle. He didn't attempt to defend himself. "Have you got another bottle?" Annie asked.

"No," he lied.

Once he saw the last wagon safely across the river, Grissom pulled up to the Rices' wagon to check on them after their little problem during the crossing. "You folks all right?" he asked as he stepped down.

"Is it time to put our fire out and get started?" Annie asked. "We just thought we'd make a little coffee while we're waiting."

"That's a good idea," Grissom said. "You don't need to put out your fire yet. We just got the last wagon across and we'll let those horses pullin' the end of the train rest a little bit before we get goin' again. I just wanted to make sure you folks were all right. What happened, anyway?"

Annie piped up right away and told him the same story she had told Ike about the girls and herself getting a little frightened when the wagon reached the deep part and that they had distracted her husband. When Jenny started to protest, Annie stopped her with a frown. Then she immediately changed the subject. "Would you like a cup of coffee, Mr. Grissom?"

"I 'preciate the offer, ma'am," Grissom replied, "but I wouldn't wanna drink up your coffee."

"We've got plenty," Annie said. "Alice brought the pot back full of water and I just made the whole pot. If I wasn't gonna throw a lot of it out, I wouldn't have offered you any," she joked.

He chuckled. "In that case, I'll have a cup. Always hard to pass up a cup of fresh coffee."

"Good," Annie said. "Alice, get a coffee cup out of the wagon for Mr. Grissom, will you, honey?"

"No need to do that, Alice," Grissom said. He reached in his saddlebag and pulled out a cup. He grinned at Annie and said, "I only keep emergency equipment in here." He held the cup while she filled it and declined when she offered sugar. "Just like it comes outta the pot," he said. He really had no particular urge for coffee at the moment, but he used it as an excuse to spend a few minutes with them. After Harlan's wagon had trouble with the crossing, he recalled how flippant Harlan was before he started across the river. He remembered thinking Harlan sounded like he'd been drinking. Now, after the crossing, Annie didn't give him a chance to speak. Grissom had a suspicion that Harlan might have been drinking and he wondered if that was going to create a problem before they reached Oregon. It seemed like there always had to be at least one drunk on the trip across the country. Maybe Annie was strong enough to keep Harlan within the traces. It appeared she might be, because Ike said she drove the wagon out of the river and handed the reins to Harlan when they came up the bank. "Well, thank you for the coffee. I'd best be gettin' along. We'll start out again in thirty minutes. I reckon you know now that your wagon will float." He started to climb up in the saddle again but paused to say, "By the way, it was John Henry Hyde that went in the river and tied that rope on your wagon when it got sideways with the current." He thought they must surely have seen the big man charging down the bank with the rope. But he decided to remind them that maybe they ought to thank him for coming to their rescue.

After leaving the Kansas River, most of the emigrants felt like veteran wagon train pioneers as they traveled several weeks across Kansas toward Fort Kearny. Well into the routine of the wagon train now, they followed the Little Blue River. Water was plentiful and good, and the new grass was growing in strong. At the end of each day, after supper, the social hour in the middle of the circle of wagons was the time when most everyone gathered to hear Vernon Tatum on the fiddle, John Henry Hyde on the banjo, Bryan Roland and Paul Courtland on the guitar. Dancing was popular, and with some, competitive. The social hour never lasted very long, however, for four o'clock came pretty early the next morning.

Roughly about halfway between Independence, Missouri, and Fort Kearny there was a favorite camping spot on the Oregon Trail called Alcove Spring. It was a parklike setting where Grissom would try to plan an overnight camp if he could, just so his travelers could enjoy the peaceful surroundings. They had made excellent travel time after leaving the Kansas River and as a result, they reached Alcove Spring at noontime and not the end of the day. Instead of continuing on after the noon rest, however, he decided to camp there overnight, anyway. His decision was met with enthusiasm for the opportunity to bathe and wash clothes.

Not far from Alcove Spring, there was a little town called Marysville and Grissom had learned from experience that it was a town to be avoided. In many places, the trail to Oregon was not one single path but several branches, all leading back to a single trail or passage. The forks of the Blue River was one such a place. As a result, on one occasion when he had followed another branch of the trail, he discovered Marysville. At first, he thought it a lucky find and maybe it was a town where his travelers could restock supplies and fix any repairs needed on their wagons. But he found that the few merchants there were primed to take advantage of the emigrants and the main business seemed to be to sell whiskey. So forever after that one time, he never mentioned the town of Marysville to the folks on his train.

As was usually the case, the folks on this train enjoyed the peaceful serenity of Alcove Spring and would leave it with reluctance the next morning.

Chapter 3

With no way of knowing how far behind the wagon train he was, Clay Moran continued to follow the trail itself, hoping to meet someone traveling east who might tell him. He found himself hoping Matt and Katie hadn't changed their plans about going to Oregon with Virgil Grissom. To add to his troubles, he had come to several places where the trail might be a hundred yards wide. There were others where the trail seemed to split, still going in the same direction, but not quite, and he had to make a choice. He was at one of those places right now. The trail had just recently struck another river and now he had come to a fork in that river. He had pulled his horse to a stop because a trail followed both forks of the river. The one to the left looked to be the more traveled, but there were more recent wagon tracks on the trail to the right and it was the bigger fork. "Hell," he declared, looking at the lefthand trail, "that's the main trail." But he was still curious about the fresher tracks taking the right fork. "Well, I can't sit here for the rest of the day," he announced. So he decided to take the right-hand fork and follow it as long as it didn't veer off to the north at some point. And if it did, he would head back to the south until he struck the main trail again.

After following the right-hand fork of the river for what he estimated to be around six miles or more, he spotted a wagon in the distance coming toward him. *Finally*, he thought, *another human being.* At a distance, it appeared to be two men or possibly one man and an older boy on the wagon seat. When they got a little closer, he could see that it was a man and a boy. The man handed the reins to the boy, reached over behind him, and pulled a rifle up to rest across his thighs. "Howdy," Clay called out, reined his horse to a stop, and waited for the wagon to come up to him. "I'm tryin' to catch up with a wagon train on its way to Oregon Territory. You ain't by any chance met one back the way you came, have you?"

The man told his son to stop the wagon, having decided that Clay looked to be honest, but he kept his rifle lying across his thighs just in case he was wrong. "Nope," he said. "We ain't seen no wagon train. Most likely a wagon train woulda followed the other fork of the river back yonder where you took this one."

"I had a feeling that other fork was the right one," Clay admitted. "It looked a lot more traveled."

"Yep," the man said. "That's the Little Blue River. That's the one the wagon trains follow. This fork is the Big Blue River. It'll take you to Marysville."

"You mean there's a town up this road?"

"About four miles," the man said.

"I didn't think there was any place to buy anything before I got to Fort Kearny," Clay said. "I'm plumb outta coffee and gettin' low on bacon. Is there a trail from, what did you say it was, Marysville? To take me back to the Little Blue? Although, if there ain't, I reckon I can just head south until I reach it."

"There's a trail," the man said. "And some of the wagon trains used to come this way. So you could stay on this trail and it'd lead you back to the Little Blue."

"Much obliged," Clay said. "I 'preciate the information."

"How's that war comin' along down there?" the man asked, no longer able to keep from asking the question, since Clay was in uniform.

"It's over," Clay said, "and I'm chasin' the wagon train that my brother and his family are on, headin' for the Willamette Valley out in Oregon."

"Well, good luck to ya, Lieutenant. I hope you find what you're lookin' for out there."

"Thanks again," Clay said and they parted company. He continued down the road and after four miles, he saw the small settlement. It didn't strike him as a thriving town. There were a few business establishments, one of which was a general store called Krebs's Merchandise. That was enough to serve his purposes. There were three places with saloon signs on the front. One of them up ahead was quite a bit larger than the other two and it also had a sign that said *Eats*. It reminded him that he had not had a regular dinner since he was in Independence, Missouri.

He pulled up to the hitching rail in front of Krebs's Merchandise, dismounted, and tied his horses. When he walked inside the store, he was greeted by Walter Krebs who was behind the counter. "Howdy. Looks like the army's rode into town."

"Nope, just me," Clay responded.

"Well, what can I do for you, Lieutenant?"

"I ran out of coffee, so I thought I'd pick up some if the price ain't too high," Clay said. "How much you charge for ground, roasted coffee?"

"Ground, roasted coffee," Krebs repeated, "a ten-pound sack will cost you four dollars and sixty cents."

"That's forty-six cents a pound," Clay responded. "I'll give up coffee before I pay that much for it."

"That's how much it's costing now," Krebs said. "Everything's gone up since the war, especially out here in the prairie."

"Coffee's half that in Missouri," Clay said. "I paid twenty-seven cents a pound for coffee in Independence. I think I'm gettin' an idea why the wagon trains quit comin' through Marysville. It was nice talkin' to ya, but I reckon I'll give up drinkin' coffee till I get to Fort Kearny." He turned around and started for the door.

"Wait a minute," Krebs called after him. Clay stopped and looked back at him. "Are you just passin' through town?" Clay said that he was. "All right then, just to help out the boys in blue, I'll let you have the ten-pound sack for three-twenty."

"I'll tell you what I'll do," Clay offered. "I'll give you thirty-two cents for one pound of coffee."

Krebs shook his head, frustrated. "The ten-pound sacks are already packed. I'll sell you the ten-pound sack for three dollars just to keep from having to weigh you out one pound of coffee."

"That seems reasonable," Clay said. He put three dollars on the counter and picked up the sack Krebs set there. "Feels like about ten pounds," he commented. "Pleasure doin' business with you, Mr. Krebs."

He walked out the door and put his sack of coffee in one of the canvas bags on his packhorse, then stepped up into the saddle. It occurred to him that it was time to eat, so he thought he'd follow the road he came in on out the other side of town, then find a good spot to cook some bacon. When he rode past the large saloon that advertised *Eats*, he wondered if he could get any decent food there. He suddenly had a real hankering for a meal somebody brought him on a plate. *Why not?* he thought. He had money. He had four months' back pay the army had owed him, at one hundred and five dollars a month, plus his mustering-out pay upon being discharged. He turned his horse around and went back to the saloon. After he tied his horses at the hitching rail, he drew his prize possession from the saddle scabbard and carried it inside with him. It was too quick and easy for someone walking past the saloon to slip a rifle out of the scabbard. And it was especially tempting when that rifle was a genuine 1860 Henry.

"Howdy, soldier," Roy Watts greeted him cheerfully from behind the bar. "Whiskey?"

"No," Clay answered. "I was more interested in your sign that said you sell food, too. Is that a fact? Can I buy some dinner here?"

"You sure can," Roy said. "Henrietta cooked up a pot of beef stew from a cow we butchered yesterday. I just had a dish of it, myself, just before you walked in. So you have my guarantee that it's good eatin'. Matter of fact, them two fellers settin' at that table over there sold me the cow." Clay glanced at the two men, who were both eyeing him openly. They didn't impress him as cattle ranchers. He wondered if stolen beef tasted better than the other kind.

"How much do you charge for it?" Clay asked. Having just come from Krebs's Merchandise, he thought he'd better ask.

"Two bits," Roy answered, "and five cents more if you want a cup of coffee with it."

"I reckon I can afford that and I'll take the coffee with it," Clay decided.

"Set yourself down at one of the tables and I'll go tell Henrietta she's got a customer," Roy said as he walked to the kitchen door. There were only three tables at the back of the saloon, so Clay left one table empty between him and the two men already seated.

In a few minutes, a large woman of uncertain age came out of the kitchen carrying a plate of stew with two biscuits sitting on the side. In her other hand, she carried a cup of coffee. "Here you go, honey. Roy didn't tell me you was a soldier. Are there more soldiers with you?"

"No, ma'am," Clay answered. "I just got out of the army, and I'm on my way to catch up with my brother and his family. They're on a wagon train, headed for Oregon."

"You was an officer, a lieutenant, right?"

"Yes, ma'am."

She seemed to be impressed by that. "You stayin' in town tonight?"

"No, ma'am, I'm headin' outta town right after I eat. I've got a ways to go before I stop for the night."

She seemed disappointed to hear that. "You just holler if you need another biscuit or some more coffee, all right?"

"Yes, ma'am, I sure will," he replied. He had been anxious to get some new clothes, so he could shed the uniform. *Maybe I ought to keep wearing my uniform*, he thought, *but I ain't sure I could handle Henrietta.*

Lonnie Tucker and Otis Wheeler were close enough to hear all the conversation between Clay and Henrietta. Had they not been so close, they might have heard her part of the conversation, anyway, for her voice was as big as she was. "He just got outta the army," Lonnie said, talking almost in a whisper. "Reckon the army give him a whoppin' big musterin' out payday?"

"Maybe," Otis replied, "but even if they didn't, I'm admirin' that Henry rifle he propped up against the wall."

"Yeah?" Lonnie said. "I've been eyeballin' that, myself. It looks like it would fit my style perfectly."

"I reckon we're gonna have to cut the cards for it," Otis declared, "high card wins the Henry."

"We oughta be fair about it, though," Lonnie said. "Whoever wins the Henry, the other'n gets that Colt Army six-shooter."

Clay took a couple of bites of his stew just to test it, unaware that Roy was watching him closely. After those two bites, he attacked the stew wholeheartedly, causing Roy to grin, and when he took a big bite of a biscuit and smacked his lips, Roy chuckled outright. He walked over to the table and said, "She can sure as hell cook, can't she?"

"Mister, she sure as hell can," Clay replied, and took a sip of hot coffee. "I wish I had some reason to stay here to see what breakfast is like." He could see that his comments pleased Roy. "Speakin' of leavin', I wound up here in Marysville by mistake. Right now, I'm glad I did 'cause I woulda missed this dinner if I hadn't. But I should have taken the other fork back there at the split. So tell me, is there a shorter way to get back to the trail beside the Little Blue River? Can I just cut straight back to the south? Is there anything that would get in the way?"

"No," Roy said, "ain't nothin' to stop ya. 'Course, you have to cross the Big Blue to get over next to the Little Blue. You don't have to ride through the bushes and trees though. There's a road right on the other side of Krebs's Merchandise that goes straight south. You ain't the only one that wants to go to the Little Blue, and it's an easy crossing at the Big Blue."

"Well, that is convenient," Clay said. "Much obliged."

"Yes, sir, Roy," Lonnie whispered to Otis, "much obliged." Then aloud, he said, "We'd better get along now, Roy. We'll see you again when we run up on a stray cow."

"Don't you boys run off," Roy japed. "I ain't had nearly enough time to sell you the likker to pay for that cow I bought."

"We'd like to get away from here one time while we're still showin' a profit," Otis told him.

Henrietta came out of the kitchen with the coffeepot. Seeing Otis and Lonnie going out the door, she commented, "Those two leavin' already? They usually set around here till damn near closin'." She filled Clay's cup. "You need anything else, honey?"

"No, thank you, ma'am, but I've gotta tell you, that was as fine a beef stew as I've ever eaten in my entire life. And the biscuits were perfect. I wish I could take you with me."

"Look out, now," she responded. "I've got me a dandy carpet-bag in the back room and it won't take me long to pack up my clothes."

Clay laughed. "Roy wouldn't let me get as far as the door before he'd cut me down with that shotgun I know he keeps under the bar. Ain't that right, Roy?"

"That's a fact, partner," Roy said with a chuckle.

"You gonna try a slice of peach pie?" Henrietta asked.

"I'm afraid I didn't save enough room for pie," Clay said, "but I'll have it, anyway, since I've still got a full cup of coffee." She went immediately to fetch it. "And then, I've got to get back on the trail," he said to Roy.

The pie, made with dried peaches, proved to be as good as the stew. He finished the whole piece and paid Roy. Feeling as if he had just eaten the entire cow Henrietta's stew came from, he apologized to the gray gelding when he prepared to step up into the saddle. "You're gonna feel a helluva lot more load, boy. I'm sorry about that." He climbed on and wheeled the gray away from the hitching rail. "I reckon I'm gonna have to think of a name for you," he said as he rode back toward Krebs's store. When he was released from the army, he had chosen the gray from the army's horse herd, but he had not been struck by a name for the horse so far. "I reckon I'll just call you Bud until you inspire me with a proper name." He didn't know if it was standard practice for the entire army, but in his regiment, a cavalry officer was given his horse as part of his severance from the army. He was not awarded a packhorse, however, but in Clay's case, he was left alone to cut out his horse from the herd. So he decided he needed a pack-horse as well, since he had a long ride to catch up with his brother. And as long as he was going to steal one, he figured he might as well be selective in case the gray didn't turn out to suit him. So he liberated a dun gelding from the herd to accompany him and the gray to Oregon and left the army as a horse thief.

When he rode back to Krebs's, he saw the road Roy had told him about. He had noticed it when he went to the store before, but he thought it was just a little two-rut road to a storehouse be-hind the store. Now, as he guided the gray down the narrow road, a comment Henrietta made came to mind again. She had said how unusual it was for the two men Roy had bought the cow from to leave that early in the afternoon. Thinking back, it seemed that suddenly they left when he was finishing his stew. He wondered now if their sudden departure had anything to do with him. He had no doubt that they had heard every word of his conversation with Roy and Henrietta. So they were certainly aware of where he was heading when he left the saloon. *It might do me well to keep a sharp eye out*, he thought.

"I'm tellin' you they don't come along like this every day," Lonnie declared. "It's just like a gift from the army, loaded up with two fine horses, a Henry rifle, a Colt six-shooter, a load of packs full of supplies, and ain't no tellin' how much money. Whaddaya think we oughta do? Just shoot him down as soon as he crosses the river?"

"No, hell no," Otis said. "Everybody in town would hear the shots and they know we just left ahead of him. You heard what he told Roy, he wants to cut over to the Little Blue. We need to go pick us a good ambush spot two or three miles from here. And there won't be no trouble to hide his body. Don't many people cut through there. We can just drag his body over in the bushes beside the road, and the buzzards will have him et up before anybody finds him."

"I reckon you're right," Lonnie said. "Let's move on down this trail and pick us a spot." They rode along the narrow road, looking for a place where it was not so overgrown with bushes and the trees were not so close. They needed a clear shot and there were not many places on the little road that would give them one. After about a mile and a half, they found a section of the road that suited their purposes. It was where the road took a sharp turn and crossed a small clearing before entering the trees again. "Made to order," Lonnie declared. So they rode through the clearing, then when the road led into the trees again, they dismounted and tied their horses in the trees.

With their horses out of sight, they looked around for the best place to shoot from. "Right yonder," Otis said, and pointed to a large tree that had fallen to form a natural breastwork from which to shoot behind.

"Made to order," Lonnie repeated, and started toward it.

"Wait a minute," Otis said. He went to his horse and fumbled around in his saddlebag until he came out with a deck of cards. "I'm gonna shuffle 'em. Then we'll each draw one and the high card wins the Henry."

"I'll shuffle 'em," Lonnie said. "Then we'll draw one."

"What's the matter?" Otis asked. "Don't you trust me?"

"Hell, no," Lonnie said and he held out his hand. "I'll shuffle 'em." He continued to hold out his hand until Otis dealt him the cards. "I've seen you play cards before."

"Well, I'll be doggoned," Otis complained. "I can't believe you'd think I'd cheat you. I thought we was partners."

"Might as well make sure everything's on the up-and-up," Lonnie said. He turned the deck upside down and fanned them out and examined them. "I swear, I can't find the ace of spades. Reckon what happened to it?"

"It musta fell out of the box," Otis said. "I'll go look in my saddlebag."

"How could it have fell out of the pack?" Lonnie asked. He turned the cards back over and gave them a quick shuffle. "Draw your card, we gotta get ready for that soldier." They both drew and Lonnie turned his over right away. "Ten of hearts," he said. Otis took a peek at the card before he turned it over. Then he turned it over and threw it on the ground. "Eight of clubs," Lonnie said with a grin. "All right, let's get behind that tree trunk and get me my Henry rifle."

They checked their rifles to be sure they were loaded, then they got down behind the tree to wait. "He oughta be comin' along before long," Lonnie said. "If we wait to let him get out in the middle of that clearin', we can hit him with two quick shots."

"I reckon you don't have to tell me how to shoot him," Otis responded, still grumbling about his loss of the Henry rifle.

Clay was not comfortable riding the overgrown trail to the Little Blue. He took a good look at the road where it crossed the Big Blue before he rode across. Gambling mostly on the notion that if the two men were thinking about bushwhacking him, they wouldn't do it this close to town. So he forded the river and followed the road into the dense growth of trees between the forks of the river. He realized that he might be creating this whole scene in his mind, but he couldn't help the feeling that he was the target of an ambush. So he decided to assume that was the case and to act accordingly, and he became more and more cautious as he got farther away from the town. Consequently, when he approached a sharp bend in the road, he stopped because there appeared to be a clearing of some kind around the curve. And to him, that seemed like a good spot for an ambush. So instead of following the road around the curve, he turned his horse off the road and into the thick woods and angled straight across the curve. Weaving his way through the trees, he pulled up suddenly when he heard a horse greet his horses. *Damn!* he swore, thinking his presence had been discovered. He looked quickly all around him and then he saw the horses ahead of him in the trees. He quietly dismounted and led his horses forward, his rifle cocked and ready. A little closer and he realized the horses were hidden there in the woods, which meant the two bushwhackers were waiting in ambush somewhere. So he tied his horses and cautiously made his way toward the edge of the road.

He didn't see anyone at first and then he saw them. Hunkered up behind a big fallen tree on the other side of the narrow road, their rifles resting on top of the trunk, they waited for him to ride around the curve into the clearing. *They weren't going to just rob me,* he thought. There was no decision to be made on his part. He had no choice. So he stepped out in the middle of the road and asked, "Are you lookin' for me?"

Startled, both men jumped as if already shot. They grabbed their rifles off the tree trunk and spun around, Otis hitting Lonnie in the back with his rifle when he tried to turn. Clay cut Lonnie down, cranked a second round in and cut Otis down before he could recover and raise his rifle to aim. He cranked in another round and walked cautiously toward the two bodies, having no wish to be shot by a dying man. Neither man had gotten off a shot, so Clay was quick to take their rifles out of their reach. Both men were still alive, but both shots were kill shots. The first man he shot was hit in the chest and he was rapidly dying, so Clay drew his pistol and put a bullet in his head. The second man was gut-shot and in extreme pain. "There ain't nothin' I can do for you. I'll get you some water and leave you here if you want me to. I've seen men wounded like that before and the surgeon couldn't do nothin' for 'em. They usually died before mornin'. Whichever way you want."

Otis grimaced painfully. "I reckon you can go ahead and shoot me same as you did with Lonnie. I'm hurtin' pretty bad."

"That's what I would do, if it was my decision," Clay said. "You just lay there for a few minutes and I'll be right back." He walked back behind him then, held his pistol a few inches from his head and pulled the trigger before Otis had time to anticipate it. He went back across the road then and brought his horses and his bushwhackers' two horses back to the bodies. He was concerned somewhat because the two men had no packhorses and that could mean that they had a hideout close to the town. They might be part of a gang, so he saw no need to waste a lot of time. He searched their bodies for anything of value but found very little. Their horses were in fair shape, so he would take them to trade, maybe in Fort Kearny. He used one of them to drag the two bodies deeper into the woods. Then he tied the two horses on a rope behind his packhorse and got underway again.

It was only a few miles before he struck the main trail beside the Little Blue River and when he did, he decided he needed to make up some of the time he had been delayed. So he traveled later than usual that night before camping. He had thought he might catch up with the wagon train by now and he told himself that surely he would within the next day or so.

Chapter 4

Virgil Grissom led the wagons away from Alcove Spring for the start of a ten- or twelve-day journey to Fort Kearny. After their extra time in the parklike setting of Alcove Spring, everyone's spirits were high as their trek seemed almost a pleasure outing. Quincy Lewis joked that he and Mildred had decided to just settle right there. "We ain't gonna find a much nicer place out there in Oregon."

"I'm afraid you're outta luck, Quincy," Grissom told him, "the government ain't opened this land up for settlement. And you'd just end up travelin' out to Oregon without all this good company you got now."

There would be sweet water and grass along the Little Blue River all the way to Fort Kearny where they would strike the Platte River. The terrain was not difficult for the horses, the nights were pleasant with almost everyone looking forward to the social gathering every evening after supper. Grissom thought it best to let them enjoy the time they traveled the Little Blue River because that would end once they reached Fort Kearny. From that point, they would travel five hundred miles along the Platte River until reaching Independence Rock on the Sweetwater River. And they were not going to find the Platte as accommodating as the Blue. Shallow and muddy with a foul taste, it was safe to drink but unpleasant to the tongue. Thankfully, there were occasional streams and creeks where the water was good.

Many of the people were finding their supplies running short already. Grissom told them they would be able to restock when they got to Fort Kearny and they would be able to do it at reasonable prices. Fort Kearny had been built back in 1848 for the sole purpose of helping the emigrants traveling the trails west. And the government had set reasonable prices for all goods sold at the fort. Someone had named it "the Gateway to the Great Plains." And it was aptly named because in leaving Fort Kearny, the emigrants would begin a long journey over a great prairie that gradually climbed toward the Rocky Mountains.

Clay Moran did not wait to head north again as soon as he came to the Little Blue River. His horses were fresh, so he continued on toward Fort Kearny until he came to a little stream just before dark. He figured he was at least fifteen miles away from Marysville and almost that far away from the two bodies he left in the woods back there. So he picked a spot by the river in a little clump of trees to make his camp. He unsaddled his horse and the two extra horses he had. Then he unloaded his packhorse and cooked some bacon and hardtack and made some coffee. He looked at his horse and commented, "It's been an interesting day. I hope to hell tomorrow ain't half as interesting."

Morning found him ready to get started again, so he decided to pack his horses up and wait until he stopped to rest them before he made breakfast. He was still concerned that he might be starting out to Oregon totally by himself. Surely he should have overtaken that wagon train before now. Something must have happened and the reason he had not caught up with them was maybe because they never left Independence. And if that was the case, he was going to have to go back to Independence to look for them. There was also the possibility that they started earlier than they planned. He decided then, if he didn't catch up with them today, he would turn around and go back because the other possibility was that they started later than planned.

He maintained a pace just a little faster than a wagon and rode for twelve or thirteen miles before he decided he was ready to eat. He was picking a place to stop when he caught sight of a building off the side of the trail up ahead. *People*, he thought, *they can tell me if a wagon train came through recently.* So he led his string of horses a little farther up the trail. As he approached what looked to be a creek up ahead, he saw that there were several buildings and there was even a bridge over the creek. He didn't expect that. One building stood apart from the others and it had a sign over the door. He wondered who would put a business out in the middle of nowhere. "I reckon I'll find out," he said.

He pulled his horses up to a stop in front of the building and read the sign. Rock Creek Station, the sign didn't tell him much. "Looks like you forgot somebody, soldier." The voice came from behind him. He looked back to see a man coming from around the corner of the building.

Puzzled by the man's remark at first, Clay realized he was referring to the absence of a platoon of soldiers behind him. "They'll be along directly," he said then nodded up toward the sign and asked, "What kind of business is Rock Creek Station?"

"Well, it started out as a store for emigrants on the trail here to buy supplies. It was a Pony Express stop till the government shut that down. It's still a stop for the Overland Stage, and that ain't gonna last much longer after they build the railroad. It is still a store to buy supplies, though, if you're needin' something. But the men who own it now are Hagenstein and Wolfe. They're freighters. They're the people I work for. What can I do for ya?"

"One thing I'd appreciate," Clay said first thing, "can you tell me how long it's been since a wagon train passed by here?"

"Sure can," the man said, and he paused to recall. "Let's see, today's Thursday and they came through here on a Sunday. So it'll be two weeks Sunday. It was one of the first we've seen this spring." This was the news Clay was afraid he might hear. He didn't know if they started late or not at all, but he knew for sure they didn't start when Matt said and get that far ahead of him. The man could see that Clay was perplexed by his answer. "Have you got some more soldiers with you somewhere? You lookin' for somebody on a wagon train or a stagecoach? 'Cause a stagecoach is due in here within a half hour. They'll be stopping here to eat and change horses."

"What?" Clay asked, then realized what the man was thinking, since he'd told him they'd be along directly. "No, there ain't nobody but me. I'm not in the army anymore. I just got out and I'm supposed to be catchin' up with my brother and his family on a wagon train. I'm going to Oregon with 'em. Only trouble is, if they were where they were supposed to be, you mighta seen 'em yesterday or the day before, but not as long ago as you saw that last one."

"Well, that is something," the man declared. "Did you ride the Oregon Trail all the way from Independence? Stayed right on the wagon trail?" Clay nodded yes. "And you've gotten this far, and no wagon train?"

"That's a fact," Clay said.

"Whaddaya gonna do?"

"I reckon I'll head back the way I came," Clay said. "Right now, though, I need to take care of my horses. You mind if I make a little camp over there on the other side of that bridge while I let my horses rest? And maybe I'll make a little coffee and cook some bacon."

"No, don't mind a-tall. Excuse my manners. My name's Thomas Simpson. If you ain't ate, why don't you wait just a few minutes and eat with us. My wife cooks a meal for the stagecoach passengers and the driver and the guard. I'll charge you a quarter, same as we charge the passengers. If you're a little short right now, I won't charge you nothin'."

"My name's Clay Moran and that sounds like a good idea to me."

"Now that me and you are good friends, Clay, can I ask you

what happened to the two fannies who were settin' in those two empty saddles?"

"Why? Do you recognize the saddles?"

"No, can't say as I do." Simpson said.

"Good," Clay said. "I stopped in Marysville and ate some dinner at a saloon there yesterday. The two fellows who used to ride those horses decided it would be a good idea to leave a little ahead of me and set up an ambush for me. I decided to go around the ambush. Even when I caught 'em dead to rights, they chose to shoot it out."

"Well, I'll be . . . Whaddaya gonna do with the horses?"

"I figure I'll sell 'em when I get to Fort Kearny, if I go to Fort Kearny," Clay said. "I don't wanna bother with the extra horses."

"I'll take 'em off your hands, if you're not askin' too much for 'em," Simpson said. "Changing horses for the stagecoach and workin' horses in the freight business, I can always use good horses and those look in pretty good shape."

"Well, that would make it a lot easier for me," Clay said. "Since you know how I came by them, why don't you make me an offer and I'll see if it's enough to be free of 'em."

"All right," Simpson said, "let me take a closer look at 'em now." He looked both horses over a little more thoroughly, then turned to Clay and said, "I'll give you twenty apiece for 'em."

"Twenty-five," Clay countered.

"Throw in the saddles," Simpson answered.

"Done," Clay said, "but only the saddles. I keep the guns."

"Pleasure doin' business with you," Simpson said. "You go ahead and take care of your horses and I'll take these two to the barn. When you get done, come on into the house and we can set down and eat maybe before the stage pulls in." He untied the two horses and started to lead them away, then he stopped suddenly and turned back toward Clay. "You said you went through Marysville. Did you go back to Alcove Spring?"

"Where's Alcove Spring?"

"That's the way the wagon trains go. They usually camp overnight at Alcove Spring. They don't go through Marysville any-more. That wagon train you're chasin' might be between Alcove Spring and Rock Creek right now. You might as well camp here tonight and wait to see if that ain't what happened to your wagon train."

"I had a feelin' I was takin' the wrong way back there where the river forked off," Clay recalled. "I don't know why I did it. The other trail was obviously more heavily traveled. I hope you're right and that wagon train is right behind me." He shook his head in exasperation. "I sure could have saved myself a hel-luva lot of trouble if I'd just taken the other fork. I mighta caught up with the wagon train and I wouldn't have shot two men."

"I think things happen the way they're supposed to," Simpson said. "Most likely you rid the world of two of that sorry bunch of outlaws that hang around Marysville." He chuckled then and said, "And I got two pretty good horses at a reasonable price, so go take care of your horses and we'll have some dinner."

Clay took his two horses to water at the creek, then he decided to hobble them, since he hadn't had either of them for very long. When he went back to the main building, Simpson was still at the barn, so he sat down on the porch and waited for him. He had barely gotten comfortable when the stagecoach pulled into the station. Simpson came out of the barn with two young men right behind him. The two young men started unhitching the horses while Simpson greeted the passengers, who were climbing out immediately, half of them asking where the outhouses were. It occurred to Clay that it might be worth his while to go ahead in-side and maybe get a head start on the stage passengers.

When he went inside, he saw a long table in the middle of the room, set for dinner. There was no one else in the room, so he hesitated to sit down. He could hear someone in the kitchen, working pretty hard, from the sound of it. He decided he'd bet-ter go and ask if he should sit down at the table. So he went over to the kitchen door and stepped inside. He saw one woman, her back to him, moving pots around on the stove. "Excuse me, ma'am," he said. She turned around, startled to see an army officer standing in her kitchen door. "Mr. Simpson said I could get some dinner here."

"Are you one of the passengers? Just sit down at the table. I'm getting ready to fill some serving bowls right now," she told him.

"He ain't a passenger, hon," Simpson said as he walked in the back door. "Meet Clay Moran. Clay, this is my wife, Isabelle. Clay's been trying to catch up with a wagon train outta Independence and we think he mighta got in front of it when he went through Marysville. I told him he could eat with us."

"How many's on the stage?" Isabelle asked.

"Seven passengers and Buck and Wilbur," Simpson answered.

"We'll have plenty," she said, and looked at Clay. "You wanna eat in the dining room with the passengers, or you wanna eat in the kitchen?"

"I'll eat wherever you say," Clay answered. "If it tastes as good as it smells, I'd eat it out in the yard if you want me to."

Isabelle laughed. "I don't think you need to go that far. Why don't I fill you a plate right now and you can go in the dining room and sit at the table with the passengers? Thomas, are you going to eat now, or wait till later?"

"I'll eat with Clay," he said. So she filled two plates and they went into the dining room and sat down at one end of the big table. They weren't there long before the passengers filed into the dining room and sat down at the table. Isabelle started circling the table with her large serving bowls until everybody was served. Then she made the rounds with the coffeepot and a pitcher of water. She served the whole meal with no help from anyone and no one had any complaints about the service. The food was good. He couldn't rate it above Henrietta's cooking in the saloon in Marysville, but it was good eating. Of course, he didn't share that opinion with Isabelle. They had invited him to eat with them while he was waiting for the wagon train to arrive, but he was reluctant to when she wasn't cooking for a stagecoach. So he made his camp on the other side of the bridge while he

waited to see if a wagon train would appear. He built his fire
where he could sit beside it and see a long way down the road.

It was a good while after the nooning time when he saw the
first wagon appear in the distance. He watched for a moment
longer until he saw a second wagon behind the first one and he
was sure it was a wagon train. He just hoped it was the right one.
He was leaving Rock Creek Station regardless, so he was all
packed up. All he had to do was saddle the gray and hang his
packs on his packhorse and put out his fire. Ready to go now, he
could see the line of wagons growing in number. There was a
man riding beside the lead wagon riding a buckskin horse. If this
was the right train, that would be Virgil Grissom. He let him get
a little bit closer before he stepped up into the saddle and rode
down the trail to meet them.

"Now, what we got here?" Grissom remarked to Ike Yocum,
when he saw the young army officer riding to meet them.

"You want me to stop?" Ike asked.

"No, keep goin' till he tells us what he wants," Grissom said.

Clay pulled up in front of Grissom, then turned and fell in beside him. "Are you Virgil Grissom?"

"Yeah, I'm Grissom. I hope to hell you ain't come to tell me
there's Injun trouble up ahead."

"To tell you the truth, I ain't got any idea whether there is or
not. I'm just hopin' one of these wagons belongs to Matt Moran
and his family."

Grissom and Ike both laughed heartily. "You're Clay Moran,
right?" Grissom asked.

"That's a fact," Clay said, laughing with them.

"What in the world are you doin' up here?" Grissom asked. "I
thought you were behind us, tryin' to catch up."

"I was until I decided to go see what Marysville looks like,"
Clay said. "And I jumped right around you."

"Well, I'll be . . ." Grissom said. "Matt's gonna be tickled to
see you. I think he was startin' to think you'd changed your mind
about going. His wagon is just about in the middle of the train.

We're gonna keep movin' right on through Rock Creek Station. There's another nice creek about seven miles up the trail and I wanna make camp there tonight. Welcome to the train."

"Thank you," Clay said. He wheeled his horse around and rode back toward the end of the train, nodding or offering a "Howdy" to the wagon drivers and the women walking he passed on the way back to Matt's wagon. Matt saw him coming and knew right away who it was. A big grin broke out on his face and he started to shout to him, but when he looked at Katie, walking beside the wagon, he realized that she didn't recognize him. She was more concerned with keeping Sarah and Hannah out of the way of the soldier's horses. So he didn't tell her. When Clay pulled up short of Matt's horses to wait for him, Matt called out, "Hey, soldier, are you lost?"

It was young Jim who said it first. "Uncle Clay?"

Katie took a direct look at the lieutenant's face then and exclaimed, "Clay! Where did you come from?" She looked at Matt, who still had an impish grin on his face. "You low-down dog, you recognized him." She didn't wait for his answer but went right back to Clay. "But what are you doing coming from ahead of us?"

"That's a long story," Clay responded. He turned his horses to ride along beside the wagon and Matt stopped the wagon just long enough for Katie to climb on, so she could sit beside him and talk to Clay. He told them how he happened to pass them while they were camped at Alcove Spring and had to camp overnight at Rock Creek Station to wait for them.

When they came up even with the main building, Thomas Simpson was standing out by the road watching the wagon train roll past. "Is that the train you were lookin' for?" Simpson called out to Clay.

"Yep," Clay answered. "This is my brother Matt and his wife, Katie, and we're headin' to Oregon country." To Matt and Katie, he said, "That's Thomas Simpson. He manages this place. Thanks for your hospitality, Mr. Simpson."

"You bet," Simpson answered. "You folks have a good trip and

I hope you find what you're looking for out there. By the way, I'm already working those horses I bought from you."

"Good, glad to hear they're workin' all right," Clay said.

"You sold him some horses?" Matt asked.

"It was just a couple extras I had," Clay said. He really didn't want to say how he happened to come by them with Katie sitting there, so he quickly changed the subject. "You see that little bridge over there? Simpson told me that years ago the fellow who used to own this place built that bridge and charged ten cents a wagon to cross it."

"Is that a fact?" Matt responded. "I wonder if ol' Grissom was the first wagon master to just ride right through the creek."

"I wouldn't be surprised," Katie said.

They continued on for almost a couple of hours, passing several creeks before coming to the one Grissom had in mind for the camp that night. It was better than the ones he passed up. He confessed that he learned that because he had stopped at one of the others before and found out the next morning that he should have waited. They circled up the wagons, primarily to pen their animals up, since there was no threat of Indians in this part of the country. Clay turned his horses out with all the others, although he might still need his packhorse, since there was very little room left in the wagon. Most of what he was packing, however, was food supplies and there was room to combine that with Katie's supplies. They had started out with a small bit of room in the wagon reserved for Clay's personal storage, but it had already been trespassed upon. Clay told them not to worry, he would lead a packhorse to Oregon if necessary.

The first night, after supper, Clay was introduced to more people than he could possibly remember, so he promptly forgot everybody's name. Grissom officially welcomed him to the train again and many of the other people welcomed him as well. One problem he hoped to fix at Fort Kearny was to buy some civilian clothes. He had nothing but his uniforms and he was anxious to get out of them. It was almost one hundred and fifty miles to Fort Kearny. That was over a week, most likely. Maybe Matt had an extra shirt he could borrow. He was a little taller than his brother and maybe a little heavier, but he should be able to wear his shirt.

So he sat with Matt and Katie, listened to the music and watched the dancing, and laughed at the jokes about the wagon train now having a military escort from several wits. When it was time for bed, he spread his bedroll under the wagon with Jim. And the next morning he was awakened by a bugle for the first time in a while. This time it was at four o'clock, an hour and a half earlier than when he was in the army.

Chapter 5

They traveled the Little Blue River for the next eight days before striking the Platte River and Fort Kearny late in the afternoon. Grissom led them to a grassy field by a strong creek where they circled the wagons. They planned to camp for two days to give those who needed repairs on their wagons, or have their horses reshod, time to get it done. They had the regular social hour after supper that night, but there was no reason to end it at the usual time. Grissom said there would be no bugle in the morning, since they were going to stay there all day. Clay was watching Paul and Evelyn Courtland entertain the crowd with a demonstration of buck dancing when Grissom and Ike came over to sit with him. "You gettin' adjusted to being outta the army and livin' a regular life again?" Grissom asked him. "Although I don't reckon ridin' a wagon train is what you'd call a regular life, is it?"

"I reckon not," Clay said, "but it's better'n being in the army." He laughed then and said, "Some things ain't much different. I've already had guard duty, the midnight to four shift at that."

Grissom chuckled. "Yeah, I figured I'd put you on the list, so you wouldn't get homesick for the army." They talked for quite a while and by the time they decided it was time to turn in for the night, Grissom decided Clay Moran was a welcome addition to the train. "Well, I reckon I'd best go talk to the guards now. Tomorrow night, me and Ike are goin' to eat supper at a place called

Leo's Road Ranch. Fellow named Leo Stern owns it and to tell you the truth, it's really a hog ranch, but me and Ike just look at the merchandise. We ain't customers. We go there to get a good supper. Leo always has a good cook. He had this ol' gal named Lulu Belle that did the cookin' for quite a few years. It was hard to beat Lulu Belle's cookin', ain't that right, Ike?"

"I ain't ever et better," Ike answered.

"Then I heard last spring Lulu Belle left Leo's, ran off with some fellow and got married. So me and Ike are gonna go up the creek to Leo's and see what kinda cook he hired to take Lulu Belle's place. Seein' as how you, me, and Ike are the only single men on this wagon train, maybe you'd like to go with us. Whaddaya say? Have us a big meal and maybe a drink of likker?"

Clay nodded and said, "That sounds like a good idea. Count me in."

"Good," Grissom said, "Leo's is just about a mile straight up this creek. We usually walk up there. Is that all right with you?"

Clay said that suited him just fine and they called it a night.

After breakfast the next morning, the whole family went over to the fort to the post trader's store. Clay gave his brother the fifty dollars he got from the sale of the two horses to Thomas Simpson. Matt reminded him that he had sent him money for supplies before they left Missouri, but Clay said he was sure that hadn't been enough. There were already a lot of things Katie had run out of and they were still on the first part of their trip. Clay led his packhorse over to the store to carry all the supplies back to the wagon. While Katie and Matt were getting their supplies, Clay was looking through the small inventory of men's clothes the store offered. He found a couple of cotton shirts that were satisfactory, but he didn't find replacements for his trousers and boots. He considered a hat with a flat crown and a four-inch brim for five dollars and a bandanna for twenty-five cents. After thinking about it for a few minutes, he decided he would just take the insignia and the hatband off his old cavalry hat and wear it, but he bought the bandanna. He figured he could still use his army coat when the weather got cold. The only other purchase he made was for three large peppermint sticks for Jim, Sarah, and Hannah. Katie wouldn't let them eat them until after they had dinner. He changed into one of his new shirts there in the store, which disappointed the kids because the soldiers they passed when they left the store failed to salute him.

Clay told Katie at the noon meal that he would not be eating supper with them that night because he was going to eat at Leo's Road Ranch with Mr. Grissom and Mr. Yocum. He looked at Matt then and said, "They invited me to go with 'em and I thought about askin' you if you wanted to go. But I imagine it ain't the kind of establishment you'd wanna take your wife to."

"I'll bet it isn't," Katie said.

"I reckon I'll pass it up," Matt said, "although Katie might want me to go with you and have myself a good time. Ain't that right, love?"

"That's right," Katie said, "if you don't mind the whipping with the axe handle that'd be waiting for you when you came home."

"Man, that married life is rougher than I thought it was," Clay declared. "Well, if I'm gonna go with 'em, I've got to take my horse for some new shoes this afternoon. They're not too bad right now, but it's three hundred miles to Fort Laramie, and I'll bet there ain't a blacksmith or a farrier between here and there." He winked at Katie and said, "And I don't wanna be late for my night out with the bachelors."

He rode the gray gelding back over to the post and waited for the farrier to finish one customer ahead of him. When it was his turn, there was no problem with the gray's hooves, so when the job was done, Clay paid the farrier, then took the horse for a spirited little run to make sure the shoes were comfortable. When he got back to the wagons, Grissom was already looking for him. Clay threw his saddle under Matt's wagon and said, "Don't wait up for me."

"You be back before ten o'clock," Katie yelled at him. "Don't you keep our wagon master out too late. He's got to get this wagon train started out of here in the morning."

"They givin' you a hard time?" Grissom laughed.

"Katie is. I think one of her missions in life is to get me married. That's the main reason I joined the army," he joked. "She married Matt, then I think she tried to hook me up with every little girl over twelve years old in that town we lived near. I've gotta admit, she's the best thing that ever happened to Matt, but I ain't ready to ride down that trail."

"Hell," Ike swore. "I reckon I'm ready to get married just as soon as I find a woman who can support me in the fashion I'm accustomed to." They started walking toward the creek and when they got to it, they followed a path that ran alongside it. "Hell," Ike swore again, "Grissom's married. Ain't that right, Grissom?" Clay began to notice that almost every statement Ike made began with the word *hell*.

"Yep, that's a fact," Grissom said.

"No foolin'?" Clay was surprised. "You don't spend a helluva lotta time at home, do you?"

"About a couple of months outta the year, and that's about as much as either one of us can stand," Grissom declared. "The rest of the time she pretty much lives her life and I live mine. I support her, so she's satisfied with that."

Clay couldn't help but feel sorry for them both. "Where does your wife live?"

"I built her a nice little house right there in Independence, so I stay with her while I'm puttin' a wagon train together every spring. It seems to be about enough time to satisfy both of us."

They followed the path through a section of thick woods on both sides of the creek and Grissom said that was a spot where an occasional member of a wagon train was robbed on his way to Leo's. "So it's always a good idea to be on guard when you're walking through here."

"It looks like a good spot to rob somebody. I'm glad I'm

wearin' my sidearm," Clay remarked. "Maybe I shoulda brought my rifle, too," he joked.

"Hell," Ike said, "I thought that was the reason Grissom asked you to come with us, to protect us. Hell, I figured we didn't have nothin' to worry about with the U.S. Cavalry escortin' us."

"And I thought you asked me to go with you because you thought I was such good company," Clay responded.

After almost a mile, they came out to an open pasture with a large, two-story house sitting at the end of a narrow road that went directly back to the fort. There was a barn, a smokehouse, and two outhouses behind the house. "That side door goes right into the saloon and the place to eat," Grissom said, "but we always go in the front door, just to take a look at the merchandise. With me and Ike, that's about all we're any good for. Now you, young stud like you are, if you're interested in buyin' anything besides supper, that's up to you."

Clay chuckled at the thought. "I ain't plannin' on buyin' anything but some supper and maybe a drink of whiskey, either before or after supper, doesn't make any difference."

They went in the front door which led into a sizable parlor where there were half a dozen women sitting on several sofas. A couple of soldiers were talking to two of them. The other women looked at Grissom and Ike with little interest, but two of them offered a bored hello. All six perked up when young Clay came in behind the two older men. The two doves nearest the front door jumped up and each took hold of an arm. "Hello, sweetie, I've been waiting for you to come in," one of them said.

"I can tell a man who likes a redheaded woman," said the red-haired woman holding his other arm. "I know just what you need."

"I'm grateful for your kindness, both of you, but I'm afraid you can't do nothin' for me," Clay told them. "I just got mustered out cf the army after a month in the hospital. We were chargin' an enemy position that was firing cannon at us. One of the cannon misfired and the cannonball went right between my legs and took out all my business down there. So I just came in here to eat some supper. But I appreciate your attention." They both looked horrified and both gentled their grip on his arms at once. He nodded politely and followed Ike and Grissom across the room and through the door to the saloon. The bartender recognized Grissom and Ike.

"I reckon it is that time of the year again, ain't it?" Floyd Trainer greeted them. "Where you headed this year, Oregon or California?"

"Oregon," Grissom replied, "we always go to Oregon." He could see that Floyd was straining, trying to remember his name, so he started to tell him.

"Grissom!" Floyd spat it out before Grissom had a chance to tell him. "And Ike, right?"

"That's a fact," Grissom said. "And this young fellow is goin' to the Willamette Valley with us this year. Floyd, this is Clay Moran. We came to see if you got a cook that can come close to Lulu Belle."

"We sure did," Floyd declared. "I'll let you try her cookin' and you can tell me what you think. Her name's Darcy Johnson and she can make that stove talk. You gonna want anything to drink before you eat?"

"Whaddaya think?" Grissom turned to ask Clay and Ike. "You want a little drink before we eat or after?"

"I don't really care," Clay said. "Maybe if we had it after supper, though, we could tell if Darcy Johnson can really cook."

"That sounds like a good idea," Grissom said, "and she can't blame it on the whiskey."

"Go on back to the table," Floyd said, "and I'll tell Darcy she's got some hungry customers out here." They went back to a little partitioned-off section of the saloon where a long table was set with plates and utensils.

"Good evening, gentlemen," Darcy said when she came out of the kitchen. "You've got a choice tonight. You can have venison if you want it. If you don't want deer meat, I can give you ham, either one of them served with red beans and rice and hot biscuits out of the oven about five minutes ago." They all chose venison. "Three coffees?" They all nodded. She spun on her heel and was back right away with the coffee. A few minutes after that, she was back with the three plates. She was all business until she saw them all served and eating, then she sat down at the end of the table to judge their satisfaction with the food.

"That's mighty good deer meat, ma'am." Grissom was the first to compliment the food.

"Hell, it's all good," Ike remarked.

She looked at Clay then for his endorsement, so he willingly gave it. She obviously very much wanted to please. "Yes, ma'am, it is good and you sure bake some good biscuits."

"Why thank you, sir," Darcy said. "I'm glad you're enjoying it. Might you be regular customers?"

"No, I wish we were," Grissom said. "I'd eat here every night. We're on a wagon train and we'll be leavin' at seven o'clock in the morning."

Clay thought she looked genuinely disappointed to hear that. "How long have you been doin' the cookin' here?" He understood her concern when he heard her answer.

"I just started a little over a month ago," she said, and looked around before continuing, as if she was afraid someone might overhear. "Leo's had two cooks since Lulu Belle left and he fired both of them. I'm just hoping I can satisfy his customers."

"I don't think you've got any reason to worry about it," Grissom told her. "This is first-class cookin' and there's one thing I can guarantee you, word gets around fast about good cookin'. And it ain't gonna be long before word's gonna get around about you. I know I'm sure gonna tell it."

"I can't tell you how much I appreciate everything you've said about the food," Darcy said. "You fellows have made my whole day."

"Hell, we didn't say nothin' that weren't the truth," Ike said.

"And I thank you for it," Darcy said. "And now, I've got to get back to work," she said when two more customers walked in and sat down at the table. "Do you want more coffee?"

"Just when you get a chance, I could use about a half a cup more," Grissom said.

"I'll bring the pot right out," Darcy said to Grissom, then to the two new customers, she said, "Good evening, gentlemen. Are you drinking coffee?"

"Do you see me drinkin' coffee? I ain't drinkin' a damn thing right now and I'm wonderin' if I'm ever gonna get some."

"I'll get your coffee right away," Darcy said, and hurried away.

Clay thought that was downright rude and uncalled for. Evidently, the two men had their whiskey before they came to supper. He glanced at Grissom and he could tell he was thinking the same as he was. The two men weren't soldiers. They looked more like cowhands. When Darcy came back, she was carrying the coffeepot and two cups. She put the cups on the table and filled them, then she came to the other end of the table and filled Grissom's and Ike's cups. Clay waved her away from his. She then told the two new customers what the choices were for supper.

"I'll just have a steak," one of the men said. A heavyset fellow with a thick neck and a heavy black beard, he looked as if he was accustomed to giving orders.

His companion, a younger-looking man, slim with shoulder-length hair and no facial hair except a thin mustache, said, "I'll have a steak, too."

"I'm sorry, gentlemen, I don't have any fresh beef tonight, so I can't give you a steak," Darcy told them.

"You don't have any, or you just don't wanna fry a steak?" the heavyset man asked. "What kinda eatin' joint can't fry a man a steak?"

"Not mucha one," his partner answered.

"Hell, you fellers oughta try that venison," Ike spoke up, "it's pretty good eatin'."

His suggestion caused both men to glare at him. "Who the hell asked you to open your mouth, old man?"

"No need to get riled up, friend," Grissom said. "He was just tryin' to be neighborly. The deer meat is pretty good eatin'. The fact is the lady ain't got any fresh beef to cook for you."

Grissom's remarks seemed only to further irritate the big man. Clay looked at Darcy, who was obviously distressed. He could see that she was going to have to grow a harder shell if she was going to last in her new job. It might have been better if Grissom hadn't said anything. A no-nonsense-talking woman would have been more effective with rough characters like these two. He decided if he made any remarks it would only make matters worse, so he held his tongue.

"Since I don't want to go all the way back to the fort to get somethin' to eat," the disgruntled man told Darcy, "I'll eat the ham. But it better be damn good." He looked at his partner. "What about you, Slim?"

"I don't know, Jake, I reckon maybe I'll try the deer meat."

Jake looked at Darcy, who was still standing there uncertain. "Well, you heard him. What the hell are you still standing there for?"

Shaken from her trance then, she said, "Yes, sir," and fled to the kitchen.

When she left, Jake looked down the table at Grissom. "Mister, you look like you've got a bad habit of openin' your mouth when there ain't nobody talkin' to you. I'd advise you to lose that habit, especially around me, 'cause the next time you stick your nose in my business, I'm liable to cut it off."

"Well, Jake, I feel like that was my business," Grissom said. "I'm that young lady's uncle and I thought you was being a little too hard on her. She ain't the one responsible for buyin' the meat. She just cooks it. All she's tryin' to do is give you a good supper."

"I swear, maybe he's right, Jake," Slim said. "Maybe it ain't her fault."

Jake simmered down a little bit. "Maybe so, but if that ham ain't damn good, I ain't payin' 'em one red cent for it."

Darcy came back in with the two supper plates and there was no more said between Jake and Grissom. Although they had finished their coffee, they sat there for a little longer while Slim and Jake attacked their plates. It appeared they were happy with the quality of their supper, so Grissom said, "I reckon we might as well go get that drink now. It looks like ol' grumpy is satisfied with his grub." So they got up and left the dining area and went to the bar, paid Floyd for their supper and ordered a shot of whiskey.

Darcy came back in the dining section with a fresh pot of coffee and asked Jake if they wanted more coffee and he said no. She asked then if the food was all right. Jake just shrugged indifferently, but Slim said, "Your uncle was right about the deer meat. It was mighty good."

"My uncle?" Darcy asked.

"Yeah, your uncle," Slim said, "just walked outta here. He said he had the deer meat and it was good. That's why I got it."

"My uncle wasn't in here," Darcy insisted. "My uncle doesn't live here."

"He said he was your uncle," Slim said. "Didn't he, Jake?"

"One of the three men who just ate supper here?" Darcy asked. Slim nodded. "I don't know why they would have said that. Tonight is the first time they've been in."

"I know why he said it," Jake said, getting angry all over again. "He was tryin' to make a fool outta me. What he needs is his ass kicked. Let's go, Slim. They might still be here."

"You can pay Floyd at the bar for your supper," Darcy called after them. She hoped the other three men had paid Floyd.

Jake stormed out of the dining area with Slim right behind. He could see the three men from the wagon train standing at the bar, talking to Floyd. So he slowed his pace down to a more intimidating swagger. "Hey, Uncle Jackass, the woman in the dinin' room says you're a low-down rotten liar. Whaddaya say about that?"

"Well, I'd say that's no way for a nice young lady like Darcy to talk," Grissom said. "I'll have to give her a talkin'-to. Did you pay her for your supper?"

"None of your business, and them is my words. I'm callin' you a dirty, low-down liar, and I wanna know what you're gonna do about it," Jake challenged.

"Well, I reckon I'll just have to practice a little more on what I claim to be true and maybe check my facts a little closer," Grissom said. His refusal to take Jake's challenge seriously only added fuel to the fire of frustration in Jake's brain.

"By Ned, I'll have you face me in the street or in this saloon," Jake threatened. "You're wearin' a gun. Let's see if you've got the guts to use it."

"You know, Jake, I can't think of anybody I'd rather shoot than you," Grissom said. "But I don't indulge in that sort of nonsense. It's just foolishness. You could get yourself killed doin' that. So let's just say you won and forget about it."

Jake stared at him in disbelief for a few moments. Then a wicked smile broke out across his face. "That's what I thought. You're a low-down coward. Well, you ain't gonna get away with it, yellow belly. I'll shoot you down where you stand."

"All right, I've had enough of this foolishness," Clay interrupted the face-off. "There ain't gonna be no showdown." He drew his Colt .44 and held it on Jake. "You pull that weapon and I'll shoot you down. Ike, draw your weapon and hold it on Slim there. If he goes for his gun, shoot him."

"I ain't gonna draw my gun," Slim quickly assured him.

"That's good thinkin', Slim," Clay said. "Grissom, walk around behind them and take their guns outta the holsters." Clay's manner was so much in command that Grissom and Ike didn't hesitate to do as he said. "Now, Floyd, what's that door in the back there with the padlock on it?"

"That's the storeroom where we keep the whiskey," Floyd answered.

"You got the key?" Clay asked.

"You can't put them in the storeroom," Floyd said, realizing what he had in mind.

"It's better than shootin' 'em down right here, and that's what I'm gonna do otherwise. So have you got the key?"

"Yeah, I got the key," Floyd said, "but I don't want 'em in my storeroom."

"You can let 'em out after we're gone and you won't have any bodies to take care of," Clay told him.

By this time, most of the other customers in the saloon were conscious of the bizarre incident taking place at the bar, so everyone's attention was focused on the drama. Aware of this as well, Jake had to make a show of defiance. "You ain't lockin' me up in no damn storeroom."

"Wait a minute, Floyd, he ain't gonna go in the storeroom," Clay said. "I'm gonna have to shoot him." He cocked the hammer back on his .44 and aimed it at Jake's head.

"Hold on, damn it!" Jake exclaimed. "I'll go in the storeroom!"

"I'm startin' to lose my patience with you," Clay told him. "It'd be a helluva lot less trouble for me to just pull this trigger and be done with you."

"I said I'd go," Jake protested.

"All right," Clay said, "come on, Floyd, bring the key." Floyd came from behind the bar and Clay, Grissom, and Ike marched Jake and Slim to the storeroom. Floyd unlocked it and the two prisoners walked inside.

When Clay started to close the door, Jake protested. "Hey, there ain't no light in here!"

"Now, don't tell me a big boy like you is afraid of the dark," Clay said. "It won't be for long, anyway. Floyd's gonna let you out in half an hour, long enough for us to be gone. That's better than being dead." He closed the door and put the padlock back on it. They went back to the bar then. Clay gave Floyd back his key and told him to give them their guns back when he let them out in about thirty or forty minutes. "You and Ike ready to go?" They said they were. "Here's the money for our supper and Jake and Slim's, too, and I reckon we'll bid you farewell." They left Jake's and Slim's guns with Floyd and went out the door. They got a round of applause on their way out.

Chapter 6

Both Grissom and Ike were still trying to recover from the unexpected performance by their young friend after Grissom's attempt to ignore Jake's challenge to duel. "I reckon I owe you my thanks for keepin' that big ox from shootin' me," Grissom said as they started back down the path by the creek.

"Glad to help," Clay said. "I'll admit, though, you had me worried for a while 'cause I don't know the way to the Willamette Valley. Maybe those two ain't got no idea that we're walkin' back to the wagon train. But if Floyd keeps 'em locked up for thirty or forty minutes, we'll be back. I just didn't wanna have to run all the way back."

"Hell, I reckon you didn't," Ike said, "what with your condition and all."

Clay thought that an odd comment. "Why do you say that? I figure I'm in pretty good condition."

"Hell, I didn't mean you wasn't in good condition for the condition you're in," Ike said. "I meant with your special problem and all."

It was obvious he didn't want to spell it out, but Clay was curious enough to want to know what his problem was. "I reckon I've got a lotta problems I don't know about," he said.

"Hell, I was talkin' about the wounds you got in the war," Ike finally said, "you know, when that cannonball bounced between your legs."

"What?" Clay exclaimed, then he remembered. "You heard me tell that red-haired whore that. I didn't get any wounds in the war. I was lucky that way. I just didn't want whatever she was passin' around."

"Hell," Ike said, "and you had me feelin' sorry for you, you being in the cavalry and havin' to ride a horse and all." Grissom was chuckling at the thought. "Hell, it coulda been," Ike insisted.

"Not likely," Grissom replied.

Back at the saloon, Leo Stern, the owner of the Road Ranch, who was upstairs spending some time with Sally Brown, was finally curious enough to put on his shoes and go downstairs. The usual grumbling noise of his busy saloon had been constant the whole time he had been upstairs. But then, it suddenly became quiet for quite a while before a wave of what sounded like applause rose up from below. That was too much. He had to go downstairs to see what was going on in his saloon. "Are you coming back?" Sally asked.

"No, I'm satisfied for a while," he answered, and left some money on the dresser.

"Thank you, Leo," she said. He always paid her for her time, even though she worked for him.

Leo walked down the steps and saw Floyd standing in the middle of the saloon, instead of behind the bar. Other than that, nothing looked amiss. "What's going on, Floyd?"

"We had a little set-to between a couple of drifters and three fellows from the wagon train that pulled in last night. It started in the dining room and spilled over in the saloon. One of the drifters called Virgil Grissom out to face him in a duel."

"Grissom don't participate in shoot-outs," Leo said. "What did he do?"

"A young fellow that was with him took over and locked the

two drifters up, then him and Grissom and another fellow that was with 'em went back to the wagon train, I reckon."

"Good," Leo said, "the young fellow prevented a shooting here." He thought about that a minute, then asked, "Where did he lock the drifters up?"

"In the storeroom," Floyd said.

Leo turned and pointed. "In the storeroom? Where we keep our whiskey? Are they still in there?"

Floyd said they were. "He said to keep 'em locked up for thirty or forty minutes, then let 'em go."

"Get them the hell outta there right now!" Leo exclaimed. "There ain't no tellin' how much damage they'll do with our liquor supply!"

"Yes, sir!" Floyd responded, and hurried to the storeroom door where he fumbled in his excitement to get the key inserted into the padlock.

As soon as the padlock was off the latch the door was flung open from the inside and Jake charged out into the saloon with Slim right behind. "Where are they?" Jake demanded.

"They ain't here no more," Floyd answered him. "They've done gone back to the wagons."

"You men can't stay in my storeroom," Leo said, thinking he should say something.

"It weren't my idea, Grandpa," Jake replied. He looked at Floyd and demanded, "Where's our guns?"

"I'll get 'em!" Floyd responded, and hurried back behind the bar, pulled the two pistols from under it, and laid them on top.

Jake and Slim picked up their weapons and checked to make sure they were loaded. "Come on, Slim, we're got some unfinished business to attend to."

"Where we goin'?" Slim asked.

"After that coward that put us in that damn storeroom. He thought he was pretty slick, gittin' the jump on me like that. I'm aimin' to see just how good he is when I'm lookin' him right in the eye."

They left the saloon and climbed on their horses. "Where you reckon they headed?" Slim asked. "We don't know where they came from."

"I know where they're headed," Jake said. "Didn't you hear that bartender say they'd gone back to the wagons? They're on a wagon train, and if you follow that path by the creek yonder, it'll take you right to that wagon train. They ain't been gone that long and thanks to ol' blowhard back there, we got outta that storeroom a lot sooner than those fellers think. Chances are they ain't gonna be pushin' their horses, but we're gonna be gallopin' ours. I'll bet we catch 'em before they get back to that wagon train. So let's go!" He gave his horse his heels and tore off down the path, immediately gobbled up by the thick woods and the growing darkness.

The three men they pursued, contrary to their belief, were walking and not on horseback. They were walking at a brisk pace but feeling no urgency, thinking that Floyd had no reason to let the two drifters out of the storeroom any sooner than Clay had requested. They figured that Floyd, like them, was intent upon preventing a gunfight. For that reason, they were surprised when they heard the sound of the horses' hooves pounding the path behind them. "That son of a . . . ." Grissom started. "He let 'em out!"

"Well, let's get the hell offa this path and get a look at 'em," Clay said, "and be quick about it. They're not sparin' the horses." They followed his lead, jumped off the path, and plunged into a bank of thick bushes. In less than a minute, the two horses galloped past, Jake in the lead and Slim close behind. "They've got about three-quarters of a mile to the wagons, and when they don't see us, they'll be a little more careful on the way back. They're bound to know we wouldn't have made it there already."

"Hell," Ike said, "we shoulda shot 'em outta the saddle when they rode by."

"I expect you're right," Clay said, "because they've got it in mind to kill us. There ain't any other reason to keep after us." He had feelings just like he had when he circled around the ambush back near Marysville. He felt a need to justify his reason to kill. Grissom's thoughts were more in line with Ike's. If the buzzards intended to keep on coming after him, then he was happy to send them to hell to be with others of their kind. "I think it'd be a good idea if we're all in agreement on what we want to do," Clay said. "Do we want to kill them, or do we just want to avoid them?"

"Let's leave it up to them," Grissom said. "Let's stay under cover and see what they do after they ride down to that field where the wagons are. If they just turn around and go back the way they came, then so be it, we'll let 'em go. But if they hang around in the field where the wagons are, then we go get 'em."

"I'm all right with that, if that's what you and Ike favor," Clay offered.

Ike shrugged indifferently, so Grissom said, "All right, let's just wait and see what they choose to do."

"All right," Clay said, "but let's find something a little more solid to wait behind in case we do get into a gunfight."

"I'll drink to that," Grissom said.

"How 'bout the other side of the path," Clay suggested, "down behind the creek bank?" That made sense, so they abandoned the bushes and crossed over the path to drop down below the bank and work on their firing positions. When they were satisfied that they were ready to defend themselves, they decided on their battle plan. Obviously, if the two drifters turned around and rode all the way back the way they came, they would give up the notion of attacking them and let them pass unharmed. But if they searched all the way along the path on their way back, then it was going to be their misfortune when they found them.

It wasn't long before they heard the horses approaching again in the darkness. "Here they come!" Grissom whispered. "It don't sound like they're searching for us a-tall. I reckon he ain't as determined to shoot me as he said." They waited, and in a few

seconds, the two horses appeared out of the darkness, just opposite their position, and passed right on by. They continued to listen until they could no longer hear the horses. Grissom exhaled a
breath of relief, for he really had no desire to take a stranger's life
for no justifiable reason. Clay sensed it and changed his mind
about him. Maybe he wasn't as much like Ike as he thought; he
respected the man for it. He was frankly surprised that the man
named Jake had given up his notion of extracting vengeance for
what he considered insults from Grissom, however. "I reckon we
can go on back to the wagons now," Grissom announced and they
climbed up from the creek bank and started back down the path.

"Hell," Ike said, "we just passed up a chance to get a couple of
good horses for the price of a couple of cartridges, didn't we?"

"I'm glad I ain't that hard up for horses," Grissom said. They
could hear the music now from Vernon Tatum and the boys, and
that meant social hour was already underway. "Sounds like we're
gettin' back just in time for Ike to show off some of his buck
dancin' steps," Grissom japed. They were out of the dark woods
now at the edge of the open field where the wagons were parked,
and they heard John Henry Hyde come in after Vernon with his
banjo. The song was an old favorite of Grissom's. "There you go,
Ike, I'll bet you could buck dance to that tune."

"I wanna see you dance, yellow belly." The gruff voice came
from behind them in the darkness. All three of them stopped
dead still and turned to encounter the hulking form of Jake Pur-
cell, his pistol already drawn. A few yards behind him with a
smirk of amusement on his face, Slim Fry stood holding the
horses.

"We let you live twice already, when you rode south on this
path, and again when you rode north," Grissom told him. "We
could have shot the both of you either time, but we let you pass
unhurt. If I wanted to kill you, I would have done it then. So why
don't you and your friend just go and leave us in peace?"

"'Cause I just don't like you," Jake answered, "and I wanna
see you dance."

"Well, I'm not gonna dance for you," Grissom said, "and I'm not gonna draw on you."

"All right then," Jake said, "I'll give you one more chance." He holstered his pistol but his hand still hovered over it. "I'm gonna count to three, and when this .45 comes out of the holster, I'm gonna shoot you down." He started counting, "One, two . . ." That was as far as he got before Clay very casually pulled his .44 from his holster and sent one round to land squarely in the middle of Jake's chest. The big man took a step backward, his six-gun still in the holster. He looked down in disbelief at the hole in his shirt and the blood that began to form around it. Then his knees began to fail him and he sank slowly to the ground. Ike walked over to him and pulled his six-gun out of his holster.

Meanwhile, Clay was watching Slim closely, waiting for him to commit or to back down. Slim did not have a weapon out. He looked at Clay, who was showing no sign of emotion as he waited for him to make a move. Then he looked at Ike, holding Jake's .45 in his direction, just waiting for a signal to fire. "I ain't got no score to settle with you fellers. This here was all Jake's party. I weren't gonna shoot nobody."

"All right then," Clay said, "pull that gun outta your holster with your left hand and put it in your saddlebag. Then I'll help you put his body on his horse and you can take him the hell away from here." Slim did as he was told. He put his six-gun in his saddle bag, then with Clay's help, he laid Jake's body across the saddle of his horse, fully expecting Clay to search the body for anything of value. When he didn't, Slim sought to ride away as quickly as possible before Clay thought to claim the inheritance.

"Well, gentlemen," Grissom commented as they stood watching Slim depart, "I'd like to say I enjoyed that supper, but I believe it's gonna be a long time digestin'."

"I reckon I'll walk on over and listen to the music for a while," Clay said. "Matt and Katie are probably out there already." He turned to look at Grissom. "You and Ike goin' to social hour?"

"I'm going to my wagon first to see who's got the guard duty tonight," Grissom said. "Then I expect I'll be over to join you." Clay nodded. "How 'bout you, Ike?"

"Hell, I'm goin' to the wagon with Grissom. I'm goin' to bed," Ike answered.

So they parted, and as Clay headed toward the big fire in the middle of the wagon circle, Grissom and Ike walked toward their wagon. "You know, Ike," Grissom was inspired to comment, "we ain't a fourth of the way on this trip. We ain't nowhere near far enough to find out what kinda people we've got on this train. But I'm pretty damn sure I know what kinda man that tall young fellow is."

"Hell," Ike said, "I knew that the day he hooked up with us at Rock Creek Station."

Chapter 7

They pulled out of Fort Kearny the next morning for the beginning of a journey across the real plains. The wagon trail followed the Platte River west across almost treeless plains which meant there was no wood for campfires, but Mother Nature in her thoughtfulness provided fuel for fires in the form of dried buffalo chips. They burned brightly and surprisingly without an offensive odor. The trouble was, about two bushel baskets full were needed to cook your breakfast. The gathering of the dried buffalo pies soon became the number one chore for all children big enough to carry a basket or a sack. Building a fire with buffalo dung was easier to get accustomed to than using water from the Platte River. As soon as the wagon train left Fort Kearny, the emigrants unfortunately discovered how foul river water could be. The river was wide and shallow to the extent that it could not be traveled by boat. Only inches deep in many places, it was muddy with a silty taste, fit for drinking or cooking. Fortunately, they were not completely dependent on the Platte, for there were numerous streams and creeks with clean, sweet water that fed into the Platte. So it soon became of the utmost importance to find containers suitable for holding water to save for cooking and drinking to be filled whenever they came to a stream. For they could never be sure when they would approach another one.

On the sixth day out from Fort Kearny, they stopped for the noon rest when they came to a sizable stream. The water looked so clean that Annie Rice remarked to her husband, Harlan, that it was a shame they had no containers to hold water other than their one water barrel. "Well, we ain't got nothin' else to carry water and that's just the way things are. I already searched the whole wagon and there weren't nothin' to use to hold water. We packed everything in this wagon we thought we couldn't do without. We never thought about not being able to find water fit to drink." He unhitched the horses and took them to the stream with all the other horses.

Thirteen-year-old Alice waited until her father took the horses before telling on her father. "I saw Papa when he searched the wagon for a container. He didn't search very hard for one. Did he, Jenny?"

Ten-year-old Jenny giggled and said, "No, he didn't."

"We'll search it again, Mama," Alice said. "Papa just didn't wanna go to the trouble of looking in all the cracks and corners behind the trunk and those food bags stacked up on top of it."

"Well, I expect you'll be wasting your time," Annie said, "but go ahead and look if you want to." Like her daughters, she didn't doubt the possibility of Harlan doing a slipshod job of it.

The two girls crawled into the wagon and tunneled in between and behind every box, bag, and bundle. As their father had said, there was nothing to be found that would do the job. Lastly, they started pulling bundles and bags of bedclothes, blankets, and towels out of the front of the wagon, even though there would not likely be a container of any kind there. And there was not, so while Alice crammed them all back the way they were, Jenny pulled a large cotton bag out from under the driver's seat. It appeared to be stuffed with more towels and blankets, but it felt heavier than it should have. When she started to stuff it back under the seat, she heard the sound of two solid objects bumping together. So she pulled it out again and untied the string keeping it closed. "Mama," she called out at once. When her mother didn't respond right away, Jenny called again, "Mama."

"What is it, Jenny?" Annie asked impatiently. "I'm busy."

"You're gonna wanna see what Jenny found, Mama," Alice called out then.

Annie walked over and looked in the back of the wagon in time to see her daughter pull a bottle half-full of whiskey out of the bag. Then she reached in and pulled a full bottle out and handed both bottles to her sister. Alice started to take them to her mother, but Jenny said, "Wait a minute, I think there's another one." She felt around in the huge bag and came out with a third bottle. "I think that's all of them," she said.

Annie couldn't believe her eyes. He had lied outright when she had asked him if he had brought any more whiskey with him, and she had trusted him. And he had three more bottles at the time and was evidently working on it whenever he got the chance, since one of them was now only half-full. "Where's your papa? Do you see him?" she asked Alice.

"Yes, ma'am," Alice answered. "He's still down the stream a ways talking to Mr. Bryan and some of the others. They're still watering the horses."

"Good," Annie said. "Crawl outta there, Jenny. We women are gonna have a ceremony." When her youngest climbed out of the wagon, Annie took the half-full bottle and had each of her daughters hold a full one. "Now, I want you to remember when your papa goes crazy because of this, that it might seem mean for us to do this. But you have to trust your mama, it's better for him in the long run. There are some men who can't handle whiskey and it's unfortunate, but your daddy's one of them. So we have to help him fight it. Do you understand?" They both nodded solemnly. "Good," Annie continued, "now pull those corks out of the bottles and empty them on the ground." They emptied the whiskey out. "Now let's go to the stream and rinse 'em out real good." The three of them walked upstream, opposite the direction in which Harlan and the other men were watching the horses drink. After the whiskey bottles were rinsed to Annie's satisfaction, she had the girls fill them with water and cork them again. Unable to resist a measure of payback for his lying, she only filled the third bottle half-full, as close to the level it had been with whiskey. "Now, we at least found some containers to hold extra water, didn't we? It's not much, but it's a little bit more than we had. We were lucky to find them. Now, Jenny, see if you can put the bottles back in that bag as near as you can to the way you found them. And we don't need to say anything about this. Do we?"

"No, ma'am," both girls replied.

"Now, I reckon we'd best get some food on this fire if we're gonna have any dinner," Annie said. "I think we're gonna need some more buffalo chips."

"She's talking to you, Alice. It's your turn," Jenny said.

At one o'clock, Grissom sounded his bugle and the wagon train was on the road again. Annie rode beside Harlan for a couple of miles before hopping down from the wagon to walk with the girls. They walked wide of the wagons even though the prairie they were passing over on this day was grassy and there was not as much dust as on other days. It helped that today their wagon was third in line. Five o'clock came without any sight of a stream and Grissom continued on for another mile or so. But there was no sign in the distance ahead that indicated the possibility of a stream, so he called a halt for the night. That meant they would water the horses in the river and use the water in their water barrels for cooking and coffee. And that would be for supper and breakfast the next morning as well. Grissom assured them that the water from the Platte was safe to drink, if you could get past the smell and taste. So many of the people would wash their dishes in the river if they could find a spot where the water was deeper than a foot and the mud had settled to the bottom. No one washed any clothes in the river after the first time because the odor lingered in the material long after.

Ike parked Grissom's wagon and unhitched the horses. When it got dark enough to see the stars, he would point the wagon tongue toward the North Star. This was in spite of the fact he would continue to follow the Platte River west in the morning regardless. But even before the wagons were circled, the children were running out into the prairie to gather buffalo chips for the fire. On this day Alice and Jenny were competing with Skeeter Tatum and Jim Moran to see who could fill a couple of baskets full of chips first. The two boys were tough competition, but the two girls were holding their own until a cry of distress rang out from the wagons. Actually, it sounded more like a mixture of agony and rage. "That sounded like it came from your wagon," Skeeter said to Alice.

"It's Papa," Alice said to Jenny. "He's been under that wagon seat. We'd best go see." They picked up the sacks they each carried and ran toward the wagon.

"We were way ahead of ya, anyway," Skeeter yelled after them.

When they got back to the wagon, they found their mother and father standing out beside it. One empty bottle was lying on the ground between them and their father was holding one of the full bottles while staring daggers at their mother as he pulled the cork out of it. Still watching her carefully, he held the dark bottle up as if trying to see what was in it. Then he held it to his lips and took a big gulp, only to spit it out immediately as if it tasted foul. "You're wastin' good water," Annie said.

"I oughta beat the livin' hell outta you, you wicked bitch," he threatened.

"You oughta try," she replied, deadly serious.

"I needed that to help my back," he claimed. "It takes a special kind of evil witch to pull a trick like that."

"What kind of low-down man does it take to spend the family's money on rotgut whiskey? And then lie about it when you tell me you didn't buy any more?" Aware of the two girls standing there watching them then, she said, "You don't need to be hearing all this disgraceful goings-on between your mother and your father. Go on back and get some more fuel for the fire."

Alice, aware now that some of the other people on the train had stopped to witness the fight between her parents, answered her. "Mama, I don't wanna leave you when Papa's so mad." She motioned with her head. "People are watching."

"Don't worry about me, honey," Annie told her. "Your papa's not going to hurt me. He knows if he did, I'd beat him to death with my broom."

"Mama," Alice persisted, "people are watching you and Papa."

Alice turned to address the closest people who had stopped to watch the altercation between husband and wife. "Is there something I can do for you folks? I expect you must have something else you need to do right now." It served to embarrass them enough to move a little farther away from their wagon.

And then, Virgil Grissom, astride his buckskin gelding, pulled slowly up to a stop beside their wagon. "Is everything all right, Miz Rice?" He saw the whiskey bottles on the ground and remembered when he had suspected Harlan of being drunk when they had crossed the Kansas River.

"Oh, just a little family squabble, Mr. Grissom," Annie answered. "I'm kinda embarrassed it called attention to us."

"Well, you folks let me know if there's anything you need from me to help you. I wanna do whatever I can to make this journey as pleasant as possible for everybody on the whole train."

"Don't worry about these bottles," Annie said. "They were just filled with water." She reached over and took the only full bottle out of Harlan's hand and gave it to Alice. "Here, show him, honey." Alice didn't understand until her mother motioned for her to drink. Then she pulled the cork and took a drink from the bottle.

Grissom smiled. "Better not let her get used to drinkin' outta that bottle, she might get herself a reputation." He turned his horse away from the wagon. "I'm glad everything's all right." He was pretty sure he knew what the spat between Harlan and

Annie was about. When Ike asked him about it later at supper, he told him what he suspected. "I think Annie found some bottles of whiskey Harlan had hidden somewhere in that wagon and she poured the likker out and filled 'em up with water. That noise we heard was the noise Harlan made when he went to take a drink of likker and he got a mouthful of water."

"Hell," Ike said, chuckling, "I bet you're right."

"I bet I am, too," Grissom said, "unless that little daughter of theirs can down a full shot of whiskey with a straight face." He clenched his lower lip and shook his head and said, "We've got a long way to go yet. And there's one thing I've found out you can always depend on, and that's for a damn drunk to act like a damn drunk sooner or later. I'm a little concerned for Annie and those two little girls."

That night at the social hour, Grissom promised his people that there was a place ahead to provide them some relief. They would take a day and a night there to rest from the weariness of the hot, dry travel they had endured along the South Platte for the last week and a half. It would still be about a week before they got there, but he decided it would be good to tell them now. He told them that when they reached this camp, there would be sweet water and shade and grass for the animals. He said it was called Ash Hollow and there might even be a chance to hunt for deer, because there had been deer there in the past.

"Well, then, I say that's reason enough to celebrate with some lively music tonight," John Henry Hyde announced. "So I'm tellin' you boys you're gonna have to work hard to keep up with me." The rest of the band responded to his challenge and in no time at all the couples who could dance to the up-tempo music were locked in competition with each other.

"I'm surprised to see you and Katie sittin' and watchin'," Clay Moran said when he came over and sat down beside his brother and his sister-in-law.

"I'm gonna tell you the truth," Matt said; "it's tiresome enough just watchin' some of these folks tryin' to dance. Look at ol' Elmo Steptoe. No wonder he can't give Cora nothing but girls. He's got two left feet."

"You're one to talk," Katie said. "At least Elmo will get out there and try."

"If I got out there and showed those folks a few of my special steps, everybody'd be too ashamed to show what little mess they've got, and it'd spoil the trip for Elmo and Cora," Matt declared. "Why don't you get out there and dance?" he asked Clay. "Ain't that part of the trainin' an officer gets in the army? Ballroom dancin' or something? Looka there, you could go over and ask ol' Steptoe's daughter to dance with you." He turned to ask Katie, "How old did she say her oldest daughter was? Fifteen, right? Marryin' age." Back to Clay then, he said, "She's been gapin' at you ever since you walked over here."

Clay just ignored him, shook his head, and asked Katie, "He ain't improved a lick since I was away in the army, has he?"

Katie laughed, shook her head, and said, "If anything, he's gotten worse."

Once the wagon train reached a long line of bluffs along the south side of the river that Grissom called O'Fallon's Bluffs, the trail began a turn to the south, following the South Platte River. It was necessary to cross the South Platte and cross the divide between the two branches in order to follow the North Platte River westward toward Fort Laramie. Because of the danger involved in crossing the South Platte, they continued to follow it to the best possible crossing point. It had been given the name of the California Crossing and required four days' travel from O'Fallon's Bluffs in what would seem the wrong direction. The South Platte was not deep, but it was a difficult crossing because of the river's sandy bottom. The wheels of the heavily loaded wagons were prone to sink in the mushy bottom of the river. It was typically swollen this time of year from the spring melts from the mountains and there were numerous spots of quicksand that could turn a wagon over. As they contemplated the problem on the morning of crossing, John Henry Hyde half seriously quipped, "You teased us back there about this Garden of Eden called Ash Hollow. Now here we stand lookin' at a river waitin' to gobble our wagons up."

Grissom laughed. "I reckon it does seem like a rotten thing to do, but I wanted to keep your spirits up. But if it'll make you feel any better, we've made it across without losing anybody every time before. Right, Ike?"

"That's a fact," Ike said. "Hell, as soon as we cross this river, then we're gonna climb the first real hill we've come to."

"That's right," Grissom said. "It's called California Hill and it's pretty steep, but it ain't nothin' your horses can't handle. It ain't gonna give you any trouble. We're savin' that for the hill you're gonna have to descend to get into Ash Hollow. Right, Ike?" Ike just grinned and nodded slowly. "That hill's got a name, too," Grissom continued. "Windlass Hill is what somebody started callin' it."

"When are we gonna get to Ash Hollow is what I want to know," Quincy Lewis declared.

"Settin' right here, we ain't but about twenty miles from Ash Hollow," Grissom answered. "So get your wagons ready to roll. I've asked Clay Moran to give me a hand to pick out the best way across the river. We'll ride our horses across the best-lookin' place to see how the bottom is. You ready, Clay?"

"I'm ready," Clay answered, and climbed up into the saddle. Grissom climbed up on his buckskin and they rode down to the edge of the river. Following Grissom's instructions, Clay kept his horse parallel to Grissom's approximately the same distance a team of horses pulling a wagon would be. They rode all the way across the river like this, then keeping the same distance between them, moved a few yards farther up and rode back across, testing the bottom for holes or quicksand. When they got back, they were of the opinion that there would not likely be any place that was better. So the wagon train prepared to cross.

Grissom yanked up a couple of sunflowers and placed them on the bank to mark the width of the two crossings he and Clay had made. "All right, Ike, get 'em rollin'. Just drive 'em between those two markers and you oughta be okay."

As they had hoped, it turned out to be an uneventful crossing. The sandy bottom was soft but the wagon wheels sank no more than a few inches at the worst spots. As a precaution, Grissom made it a point to cross on his horse again at the same time Harlan Rice drove his wagon across. She said nothing about it, but Annie Rice was certain it was not by chance. Once the South Platte crossing was completed, they drove straight up California Hill, a climb of about two hundred and forty feet to reach the plateau between the two forks of the river. From that point, they drove north again to arrive at Windlass Hill and the entryway to Ash Hollow.

Grissom stopped the wagons at the top of the hill and the migrants got their first look at the almost vertical decline necessary to descend to the North Platte River Valley below. It was a drop of two hundred and fifty to three hundred feet. There was only one section of the steep hill where it was possible to descend, for it was the only point with no shelves of rock protruding from the face. To the faint of heart, this looked like the end of their journey, for there was no apparent route down this cliff. When asked where the road was that led down to the valley, Grissom replied, "You're lookin' at it." And he pointed to the many deep ruts cut into the face of the hill.

"We're gonna have to slide 'em down on ropes," Matt Moran declared.

"That's right," Grissom confirmed. "There ain't no other way. It's a lotta work and you have to keep your mind on what you're doing, but we'll all be helpin' to get each wagon safely to the bottom without losin' it. On every journey we've made on this trail, we ain't never lost a wagon. Have we, Ike?"

"That's a fact," Ike answered. "Hell, when we camp in Ash Hollow, you'll think it was worth the work to get your wagon down this steep hill." He didn't express the fact that Grissom was one of only a couple of wagon masters who chose to continue to face the challenge of Windlass Hill, as it was now called. For about the last five years, most trains were avoiding Ash Hollow and taking another route through Julesburg. Ike agreed with Grissom, however. After the long, hot days, gradually climbing the treeless prairie toward the Rockies and drinking the foul Platte River water, the emigrants needed Ash Hollow. With its sweet spring water, trees and wood for their fires, it would give them heart to again face the harsh trail along the Platte still waiting ahead. Ash Hollow was actually a deep, wooded valley about four miles long, an Eden totally unexpected in the middle of a treeless prairie. There was even the possibility of game in the little valley because animals were attracted to it no less than humans. Years ago it was buffalo. Today, it was most likely pronghorn antelope or deer.

Chapter 8

It was too late to start the descent down Windlass Hill on this day, so they went into camp on top of the hill. The social hour that night was in great part a discussion hour with the main topic the best way to safely get wagons, horses, and people down that hill. Some wondered if they should try to lower the wagons down with the horses still hitched up. Vernon Tatum was in favor of this method. "So you're sayin' tomorrow mornin', you're just gonna hitch your horses up, hop up on the seat, and drive 'em down that cliff?" Quincy Lewis asked, sarcastically.

"I'm not sayin' any such thing," Tatum replied. "You know we're gonna tie the wheels so they won't turn. And we're gonna tie ropes on the wagon to hold it back. I'm just sayin' if the horses were hitched up, their weight might help hold the wagon back."

"Damn, Vernon," Quincy said, "go take another look at that cliff. Do you think your horses could just walk down that hill?"

"I expect we'll just lower those wagons the way Grissom says, since he's done it a few times before," Matt said. "I notice he's carryin' quite a bit of rope on his wagon. I've got quite a bit, myself. Looks like we're gonna need it." The discussion continued for a while, but the social hour ended a little earlier than usual. It was as if everyone wanted to hurry the night along, so they could get started lowering those wagons down into the valley.

The next morning started as every other morning on the trail with a four o'clock wake-up call from Grissom's bugle, but the horses were not hitched up as usual. Instead, most of them were herded down the hill, with only a few left on top to move the wagons into position. The men ate breakfast before starting the labor of sliding the wagons down through the ruts of the many wagons before. Grissom's was always the lead wagon, so they readied it to challenge the hill. Ike preferred to back the wagon down so the wagon tongue could act as a drag to help slow it down. "It'd be even better if you was to sit on the tongue, John Henry," Vernon Tatum japed. "Big as you are, that'd slow it down."

"I thought you was gonna show us how to hitch up your horses and just drive it down," John Henry replied.

Since the wagon was going down backward, they tied the front wheels so they couldn't turn and tied ropes on the axles and the tongue. Then every man who could get on a rope grabbed hold and they lowered Grissom's wagon down the hill without mishap. One by one after that, the wagons slid to the floor of the North Platte River Valley. To everyone's satisfaction, especially Grissom's, it was accomplished without major damage or personal injury, save some cases of rope burn. When the last wagon was down and hitched up, Grissom led them to a camping area beside one of several springs. "I declare," Katie Moran marveled, "it's even better than Grissom said it would be." There were shade trees and flowers and the water was sweet to the taste. It was well on to suppertime by the time they were camped, so the women started cooking right away.

"Listen, folks," Grissom called out, "I think we can afford to stay here two days and two nights to rest up a little. And I know some of you have got some work to do on your wagons. Oh, and there's plenty of wood for your cookfires, but if you prefer buffalo chips, I think you can find some of them, too." He got the loud razzing he expected. Pleased with the emigrants' reaction to Ash

Hollow, he turned to go to his wagon. Clay Moran stepped up beside him and walked with him.

"I thought I'd better tell you I'm gonna do a little scoutin' about tonight after supper," Clay told him. "There's deer sign all over the side of that spring where we watered the horses. I figured I'd ride on down this canyon a ways, since you said it was about four miles or more, and see if I can scare up a deer. If I do, I'll take a shot at it."

"I don't blame you," Grissom said. "I 'preciate you tellin' me. If I hear a shot, I won't grab my rifle and get ready to defend myself."

Clay laughed. "Right, and I'd appreciate it if somebody else tells you they're goin' huntin', you'd tell 'em that I'm out there, too."

"I'll tell 'em," Grissom said, "but I'll expect a big enough cut of the backstrap to slice a steak for me and one for Ike, if you get a deer."

"You got it," Clay said. "If I was to be lucky enough to get a shot at more than one, I'd be happy to share it with whoever wants some."

"I was wondering if I was gonna have to throw yours out," Katie said when Clay returned to the wagon. His brother and the children were already halfway finished with supper.

"Sorry I'm late," Clay said. "I was talking to Grissom."

"What didja bring your horse for?" Matt asked, noticing also that his horse was saddled.

"I'm goin' huntin' after I eat something," Clay answered. "I've seen so much deer sign around here I'm gonna ride down toward the other end of the canyon and see if there's just as much down there. You wanna go with me? It's been a long time since we went huntin' together."

"No, I reckon not, I've got a few little things I need to fix on the wagon that didn't take the ride down the hill too well."

"Is it something you need some help with?" Clay asked.

"No," Matt replied. "It's just some little things, and if I do 'em tonight, I won't have to do 'em tomorrow."

"In other words, you're gettin' too old and lazy to go huntin', is that about right?" Clay said.

"Yeah, that's about the size of it," Matt answered.

"I'll go with you, Uncle Clay," ten-year-old Jim spoke up.

"Uncle Clay may not want to have you in the way if he's trying to track a deer," Katie said.

"He can go if he wants to," Clay said at once. "I could use some help and it's about time for him to start learning how to hunt." He could see the excitement in the boy's eyes. "If you don't mind him wanderin' off in the woods with somebody who ain't ever been in these woods before, I'd be glad to have him." He looked the boy in the eye and asked, "You really wanna go, Jim?" Jim nodded his head vigorously.

"You can go," Matt stated, not giving his wife a chance to say no, in case that was her intention. "You mind your uncle, boy."

"Yes, sir," Jim said, beaming from ear to ear.

"Finish your supper," Clay said. "We might be late gettin' back."

They left as soon as Clay finished eating supper. He wanted to ride down the valley before darkness set in because he wanted to be able to spot game paths coming down from the heavily forested hills on either side of the valley. He climbed up on the gray gelding then reached down and pulled Jim up behind him. Jim put his arms around Clay's waist and they left the camp and headed down the valley.

When they were about half a mile away from the wagons, they came to a healthy stream that ran along the base of a tree-covered ridge. The floor of the valley was green grass, a perfect place to hunt, Clay thought. And as they rode, he saw many little game trails that likely brought the deer down to water and feed in the meadow. When they came to a place where the stream had formed a small pond, he knew that was where he would wait for his deer. He helped Jim down, dismounted, and led his horse partway up the ridge, just far enough to hide him, the boy, and himself.

"Now we're gonna find out if I know how to find deer or not," he told Jim. "It's gettin' darker now. Those deer have been layin' around and sleepin' up on that slope in the woods. They're gonna wanna come down now to get water and food. If we're lucky, we'll get a shot at one. If we're really lucky, we might get more than one. Then we could take fresh meat back to share. Ain't nothing to do now but wait, so sit down and make yourself comfortable." Clay pulled his rifle out of the saddle scabbard and cranked a cartridge into the chamber, ready to fire. Then he seated himself where he could clearly see the pond through a gap in the foliage. Jim sat down beside him. Clay looked at him and smiled. "Ain't very excitin', is it? We have to be real quiet. A deer's got good ears, they can hear the slightest sound." Jim nodded his understanding.

They sat and waited as it gradually grew darker. Clay was beginning to wonder if he had picked the wrong place to wait when Jim gently tapped him on the arm. When he turned to look at him, Jim said nothing but pointed to a clump of trees on the other side of the little pond. Clay looked in the direction the boy pointed in but saw nothing at first. Then he saw the eight-point buck move cautiously out of the trees and look around him. Clay put his index finger to his lips to signal Jim to remain quiet and they watched the buck lead his harem of six does out of the trees to follow him to the pond. When they were all at the edge of the pond, drinking, Clay knew he could get at least two of them, but he looked at Jim and changed his mind. "Have you ever shot a rifle?" he whispered softly. Jim nodded and held up one finger. "Do you wanna shoot a deer?" Clay whispered again, and received a vigorous nodding of Jim's head in response.

He put the rifle up to Jim's shoulder, holding his hand over the trigger guard to make sure Jim didn't pull the trigger too soon. "You're gonna aim at that biggest doe," he whispered. "Aim at the shoulder and as soon as you pull the trigger, let me take the rifle. All right?" Again, a nod from Jim as he aimed the rifle at the big doe and Clay removed his hand from the trigger guard. As if suddenly aware of danger, the buck lifted his head from the water and snorted. Jim pulled the trigger and the Henry rifle spoke. "You got her!" Clay exclaimed as he snatched the rifle away, cranked in a new round, and knocked another doe down as they bolted toward the slope on the other side of the pond. Cocking the rifle as he ran, Clay sprinted out of the trees in time to take one more shot before the deer disappeared up the slope. He made it count, a shot behind the doe's front leg just above the heart that dropped her short of the slope. He went after the big doe that Jim shot then. Jim had hit her in the left back leg. She stumbled and fell but then got up again and started hobbling after the other deer. Clay managed to catch up to her and finish her with a close-range high-shoulder shot. He came back then to check the first deer he had shot. She was down but still alive, so he put her out of her misery.

He looked up to see Jim running toward him, his eyes wide with the excitement of the slaughter. "We got three of 'em," Clay said. "I never expected to get three deer. We make a helluva team of hunters." The immediate task now was to get them back to camp as soon as possible. It was lucky that camp was only a little over a half mile away. He didn't want to load all three carcasses on his horse. He could get some help from Matt and maybe one of the other men, but he didn't want to leave two deer lying dead while he took one to the wagons. If there were deer in this valley, there were other critters, too. The other two deer might not be here when he got back. "Jim, do you think you can lead my horse back to the wagons?"

"Sure," Jim answered, "it ain't that far back."

"Good boy," Clay said. "If I load a couple of these carcasses on my horse, you reckon you could lead him back? And I'll tote the other one."

"Yes, sir, I can do that," Jim answered, "but how we gonna get the deer on the horse?"

"Oh, two big men like us, we'll get 'em on the horse," Clay said, guessing the larger doe wouldn't go over a hundred and twenty-five pounds. His horse could carry all three of them, but he preferred not to handle them roughly and risk them falling off the horse. To the boy's amazement, Clay bent down and picked the large doe up in his arms and stood straight up. "She's pretty heavy," he said. "She might go one-twenty or a little more." He carried her over and laid her across his saddle. Then he picked up another one of the deer and laid her behind the saddle. "I'm sure glad you came along with me," he said to Jim. "You can start back now. The sooner we get these deer bled and skinned, the better the meat'll be. I'll come along behind you." Jim started back, so Clay went over and picked up the last deer and settled it on his shoulders. "I saved you to go with me, darlin', 'cause you're the smallest." They started back the way they had come earlier, but it was getting pretty dark by then. So he had to be more careful where he stepped. The deer on his shoulders was not a big doe, she was heavy enough to keep his feet planted solidly on the ground. And it made the trip back seem quite a bit longer than it had seemed going the other way.

"What the hell is that?" Grissom blurted when he saw the small boy approaching the circle of wagons leading a horse. He was already concerned, having heard the shots fired earlier. Clay Moran had gone down that way to hunt deer, but the shots they heard didn't sound like someone taking a shot at a deer. It was five quick shots and then nothing. It sounded more like a brief gunfight and it was the reason he and Ike were standing guard beside the wagon.

"Hell," Ike declared when Jim got a little closer, "it's the Moran kid. He went with Clay to go huntin'. That's Clay's horse and there's somethin' that looks like a body layin' across the saddle." He turned to Grissom and said, "Hell, that don't look too good."

They both started walking to meet Jim. "I swear, what happened, boy?" Grissom asked when he was close enough for Jim to hear. "Well, I'll be . . ." he started then when he saw what the horse was carrying, then saw Clay coming behind with the deer on his shoulders. "Well, I'll be . . ." Grissom repeated. Some of the other men came to join them, having become aware of someone approaching. Like Grissom, they had thought the shots they heard unusual.

"Who's ready to roast up some venison?" Clay sang out. "We need to get these deer bled and skinned right away. I could use some help."

He received a rousing cheer that alerted everyone else on the wagon train. "I'll help you butcher!" John Henry Hyde yelled. There were several other volunteers, including Matt Moran.

"You have to volunteer, Matt," Clay shouted back, "your son Jim shot one of 'em." He grinned when he saw the look of pride on Jim's face.

"Three deer!" Molly Tatum exclaimed to her husband. "He got three deer!"

"You don't play around when you go huntin', do you, Clay?" Vernon yelled at him.

"Nope," Clay replied, "not when I've got my huntin' partner with me. Jim said he wanted to get enough to feed everybody."

There were several men who volunteered to butcher the deer, so there was no further delay in draining the blood and cutting the hides away. Unlike the prairie they traveled before reaching Ash Hollow, finding a tree limb to hang the carcasses from was no problem. Some of the men who were not doing the butchering set up a couple of small tables to do the butchering on. In a short time, slices of fresh venison were roasting over the large fire built for the social hour. Even though the women had just cleaned up the dishes from supper, everyone was eager to have some of the fresh roasted meat. Social hour turned out to be a big feast in celebration of descending Windlass Hill with no fatalities or serious damage to the wagons. Young Jim Moran was basking in the envy of his friend, Skeeter Tatum, for having shot one of the deer. Clay made sure he skinned and butchered that particular deer, so no one might notice the bullet hole in the deer's ham. Everyone who wanted venison got some and there was meat left over, so that was cut up in strips, smoked over the fire, and divided up among the butchers. Even after all that, there was still time for some music before the night was done. It was minus the banjo's part, however, since John Henry Hyde was one of the butchers.

"I swear," Grissom confessed to Ike after the evening finally wound down, "I'm so damn full I've got to loosen my belt. I wish he'd gone huntin' before you cooked our supper."

"Hell," Ike said, "that was worth tacklin' Windlass Hill right there. Makes you glad we didn't go the other way so we'd miss Ash Hollow."

"That's just what I was thinkin'," Grissom said. "These folks are gonna be right back on that prairie beside the Platte when we leave here. This'll give 'em something to remember."

The next day was spent primarily enjoying the beauty of Ash Hollow and taking care of any repairs that didn't require a blacksmith or a harness maker, services that would have to wait until reaching Fort Laramie. There was one more night spent in the pleasant camp, then at seven o'clock the next morning the wagons rolled out of Ash Hollow and started following the North Platte River west toward Fort Laramie. It would take them a week to reach Scott's Bluff, passing Courthouse Rock and Chimney Rock, both already famous landmarks on this dusty trail.

Scott's Bluff, a towering rock formation that stood eight hundred feet above the North Platte River, was actually two bluffs, Scott's Bluff and South Bluff, but it was generally referred to as Scott's Bluff. It was a significant point to reach in the minds of the emigrants only for the fact that, upon reaching it, they knew they had completed one third of their journey. The pleasant stop they made at Ash Hollow, although only seven days behind them, seemed like months. Every day was once again a hot, dry trek over a mixed grass prairie, following the North Platte with its foul-tasting water, and scouting each day for buffalo chips for their fires.

Supplies were running short in many of the wagons, so they were looking forward to reaching Fort Laramie, which should be in four days after leaving Scott's Bluff, according to Grissom. The fort, at the confluence of the Platte and Laramie rivers, was a major post for the army in the Indian wars and a supply base for fur trappers and buffalo hunters, as well as emigrants on the Oregon Trail. Grissom was accurate with his estimation and at the end of the fourth day after leaving Scott's Bluff, they rolled into Fort Laramie. According to his calendar, it was the twenty-sixth of May, which gave him a great deal of satisfaction. They were making good time, even though they had started later than he normally would have. He led them to a campground not far from the fort on the Laramie River and circled the wagons. While the men took care of the horses, the women prepared to fix supper. There was plenty of wood along the riverbank for the cookfires, so everything seemed to be humming effortlessly until a loud scream rang out from down at the edge of the river. Those close by ran to the source. Clay Moran was one of them. With his rifle in hand, he ran down the bank to be suddenly met by Annie Rice, soaking wet, coming up the bank. "What is it?" he exclaimed.

"It's good!" she answered him, truly excited. "It's good! It ain't like the Platte! You can drink it!"

"Did you fall in?" Clay asked. "Are you all right?"

"No, I didn't fall in. I jumped in after I took a little taste of the water. I'm gonna take a bath and wash all our clothes," she declared. It didn't take long for the folks following close behind Clay to spread the word about the water. So under Grissom's direction, two areas of the river were designated, one for the men, the other for the women. The only problem, for the women but not so much for the men, was the path that ran along the riverbank. It led directly to a saloon and hog ranch called Jake's Place, located a mile up the river. Grissom tried to give the ladies the section with the best screen of vegetation along the bank. Cora Steptoe took it upon herself to organize a guard detail of women to guard the path along the river at a certain hour of the day to ensure the women had privacy. She figured there wouldn't be that much traffic on the path during the earlier hours of the day, that most of the use would be after supper at night.

The field where the wagons were parked was about half a mile from the fort. Grissom told them that first night at the social hour how to find the post trader's store, as well as the blacksmith and harness shop. "Last year, there was a regular farrier here, if your horses need shoein'. Those of you who need some work done, better get into the fort early in the morning. We need to pull outta here day after tomorrow. I expect most all of you will wanna go into the fort tomorrow, but I think it'd be a good idea if we didn't all go at the same time. Let them that has to get work done, or horses shod, go early and the rest of us can go later. That way, we'll always have enough folks here to keep an eye on things."

Chapter 9

"Lookee yonder, Troy, it's the wagon train that pulled in here today." He pointed to the circle of wagons in the field close to the river. "It sounds like they're havin' a big ol' time over there, don't it?"

"That's where the music was comin' from," Private Troy replied. "I thought we was both hearin' things for a while there." The two soldiers were on their way to Jake's Place and they could see the big fire in the center of the circle. "I wonder if they've got any likker over there. Might be a place to get a drink without payin' for it. Maybe they'd be proud to offer a drink to a couple of soldier boys."

"And maybe somethin' else, if there's some women that ain't too bad-lookin'," Private Lister said.

"You wanna go over there and see?" Troy asked.

"Couldn't hurt nothin'," Lister replied, "and it might save walkin' a mile and some money, too."

"You talked me into it," Troy said, and promptly left the path and started toward the circle of wagons. Lister hurried after him.

Vernon Tatum was sawing away on his fiddle when he became aware of his wife trying to get his attention. When he looked at her, she pointed to the two soldiers who had just come between two of the wagons and were approaching them. Vernon pulled his bow down, and since he was the leader of the group, the others stopped playing, too. By that time, the two soldiers were nearing the fire. "Hey there, folks," Troy said, "don't stop the music."

"That's right," Lister added, "we came over to welcome you to Fort Laramie." The two soldiers looked around them at the group gathered there, all of whom were staring back at them.

Finally, Vernon spoke. "Is there something we can do for you boys?"

"Well," Lister answered, uncertain what to say now, "we was headin' up to Jake's Place to get a drink of likker. It looked like you was havin' a party over here, so we decided we'd go to your party instead." He grinned as he searched the group of older couples gathered around the fire, looking for younger women.

Since it appeared that no one was going to address the situation, Clay got up from the log he was sitting on. "We appreciate your welcome, soldiers, but we don't have any alcohol. We're Mormons and we're gettin' ready to have a prayer service and Bible study, and you're welcome to participate."

Neither Lister nor Troy responded for a few moments until they slowly started to back away. "Thank you just the same," Troy finally said, "but I expect we'd best be gittin' along." Then they turned and headed back to the path by the river.

"Well said, Brother Clay," John Henry Hyde remarked. "That coulda been a problem."

"Amen," Vernon said. It was followed by several amens from the gathering, followed by some giggles.

Morning brought a small caravan of wagons out of the circle and over to the fort. The members of the migrant train were not awakened at four o'clock by Grissom's tortured bugle as usual, however. Grissom said he wanted them to sleep as late as they wanted, since they were not on the move that day. The common belief was that he was afraid the army bugler might hear his efforts, since they were so close to the fort. He was one of the first to visit the post trader's store, but it was not to buy supplies. He left that up to Ike since Ike was the one who did all the cooking. The purpose of Grissom's visit to the store was to talk to the post trader, Seth Ward. He needed information on a subject he had not discussed with any of the people on his train except Ike. And he could get that information from Seth just as well as he could from the post commander, and a hell of a lot easier.

Ever since the Sand Creek Massacre last November on a peaceful Cheyenne and Arapaho village in Colorado Territory, there had been an uprising among the Plains Indians. It had resulted in raids on army posts and wagon trains. Grissom wanted to know if there was any trouble with the Indians along the trail he traveled. There had been no reports when they passed through Fort Kearny, so he wanted to know what the word was at Fort Laramie. Seth told him there was no sign of trouble so far. In fact, he told him that about fifteen hundred Lakota Sioux, under Spotted Tail, had moved close to Fort Laramie this past spring to live in peace with the army. This was enough to ease Grissom's concerns about going forward.

Clay went over to the post trader's store with Matt, Katie, and the kids. He led his packhorse over as he had done at Fort Kearny, since that had proven handy on that occasion. Sarah and Hannah rode over to the fort on the packhorse, but Jim declared he was too old to ride up there behind his two sisters. They spent some time in the store, since there were quite a few folks from the wagon train. When they came out of the store, Matt and Clay loaded their purchases on the packhorse. Then to please the kids, they took a little walk around the fort. A patrol of cavalry of fifteen men with one officer rode past them and they stopped while Jim saluted. The officer returned his salute. "Is that what you used to do, Uncle Clay?" Jim asked.

"Yep, sometimes," Clay answered. "Looks like they're goin' on a patrol of some kind."

"Why didn't you stay in the army?" Sarah asked. "Didn't you like being a soldier?"

"Oh, I liked bein' a soldier all right, I guess, but I wanted to go help your daddy build a big farm and cattle ranch out in the Oregon country. I wanted to see you and Hannah and Jim grow up and go to your wedding."

"Fiddle!" Sarah said. "I'm not ever gonna get married."

Katie laughed when she heard that. "I'm going to remind her of that when she gets a few years older."

When they had seen enough of Fort Laramie to cure their curiosity, they walked back to the wagon train. Katie wanted to get back in time to wash some dirty clothes while there was still enough daylight left to dry them. And Matt, Clay, and Jim had committed to taking a bath because Grissom had told Clay that the Laramie was going to be the last good river they were going to see for a long stretch. So when they got back to the wagon, they unloaded the supplies they had just bought. Then they all went down to the river where they split up. Katie and the girls went to the heavily wooded section, reserved for the women to wash the clothes. She and the girls had already bathed that morning after breakfast with the other women. Matt, Clay, and Jim went down the river until finding a spot that offered enough privacy for them. The spot they picked was already occupied by Ike Yocum, which was somewhat surprising to Clay, although he had to admit he had no reason to be surprised. "Mind if we join you?" Matt asked.

"Hell," Ike replied, "I think the river's big enough to hold all of us. Come on in. I was just gittin' ready to get out, anyway. I got to get back and start fixin' my and Grissom's supper." So they peeled off their clothes and jumped in the river. When Ike got into some dry pants and a dry shirt, he came back over to where Clay was scrubbing himself with a washcloth. "Hell," he said, "now that I'm all cleaned up, I think I'll walk up to Jake's Place after supper and get me a drink of likker. How 'bout it, Clay, you wanna go with me?"

"I don't know," Clay responded. "That's something I hadn't thought about doin'."

LEAVING INDEPENDENCE   91

"Hell, well, think about it. I asked Grissom, but he don't wanna go." He looked over at Matt. "I'd ask you to go, but I know you got trouble."

"Trouble?" Matt asked. "Whaddaya mean I got trouble?"

"Hell, you're married," Ike answered.

"Oh," Matt replied, "you're right. I've got trouble."

"Come on and go with me, Clay. I need some company," Ike urged.

"All right, what the hell," Clay said. "It ain't like I've got any important business to take care of tonight. And I reckon I can afford a couple of shots of whiskey. Long as you ain't plannin' on stayin' too late 'cause you know we're pullin' outta here in the mornin'."

"Hell, I know that. I ain't plannin' on stayin' late, just long enough to enjoy a drink of likker." He looked behind him to make sure Jim couldn't hear him. "And anything else if it's available and reasonable, if you know what I mean."

"I know what you mean," Clay said, "but I'm just goin' for the whiskey, that's all. I ain't brave enough to have anything to do with any female who works at Jake's. I didn't know you were that fearless."

"Hell, I ain't got that much to lose and it ain't gonna be many more years before I ain't got no chips to bet with. But you're goin' with me, right?"

"Yeah, I'll go with you," Clay said. "You might need some help findin' your way back to the wagons."

"Right after supper," Ike pressed. "I'll come by your wagon."

"Right after supper," Clay confirmed. Ike nodded and left then.

"Damn," Matt swore. "Are you sure you wanna go up there with him? He sounds like he expects you to take care of him."

"He's not as bad as he makes out," Clay said. "I've been with him before. I was with him at that place at Fort Kearny, Leo Stern's Road Ranch. He talked big then, but he didn't do anything but look at the merchandise. We'll have a couple of drinks and call it a night."

"I reckon you know what you're doin'," Matt said. "But if you're wrong, at least we got you all cleaned up for your funeral."

They finished up their baths and waited a little while longer to let Jim play in the river till he was ready to go. When they walked back up the river to the spot where they left Katie and the girls, they found that they had already finished washing the clothes and gone back to the wagon. "Good," Matt said, "I hope they've got supper started. I'm hungry after all that wallowin' in the river."

Just as he had threatened, Ike showed up at Matt's wagon shortly after they finished supper. Clay noticed that he was wearing his sidearm, so he strapped his gun belt on as well. "You've been to this place before," he japed, "do I need to take my rifle, too?"

"Hell," Ike replied, "ain't no sense in takin' a chance on needin' one and not havin' it."

"You two boys stay out of trouble," Katie teased, "and don't stay out too late. I don't wanna have to send Matt to get you."

"I'll try to bring him back in one piece, ma'am," Ike tossed back to her as he and Clay left to take the path up the Laramie River in the gathering darkness. Halfway there, they could hear the sound of the saloon already cranking up for the evening. "Feller name of Jake Plummer owns this place," Ike said. "It ain't really a hog ranch. It ain't big enough to support many women, but last year Jake had a couple of gals here that stayed pretty busy. The army made him build it at least a mile away from the fort. Hell, the soldiers would walk to it if it was five miles from the fort."

"So would the drunks, I expect," Clay said. They heard the sound of horses approaching from behind them and looking back, they saw two riders, so they moved off the path to let them pass. From their appearance, Clay figured them to be ranch hands or drifters. And when they caught up to him and Ike, they didn't bother to say howdy but loped on past as if they were invisible. "It's a good thing we got off the path, ain't it?" Clay remarked. "We mighta got run over."

"Hell," Ike said, "it's dangerous to get between a man and his likker."

When they reached the saloon, Clay saw that it was nothing fancy, even though Ike said Jake had added another room on the back of it. It was a plain structure with a single door and a sign over it that read *Jake's Place*. The two horses that just loped past them were tied at a hitching rail in front of the door. When they stepped inside, Ike went directly to the bar, but Clay stopped just inside the door to look the room over. It was still early in the evening, but there were more customers than he expected, considering there were only two horses tied out front. Then it occurred to him that the other customers were soldiers who had to walk from the fort. There were seven of them, seated at two tables. *They must have walked up here right after mess call,* he thought. The two men who passed them on horses were sitting at a table in the center of the room. They were working on a bottle of whiskey. Clay walked over to join Ike at the bar then.

"Say howdy to Elmo," Ike said when Clay walked up. "He's been the bartender here forever."

"Howdy, Elmo," he said, "Clay Moran."

"Welcome to Jake's, Clay," Elmo greeted him. "What can I pour for you? I can give you any kind of whiskey you want as long as it's corn or rye."

"I'll be honest with you, Elmo," Clay confessed. "I'm not much of a drinker, so I don't know what kind of likker I like best. So whatever Ike's drinkin', I'll have the same."

"An honest man," Elmo remarked, then picked up the bottle and poured two shots. "Ike's drinkin' corn whiskey." Back to Ike then, he continued, "Like I said, Lola and Thelma oughta be comin' in pretty soon now. They're in the back eatin' supper." As if on cue then, a door in the back of the room opened and a woman walked into the room. A minor rising of enthusiasm went up from the two tables the soldiers were occupying, so she went over to say hello. "That's Thelma," Elmo said, "Lola usually stays longer at the supper table."

They stood at the bar for a while with Ike watching the door in the back of the room and Clay making idle conversation with Elmo until Clay grew impatient waiting for Ike to make a move in some direction. "Let me just buy the rest of that bottle," he suggested, "and we'll take it over and sit down at a table." So that's what they did and Clay told Ike to pick out the table he preferred. Ike picked one and sat down in a chair that faced the back door. Clay poured them both another drink from his bottle. "So tell me, Ike," he asked, "do you know this other woman, this Lola?"

"Nope," Ike replied.

"Well, why are you waitin' for her to come out the back door then? She might not even be workin' tonight. And none of those soldiers are lookin' like they wanna invest any money in Thelma's company. Why don't you wave her over here and see if she'll have a drink with us."

"Hell," Ike said, "she's a little too bony to suit me. I like 'em with a little more cushion on 'em." So they poured another drink from Clay's bottle and waited. And Clay swore that was the last drink he was going to have. Ike, on the other hand, was getting a little tense and said he needed another to relax him. Clay poured it for him but none for himself, and they waited.

Then one of the two men sitting at the table in the center of the room yelled at Thelma to come over to his table. Thelma gave him a fearful look, then looked down at one of the soldiers and said something. The soldier pulled her down to sit in his lap and yelled back at the man who called for her, "She's busy." Clay figured Thelma knew the first man and had had a bad experience with him. He took another look at the man. He was a rough-looking individual, the kind that might be brutal with women and children.

The man pushed his chair back and got to his feet. He was a big man and he was wearing what looked like a Colt .45 Navy revolver. His partner was also wearing a sidearm and they were obviously unimpressed by seven soldiers they knew were unarmed. "Thelma," the brute threatened, "don't make me come over there and pull you off that soldier-boy's lap. 'Cause if I do, it's gonna be bad for both of ya."

One of the other soldiers, a sizable man, himself, stood up. "Look here, mister, the lady's already engaged for the evenin'. She obviously doesn't want to visit with you, anyway. So why don't you just set yourself back down, drink your likker, and quit botherin' her."

"Well, now," the brute replied. "Whaddaya think about that, Red? Little Thelma's got herself some soldiers to look after her, but there ain't none of 'em wearin' a gun."

"I reckon they figure they got us outnumbered, Jack," Red responded. "I count seven of 'em, if you're talkin' 'bout both tables, and there ain't but two of us."

"That is a fact," Jack said. "I got five bullets in my gun. How many you got in yours?"

"I've got five, too, with the hammer settin' on an empty chamber," Red answered.

"My 'rithmetic ain't ever been too strong," Jack said, "but I believe we can take care of all of 'em and have three bullets left over." Their little performance over then, Jack directed his threat back to the soldier who had spoken out in Thelma's defense. "All right, General, I'm gonna give you a chance to show everybody how tough you are. If you can borrow a gun from one of them fellers settin' over at that table"—he nodded toward Clay and Ike—"then you can stand up and face me. And the winner gets Thelma."

"I'm not gonna face you in a duel," the soldier said. "You've no doubt practiced drawing that gun you're wearin'. It wouldn't be a fair fight. I'm sure you'd win."

"Damn right I'd win," Jack said. "But I'm gonna shoot you if you don't stand up like a man and face me, anyway. I can't abide a low-down coward like you, so get yourself a gun or get ready to meet your maker."

"I've had about as much of this as I care to watch," Clay finally declared. "Ike, keep your eye on that one he called Red. If he makes a move, shoot him."

"Hell," Ike said, "it'd be my pleasure." He eased his six-gun out of his holster and held it beside his leg.

Clay got up from the table and walked over to stand right in front of the man called Jack. "What tha . . . ?" Jack blurted. "You lookin' to get yourself shot?"

"Nope," Clay said. "I brought a gun for the soldier, since he needs to borrow one." Then before Jack could react, Clay whipped his Colt out of his holster and flipped it upside down, so he was holding it by the barrel. Jack almost drew his gun but stopped when Clay just stood almost toe to toe with him, holding the gun by the barrel. Clay smiled and said, "This is the gun for the soldier in your duel. Is that all right?"

Jack grinned back at him. "Yeah, that's perfect."

"Good," Clay said, and striking like a rattlesnake, he hit Jack in the temple with the butt of the pistol, dropping him like a rock to the floor. Without missing a beat, he flipped the gun around and held it on Red, who had no time to act. Clay nodded to Ike, who had his six-gun in hand as well. "Ike, take his gun."

"Hell, right," he said, and hustled over behind Red and relieved him of the weapon.

Clay looked down at Jack, who was beginning to stir slightly as if starting to wake up, so Clay motioned toward the two tables where the soldiers were all standing gaping. "Some of you soldiers get over here and hold these two jackasses down." They responded to his commands at once. "You, soldier," he told one who had not piled on the two men to hold them down, "go outside and get the rope off their saddles."

"Yes, sir!" the soldier responded, and ran out the door.

Standing dumbfounded behind the bar throughout the entire capture of the two men, the bartender finally sought to find out what he should do. He walked out from the bar and approached Clay. "Whaddaya gonna do with 'em?" he asked.

"I'm not gonna do anything with 'em," Clay told him. "I was only interested in stopping a senseless murder of one of those soldiers. I'm gonna tie those two up and turn them over to the soldiers to take care of. Or give 'em to you if you've got something to do with 'em. I don't reckon there's any sheriff or marshal or anybody like that at Fort Laramie, is there?"

"No," Elmo said, "far as I know, everything is handled by the military."

"How do you usually handle trouble that happens like that?"

"Usually, Mr. Plummer tells 'em to take it outside and settle it themselves," Elmo said. "If it had happened at the fort, they'd put the two of 'em in the guardhouse."

"Well, there's your answer," Clay said. "We'll give 'em to the soldiers." When Elmo didn't understand that logic, Clay said, "Come on, you'll see what I mean."

The soldiers were already in the process of tying Jack and Red up like two mummies. So Clay remarked to the soldier who had first stood up and told Jack he wouldn't shoot it out with him what they were to do. "I'm leaving these two in the hands of you men now. What you are to do with them is lay them over their saddles and when you walk back to the fort tonight, lead their horses back with you. And when you get back, turn them over to the officer of the guard, and he'll throw them in the guardhouse. Can you do that?"

"Yes, sir, we sure can, and thank you, sir."

"You're welcome. They're in your hands now," Clay said. That done, he pulled Ike off to the side. "What do you want to do now? You wanna talk to that woman, Lola, if she ever shows up?"

"Hell, if it's all the same to you, I'd just as soon go on back to the wagons. I've had enough excitement for the night."

"Glad to hear it. Come on, let's go," Clay said, and headed for the door.

The soldier who had been threatened by Jack commented to those standing near him when he saw them go out the door. "I don't know what we woulda done if that man hadn't been here."

"Boy, that's the truth," Private Troy said.

"You best not mess around with those Mormons," Private Lister said. "They don't put up with troublemakers."

Chapter 10

Clay and Ike got back to the wagons while the social hour was still in progress. Ike decided he was ready for bed so he went directly to Grissom's wagon, while Clay chose to join Matt and Katie at the social gathering. He was pretty sure they would be out there with the other folks, so he didn't bother going by the wagon first. His mind was occupied with the unexpected encounter he had experienced at Jake's Place and he was halfway to the gathering when he realized that he was carrying a bottle half-filled with corn whiskey. He had intended to give it to Ike, and by the time they walked back, he just forgot he was holding it. He paused and started to turn around and go to Grissom's wagon. Then he decided social hour would soon be over. He would just hold on to the bottle until tomorrow, or maybe Matt would like a couple of shots. I must be getting old, he thought, to forget I was holding something in my hand. I'll give it to Ike tomorrow, he decided, and held the bottle close against the side of his leg while he looked ahead to locate Matt and Katie. Good, he thought, for they were sitting off to the side with a small group consisting of the Courtlands, the Steptoes, the Rices, and Eleanor Hyde, whose husband was playing the banjo.

"Hey, Clay," Matt called out when Clay slipped up beside him and sat down. "I didn't expect you back so soon. Whata you tryin' to hide there?"

"About half a bottle of corn likker that I was gonna give Ike and forgot I still had it," Clay whispered. "There ain't enough to pass around, if that's what you're thinkin'."

"Just stick it down behind this box I'm sittin' on and nobody will see it," Matt said. "What about Ike? Did he get his itch scratched?"

Clay chuckled. "No, they had two doves workin' there, but we only saw one of 'em, and she spent the whole time with a bunch of soldiers from the fort. Ike said she was too bony, anyway. The bartender, Elmo, said there was another one in the kitchen eatin' supper, but she never came out before we left. I told him I was in no hurry, if he wanted to wait her out, but he said he'd lost the urge."

"Well, maybe Grissom will take another load of folks out to Oregon next year and Ike can try it again," Matt suggested.

"It might take him that long to work up the urge again," Clay said, and they both chuckled over that.

"What are you two giggling about over there?" Katie asked.

"Oh, the weather tomorrow and the next leg of the journey, and things like that," Matt answered her.

"Well, pay attention," Katie scolded, "Grissom's getting ready to say something about that right now." They looked over toward the fire and saw the wagon master walking up.

Grissom stood by the fire and waited until Vernon and the boys finished the tune they were punishing at the moment. "Mighty fine," he complimented them when they finished. "You boys sound better every night. You might wanna go professional by the time we reach Oregon City and let the women work the farms." He waited for the chuckling and the catcalls to subside before he continued. "Tomorrow mornin' we're pullin' outta here to keep headin' for the Continental Divide. I know we're all anxious to get back to the North Platte road and leave this nasty Laramie River water behind." He waited again for the boos and catcalls. "So I wanted to give you a choice about tomorrow's travel. When we leave here, we ain't gonna travel but eight miles before we come to a line of high bluffs on the south side of the Platte. One of 'em is about a hundred-foot-high sandstone cliff and they've took to callin' it Register Cliff. And the reason is because every wagon train that passes this way stops so everybody can leave a message or carve their name on it. A lot of 'em camp overnight there because it does have good grassy pasture to camp in. What I'm tryin' to say is we'll stop there so you can all carve your name on the face of that cliff if you want to. But it ain't but eight miles. So I don't want to spend the night there, so I want you to know that we'll be noonin' there and drivin' another four miles to a freshwater creek to overnight."

No one saw fit to make any comment on his announcement. For the most part, they just looked at each other and shrugged indifferently. Finally, Bryan Roland spoke. "But you say we will stop there and have some time to write our names and the date? Because we'll be part of the country's history."

"That's what I'm tellin' you," Grissom answered. "I'm just sayin' let's don't waste half a day just so everybody can be part of the country's history. We'll make the noon stop there and that oughta give everybody time to carve up that bluff. That half a day might mean the difference between catchin' an early blizzard in the Blue Mountains and missin' one."

There was some conversation about the noontime stop at Register Cliff planned for the next day, but no one seemed to care if they stayed there overnight or not. Most of them wondered why Grissom brought it up at all. The music started up again and there was some dancing, mostly two women dancing together, while their lead-footed husbands sat and watched, or went back to the wagon to go to bed. Harlan Rice was one of the lead-feet. When Annie and Katie came back to join their men, after a buck dancing duel, Evelyn Courtland told Annie that Harlan went back to the wagon. "Said he was feelin' poorly, otherwise he'da been dancin' with you."

"Well, I'da loved to see that, myself," Annie replied. "I tried to teach him a few simple little steps right after we first got married. It was hard to teach him because when you said, stick your left foot out, he had to stick both feet out."

"Sounds about like Matt," Katie said. "He won't even try."

"I'd dance, if the pay was better," Matt remarked. "How 'bout you, Clay?"

Clay replied, "Just thinkin' about dancin' has tired me out." He got up on his feet. "I think I'll go crawl in my blanket. Four o'clock comes mighty early in the morning. Good night, all." He remembered his whiskey bottle behind the box Matt was using for a seat.

"Katie and I'll be along pretty soon, I expect," Matt told him when he reached down behind him to pick it up.

"Did you move it?" Clay whispered as he felt around behind the box.

"Move what?" Matt asked, having forgotten all about it.

"My damn likker bottle!" Clay responded, almost loud enough for everybody to hear. "It's gone!"

"What?" Matt jumped up and picked up the box, and like Clay, started looking all around in the weeds behind them. "How the hell could it be gone? We've been sittin' here the whole time."

By this time, everyone who was sitting in their little group was aware of their strange behavior. "Matt!" Katie demanded. "What on earth has got into you two? What's gone? What are you talking about?"

"Oh, nothin', Katie," Matt responded. "Just something Clay had and we can't find it."

"Sounded like he said something about a likker bottle," Eleanor Hyde offered.

"Yeah," Matt said. "It sounded like . . . Tell 'em, Clay."

Clay didn't know whether to laugh or not, but he knew he had to save Matt, because Katie was already building up some mischief that he was evidently guilty of. "Here's the thing, Katie. When I came back from the saloon, I had half a bottle of corn whiskey I intended to give to Ike. I saw everybody out here with the musicians and I plumb forgot I was holdin' that bottle in my hand. I forgot to give it to Ike. I didn't want anybody to see it because there wasn't enough to offer everybody a drink. Besides that, I still wanted to give it to Ike. So I put it behind that box Matt was sittin' on and it disappeared."

It was a mystery because no one had come to join their little group the entire time they had settled there. There was one, however, who automatically had a suspect in mind. *So he was feeling poorly, was he?* Annie Rice thought, and he went back to the wagon while she and Katie were dancing. *That sorry excuse for a man*, she thought. *The father of her two daughters.* She felt guilty for not doing better by them. Half a bottle of whiskey, Clay had said. She wondered how much it would take to make him crazy or mean. She decided she'd better get back to the wagon right away. Her girls were there. She hoped he'd sneaked off to hide somewhere while he drank it all up. "Well, I'll say good night," she suddenly announced. "I've gotta be getting back." She looked at Clay when she walked by him and said, "I sincerely hope you find that bottle of whiskey."

"I doubt I will," he replied. "It didn't just walk off by itself." He thought it best not to say anything, but like her, he remembered that Harlan had left early.

Annie hurried back to her wagon where she found both girls sitting beside their sleeping tent with one small candle providing some light. "Where's your papa?" Annie asked.

"I thought he was with you at the social hour," Alice answered.

"He didn't come back to the wagon?" Annie asked.

"No, ma'am."

That was good news to Annie. She didn't want him around her girls when she wasn't there and he'd been drinking. "I'm surprised your candle doesn't blow out, settin' out here in the breeze," she said, preferring not to let them know what was on her mind.

"It did blow out a couple of times," Alice said. "Then I moved it over to this side of the tent and the tent blocks the wind."

"Well, that was smart," Annie said. "I expect it's about time for you girls to think about going to bed. We're gonna be back on the trail schedule in the morning. That means four o'clock when Mr. Grissom blows that bugle."

"I wish one morning Mr. Grissom would oversleep," Jenny said. "Then we'd all sleep on until the sun came up."

Annie laughed. "I don't know how long it would take us to get to Oregon if we slept that late every morning. You girls get ready for bed now."

"Where's Papa?" Alice asked.

"I don't know," Annie answered. "He's probably talking to some of the other men somewhere. Everybody hasn't left the social hour yet. I'm sure he'll be home pretty soon." She turned when she heard something on the other side of the wagon. "See, here he is now. Get ready for bed." She went to the back of the wagon where she found her husband emptying his bladder of its contents. "Damn you, Harlan, your daughters are right on the other side of the wagon. Don't you have any sense of decency?"

"Hell, they oughta know by now how a man passes water," Harlan responded, his words properly slurred by the whiskey he had imbibed.

"You must have drank every drop in the bottle you stole," she said.

"Bottle? What bottle?" he responded. "Oh, you mean this bottle?" He held it up for her to see. "Every last drop," he confirmed. "Whaddaya mean stole? I didn't steal this bottle. I found it growin' right there in the weeds."

"Ain't you got any shame a-tall?" she demanded, disgusted with him. "You saw Clay Moran put that bottle behind his brother. Then you sneaked behind Matt like a weasel in the henhouse and stole it like a common thief. I know you don't give a damn what I think of you anymore. But think of your daughters and how they must feel, knowing everybody on this wagon train thinks you ain't worth as much as a sack of buffalo chips."

"I don't wanna hear no more outta that mouth of yours," Harlan said, turning back to his mean side again. "You don't talk to me like that, and you sure as hell don't tell me how to act in front of my daughters. All three of you better start showin' me a helluva lot more respect."

"You have to earn respect," Annie said, "and right now you ain't earned a nickel's worth. Why don't you tell Alice and Jenny how you sneaked behind Matt Moran's back like an egg-suckin' dog and stole Clay's whiskey. See how much respect that buys you." She should have been warned, standing right up in his face like she was, even though his speech was slurred and he seemed unsteady on his feet. When she refused to relent in her verbal attack on him, he suddenly struck her with his fist. The blow landed on her chin, at the corner of her mouth, knocking her to the ground.

She lay there, stunned for a couple of minutes, and he stood over her, glaring down at her, his drunken anger intense. "You ever open your mouth to me like that again and you'll get worse. It's time you learned who's the boss of this family." Then feeling as if he was about to pass out, he turned and went in search of his bedroll.

She continued to lie there on the ground for a long time, bleeding from a cut in her lip and feeling as if her jaw was dislocated. She scolded herself for getting so close up in his face. She should have known better, aware of the kind of coward he was by now. After a few moments more, she aroused her determination and struggled to her feet. She went back around to the other side of the wagon to check on the girls. She found them inside their sleeping tent but still awake. They stared at her with fearful eyes. "Mama," Alice said, "your mouth is bleeding!"

"I know, honey. It's nothing," she said, although it hurt when she spoke, "a little accident."

"We heard you and Papa fighting," Jenny said. "I was afraid. He was talking crazy again."

"I know, darlin', Papa got ahold of some whiskey again, but it's all gone now and I think he's gone to bed. I'm gonna go check on him right now. So you and Alice go to sleep now. We'll be gettin' up early in the morning." She gave each of them a peck on the cheek with the side of her mouth that wasn't bleeding and tucked their covers up close to their chins.

Satisfied that her girls were all right, she went back to the other side of the wagon where she found Harlan, passed out cold. He didn't make it inside the sleeping tent set up there. Instead, he simply pulled the blanket, lying on top of the tent to air out, off the tent and dropped down on it, and was already snoring away. *The peaceful sleep of the innocent,* she thought to herself, sarcastically. She kicked the sole of one of his boots lightly with the toe of her shoe. He didn't respond. So she went to the back of the wagon and got the coil of rope from the tailgate. She returned to Harlan and tied his boots together tightly with one end of the rope. He paused for a brief moment before continuing with his snoring. Then she gently rolled him onto his side and held him there. He grunted and stopped snoring, but after a few moments, he began snoring again in earnest, so she rolled him all the way over on his stomach. Now, she could tie his hands together behind his back, so she did so, then she took the loose end of the rope and tied his hands to his feet.

Content that he was secure for the night, she hung what was left of the coil of rope on the side of the wagon and proceeded to get ready for bed. She checked to make sure the coffeepot was filled with water and the fire was set, ready to light. She then climbed out of her clothes and into her nightgown, did what she could for her swollen lip, and went to bed, satisfied that she would not be disturbed during the night.

She was awake with the first few rusty notes of Grissom's

bugle, so she got up at once and crawled out of the tent to take a look at her husband. He was just stirring, in the process of waking up, but obviously confused by his inability to turn his body to a more comfortable position. She decided he was all right there for the moment, so she went to the other side of the wagon to check on the girls. They were awake, so she said good morning and suggested that they might take an extra quarter hour of rest if they'd like. "And I thought we might have some pancakes this morning, since we've got the makings for once." That suggestion was met with enthusiasm from both girls. "I've got a couple of little things to take care of first and then we'll get started on them."

She left them to snuggle back down in their blankets while she went back around to check on Harlan. "Well, good morning, Harlan, I see you finally woke up."

"Annie, what the hell . . . ?" He struggled to free himself and realized that he was not just tangled up in his blanket, he was tied hand and foot. "What the hell is goin' on here?" he demanded this time. "Get me outta these ropes!"

"You got some punishment coming first for slugging me in the face. You liked to broke my jaw. So you'll have to answer for that. I'll bet when you were a little boy your mama and daddy told you boys weren't supposed to hit little girls. You probably got a whippin' for it if you did, didn't you?"

"You're talkin' crazy," Harlan said. "Untie me. I gotta go take care of the horses."

"That's right, you've got chores to do, so I expect we'd better get on with it." She took her butcher knife and cut a handy length off the coil of rope for her purpose. Then she tied a double knot in the end of it and started walking toward him, swinging the rope round and round.

"Wait a minute," he blurted nervously. "I don't know what you're thinking about doin'. You'd do well to just untie me and let me go take care of the horses."

"I'm going to," she said, twirling the end of her rope faster, "but first there's a little matter of you hittin' me in the face with your fist. You gotta pay for that. Then there is that business about stealin' likker." Then she suddenly whipped him across his shoulders.

"Ow," he yelped, then, "Ow, ow, ow," as she warmed to her task, his clothes offering less and less protection as she gained determination. "Stop, Annie, it weren't me that hit you. It was the whiskey doin' it. I swear!"

"I know that, Harlan. I ain't whuppin' you, I'm whuppin' the whiskey. If you hit me like that, I'd shoot you," she said as she continued swinging the knotted rope.

"Cut me loose, damn it, I'm warnin' you, you'll be sorry for this."

She gave him one across the neck then. "You warnin' me? Anything happens to me, you're gonna have to be the mama for our two daughters, do the cookin' and the washin', and everything else they need. You better hope nothing happens to me before we get to Oregon. If something happens to you, I can drive this wagon. You oughta keep that in mind, you ain't needed for a damn thing." She untied him then and when he was free of her ropes, she said, "Now, go take care of the horses. The girls and I are gonna make pancakes this morning, so you don't wanna be late for breakfast."

Harlan wisely kept his thoughts to himself as he struggled up from the shoddy bed he had passed the night in. He hurried out after the other men to make sure the horses got water and grazed before leaving Fort Laramie. He made it a point to avoid saying good morning to Dick Batson, whose wagon was parked in line in front of his, as well as Henry Corbett, whose wagon was right behind. They were bound to have heard the confrontation between him and Annie.

Seven o'clock according to Grissom's railroad pocket watch saw the wagons roll away from the pasture on the Laramie River and return to the emigrant road following the North Platte. Clay

Moran rode his gray gelding up beside Ike Yokum, driving Grissom's wagon. "Mornin'," Clay said and Ike returned it. "I thought you mighta been wonderin' what happened to that half a bottle of corn whiskey I brought back last night."

"Hell," Ike responded, "you bought it, so I figure you could do what you wanted to, but I was wonderin' if you drank it all last night."

Clay chuckled at his response. "I meant to give that bottle of whiskey to you, but I plumb forgot I was holdin' it when we got back. I walked right on out to the social hour carryin' that bottle." He went on to tell Ike the whole story about the missing bottle. "You know, I didn't wanna say for sure that Harlan Rice stole that bottle of likker, but it sure is easy to suspect he did. I wouldn't say anything about it to him. I think that poor wife of his has suffered enough embarrassment because of his drinkin'."

They were joined by Grissom then as he pulled up beside Clay. "I didn't see you up here at the head of the train," Clay joked. "So I thought I'd take over as the wagon master."

"I was back at the last wagons, trying to convince Steptoe that we wanted him to join the rest of the wagon train, instead of creatin' his own little wagon train. He's got three wagons behind him and a gap gettin' bigger and bigger between him and Bowen's wagon."

"Steptoe and some of them behind him might not have agreed with what you said last night about Register Cliff and it not being but eight miles," Clay said. "Maybe they're thinkin' more about campin' overnight there, instead of just noonin' there like you said."

Grissom laughed. "Now, I never thought about that. You could be right."

"I reckon I'll drop back and see how my brother and sister-in-law are gettin' along this mornin'," Clay said, and started to wheel the gray around, but Grissom stopped him.

"Ike said you two ran into a little trouble up at Jake's Place last night," Grissom said.

"Yep, that's right, we did," Clay replied. "We had a couple of drinks, but the one whore we saw was captured by a bunch of soldiers. Ike said she was too scrawny for his needs, anyway. There was supposed to be another one who was a little more to Ike's liking. You know, with more padding, but she never came outta the kitchen. So Ike kinda lost his enthusiasm."

Grissom looked at him and shook his head as if confused. "Ike said there was two drifters there who tried to get one of the soldiers to shoot it out with him, and you knocked him out with the butt of your six-gun. He said you had the soldiers tie the two drifters up and take 'em back to the fort."

"Well, yeah, there was that, too," Clay said. He wheeled the gray around then and headed back to join with his brother's wagon. Ike looked at Grissom and grinned in response to Grissom's look of disbelief.

Clay pulled over beside his brother Matt on the driver's seat of his wagon. "Don't reckon your bottle of whiskey ever showed up, did it?" Matt asked.

"Nope," Clay answered, "but I'm pretty sure I know where it ended up." Jim, who was walking a little ahead of his mother and his sisters, came over to walk next to Clay's horse. "You want a ride?" Clay asked, and reached down for him. Jim grabbed his arm and Clay pulled him up behind him.

"When we gonna go deer huntin' again, Uncle Clay?" Jim asked.

"I don't know," Clay answered. "I expect it'll depend on whether or not we find some deer and we have a chance to go after 'em."

Chapter 11

The wagon train traveled the short distance to Register Cliff and paused there as Grissom had promised, and as he expected, almost everyone wanted to carve their names and the date they passed the sandstone cliff standing one hundred and fifty feet above the plains. They remained there for the noon meal before pushing on another four miles to camp overnight at a stream that Grissom had used before and that provided better water than they had experienced at Register Cliff. Pushing on the next morning, they traveled the monotony of the North Platte for five more days before reaching La Prele Creek a little earlier than the usual five o'clock stopping time.

It was a strong creek, looking more like a small river, with pure water, wide and about two feet deep at the crossing. It was no wonder that Grissom chose to camp there, instead of pushing on until five o'clock. He said it was called La Prele Creek. Clay thought it odd that Grissom knew the name of the creek, when he didn't know the names of other creeks they crossed. So he asked the reason. "There's a lot of people that know about La Prele Creek because of the natural bridge," Grissom told him.

"What natural bridge?" Clay asked.

Grissom turned and pointed down the creek to the south. "Yonder way," he said, "'bout two miles down the creek. I ain't never gone down there to see it, myself, but it's down yonder at the foot of that mountain you can see there. It's a bridge this creek carved outta solid rock about a hundred feet long and standin' about fifty feet over the creek."

"Damn," Clay replied, "I'd like to see that. Why haven't you ever gone down there to see it?"

"Hell," Ike interrupted, "'cause it's too blame much trouble to get down in that gorge where it is. We've had some folks go to the trouble to see it. They had to go down a steep mountainside to get down to the creek. Then they had to push through brush so thick they thought they was gonna have to set it on fire to get out."

"That is a problem," Clay declared, but he still had enough curiosity to want to see it. "Anybody ever ride down the creek to it, instead of goin' down the mountain?"

"I don't know," Grissom said. "Least not that I know of, but I reckon you could get there that way. It's a strong creek, but it ain't but about two feet deep."

"I think I'll take my horse for a little ride down that creek, just to see how far we can get," Clay decided. "I didn't ride him much today, anyway, so he ought not complain."

"If you ain't back by the time we roll outta here in the mornin', I'll send Ike down that creek to find you," Grissom japed.

"Don't count on that," Ike said.

Clay got the gray out of the horse herd and led him back to the wagon to saddle him. "Where you goin'?" Matt asked when he saw what Clay was doing. Clay told him about the natural bridge that was supposedly over the creek and said he was going to ride down the creek to see it.

"You say it's two miles down the creek?" Katie asked. Clay said that was correct so she said, "I'm just starting to fix supper, you won't have much time if you wait till after supper."

"No, I wouldn't," Clay said, "so I'm gonna go ahead and go now. Grissom said folks that have seen that bridge say it's one of nature's wonders. And I ain't seen many of nature's wonders in my life, so I'm gonna go see it." He nodded firmly to confirm it. "Of course, I wasn't countin' you when I said I hadn't seen many of nature's wonders, Katie."

"That won't work," Katie said. "I haven't even started supper yet. Take some of that smoked deer jerky with you, if it's still fit to eat." She got a couple of strips for him and wrapped them in a cloth. "I was saving that jerky for an emergency. I guess this is a little bit of an emergency when somebody wants to ride a horse up a river. Bring the cloth back with you."

"Thank you, doll," Clay said.

"I wish she'd fuss over me like that," Matt grumbled.

"I thought you knew that when you marry a woman, she doesn't have to fuss over you anymore," Clay said. "That's the reason I ain't hitched yet."

"That and the fact that you ain't ever found a gal that'll have you yet," Matt said.

"Yeah, then there's that. I think I'll say goodbye now." He climbed on his horse and rode down to the creek. He followed the creek south, upstream, walking the gray along the bank when it was passable on horseback, walking him in the water when it was not. He couldn't help but admire the beauty of the creek as it approached the sandstone bluffs. The water was pure and clear. He could see the rocky bottom clearly enough to avoid the larger and sharp-edged stones that might damage the gray's hooves. The deeper he rode into the gorge formed by nature, the more powerful the water seemed to be, and the more noise it produced as it surged through the rocky crevices. He was surprised to see grass-covered banks and trees and bushes when he rode deeper into the gorge. And then he saw the bridge. It looked monstrous! Perfectly formed, like a stone sculpture, and it spanned the wide creek, maybe a hundred feet long and standing fifty feet above the water. He realized then that he had been standing still in the creek for several minutes, captured by his first sight of the natural bridge. He had not expected to see a work so extraordinary hidden away in this gorge. He was at once glad that he had decided to come.

He started to nudge his horse to continue but he hesitated because he just then noticed the thin gray ribbon of smoke wafting up from a grassy bank that sloped down to the water, on the other side of the bridge. Alert now, he peered at the spot where the smoke originated and discovered the form of a man sitting there. Evidently, just sighting him as well, the man stood up and peered back at him. He was an Indian, Clay could see that at once, even though the light was fading rapidly in the gorge. He showed no sign of alarm, he just remained standing there watching Clay. Clay looked quickly around him. Were there more Indians closing in around him now? He slowly eased the Henry rifle from its saddle scabbard and let it rest across his thighs as he prodded the gray gently and began moving forward again. He figured he would already be dead now if he had, in fact, ridden into an ambush. He felt pretty sure the Indian was alone. The size of his fire should have told him that. *Might as well see if we can make this a friendly visit*, he thought.

He rode under the bridge and up on the bank while the Indian remained standing holding a rifle in one hand, hanging down by his leg. Clay stepped down, one hand still holding his rifle. The Indian continued to stand motionless as if waiting for him to speak, so Clay wasn't sure if he was friend or foe. So for sake of any better idea, he made the peace sign with his free hand, a Sioux sign he had been taught in the army. He had no idea what tribe this man he was facing now belonged to. He wasn't even sure he was making the sign correctly, since he had never had an occasion to use it before. He had never fought the Sioux. The Indian standing before him now was a fine specimen of a man, maybe his brother Matt's age, and he looked surprised when Clay had given him a sign of peace. When it appeared they were at a silent standoff, Clay finally asked, "You speak white man?"

Another flicker of surprise appeared in the Indian's eyes and he nodded, then spoke. "I speak white man talk."

Thank goodness for that, Clay thought, because he didn't know any sign language. "My name is Clay Moran."

"I am Black Bear of the Cheyenne nation. I have come to fight you."

Properly startled by that announcement, Clay asked, "Why have you come to fight me? I come in peace. I don't have any reason to fight you." There hadn't been any reports of Indian trouble when they were at Fort Laramie, especially Cheyenne. They would have been warned if that was the case.

Black Bear looked confused at that point. "Then why have you come to this sacred place?"

"I don't mean to offend you," Clay said. "I didn't know this place was sacred to the Cheyenne."

"Not long ago, the Cheyenne ruled all this land, all the way down to what your people call Texas. This land here between the two forks of the river was a Cheyenne hunting ground. The white man has changed all that and has taken our land. I came to this sacred place to fast and make my medicine. In my dream, the Great Father said a white warrior would come to challenge me and test my faith. And then you came."

That didn't sound too good to Clay. "I'm not the man you saw in your dream. I simply came to see the natural bridge over this creek. I didn't know it was a sacred place. I know the white man has stolen land that belonged to the Cheyenne, but I am just passing through on my way to the far west. I will leave this sacred place now. I did not come to fight."

Clay's talking only served to confuse Black Bear. He had ridden a long way from the reservation to come to this special place to make his medicine. He had fasted and meditated for three nights and days until his dreams came to him, telling him that a white man would appear, and that he must kill this white man. Now this white man had turned his back and was walking back to his horse. *What trick is this?* He dropped his rifle, drew his scalping knife, and charged after him. Clay turned, cocking his rifle, when he heard Black Bear's rifle drop to the ground. "Stop!" he warned, but the Indian kept coming, his knife raised to strike, so Clay pulled the trigger and stepped aside as Black Bear collapsed on the grassy bank, a bullet in his chest.

"Why didn't you listen to me?" Clay urged. "I didn't wish you any harm." He knelt down beside the dying man, feeling sick in his stomach for the senseless killing. "You should have shot me in the back, instead of comin' at me like a crazy man." He had been given no time to place his shot, or even think about placing it. His natural reflexes overrode his conscious thoughts and delivered the kill shot. As a consequence, there was nothing he could do to save him, so he remained by his side and watched him finally die.

He had no tools with him to bury Black Bear, so he was going to have to leave him for the scavengers to deal with. Wishing to give him some form of a grave, he dragged his body off the bank and rolled it over into a deep gully. Then he caught his horse and relieved it of a crude Indian saddle and bridle and let it go free. He had no desire to take it back to the wagon train with him to remind him of the useless killing he had performed on this misguided Indian. He felt like he would have felt if he had killed an innocent child.

As he rode back down the creek, it seemed like the distance back to the crossing was much greater than when he was riding upstream to the bridge. "I wish to hell I had never thought about going to see that damn bridge," he suddenly blurted to the gray gelding. Then he heard the fiddle and the banjo crank up and figured he was about halfway back. *They're getting started a little late tonight*, he thought as the guitar players joined Vernon and John Henry. He wondered then why he wasn't hungry. "A night like tonight will make you lose your appetite, I reckon."

"Hey, Clay," Ike yelled to him when he rode into the circle of wagons, "did you find that there natural bridge?"

"Yep, I found it," Clay answered, and continued on to the horse herd to leave the gray with the other horses. When he carried his saddle back to the wagon, he found Katie and Matt still there. Surprised, he said, "I thought I'd find you two over there listening to the music."

"We decided to wait till you showed up," Katie said. "Thought you might be hungry, so I've still got some beans and rice in that kettle hanging over the fire. And Matt left a little bit of coffee in the pot."

He decided that he was hungry then. "I swear, that's mighty nice of you, Katie. It was even thoughtful of you, Matt, leavin' me a little coffee. So, one thing led to another and I never even got around to eatin' the deer jerky you gave me. So I brought it back. I'll tell you what I'll do. You and Matt go on out to the social hour and I'll clean up your kettle and coffeepot and things when I'm finished."

"No such a thing," Katie responded. "You'd likely be as bad at it as your brother. If you wanna save me a step or two, just eat right outta the kettle and I won't have to wash another dish. There's not but about one good serving in the kettle."

"I want to hear about the natural bridge," Matt said. "Did you find it?"

"Yeah, I did," Clay answered him. He shook his head slowly and said, "I found it, but I wish to hell I hadn't." He went on to tell Matt and Katie about the incident at the bridge and the fact that he was forced to kill a man for no good reason at all.

"We heard the shot," Matt said. "It sounded like that Henry rifle of yours and there wasn't but one shot, so I figured you might come back with a deer or something. I understand why you wish you hadn't gone to look at that bridge, but you got no call to beat yourself up over it. And I disagree, you had the best reason I can think of to kill him, to keep from being stabbed to death. Ain't that right, Katie?"

"I'd have to agree with Matt on that," Katie said. "Sounds to me like you weren't given any choice." She didn't say everything she was thinking, however, and that was the fact that he did have a conscience. "Was the bridge as fascinating as they said?"

"Yes it was," Clay answered, "a magnificent work of nature. I can understand why the Cheyenne thought it was a sacred place. And now it's his burial ground."

The wagon train pulled out the next morning, heading for Independence Rock, a leg of their journey that would take them about six or six and a half days. Their first stop would be the nooning stop to rest the horses and to fix the midday meal. They were not the first wagon train to camp there for any period of time, for there was a stone marker not far from the road with the name of Alvah Unthank carved on it. A young man, nineteen years old, he had died of cholera on June 28, 1850, and was buried there. "Cholera," Vernon Tatum said, "that's the number one killer on the Oregon Trail."

"You might be right," Grissom remarked. "But I ain't ever had a case of cholera on any train I've ever took on this trail. So I must be doin' something right. You oughta be countin' yourself lucky you came with me."

About thirty miles past the Unthank gravesite they came to the bridge across the Platte River, built by the Mormons where the Mormons departed from the Oregon Trail. They rested the horses there and ate the noon meal before pushing on toward Independence Rock. Ever since leaving Register Cliff, Grissom had been pushing a little harder each day. His purpose was to reach Independence Rock by the Fourth of July, because it was a given that if you reached the rock by the Fourth, you were likely to get through the Blue Mountains before the first snowfall. It had been of some concern to him, even though they had been making good progress all along. They had left Independence, Missouri, later this year than in years past, but they circled up the wagons at the massive rock on the fifth of July, which was close enough to celebrate the Fourth as far as he was concerned. It was his custom to camp at Independence Rock two days to celebrate the Fourth of July to let his people rejoice in the knowledge that they had completed one half of their long journey. There was even more cause to celebrate reaching the rock, which was nineteen hundred feet long, seven hundred feet wide, and stood one hundred and twenty-eight feet high. For the rock was on the Sweetwater River and their days of tolerating the muddy water of the Platte were behind them. They had no way of knowing, but there was one thing more to celebrate. And that was the fact that the Platte Bridge Station, where they had stopped for a noon rest, was far behind them. For later in that month, the soldiers stationed there would be attacked by a force of thousands of Cheyenne and Sioux Indians in a bloody fight that became known as the Battle of Platte Bridge Station. When Grissom had talked to Seth Ward, word had not reached Fort Laramie of the increased attacks along the North Platte. And the army closed the Oregon Trail to wagon train traffic on May thirtieth, two days after Grissom's wagon train left Fort Laramie.

Totally unaware of the chaos behind them on the trail, there were two days of patriotic celebration with gunshots in the air and the singing of songs about Old Glory at Independence Rock. Some hidden bottles of whiskey were brought out of hiding to toast the Union and Harlan Rice was literally slinking about like a stray dog at a packing house, much to Annie's embarrassment. Of course, many of the emigrants desired to record their names and the date they passed through, and by this day and age it was hard to find a spot to carve another name.

Independence Rock was also the place where the members of Grissom's wagon train met Worley Branch. "Look comin' yonder," Grissom called Ike's attention to a stranger riding up from the river and heading straight toward them. Dressed all in animal hides, he was riding a paint horse and leading a sorrel packhorse.

Ike twisted around to look behind him. "Hell, whatever he's sellin', I don't want none of it," he remarked. They didn't bother to get up and waited for the stranger to pull the paint up before their wagon.

"How do," the stranger said and both Grissom and Ike returned the greeting. "My name's Worley Branch," he said, "and I figure one of you is the boss of this here train, since you're settin' beside the first wagon in the circle. Mind if I step down?"

"You're welcome to," Grissom said as he got to his feet. "I'm the wagon master, what can I do for you?"

"I'm just lookin' for a little company," Worley answered and he slid off his horse. "Since we're headin' in the same direction, I was wonderin' if I might tag along with you folks."

"Why would you wanna do that?" Grissom asked as he considered the odd-looking little man. "With the next hundred miles ahead of us and all the river crossin's we'll be makin', you'd make a lot better time by yourself since you're ridin' a horse."

"Yes, sir, that's a fact, but there ain't but one of me and there's a whole lot more of you," Worley said. "And you made it this far, so you must be pretty good about fightin' the Injuns. By myself, I ain't got much of a chance."

"Indians?" Grissom responded. "We ain't seen any Indians."

Worley looked at him in disbelief, then looked at Ike to see if Grissom was telling the truth. "You're japin' me, ain'tcha?" Grissom and Ike just looked at each other at a loss, so Worley asked another question. "You know the Oregon Trail is closed to wagon trains as of May thirtieth, right? And big war parties of Cheyenne, Sioux, and Arapaho have been attackin' army stations on the North Platte, don't you?" He could tell by their expressions that this was news to them. "Now I know I wanna tag along with you folks. You gotta be the luckiest folks I ever met."

"Are you sure you know what you're talkin' about?" Grissom asked. "Where did you hear all this about the raids?" He saw Clay walking by on his way to the horse herd and yelled, "Hey, Clay!" Clay turned and came over to the wagon. "This fellow here says the Cheyenne and the Sioux are raidin' all along the North Platte. What did you say your name was?" Worley told him and Grissom continued. "I told him we ain't seen any sign of an

Indian between Fort Laramie and here. Have you seen any Indians? I don't think Worley believes me."

Clay hesitated just a moment, then answered. "Well, I saw one, a Cheyenne."

That surprised Grissom. "You did? Where?"

"At that natural bridge where we camped that night." He had not planned to ever say anything about his unexpected meeting with the Cheyenne warrior, Black Bear. It still didn't sit right on his conscience.

"You never said a word about seein' a Cheyenne Indian at that bridge," Grissom said.

"Hell," Ike finally spoke up, "I knew he was actin' kinda strange when he rode up outta the creek that night. He didn't stop to say nothin' to me and you."

"That natural bridge is a sacred place to the Cheyenne," Worley said, "big medicine."

"You know about the natural bridge?" Grissom asked. "How do you know it's sacred to the Cheyenne?"

"The same way I know the Cheyenne and the Sioux are attackin' stations where the soldiers have horses and any wagon trains they find," Worley answered. "Because I was livin' with a Cheyenne woman in a Cheyenne village and I saw some of the warriors when they came back from their raids. That's the reason I left. There was too much of it goin' on and I couldn't side with the Injuns against the white man." He looked at Clay then and asked, "Did you talk to the Cheyenne warrior at the medicine bridge?"

"Yes, I did," Clay answered.

"Was his name Black Bear?"

"Yes, it was," Clay answered. "You knew him?"

"He was my woman's brother," Worley said, "and now I reckon I know why he never came back. You killed him?"

"I had to," Clay said. "He gave me no choice. He came at me with a knife. I told him I didn't go there to fight him, but he wouldn't listen, said he had a dream that he had to kill me." Grissom and Ike exchanged stares of amazement.

"So you're tellin' me we'd best be ready for some Indian trouble, is that right?" Grissom asked when he found his voice again.

"I'd say you sure as hell oughta be on the lookout and be ready if it does come," Worley said. "'Cause it sure could, but on the other hand, you've already drove through the territory where most of the raids are planned. But you can't never tell about Injuns. They get a wild fever to fight, they'll go anywhere. So, is it all right if I tag along with you folks? If we do see Injuns, I'll be an extra gun for you, and I ain't askin' for nothin' else. I'll feed myself. I just want the company."

"Well, I don't see any reason why you can't," Grissom said. "Do you, Clay? Ike?" No one objected. "Long as you're takin' care of yourself, welcome to the family."

"Thank you, gents, I won't cause you no trouble," Worley said. "I'm gonna go along now and find me a place to unload my packhorse and make my camp." He rode on toward the back of the circle.

"Now, I'd appreciate it, Clay, if you'd help me and Ike keep an eye on this character to make sure he ain't thinkin' about stealin' all our horses. But first we'd like to hear a little more about you killin' an Indian at the natural bridge."

"Hell, why didn't you say somethin' about it that night?" Ike asked.

"I don't know," Clay answered. "I reckon I was hungry, so I was in a hurry to get back to the wagon to eat." He had actually had no desire to discuss his killing of a Cheyenne warrior.

Chapter 12

Grissom made it a point to visit Worley after the odd little man unpacked his horses and made himself a camp as far out of the way as he could. "Is this all right with you?" Worley asked before Grissom had a chance to speak. "'Cause if it ain't, I can move it anywhere you say."

"No, you ain't gotta move. Right here's as good a place as any. I just came over to let you know about social hour. That's what we call a little get-together we have every night after supper. Some of the men play musical instruments and most of the folks like to sit around and talk after a day on the trail. I just thought I'd let you know what was goin' on when it starts up and let you know you're welcome to join in, if you want to."

"Why, that's mighty neighborly of you," Worley said, "I 'preciate that, I surely do."

The man looked so harmless that Grissom found it difficult to believe that he might be setting himself up to get some horses stolen. "How long did you live with that Cheyenne village?"

"About two and a half years," Worley answered.

"And didn't you say you were livin' with a Cheyenne woman?"

"That's right, I was."

"It musta been kinda hard to leave, after you'd been livin' with 'em that long," Grissom wondered. "Didn't your woman wanna come with you?"

"Oh, no, she wouldn't leave her people to go with me," Worley replied. "Matter of fact, I didn't tell anybody I was leavin', not even her, on account they mighta treated me like just another white man and lifted my hair."

Grissom had only planned to tell Worley about the social hour. He hadn't wanted a long conversation, but now he found himself intrigued by the man's story. "You think the people in the village would have turned on you, after you'd been with them that long?"

"Well, ya see, it weren't like I was a friend of ever'body in the village. It was more like I was doin' the village a service they couldn't get nobody else to do. I was livin' in Mud Turtle's tipi, that's her name, and they was happy about that. Ya see, Mud Turtle's kinda like me. When she was born, there musta been a big shortage of good looks. And in her case, they tried to make up for it by givin' her an extra helpin' of ugly. To top it off, they gave her a wart about the size of her thumb, right in the middle of her forehead. Well, when she was at the marryin' age, there weren't no young bucks who wanted poor Mud Turtle. By the time I met her, she was to the age where she didn't give a damn. So we kinda helped each other out for a while and it worked out for both of us. Tell ya the truth, I mighta left before this, but her brother, Black Bear, mighta come after me, even though I think Mud Turtle was gittin' kinda tired of me. You can tell when somebody's tired of havin' you around."

"I reckon so," Grissom remarked. "But you're welcome to ride along with us till you get tired of it. We work on a regular schedule. I'll blow my bugle at four o'clock in the mornin', so everybody can take care of their horses and eat their breakfast. Then we pull out at seven, stop at noon to eat dinner and rest the horses. Then it's back on the road until five, and that's when we stop for the day. That's about as much as I wanna push these families with their children and all to do in a day's time. Like I said, you could make a lot better time, just you on a horse."

"I ain't in no particular hurry to get where I'm goin'," Worley said.

"Where are you goin'?" Grissom asked. "I don't believe you ever said."

"I figured I'd go to Fort Hall. I've done some huntin' and trappin' around there. It's been a while since I left there, but I reckon it ain't trapped out yet."

"Good enough," Grissom said. "Well we'll be startin' out in the mornin' for the Narrows and Three Crossings and see what kind of spring the Sweetwater had."

"I don't expect the river will be up too high after the spring we just had," Worley said. "I don't believe we had as much rain as usual."

"I hope you're right," Grissom said, and got back on his horse. "You got something to eat?"

"Yes, sir, like I said, I ain't lookin' for no handouts. I can feed myself." Grissom nodded and rode back toward the front of the circle.

Worley built his campfire and roasted some strips of smoked venison over it. It was a skimpy supper, but he seldom ate much, anyway. What he missed most was the coffee. He had taken a small amount of the coffee beans that Mud Turtle had, but they were only enough for two pots and they were gone before he reached Independence Rock. He had a little bit of money but it was going to be a long time before this wagon train he had joined would come to any place where he could buy coffee. His supply of smoked meat was getting low as well, but he knew there were deer in the Sweetwater Valley, so he would go hunting, probably when this wagon train camped somewhere on the other side of Devil's Gate. His thoughts of food were interrupted when he saw a huge man come from one of the wagons carrying an axe. He walked to a spot in the middle of the circle where the remains of a fire could be seen and looked at a pile of firewood nearby. "He don't think it's enough," Worley said to himself when John Henry Hyde headed for the trees outside the circle of wagons. He could no longer see him but he could hear his axe for quite some time. When it stopped, Worley said, "He's cut as much as he needs." And in a couple of minutes, he saw him come back between two of the wagons with a double armload of wood. "Got enough to last for a while now," Worley said, "but he's gotta go back and get his axe." John Henry laid some kindling that was already there and built his fire. Worley watched as he got the kindling started really strong, then left it and headed back toward the trees. "Got the kindlin' burnin' good," Worley said. "Now, going back to get the axe and when he gets back, he can see if his new wood is catchin' on good." John Henry stood watching the fire for a minute or two, then went back to his wagon, carrying his axe. "Fire's burnin' good now," Worley said, satisfied the big man had done a good job. He was not really conscious of the fact that he often spoke all his thoughts aloud when he was alone. He had spent most of his life alone since the age of eleven after his mother was killed in a bar fight at the whorehouse she worked in. He learned to live in the woods when an old trapper took pity on him and took him to raise. The old trapper was killed by a grizzly bear when Worley was fourteen and he'd been alone ever since, until he met someone else that nobody wanted. And that was Mud Turtle. He couldn't be certain because he was not sure of the date of his birth. But he figured he was between the age of thirty-one and thirty-three when he met Mud Turtle.

His thoughts were distracted then when he saw two other men walking out to the fire carrying guitars. "Social hour," he repeated, remembering what Grissom had told him. It wasn't long then when a lot more folks started coming out to the fire, some of them carrying stools and boxes to sit on. Then he saw the big man who had built the fire returning, this time carrying what Worley guessed was a banjo. He had seen one of those in the place where his mother used to work. When a man came out there with a fiddle, it wasn't long before they all started playing together, and then a lot more people came out to listen to the music. Worley was impressed. He liked the music and the folks from the wagons looked like they liked it, too. Some of them were dancing and some of them were singing. To his simple mind, it was a wonderful sight to see. He would have liked to get closer to the music, but he was afraid an ignorant backwoodsman like himself might not be welcome.

"How you doin', Worley? You got your camp all set up?" He was surprised when the tall young fellow who had killed Black Bear walked up to his little fire.

"Yes, sir," Worley answered. "The boss of the wagon train came over here and he said it was all right if I camped here. He never told me his name, but he said I wouldn't bother nobody over here."

"His name's Grissom. My name's Clay Moran. I just thought I'd come over to tell you you're welcome to come up by the fire with the rest of the folks." He had suspected Worley was such an innocent soul that he was reluctant to mingle with the people who owned the wagons. "If you like to hear the music, you can come on up where the other people are and you'll hear it much better."

"Oh, thank you, sir, but I wouldn't wanna bother them folks when they're havin' their evenin' time. I might scare the young'uns."

"Come on, Worley, you can walk up there with me." Clay sus-pected he would like to go up close to see the dancing and hear the music, but he was too self-conscious to approach the group alone. "Whaddaya say? They won't bite."

"I'm skeered they might think I bite," Worley said. "All right, let's go, then." In spite of Grissom's concerns that Worley might be scheming to escape with some of their horses, Clay no longer had any suspicions along those lines. The simple man could not be that great an actor. He walked up to the fire with Clay and Clay introduced him to a few of the folks. All were quite happy to make his acquaintance, much to Worley's delight, and Clay told them that Worley would be accompanying the wagon train when it pulled out in the morning. It turned out that the emigrants found the odd-looking little man dressed in animal skins fully as fascinating as he found them to be. When Clay left the gathering to check on his horses, Worley wasn't even aware of his leaving.

When Grissom gave the signal at seven o'clock the next morning, the wagons rolled away from Independence Rock to follow the winding Sweetwater River to South Pass. It was a trip of about a hundred miles, but it was going to seem longer because of the many crossings of the winding river. Just five miles after leaving Independence Rock, they would come to a freak of nature called Devil's Gate. It was actually a cleft that the river had cut through the granite mountain, leaving a narrow passage about thirty feet wide at the base and about three hundred feet at the top, which stood three hundred and seventy feet above the river. They could hear the river's roar well before they reached the Devil's Gate, as it surged through the cleft it had carved over the centuries.

When they got to the Devil's Gate, they found they would have to ride around it because it was not wide enough for a wagon to pass through it beside the river. As they rode around the rock formation, Katie couldn't help but wonder, *Why didn't the river go around the huge chunk of rock, instead of cutting through the center of it?* There was plenty of room around it. There were the old remains of a trading post close by, many of the timbers still standing, although there was evidence that some had been burned. When asked about the standing timbers, Grissom said there used to be a quite successful trading post there. He was told that several French traders had operated it over the years, but the last to run it closed it down about ten years ago.

Although the base of the cleft was not wide enough for a wagon to go through Devil's Gate beside the river, there was enough room for a man on a horse, so Clay rode straight through the mountain. Following his lead, Worley Branch took his horses through as well. Like every other landmark on the Oregon Trail, the wall of stone beside the narrow path bore the evidence of hundreds of emigrants passing. Their names and the dates they were there were carved into the stone, giving evidence that they had stopped there long enough to walk into the cleft.

When they got to the point where the water was forced into the narrow part and the bottom was a maze of large rocks, the noise was deafening. Clay turned to look at Worley behind him and tried to ask him if he was going to carve his name on the mountain. But the noise the water was making made it impossible for him to hear. So Clay just shook his head and rode on out of the mountain. He pulled on up from the river and waited beside the ruins of the trading post for the wagons to come around. Worley pulled his paint pony up beside him. "I couldn't hear what you was askin' me back yonder," he said to Clay.

Clay laughed. "It was pretty doggone loud in there, wasn't it? It was nothin'. I just asked you if you were gonna carve your name back there with all those others. Sittin' on a horse, you had space above most of the other names of those folks who walked through there."

"Nah," Worley said, "I wouldn'ta done that."

"I feel the same way you do, I reckon," Clay told him. "I don't want to mess up Mother Nature's work, either. If she'da wanted names and numbers all over it, she'da made it that way."

Worley looked at him as if he didn't understand. "I reckon," he said. "I didn't carve my name in there 'cause I can't write."

"That's a better reason than mine," Clay said. "Here they come!" He nudged his horse and loped off to meet Grissom. Worley waited there. Clay wheeled the gray around to come up beside Grissom. "Are you plannin' to stop here to let everybody take a look at the inside of the Devil's Gate?"

"I was hopin' not to," Grissom told him. "We ain't hardly ready for a noonin', so I'd like to get a little way up the road before we stop." He turned his head to look back at the wagons.

"There ain't nobody makin' any noise about wantin' to stop, so far. But if enough of 'em want to, I reckon I'll call a halt. We'll know for sure when we get to where ol' Worley's settin' up ahead and I don't stop."

"Right," Clay said, understanding. So they rode along in silence until they came up even with Worley. When they didn't stop, he pulled in behind them, and to Grissom's disappointment, the yelling started.

Unfortunately, John Henry Hyde was only two wagons behind Ike in the lead wagon. He gave the reins to Eleanor, jumped off his wagon, then stretched his long legs out and ran past Dick Batson's wagon to catch up to Grissom. "Reckon could we stop for just a little while? There's a lot of folks behind me that want to take a look in the Devil's Gate."

"Why, sure," Grissom told him. "We just got started, so it's too early for the noonin'. We'll stop for thirty minutes so everybody can go scratch their names on that rock. I'll go tell 'em right now." He turned his horse around and rode back along the train of wagons to tell each one that they were going to take a thirty-minute rest, then they'd do the nooning up ahead a few miles. "Just let the horses stand in the traces. We'll water and graze 'em when we stop to eat." Then he watched a pretty good number of people running from the wagons to see the inside of the Devil's Gate and the cause of the angry noise the water made.

As Grissom had feared, his thirty-minute stop at Devil's Gate turned into one that was closer to an hour before he got all the people ready to roll again. They had traveled several miles again when Clay noticed a large mountain in the distance with a V-shaped gap in the top of it like a gunsight. When Grissom signaled the noon stop, he rode up to the front of the column beside him. "I've been lookin' at that big mountain up ahead with a notch cut out of the top. It seems like this trail we're followin' is headin' right at it."

"That's Split Rock," Grissom said, "and you're right, we're headin' straight for it. When the trappers and whoever first struck this trail, they musta used Split Rock as their compass 'cause this road don't veer off that line between Split Rock and Devil's Gate. I'da liked to camp overnight at Split Rock, but it's still twelve or thirteen miles ahead."

Clay went back to the wagon then to help Matt water the horses and build a fire for Katie to cook the noon meal. He told them what Grissom had told him about Split Rock and Matt wondered if they were going to have to stop so everyone could scratch their name somewhere on the mountain. "I see you got yourself a new friend," Matt said to Clay.

"Who?" Clay responded. "You talkin' about Worley?"

"Yeah, you two seemed to be hangin' out together," Matt said.

"Is that so? I reckon it's because we're both on horseback and not on a wagon."

"He's a strange one," Matt said.

"You're right about that," Clay conceded. "It's like he just popped outta the egg, and on the other hand, he's smart as can be about anything that lives in the woods."

"Has he got anything to eat?" Katie asked.

"I don't know," Clay replied, "I don't think so. When I went over to his campfire last night, he was sittin' there chewin' on a piece of jerky. But I didn't see anything else to eat, and no coffee or crackers or anything like that. But he didn't seem to be worried about it. He said he's gonna go kill a deer when we get over to the Narrows."

"That poor little man," Katie said. "I'm making corn cakes. I'll make a couple extra. Why don't you take 'em to him, Clay, and maybe a cup of coffee?"

"Whoa, Katie!" Matt exclaimed. "We can't start feedin' an extra mouth. We'll be runnin' outta food before we get to any place to buy more."

"I'm not gonna take him to raise," Katie insisted. "I'm just talking about giving him some corn cakes and a cup of coffee today to help hold him a little bit till he kills his deer. If you're worried about it, we can give him my cup of coffee."

Matt chuckled. "No, let's give him Clay's cup of coffee. How 'bout it, Brother? You wanna donate your coffee to your little friend?"

"I've got a better idea," Katie said. "Let's give him your second or third cup."

"Ow," Clay yelped, "she got you there, Brother."

There was never any real question in the minds of Matt or Clay as to whether or not Worley Branch would get corn cakes and coffee for his dinner that day. Cooking was Katie's department, so she made the decisions in that area. When dinner was ready, she wrapped two corn cakes up in a cloth and poured coffee in an extra cup. And when Matt suggested she could give them to Jim to run over to Worley's fire with them, Katie said no. "Clay, he knows you. You take 'em over and give them to him. Look at him, sitting over there by himself. He wouldn't know what to do if Jim ran over there and handed this to him."

"You're right," Clay said. "I'll take it over to him and I'll charge him a quarter."

"You probably would," Katie scolded. "You're as bad as your brother."

He took the food and coffee from her and walked quickly down the riverbank where Worley had built a small fire for no particular reason that Clay could see. He wasn't cooking anything, he wasn't making any coffee, and it wasn't cold. Clay figured he had built it just for the warmth a fire could provide to your soul. At any rate, it was good he had one, because he could heat metal cup the coffee was in. Worley quickly got to his feet when he saw Clay coming. "Howdy, Clay, you need me to do somethin'?"

"No, Worley, I brought you something to eat. My brother's wife made some corn cakes and she wanted me to take a couple of 'em to you." The expression on his face told Clay the simple little man was overwhelmed. "I brought you some coffee to wash 'em down with." He started to hand him the cup, but hesitated because Worley's hand was trembling so violently with emotion Clay was afraid he would spill it. "Here, let me stick it right here at the edge of your fire to heat it up a little bit. It's just plain black coffee, no sugar in it. I hope you like it that way."

"That's the only way I ever had it," Worley said. He unwrapped the cloth Clay gave him and looked at the warm corn cakes. "Oh, I do declare, don't they look pretty?" He held them out toward Clay. "You want one?"

"No, thanks, already had mine. They're for you, from Matt and Katie Moran. She looked over here and it didn't look like you had anything to eat."

"I don't know what to say," Worley stammered. "You thank that nice lady for me. You tell her I'm goin' huntin' tonight or the next night, and I'll bring her some deer meat."

"She'd like that, Worley, but don't feel like you have to do that, she just didn't want you to be hungry while everybody else had something to eat." He started to leave but paused when he thought, "What if you don't find a deer tomorrow night or the next? Have you got anything to eat?"

"Ain't no worry about that," Worley replied right away. "I ain't gonna go hungry as long as I'm near water. There's always somethin' to eat on the river. I take my bow and get me a rabbit or a coon or a possum. Here, I'll give you your cup." He got a metal cup out of his packs and emptied the coffee into it, took a quick sip before the coffee had a chance to heat the metal cup to the point where it would burn his lips. "That's good coffee, better than what I make." He took the two corn cakes out of the cloth and handed it and the empty cup back to Clay. "Tell that nice lady thanks, and thank you, Clay."

"You're welcome, Worley, I'll tell Katie for you."

When he got back to Matt's wagon, he told Katie that she was now the mother of another son. Her gift of coffee and corn cakes had indebted Worley Branch for life. "Did he have anything to eat?" she asked.

"Not a crumb that I could see," Clay answered.

"I knew it," she said. "That man needs someone to look after him."

"He's got someone now," Clay japed.

"I'll be damned," Matt spoke up.

"He said he's gonna bring Katie some deer meat tonight or the next night," Clay said.

"In that case, Katie, you have my blessing," Matt said.

The joking went on until it was time to hitch up the horses and continue on toward Split Rock. Although clearly seen ahead of them, the one-thousand-foot mountain never seemed to get any closer until finally, Grissom called the five o'clock halt some three miles short of it.

Chapter 13

The wagon train pulled out of their camp at seven o'clock as usual the next morning, finally passing Split Rock and heading for the Narrows, or as it was more commonly called, Three Crossings. Grissom anticipated one full day's travel would take them to the first crossing in a winding segment of the Sweetwater that would require them to cross it three times to gain a lineal distance of only about two miles. His plan was to make camp that night at the first crossing and start across first thing the following morning.

The odd little man in animal skins was conspicuous by his absence. Clay, accustomed to seeing Worley more than the others, was the first to comment on the fact. "You know, I didn't see Worley anywhere when we were hitchin' up your wagon," he said to Matt. "He said he was goin' deer huntin' last night. Don't reckon he had any luck and maybe he don't wanna face Katie to tell her he didn't bring her any venison," he joked.

When the wagons first got underway, Clay had ridden up to the lead wagon to say good morning to Grissom and Ike. "I ain't seen Worley this mornin'," Grissom said to Clay when he pulled up beside him. "Reckon what's happened to him?"

"He told me yesterday that he was goin' deer huntin' last night," Clay said. "He'll probably show up somewhere along the road."

"Hell," Ike commented, "he mighta decided we was travelin' too slow and he just went on ahead."

"Maybe he just figured all that Indian trouble he was tellin' us about was all back there along the Platte, so he might as well go on by himself," Grissom suggested. "I'm hopin' that's the case, too."

The day passed as an uneventful day of travel and the wagon train circled up for the night in the grassy area before the first of the river crossings. It was only a little after five o'clock when they pulled in, so there was plenty of time before dark to inspect the crossing to make sure they picked the best spot. Clay, on his gray, gave Grissom, on his buckskin, some help in testing the river's bottom. They found it firm and the exit point on the opposite side was solid with a gentle slope. Nothing to cause Grissom any concern. "We'll just start the wagons right across in the mornin'," he said. Like the night before, there was no sign of Worley Branch, but on this night, no one said anything about it. He had vanished as suddenly as he had first appeared at Independence Rock. And for the most part, he was already forgotten, with the exception of Katie Moran, who had felt some compassion for the little misfit.

Most of the talk that night at the social hour was centered around not only the first crossing in the morning, but also what they had been told by Grissom about the coming days' travel following the Sweetwater to South Pass. With only about seventy-five miles from where they now were, they would be crossing that river ten times. It was hard to say how long it would take to reach South Pass, ten days or twenty days. It would depend on the condition of the individual crossings when they reached them.

Because of a general sense of urgency to tackle the tasks before them, they started a little earlier than the normal time of seven. At six forty-five, Ike drove Grissom's wagon into the river. John Henry Hyde followed right behind him and Vernon Tatum

close behind John Henry. Everything went smoothly as the rest
of the wagons followed in line. The canyon the river ran through
was so narrow at some points that upon leaving the water, the
wagons found the road beside the river barely wide enough for a
wagon to pass. Those emigrants who could never pass a space to
register their names and the date had to stand in the wagon bed
to carve on the granite wall of the mountain. The height of the
signatures from the wagon road testified to the fact that there
was no room to get out of the wagon to engrave.

The first two crossings were so close together that Ike and
Clay were already at the second crossing, checking the conditions while most of the wagons behind them were still making
the first crossing. Grissom, having discovered that Clay Moran
was a man he could depend on, took full advantage of Clay's will-
ingness to help. And after testing the bottom at this second loca-
tion, Clay told Ike it was as good as the first. So Ike committed
the wagon to the river again, and like the first, came out on the
other side with no problems. John Henry followed as before, and
Vernon after him. So there were two crossings going on at the
same time. There was a little more space between crossing number two and crossing number three, however, so Clay and Ike
waited for all the wagons to complete the crossing of number two.

Clay wanted Grissom to supervise the third crossing because it
was a more difficult one than the first two. The major difference
was that the river curved at the exit point on the far bank. And
the main channel of the river was right up along that bank. So the
water was deepest and the current strongest right where the
horses had to be trying to quit swimming and find firm footing.
When Grissom arrived with the rest of the wagons he asked Clay
what he thought their best place to cross would be. Clay showed
him the spot he would pick if it was his decision to make. "It's
not gonna be as easy as the first two," Clay said. "The horses are
gonna have to do some swimmin', almost right up to the bank.
And the bank is just a little bit steeper on the other side than it is
over here. The horses might need some help pullin' that wagon

out of the water, so we'll need another team hitched up on the other side to help those who can't make it."

Grissom looked at Ike and said, "In other words, it's just like it was last year. You made it across without no help last year, so you might as well see if you can do it again. We'll hitch up another team on the other side to help those that have trouble." Harlan Rice came to mind right away.

"Hell, I'm headin' across," Ike said, and started his horses down the bank.

John Henry got set to follow but Grissom told him to give him some more room. "Let's see how much trouble he's gonna have, so you'll know what to expect." As they watched, Ike's horses pulled the wagon with no trouble at all out past the middle of the river, the water rising slowly until, suddenly, the horses sank deeper and started to swim. "Now, let's see what they do," Grissom said. They slowed down but continued to pull toward the other side, with Ike threatening to cook them for supper if they didn't take that wagon outta the water. Then they saw the point where the wagon started to float and the current pulled it to the downstream side. The horses continued to struggle, however, and suddenly their hooves struck dirt again and they began to come up the opposite bank. An involuntary cheer shot up at the sight. "All right, John Henry, take 'em across," Grissom said.

The crossing actually went better than anyone expected. Three of the wagons needed assistance from an extra team of horses, but there were no casualties and no personal belongings lost in the river. A surprise to Grissom was the fact that of the three wagons that had to be helped, not one of them was Harlan Rice's wagon. It didn't set well with Harlan that Grissom, Clay, and John Henry Hyde were close by and ready to go into action at his crossing. Annie and the girls, on the other hand, very much appreciated their close surveillance, and expressed as much to the three men. Grissom was pleased to have completed the first three river crossings on the first morning of the Sweetwater segment of their long journey. They finished in time for the nooning. So he called a halt as soon as the last wagon was pulled up the bank of the river to rest the horses and prepare the noon meal.

"I don't know why I feel like I've worked all morning," Katie commented as she started arranging the wood Jim had brought for her cookfire. Matt and Clay had just come from taking care of the horses. "At least you men have been working all morning. All I've done is sit in that wagon, worrying about losing the wagon or one of the children."

"Don't you know worryin' makes you tired?" Matt said. "Get over there and get busy makin' me something to eat and you won't feel tired no more."

"I expect I'd better," Katie responded, "'cause if I didn't cook something for you, you'd starve to death."

"Before you start cookin' anything, you might wanna wait to see how many you're gonna have for dinner," Clay commented. He was standing by the wagon, staring down the road they would travel after the nooning. Matt and Katie both turned to follow his gaze up the river and spotted what had caught his eye.

He was a long way off, a man on a horse, leading a packhorse, but there was no mistaking his identity. "Worley Branch," Katie uttered, just above a whisper. "I declare, I had almost forgotten the man."

"Worley's the kind of man that's easy to forget," Matt said. "I wonder where the hell he went."

Clay chuckled at his brother's sarcasm. "Come on, Matt, you don't believe that. Worley's a man that'll never let you down. Ain't that right, Katie?"

"Bless his heart, he's a poor soul that's never had a decent chance in his whole life," Katie said. "He mighta wandered off the other night and gotten lost."

"He mighta wandered off," Clay said, "but I doubt he got lost."

They continued to watch the little man's progress as he approached the camp. He stopped to talk to Grissom and Ike for a few minutes before continuing on into the heart of the camp. "Wherever he went, it was to get something," Clay said. "That packhorse is loaded down." It occurred to him what it was, but he decided not to share it. As he expected, however, Worley turned the paint horse toward them and rode up to their wagon. "Welcome back, Worley," Clay said. "Where you been?"

"I been a ways up the Sweetwater, Clay. I had to get some deer meat for that kind lady that made me them corn cakes."

"Oh, Worley," Katie said, "you shouldn't have gone to all that trouble. You don't have to pay me anything for those corn cakes."

"It weren't no trouble, ma'am," Worley insisted. "I'm sorry it took me so long to get back here with the meat. I wanted to give you fresh meat to cook, but this time of year the meat'll turn if you don't cook it pretty quick. So I had to smoke it to keep it from turnin'."

"So that's smoked deer meat piled up on that packhorse," Matt said.

"Yes, sir," Worley answered. "It'll keep for a long time."

"Well, that was so thoughtful of you, Worley," Katie said. "I'll be happy to take enough of it to cook right now for dinner. And you can eat with us."

"I brought all of it for you and your family, ma'am," Worley said.

"No, Worley, that's way too much for those two corn cakes," Katie told him.

"And a cup of coffee," Worley reminded her.

Katie had to laugh. "Even with a cup of coffee," she said. "I'm very thankful for what you want to do for me and my family. But here's what we're gonna do. I'll take enough of that meat to feed my family for a couple of meals. And you'll keep the rest of it for yourself. We have food to cook and I know that you don't have any. So it will make me happy to know that you have food to eat, too. There, that's settled, all right?" She looked at Clay and winked. "And I'm gonna give you some ground coffee, too." She held up her hand to silence him when he started to protest. "Don't argue. Now let me see the meat."

They all walked over to his packhorse and he untied the deer hide he had packed the smoked meat in. It looked in good shape, he obviously knew how to properly smoke meat. Clay estimated that he had about fifty or sixty pounds of meat on that packhorse. "It must have been a pretty big deer," he said, knowing that only about forty to forty-five percent of a deer is meat. And Worley had probably already eaten a lot of it.

Worley nodded. "Big deer," he said.

Katie sent Sarah back to the wagon to fetch the big tray she used to bring food out by the fire. Since the venison looked fit to eat, she would do what she told Worley she would do. "You must have gone a long way before you found this deer," Clay said to Worley.

"Not far," Worley replied. "I found her followin' a big buck halfway to Three Crossings. I put one arrow in her side, but I couldn't get another shot at her."

"Didn't you have your rifle with you?" Clay asked.

"Yessir, I had my rifle, but I don't have no more cartridges, so I've just been hunting with my bow. That arrow crippled her and she fell, but she got up again, and run off. So I had to follow her. She led me past this crossin' here, up in the mountains on the other side of the river. By the time she give out, we was so far from you folks I was afraid the meat wouldn't keep till I got back to you. So I butchered her and set up a smoke fire to cure the meat. That's why it took me so long."

Clay looked at Matt, who just smiled and slowly shook his head. Then Matt looked at Katie and said, "We certainly owe this man some coffee to go with his venison."

Sarah came back with the tray then. Katie took it and selected enough cuts of the smoked meat for their dinner now and another meal tonight. When Worley urged her to take more than that, she insisted that was all she wanted. "I don't want you sitting over there at night going hungry because we ate all your venison up. Understand?"

"Yes, ma'am. Thank you, ma'am."

"Now, let me get busy cooking some of this beautiful meat," Katie said. "Looks like Jim's got a good fire going. I'll see what I can fix to go with the meat."

It was one hundred miles from Independence Rock to South Pass, a distance that Virgil Grissom might normally figure to take seven and a half to eight days. But with all the river crossings of the Sweetwater, the time it took was nearly doubled. During that time, the Moran family was unofficially adopted by Worley Branch, who kept them supplied with occasional game that fell victim to Worley's bow. In addition to that, he taught young Jim Moran how to catch fish and trap small animals. With the ten-year-old boy's father driving the wagon all day, and his uncle Clay having been drafted by Grissom to act as a scout, Matt and Clay were happy about the situation. Jim's friend Skeeter Tatum quite often joined Worley and Jim on their hunting and fishing trips, so both boys were gaining some basic skills for surviving in the wilderness. Katie believed the relationship between Worley and the two boys worked so well because she felt they were pretty much on the same level of maturity. She didn't worry about the difference in their real ages because she sensed a basic goodness in Worley that would keep the friendship wholesome. Being the innocent man that he was, she hoped he was learning some useful things from Jim. There was one incident in particular that she would always remember. One day when they had stopped for the nooning, Jim came to her and asked her how to spell Worley Branch. She told him and he repeated it several times to make sure he would remember. Then he went back to the riverbank where he and Skeeter had been sitting with Worley. Curious, she moved a little closer to eavesdrop. Jim went to a clear spot on the dirt bank and printed Worley's name in the dirt with a stick. Then he called Worley to come look at it. "Look at this, Worley," Jim had said. Worley walked over and studied it for a while, then Jim asked, "Do you know what that is?"

"Yep," Worley had answered, "that's writin'."

"Do you know what it says?" Jim had asked.

"No, I don't do no writin'," Worley answered. "Ask your mama. I bet she knows."

"That's your name, Worley." Worley had not understood, so Jim pointed to each word with the stick he had written them with. "That's your name, Worley Branch."

Worley was dumbfounded. He stared down at the two words, astonished. "Is that what my name looks like?" Jim nodded. "How do you know?"

"'Cause I can read," Jim answered and he read them again, pointing to each word as he pronounced it. Katie knew that was one scene she would never forget. Worley stared at it for so long, trying to embed it in his mind that she had written it on a piece of a paper bag, so he could keep it with him. Jim had told her later that Worley had practiced copying it until he could write it just like the name on the paper.

From Worley's perspective, it was like he had found a family at this late stage in his life. The most he remembered about living with his mother was staying out of sight all the time. The man who owned the place where his mother worked didn't want her potential customers to know she was the mother of an eleven-year-old boy.

There had been a great deal of excitement in the anticipation of reaching South Pass. It was no small accomplishment, the crossing of the Continental Divide. As the emigrants neared the end of the Sweetwater River segment, most of the conversation at the evening social hour was speculation upon the coming thrill of crossing the South Pass. In spite of Grissom's and Ike's attempts to curb their enthusiasm for the event, it was still a major disappointment when the wagon train actually reached that historic crossing of the Rocky Mountains. For what they found awaiting them was an apparently endless plain of thick sagebrush with not a tree in sight. The sagebrush was so prolific that it grew right up to the two narrow ruts that served as the wagon road across the pass. Grissom and Clay rode ahead of the train armed with hand axes to remove some of the young sagebrush that had taken root in the middle of the road. It made it impossible for the people who normally walked wide of the wagons to do so. Consequently, those who continued to walk had to walk behind the wagons, subjected to the dust they created.

When they were stopped for the evening, Grissom told them that they would soon be beyond this South Pass and the going would be better—not great, but better. And what they should appreciate is that this gradual rise over the Continental Divide was far better and less risky than climbing over the Rockies through the steep mountain passes. About a day and a half's travel after they crossed the Continental Divide, they came to a fork in the two-rut road they had followed across South Pass. It was called Parting of the Ways, Grissom told them. Someone had left a small sandstone block with directions carved on it. An arrow pointed to the left with the words *Ft. Bridger* and an arrow to the right with *Ft. Hall*. Grissom stopped the wagons there when some of the emigrants wanted to know why they didn't take the right fork to Fort Hall. "In that letter of agreement we signed before we started, it said S-Fort Hall was one of the places we would stop," Quincy Lewis said. "If the road to the right goes to Fort Hall, why don't we take that road? It looks like it heads straight west. But you stopped your wagon on the other road, and it looks like it's headin' south."

"Well, that's right, Quincy," Grissom replied, "and the letter also said we'd make a stop at Fort Bridger. That *S* on the stone in front of Fort Hall stands for Sublette Cutoff. And I'll be honest with you. We might shorten our trip to Oregon City by two and a half days if we take the cutoff. But we also have a good chance to lose some of our horses. That way is a shortcut that brings you back to the trail we're takin', but you'll have to cross forty-five or fifty miles of desert. And there ain't no grass and not a drop of water till you reach the Green River. Even if your horses make it that far without water, they're in pretty bad shape when you get there. If we take the left road, there's not a lot of good grass, but there's some, and there's water because we'll follow Big Sandy Creek all the way to the Green River. There's some grazing for the horses by the creek and there's willow wood for your fires. And about fifty miles or so south of the Green, we'll stop at Fort Bridger, so you'll have a chance to make any repairs you need and replace supplies."

While they were talking about the risks each way, Clay pulled his horse over beside Worley Branch. "What are you thinkin', Worley? When we left Independence Rock, you said you thought you'd go to Fort Hall. Are you thinkin' about headin' up that road to the right, if we take the one to Fort Bridger?"

"I think I'll stay with you folks, if that's all right," Worley said. "We can take the long way to Fort Hall."

Clay chuckled. "I thought you might. I think that's the smart thing for you to do."

Grissom waited for a few minutes while several of the men were discussing the risk involved versus the time saved. Then he said it was time to move on. "You all know which way I'm goin' and it's time to go. So I'll just say everybody who thinks I'm right just follow me. And anybody who wants to challenge the cutoff, I wish you the best of luck." He turned to face his wagon. "Head 'em out, Ike!" Then he climbed back up in the saddle and went after the wagon. The group of men that had gathered to discuss the fork in the road ran to their wagons to get back in line. No one chose to take the right fork.

They camped that night by a creek called Little Sandy Creek. There was good grass on both sides of the creek that was only about ten feet wide and two feet deep. So it was easy to graze the horses on both sides of it. They set out the next morning on a road that struck Big Sandy Creek, the creek they would follow all the way to the Green River.

Chapter 14

For the next five days, the wagon train followed Big Sandy Creek through a sandy, sagebrush plain toward its confluence with the Green River. They arrived at the north bank of the river at the end of the fifth day and went into camp while Grissom made the arrangements to start ferrying the wagons across the river in the morning. The ferry was operated by a group of Mormons, strictly as a money-making endeavor, so Grissom spent quite some time trying to negotiate a reasonable fee for his wagons. He was at a disadvantage because the competing ferry that had been there the year before was no longer in business. The best he could settle for was a price of ten dollars a wagon, which was two dollars more than he had paid the last time.

There had been some talk among his party before reaching the river. Some of the men wondered why they had to pay a ferry operator to take them across when they had been fording all the rivers they had encountered ever since leaving Independence. Now, when they saw the river, they realized the Green was the biggest river they had struck so far. It was wide and deep, and the current was strong. The prospect of losing a wagon and all possessions in it was a definite possibility. So the arrangements were made to take the first wagon across the next morning.

There remained one member of the wagon train who would

decide to challenge the river, however. "You don't have to do that, Worley," Clay told him. "We're payin' to ferry our extra horses across the river. You can just lead your two horses on the ferry with the rest of 'em. It won't cost you a cent."

"You're too good a friend for me to cost you money to do that," Worley said. "We'll swim across, just like the Cheyenne do." He had a few dollars that he had been saving for a long time, but he didn't want to spend it to cross a river. He was saving it to buy cartridges for his rifle. No matter how hard Clay tried to convince him it was all right for him to put his horses on the ferry with the others, Worley would not concede. "Don't worry 'bout me, Clay, I'll get across," he assured him.

At a little after seven the next morning, Ike drove Grissom's wagon onto the ferry. Once across, he parked it in an open pasture for the following wagons to form a circle on because they would be there past nooning. Worley stood there on the bank with Clay and Matt and Jim and watched the first three wagons go across, since their wagon was near the back of the line. Then he announced that he was going to go ahead and cross, too, so he could build a fire and dry his clothes a little before they came across. So he checked the packs on his packhorse to make sure everything was tied up good and tight. Then he climbed aboard his paint gelding and rode down the bank into the water. "Well, there goes our source for fresh venison," Matt remarked, "down the Green River."

"I wouldn't bet on it," Clay said. "Ain't that right, Jim?"

"Yes, sir," Jim responded. "Worley knows how to live like an Indian."

They watched with great anticipation as Worley's horse walked out into the river with Worley holding the reins to his packhorse in one hand as it followed along behind. The paint didn't walk far before the water was up to Worley's knees and a few feet more brought him out of the saddle and the paint swimming. And as soon as the horse was swimming, it was fighting against the current to swim straight across. The paint continued swimming, and when it reached the middle of the river where the current was strongest, man and horses were suddenly swept downstream. And in a handful of seconds, they were tiny objects in the big river, still struggling to reach the opposite bank, and then they disappeared around a bend in the river.

"Like I said," Matt remarked.

Clay shook his head. "I sure hope you're wrong," he said as Matt and Jim started back to their wagon to move it up in line. "He might just disappear for a while, then show up again, like he did last time."

The crossing took longer to complete than Grissom had figured and they ended up camping there overnight on the south side of the river. He was not at all happy about it because they were camped in a common waiting area for all wagons and livestock that crossed there. So the area was the recipient of countless emigrants' waste and garbage, and Grissom was always concerned about the possibility of cholera. His wagon trains had been fortunate enough to avoid being struck with cholera and he was convinced it was because of his habit of avoiding common camping grounds. He cautioned his people to get their water upstream from the crossing and to mind where they did their business when Mother Nature called. They wanted to have the regular social hour, anyway, so the musicians cranked up as usual.

It was during the social hour when Worley Branch rode into the circle of wagons. After he took care of his horses, he came to the social hour and sought out Clay or Matt, as was his usual habit. He found Clay sitting with Matt and Katie, watching Maurine Corbett trying to teach her husband, Henry, how to dance. "Well, look who's here," Matt said after seeing him first. "We were beginning to think you musta floated on down to the ocean."

"That current looked pretty swift," Clay said. "How far did you go before you made it across? Musta been a helluva long way."

"It was about two miles, I reckon," Worley answered.

"Did it take you this long to ride two miles back here?" Matt asked.

"Nossir," Worley replied. "But I found a good place to come outta the river and I was soakin' wet. Since there weren't nobody around to see me nekkid, I built me a fire and come outta my buckskins. And I just figured I'd wait right there till they got all the way dry. My bedroll got wet, too, so I cut some willow limbs and made me a rack to hang it on, so it could dry out. When I went to cut some more wood for my fire, two rabbits popped up outta the brush. I grabbed one of 'em before he thought to run. I threw my hand-axe at the other'n, but I missed him. Since I had me a rabbit, I went ahead and skint him, gutted him, and cooked him for my dinner. He was a good-sized rabbit and when I finished eatin' him, my bedroll still weren't dry. So I pulled on my buckskins and laid down and took a little nap. When I woke up, my bedroll was dry and my fire was about out. I figured I'd best get started back then, 'cause the sun was gittin' pretty low. I'd slept longer than I thought, so I figured I'd best get on my horse and find this place before it got too dark to see where I was goin'." He paused then and looked from Matt to Clay, confused and not sure why neither one of them said a word but just stared at him in wonder.

Finally, Clay spoke. "Well, I can see why that mighta took a little time."

"You caught the rabbit with your hand, right?" Matt asked. "You have to be pretty doggone fast to do that."

Worley shrugged. "When I pulled that brush up, they didn't run. They just popped straight up. The other one didn't run till I grabbed the first one." That was met with another void of silence from the two brothers, so he said, "I thought you'd be gone."

"We were waitin' for you," Matt said. "Katie said we couldn't ride off and leave you."

Katie decided to interrupt at that point when she saw the look of alarm immediately appear on Worley's face. She had been listening to the conversation between the three men, and knowing Matt's tendency to tease, she wanted to save this simpleminded man from her husband's japing. "He's just funning you, Worley. It took so long to get all the wagons and livestock across the river that it was too late to start. We were all wondering if you were all right, but that wasn't the reason we're still here." As soon as she said it, she wondered if what she said wasn't just as bad as what Matt said. She looked at once at Matt and found him grinning widely in amusement. But when she looked back at Worley, his expression told her that he was relieved to hear he wasn't the cause of the wagon train's delay.

They left the Green River early the next morning, following a well-defined road, formed by the many wagons and horses on their way to Fort Bridger and Salt Lake before them. Five and a half days of travel over a prairie almost devoid of trees and grass found them at Fort Bridger. The post, built by Jim Bridger on Black's Fork of the Green River as a fur-trading fort, was a crude affair, a small collection of log buildings inside a wall of pickets that had been plastered with dried mud. The center point of a war with the Mormons, called the Utah War, Fort Bridger still wore scars of that conflict. Portions of a stone wall that was built around the fort by the Mormons still remained. Also, burnt timbers of original buildings still stood as evidence of the attempt by the Mormons to burn the fort down. The Mormons were put down, but soldiers were still stationed at the fort. Now Fort Bridger served as a major supply and repair station for emigrants going to Oregon as well as Salt Lake Valley.

There was a large grassy pasture area around the fort, close to water, with plenty of room to accommodate a visiting wagon train. Grissom led his charges into the pasture and set the wagons in their customary circle. The fort offered the services of both blacksmith and farrier as well as the basic supplies the emigrants needed replaced. The sutler at Fort Bridger was a man well experienced in the business, named William A. Carter, who had a reputation as a fair and honest tradesman.

Since they had arrived close to what would have been the nooning time, most of the emigrants proceeded to treat it as such. The men turned the horses out to water and graze while the women built their cookfires for the noon meal, using wood from a giant stack of firewood near one side of the pasture. Grissom told them the wood was cut and brought in from the mountains northwest of the fort. He said the wood was furnished by the army as a gesture of good will and the soldiers were sent up there to cut it and haul it back. Clay noticed that there was a nice stand of trees along the river, but he reckoned they wouldn't last long if every wagon train that stopped here went to those trees to cut firewood. He wondered if that might have had some influence on the fort's goodwill decision on the firewood.

Those folks who needed repairs on their wagons were prone to let the nooning wait and sought out the blacksmith while the afternoon was still young. During the social hour at their last night's campsite, Grissom had advised them to get any worn parts or damaged undercarriage fixed on their wagons here at Fort Bridger. He warned them of a particularly difficult mountain crossing awaiting them. "In about a hundred miles from here we're gonna have to climb over a string of mountains to get to the Bear River Valley. The trail goes over them in the easiest spot a wagon can make it and what it amounts to is that it's the only place you can drive a wagon over those mountains. They got a name for it, they call it Big Hill, and it'll test your horses because it's straight up. But goin' down the other side is the dangerous part and if there's anything that ain't tight on your wagon, comin' down Big Hill will shake it to pieces."

"Damn, Grissom, that sounds terrible," Paul Courtland had asked, "ain't there no way to go around it?"

"Yeah, I expect you could get around it," Grissom had answered, "but that long line of mountains turns back to the northeast and who know where it ends. You have to cross over Big Hill, but once you do, you're gonna see one helluva difference on the other side of that mountain."

Grissom's sales pitch for the blacksmith was successful in generating the need for the blacksmith's services and caused quite a few to have their wagons fixed. He told them that they were going to stay over for the next day, too, in case the blacksmith couldn't handle all the business today. Clay was glad when he heard that because he wanted to visit the farrier. He wanted to go ahead and get new shoes for both of his horses. He had bought new shoes for them at Fort Kearny, but he didn't like the way the shoes had worn. So he was going to go ahead and replace them before they caused any trouble. Fort Hall was most likely the next place he might have that done and that was a hell of a long way from there. Matt was not one of those who needed work done on his wagon, but Katie did need some things at the sutler's store. So they decided they'd go over after they ate and take Clay's packhorse as they had done at Fort Laramie. That was fine with Clay because he had all day tomorrow to take the packhorse and the gray to get new shoes.

After they had eaten and Katie and the girls cleaned up the dishes, Matt, Katie, Clay, and Jim went into the fort to the sutler's store. While Katie and Matt were going over their list with Mr. Carter, Clay walked around, looking at the merchandise on the shelves. When he came to an open door in the back, he peered in to see Worley Branch talking to William Carter's clerk at a large table. Curious, he paused to watch for a few moments before he realized that Worley was in the process of getting an appraisal for a deer hide he was hoping to trade. Thinking Worley might need some help, Clay walked into the room. "Whatcha doin', Worley?"

"Howdy, Clay," Worley responded. "I'm tryin' to trade the

hide of that doe I killed on the Sweetwater for some coffee and some flour." He turned to face the clerk and said, "This is my friend Clay Moran. He's ridin' with the wagon train, too."

"Mr. Moran," the clerk acknowledged. "My name's Frank Bland."

"Glad to meet you," Clay responded. "That was a right sizable doe, wasn't it? It sure was good eatin'. Oughta be worth a good amount of coffee and flour, right, Mr. Bland?"

Bland smiled at Clay. Having already been talking to Worley, he could see that the odd little man was a little slow between the ears. And he could guess that Clay would naturally assume that he might take advantage of him. "We don't trade for a lot of fur and such this time of year, so deer hide in this condition is worth more than we'd normally pay for one. I'd say we'll allow your friend, here, five dollars' credit for this skin."

Clay had no idea what the going rate for deer hides was. He had never tried to sell one, but judging from the happy glow on Worley's face, he assumed that was a fair price. "That oughta be enough to buy you some coffee to last you a little while, Worley," he said, and left him to spend his credit. When he went back to the front counter, there was a large stack of items ready to be loaded onto his packhorse, so he said, "If you got these marked off, I'll go ahead and start loadin' 'em." He picked up a couple of sacks and walked out to his packhorse with them. While he was tying them on, he noticed Harlan Rice talking to a soldier beside his wagon in front of the blacksmith's shop. Harlan's was not the only wagon waiting to be serviced by the blacksmith. *I hope the farrier ain't backed up that bad tomorrow when I come to get my horses shod*, he thought. When he went back inside the store, Matt and Katie were settling up with Mr. Carter, so they all grabbed some of the packages and carried them out to the horse.

While they were eating supper that evening, Matt pointed out the three gaps in the circle of wagons where three wagons should be. "They're waitin' at the blacksmith shop," Clay told him. "I saw 'em parked in front of his shop when we were at the sut-ler's."

"Somebody's gonna get a cold supper tonight," Katie said. "They could have waited until tomorrow."

"I know somebody who's gonna have hot coffee with his sup-per tonight," Clay said. Then he told them about Worley trading his deer hide for some coffee.

"Good for him," Katie said. "Bless his heart, he's like a lost child. If we were good Christian people, we would have invited him to eat supper with us."

"For Pete's sake, woman!" Matt exclaimed. "We're already takin' care of Clay. We can't afford but one lost child at a time."

"You oughta be ashamed," she told him. "He pays more than his share of the food he eats, and he . . ." She stopped then when she saw the grin on his face and realized he was just trying to get her goat.

"I find it best to just ignore him," Clay said to Katie.

When supper was finished and the dishes washed, they walked out into the center of the circle when they heard Vernon Tatum's fiddle crank up and go to work on one of his favorites. He was soon joined by Bryan Roland and John Courtland on gui-tar. The only thing missing was the banjo. "John Henry must still be eatin' supper," Matt said.

"You know," Clay remarked, "there's still one of the wagons missin'." He pointed to the one gap in the circle of wagons on the lower end of the camp. "I wonder whose wagon is still gettin' worked on." He had an answer a few short minutes later when Annie Rice and her two daughters came walking up to the fire.

She was looking for Grissom but since he had not come out to the social hour yet, she went straight to Clay and Matt. But it was Katie who spoke first. "Annie, are you all right?"

"I'm worried about Harlan," Annie said. "He took the wagon to get the rims fixed on the back wheels before supper and he ain't back yet. We ain't had no supper and I can't cook anything till he gets back with the wagon. I wanna go over to the fort to see if I can find out what's holding him up so long, but I'd like to leave the girls here with you folks, if that's all right."

Clay was immediately concerned. He remembered seeing Harlan talking to a soldier earlier that afternoon. At the time, he had a half-serious thought that Harlan was probably asking him where he could get a drink. Seeing Annie and the girls here tonight, he had a bad feeling about it. "Why don't you stay here, Annie? I'll go over to the blacksmith and see if I can find out why it's takin' so long."

"Oh, I couldn't ask you to do that, Clay. Mine and the girls' evening is already messed up. There's no call to mess yours up, too."

"Clay's right, Annie," Katie said. "You and the girls stay here. You don't need to be wandering around an army post by yourself at night. We'll find something for you and the girls to eat. You must be starving."

"Now, see, we're messing everybody's evening up," Annie protested. "I didn't wanna do that. Alice and Jenny and I can wait till we get the wagon. Can't we, girls?"

"Nonsense," Katie replied. "I've got just the right thing to keep you from starving. Worley Branch gave me some more smoked venison, more than we could possibly eat. We'll let you and the girls roast it over the fire. It'll be like a picnic. Matt, you go get enough for the three of them. Clay, you go and find Harlan and the wagon."

"Yes, ma'am," Clay and Matt said simultaneously, and departed at once. Annie still looked uncertain, so Katie took her hand in hers and told her Clay would find her husband.

The two brothers headed for their wagon at a trot, Matt to get the deer meat, Clay to pick up his Henry rifle. He still had a bad feeling about the situation, so he wanted to have his rifle in case there was a need for a firearm. "Clay!" Matt shouted as his brother left the wagon. "You be careful."

Clay hurried past the sutler's store, now closed, and on to the blacksmith where he saw Harlan's wagon standing, the horses still in harness. The blacksmith was obviously closed, so Clay ran up to the wagon to see if Harlan was inside. "Can I help you?" The voice came from inside the shop. Clay spun around, his rifle ready, trying to spot the source. He saw no one in the darkness at first. Then the voice came again. "Take it easy. Ain't no need to shoot anybody."

Clay saw the source then. He was sitting in an outdoor armchair by his forge, eating his supper. "Sorry," Clay said, "you startled me. You're the blacksmith, I reckon."

"That's right, Bill Anderson's the name."

"I'm looking for the man who owns this wagon. Harlan Rice is his name," Clay said.

"So am I," Anderson replied. "I fixed his wheels this afternoon. But he wandered off somewhere and never came back to get his wagon. That's the reason I'm still here. He just left his horses standin' there in the traces. I felt sorry for 'em, so I dragged that tub of water over there so they could at least drink some. But I ain't got no idea why he ain't come back."

"Did he pay you for the work?" Clay asked.

"Yeah, it's paid for and ready to go. The work's done. He asked me how much it would cost before I started on it and I told him. So he said he better pay me then, and he did. Said he was just gonna wander around and look at things for a little while, and I ain't seen him since."

"Where can a man get a drink of likker?" Clay asked.

"There ain't but one place," Anderson said, "place called Shorty's, quarter of a mile ride down that road." He pointed to a little road running toward the river. "You figure that's what happened to him, huh?"

"It's the first thing that comes to mind," Clay said.

"You goin' there to look for him?" Clay said he was, so Anderson asked, "Do you mind takin' care of his wagon, too? I don't want to leave here with that wagon and horses standin' there with their whole life's belongings just settin' there."

"Yeah, I reckon I could drive his wagon down to Shorty's," Clay said. "And I'll apologize to you for him leavin' the damn wagon here."

"I'm obliged. Whatcha gonna do if he ain't there?" Anderson asked.

"I'll just drive the wagon back to the wagon train and tell his wife and two daughters this turned out to be the luckiest night of their lives when they lost that no-account drunk."

"Amen," Anderson said, "I know what you mean."

Chapter 15

Clay climbed up on the wagon and sat down in the driver's seat. It had been some time since he had driven a team of horses. As he took the reins in hand, he tried to remember if there had been a time since he left Matt's farm in Missouri and decided there had not been an occasion. He gave them a little slap with the reins across their rumps to wake them up, then hauled back on the reins and backed the wagon away from the blacksmith shop. He turned them and drove the wagon the short distance to the small log building with a little porch on the front. There was one horse tied at the hitching rail out front. He pulled the wagon around the building and parked it on the other side, so that he could pull straight out, instead of backing out. He sat there for just a few moments, listening. There was the typical loud talking and swearing normally heard in a saloon, but nothing that sounded out of hand. So he considered leaving his rifle in the wagon but then decided it better to have it and not need it, than the other way around.

He was about to step up on the porch when a young soldier charged out the door and lunged toward the hand railing on the side of the porch and held on while his stomach turned inside out to deposit its contents on the ground. Clay waited for the soldier to go back inside, but he remained at the handrail while his stom-

ach went through the motions to prepare for a repeat performance. So Clay stepped up on the porch and went inside. He
paused just inside the door to look the room over. There were a
few tables on one side of the room across from the bar. A group of
five soldiers were seated around two of the little tables that had
been shoved together to make one. All five of the soldiers stared
back at him, no doubt because they expected the young soldier
to come back in the door, and not a tall stranger carrying a rifle.
When they continued to stare at him, he walked over close to the
table and said, "He'll most likely be back in a minute or two.
He's still hangin' on to the handrail on the porch." They laughed
then, so he turned and walked over to the bar where he saw a tall,
gangly man awaiting his order. There was only one other man at
the bar. He was standing down at the end with two bottles and a
shot glass on the bar in front of him. He was a rough-looking man
of solid build, non-military obviously. Clay figured he belonged
to the horse tied out front. He heard a sudden cheer go up from
the soldiers behind him and he turned to see the young soldier
come back inside and head for the tables.

Clay stepped up to the bar to address the bartender, who appeared to stand a couple of inches taller than himself. "I'm gonna
take a wild guess and say you must be Shorty."

Shorty chuckled and replied, "You'd be right on the money.
What can I pour for you?"

"Well, Shorty, I'm lookin' for a fellow who came in with that
wagon train today. He went to get his wagon fixed and never
came back. He's been known to take a drink now and again, so I
thought you mighta seen him." Shorty didn't respond right away,
but his expression said that he had. "His wife and children are
worried about him," Clay continued. Shorty still didn't say anything, but he indicated with his head, nodding toward the man
standing at the end of the bar. Clay didn't understand. He
glanced at the man, who met his glance with a smirk, obviously
having heard Clay's conversation with Shorty. Clay looked back
at Shorty and asked, "Are you sayin' I should ask him?" Shorty

still didn't speak but answered with a nod of his head. "Who's he?" Clay asked.

"Ace Wilson," Shorty answered. And when it was obvious he was not going to say more, Clay walked down to confront Ace Wilson. "Ace Wilson?" Clay asked. Wilson responded with a sarcastic smile. "I reckon you heard me talkin' to Shorty about the man I'm looking for. He thinks you know where he might be. Is that a fact?"

"Yeah, that's a fact," Wilson replied.

"Where is he?" As an answer, Wilson motioned toward the wall behind the bar with his head. When Clay looked in the direction indicated, he saw Harlan slumped on the floor, his back against the wall, his face a mess of dried and fresh blood. "Son of a . . ." Clay started and turned back to Wilson. "Did you do that?"

Wilson's smirk returned and he answered. "I sure did. He ain't dead. He's just drunk. He said he hadn't had a drink since Fort Laramie and he wanted to buy me a drink, too. So he bought a bottle and we sat down at a table and finished it—least he finished it. When it was gone, he was too drunk to stand up, so he told me to go buy two more bottles to take with us, one for him and one for me, and he'd pay me for both of 'em. I had to go to the outhouse and when I came back, I caught the little rat sneakin' out the front door with both bottles of likker. He claimed he lost his money somewhere."

"I don't blame you for bein' mad," Clay said, "but from the looks of his face and clothes, it looks like you took out your vengeance on him, for whatever satisfaction you can get beatin' up a drunk. I'll take him back to his family." He started toward Harlan, who was still slumped against the wall, but Wilson stepped in front of him.

"First, you gotta give me the price of two bottles of rye whiskey," Wilson said. "He sets right where he is until I get the price of two bottles of likker."

"Why?" Clay asked. "You said you stopped him before he got away with the two bottles of whiskey. Give the whiskey back to Shorty." He turned to look at the bartender. "You'll take the whiskey back, won't you, Shorty?"

"Yeah, but he don't wanna give 'em back," Shorty said.

"Well, that's the only way you can get your money back 'cause I've gotta take him back to his family," Clay said.

"As soon as you give me the money for the whiskey, you can take him," Wilson said, and dropped his hand on the handle of the pistol he wore. "And not a second before that."

"I don't want the damn whiskey," Clay said. "Give it back to the bartender."

"I didn't say you'd get the whiskey," Wilson replied. "I'm keepin' the whiskey, but you're gonna pay for the low-down trick he tried to play on me."

Clay just stared at him for a moment, finding it hard to believe he really thought he was owed something for his trouble with Harlan. "That's just plain stupid. I don't owe you a damn thing. Maybe you need to learn that it ain't ever a good idea to make any deals with a drunk. And here's another lesson you need to learn, if that hand comes up with a gun in it, you're a dead man."

"Ha," Wilson released a contemptuous grunt, "you think you're that fast with a rifle?" As soon as he saw Wilson's hand tighten to grip the pistol, Clay struck. Holding his rifle in both hands, he jammed Wilson's hand with the butt of the rifle before his pistol cleared the holster. The force of the blow caused Wilson to pull the trigger, drilling a hole through his holster and ripping a strip of wood from the floor. Before he could recover, Clay swung the rifle in a sweeping motion like a club, striking Wilson on the side of his head with the barrel. Wilson dropped to the floor unconscious. Just as a precaution then, Clay cranked a cartridge into the chamber of the Henry and looked at Shorty to make sure he wasn't in with Wilson. Then he looked at the soldiers but saw nothing but expressions of admiration. So he figured it was safe to help Harlan get to his feet.

"Harlan, can you get up?" Clay asked. "I've got your wagon outside. I'm gonna try to get you on your feet and out the door." He paused then because a couple of the soldiers got up from the table and advanced toward him. He turned to face them.

"You look like you could use a little help," one of the soldiers, wearing corporal's stripes, said. "We heard you say that's his wagon beside the building. Let us carry this poor fellow out to the wagon for you. I'd like to say we admired the way you took care of ol' Ace Wilson, too. He's had that comin' for a long time." He took hold of Harlan's shoulders and another soldier grabbed his ankles and they carried him outside to the wagon. "Where do you want him, sir?"

"Just dump him anywhere in the back you see a space. I just have to take him to the wagon train on the other side of the fort," Clay said. When they laid Harlan in the wagon, Clay said, "I'm much obliged to you boys. I would have had a time tryin' to tote him on my shoulder while I'm carryin' my rifle with one hand. I shoulda known I could count on the army to help out."

The soldier laughed and replied, "That's right, sir. We couldn't help but notice the trousers you're wearin'. That's the kind of trousers an officer in the cavalry usually wears, ain't it, sir?"

"That's right," Clay answered.

"When was you mustered out?"

"This past April, Corporal, and I thank you and the others again for your help. This poor fellow has a wife and two daughters dependin' on him to take 'em to Oregon, so I'd better get him back."

"Yes, sir," the corporal said. "Good luck on your journey." He turned to go back inside but hesitated and turned back to face Clay again. "Are you folks pullin' out in the morning?"

"No," Clay answered, "we're gonna stay over another day. I know I've got to get some new shoes for my horses."

"Well, keep a sharp eye out for what's going on around you," the corporal warned. "That fellow you handled tonight has a reputation around here as a troublemaker and a gunslinger, and you made him look pretty stupid tonight."

"Thanks for the warning." They shook hands, then Clay climbed up in the wagon and drove the wagon back past the fort to the big pasture where the wagons were parked. He drove the wagon into the circle through the open space where it should have been parked already. Many in the group gathered around the fire ran to help when they saw the wagon pull in. Annie told Alice and Jenny to stay there by the fire until she had a chance to see if Clay had found their father. Then she ran to the wagon with the others, fearing what she was to find. When she got there, she saw Clay climbing down from the wagon seat while a couple of the men were unhitching the horses.

"Harlan?" That was Annie's single question when she ran up to Clay.

"I found him," Clay said, dreading to tell her the circumstances in which he found her husband. "He's in the back. He ain't feelin' too good right now."

It was what she expected and she immediately blamed herself for it. "Drunk?" Clay nodded. "I should have gone with him to get the wagon fixed," she said. "I don't know why I didn't. It's just because he's been so much better lately. I should have known it was just because he couldn't find any whiskey anywhere." She walked around to the back of the wagon and called to him, "Harlan?"

"I think he's totally passed out," Clay told her. "Before you look at him I need to tell you he looks pretty bad. He got into it with a fellow at the saloon and I don't know how bad he got hurt, but it looks bad. You're gonna need some help cleanin' him up."

"No," she said, "I don't need any help. I can clean him up."

"He might need some doctorin' on his face, too," Clay said.

"I can do the doctoring, too," she insisted.

"Annie, I understand how you're feeling," Clay finally told her frankly. "You don't want everybody on the wagon train to know what Harlan gets himself into. I don't blame you. But the fact of the matter is that he needs cleanin' up all over and you can't even pick him up to get him out of this wagon. And right now, he can't help himself. Ain't no tellin' when he's gonna wake up, if he drank as much likker as they said he did. I'll get Matt and maybe Worley to help me, and we'll take him to the river and clean him up. You fix his bed up and after we get him cleaned up, we'll lay him on his bed and then you can do the doctorin'. How 'bout it? Don't you think that's best?"

She hung her head and admitted it. "Yes, I didn't know how I was going to take care of him. I don't want the girls to see him like this." She raised her head to look at him. "I don't know what I would do without your help, but I'm so sorry to saddle you with my problem." Then she seemed to bounce back to her typical confidence. "Phew," she said, "he smells something awful. We need to get him outta the wagon before we have to burn everything in it."

"Right," Clay said. "I'll go get Matt. You get rid of the rest of these folks still standing around wantin' to help." He hustled back to where he had seen Matt with Katie before.

"Everything all right now?" Matt asked when Clay hustled up to them.

"I need your help with Harlan," Clay told him.

"Why didn't you tell me when I was over there at the wagon?" Matt asked. "I didn't hang around because I thought Annie would rather have everybody leave."

"She would," Clay said, then japed, "everybody but you, Matt. She sent me to get you." He glanced over and saw Worley rise up from his seat on a mound of earth and gawk at them. "And Worley," Clay said. "She said go get Matt and Worley." He raised his hand and made a "come on" motion. Worley jumped up at once and joined Clay and Matt as they hurried to Harlan's wagon.

"Poor Annie," Katie mumbled, and shook her head.

"What, Mama?" Sarah asked.

"Nothing, darlin'."

Matt and Clay pulled Harlan out of the back of the wagon as carefully as they could in an attempt to contain all his involuntary organ discharges within his trousers and leaving none to foul any surfaces his body touched inside the wagon. Once his body was clear of the wagon, Matt took a closer look and remarked, "I swear, I don't know if we ought to take him to the river and throw him in, or just dig a hole and bury him."

"Careful, Matt, Annie might hear you," Clay cautioned him.

"Shoot," Matt responded, "she's probably thinkin' the same thing."

She came from the other side of the wagon at that moment carrying a bucket with soapy water, a washcloth, towels, and a blanket in time to hear his last comment. "Probably thinking what?" she asked.

"That we better clean him up before the girls see him," Matt said. "He's lookin' in pretty bad shape."

"Oh, my Lord . . ." Annie despaired, getting a closer look at his battered face now that he was out of the wagon. As Matt had remarked, she wondered if he was dead. To settle the issue, Harlan stirred at that moment and uttered a few garbled words before passing out again.

That was signal enough for Matt. "Okay," he said, "he's alive. Let's take him to the river and clean him up!" Matt and Clay picked Harlan up, Worley took the bucket and the rest from Annie, and they headed for the river.

"Be sure you go downstream," Annie called after them, a warning that was unnecessary.

When they reached the river, the body was unceremoniously heaved into the shallow water, and like a log, it just sank to the bottom. Expecting Harlan to immediately start floundering around with the shock of landing in the river, Clay and Matt exchanged glances of alarm, then jumped in the water to retrieve the body. When they brought him to the surface, he started to sputter and spew water from his mouth, coughing and heaving frantically. "What the hell?" He slurred the words, still a little drunk. "Where'd you two come from? I gotta go get my wagon. Let go of me." He tried to pull away from Matt's grip on his arm. Not endowed with the patience of his brother Clay, Matt held him firmly and ordered, "Shut up, you damn fool. Your wagon's back in place where it's supposed to be and now you're gonna get a bath before your little daughters have to see what a disgustin' drunk their daddy is."

"You can't talk to me like that," Harlan said. "Me and my daughters ain't none of your business. You ain't givin' me no bath, either. Ain't no man givin' me a bath."

Clay could readily see that his brother's approach wasn't helping their attempt to get the job done. So he tried another approach. "Look, Harlan, I understand how you might feel about what we're trying to do. But maybe you ain't realized how bad you got hurt in that saloon. You took a bad beatin', lotta cuts and bruises on your face, and I think your nose might be broke. Now, Annie wants to do some doctorin' on your face, but she needs to have you cleaned up first. You might not realize it, but you were passed out for a helluva long time. And when you were passed out, your body kept right on crappin' and peein', just the same as if you were awake. So now, it's all in your clothes and all over you. With you passed out, you couldn't help yourself and Annie couldn't give you a good cleanin', so Matt and I volunteered to help you. Now, seein' as how you're awake, maybe you can clean yourself up. Annie gave us a bucket of soap and water and a washcloth you can use, and any places you can't reach, like your back, we can get that for you. Whaddaya think, you feel able to clean yourself up now?"

Harlan didn't respond at once, but he calmed down considerably while he thought about what Clay had just said. Finally, he decided that maybe they weren't trying to trick him. "Yeah, I can do that. I can clean myself up, but I don't want the three of you standin' right here watchin' me."

Matt rolled his eyes and shook his head, but Clay quickly said, "Understood; I don't blame you. We'll just check you over to see if you missed any spots when you're done. Good man. Worley, give him the soap bucket and we'll go up the bank a ways, so you can have some privacy." Clay put his hand on Matt's arm and turned him away. "Come on, Brother," he said, just above a whisper, "give him a chance. Hell, you don't wanna wash him." Matt let himself be led up the bank. Worley gave Harlan the bucket and washcloth. He laid the towel and blanket to wrap himself in on the bank. Then he followed Clay and Matt.

When they walked what they considered a far enough distance from Harlan's bath but were still able to see what he was doing, they sat down to wait for him to finish. Matt was still skeptical about depending on Harlan to do a decent job. "What if he does a sorry job of cleanin' himself up?" he asked. "Then what?"

"Then we switch over to your way," Clay told him. "You and I will hold him down and Worley will scrub him raw."

"I'm gonna remind myself of this night the next time you come to me and tell me you need my help," Matt told him.

"Come on, Brother, you know this beats sittin' around the fire back there and listenin' to Vernon and the boys torture those instruments."

"You know it's gonna be too dark to see what kinda job Harlan does on himself," Matt declared.

"I believe you really did want to give Harlan a bath," Clay japed. "Don't you, Worley?"

"Right," Matt spat in disgust.

Even though still half under the influence of the amount of whiskey he had imbibed, Harlan was motivated to give himself a bath, once he began to discover how badly he had fouled himself with his own bodily fluids. Before he finished, he had stripped down completely, then he toweled off and wrapped the blanket around himself. Although his boots were wet, he put them back on, since he felt he was recovered enough to walk back to the wagons. He emptied the soapy water out of the bucket and put his wet clothes and cleanup materials in it. Then he walked up from the water's edge and with no word to his escorts, started back to his wagon.

"Whoa!" Clay yelled at him. "Where you goin'?" He ran down the bank to catch him, with Matt and Worley right behind him. He caught up with Harlan right away and stopped him. "Where are you goin'?" he asked again.

"I'm goin' back to my wagon to get on some dry clothes," Harlan said, sounding much more sober now.

"That wasn't our agreement," Clay said. "We let you wash yourself, but we had to inspect you before you could go back to let Annie work on your face."

"I'm a grown man," Harlan replied. "I can damn-sure give myself a bath, and I just gave myself a good one. So you can tell my wife that you did your job and now I'd appreciate it if you'd get outta my way and let me go get some dry clothes on."

Clay was standing directly in front of him and he was considering whether to step aside or not when suddenly Matt, who was standing behind Harlan, reached up and jerked the blanket off. Mortified, Harlan tried to cover himself as best he could with his hands. "Damn you!" he cursed them.

"Looks to me like he did a pretty good job," Clay said to Matt.

"Yep," Matt agreed, "Annie oughta be pleased with the job we did. I hope you are, too, Harlan. Here's your blanket back."

Chapter 16

There was nothing more that Clay could do for Annie Rice after Harlan returned to their wagon. She thanked Clay and Matt, and Worley as well, for carrying Harlan for his bath. Before they left her to care for her husband's facial injuries, Clay made a point of confirming Harlan's claim to her that he had bathed himself. He figured they had plenty to fight about already without adding another issue. Clay, Matt, and Worley returned to the social hour to join Katie and the kids for the short time left before the musicians packed it in for the night. Tomorrow would be another morning without Grissom's bugle at four o'clock and everyone was looking forward to that.

At the Rices' wagon, Alice and Jenny lay in their sleeping tent, their pillows wrapped around their ears in an effort not to hear the argument between their mother and father. It had to do with the disappearance of a sum of money from their cash box that was more than the cost of fixing the wagon wheels. To Annie's surprise, however, there was a definite change in Harlan's attitude. In past arguments over his drinking problem, he was always defiant and abusive. Tonight, he was less offensive and even admitted that he took extra money to buy whiskey. Furthermore, he even told her that he was going to stop drinking, and she realized that this time he feared that he had almost killed himself.

Before the evening was over, he even confessed to her that he didn't remember anything after Ace Wilson beat him senseless in the saloon. The first thing he was aware of after that was when he came to and found himself lying on the bottom of the river. He told her that he thought he was dead until Clay and Matt pulled him up out of the water. Evidently it was enough to scare him sober, for he told Annie that he knew he had treated her and the girls poorly and he was going to try to make up for it. "I know I ain't done right by you. I'm gonna try to change all that I done wrong."

Annie honestly didn't know whether to believe him or not, not sure if one could ever believe the word of a drunk. But she knew the way things had been going, she and the girls were likely to be on their own in the Oregon country. So she told him, "Starting tomorrow, we'll begin a new life together, and any trouble we've had is in the past, all right?"

"All right," he quickly agreed.

"I'm glad the man I married is back," she said. "Now, I think we both need to get some sleep. You've had a pretty rough day and tomorrow's a new day."

As was usually the case on a non-traveling day, breakfast was a little later than normal, and took a little longer to finish. After the kids ate and left to pursue their interests, Matt and Clay and Katie returned to the conversation about the happenings of the night just past. Katie was concerned that yesterday's actions by Harlan would be the final spike to split Annie's marriage apart and leave her with two daughters to raise on her own. "I'm takin' my horses over to the farrier's this mornin'," Clay said. "I'll stop by their wagon to see how they're doin' after last night's bath. Harlan was pretty feisty after we left him last night."

Matt chuckled and said, "You'd best be careful he doesn't take a shot at you."

"You're the one who jerked the blanket off him," Clay replied.

"You're the one who'd best watch your back." He got up to go saddle his horse.

"Hey, wait a minute!" Katie stopped him. "I wanna hear about this!"

"After Harlan took his bath, he covered his naked body with a blanket Annie sent with him. Ask Matt about it. He'll tell you how he grabbed that blanket and shucked him like an ear of corn. I never thought to do that. I reckon Matt and I don't exactly think alike. Frankly, I preferred to keep him covered up."

"Is that so?" Matt came back at him. "It was your idea to give him a bath."

"Thank goodness the children aren't here to see their daddy and their uncle have an adult conversation," Katie said.

Clay walked away without looking back, his saddle on his shoulder, but he raised his other hand in the air to let her know he heard her. He walked over to where the horses were grazing and whistled to get the gray's attention. The horse looked toward him at once and did not move while Clay walked up to him. "How you doin' this mornin', Bud?" Clay asked, and rubbed the horse's face and neck. "You know, we've been partners ever since I got out of the army and you still won't come when I whistle. Is it because I still haven't thought of a name for you? Well, no trouble, at least you don't run away when I whistle. I'm gonna take you to get some new shoes this mornin'." He put the saddle on him and then rode into the herd to cut out his packhorse. "I could whistle all day and you wouldn't stand still for me," he told the dun after he roped him. "You're gonna get some shoes, too." Since he was only going over to the farrier's, he didn't bother with a bridle for the dun.

He rode out of the circle of wagons, then rode around the outside of it until he came to the Rices' wagon. He saw Harlan and Annie sitting beside the fire on the other side of the wagon. When they saw it was him, they both got up and walked around the wagon to greet him. He wasn't at all sure what to expect when he said, " 'Mornin', how are you folks this mornin'?"

"Good morning, Clay," Annie said. "We're havin' a late breakfast, like most everybody else this morning."

"I just got through, myself," Clay said, finding it awkward trying to make casual conversation when he really just wanted to know if Harlan had given her any trouble. "I'm takin' my horses over to the farrier's to get new shoes," he said. "So I'll let you get back to your breakfast." He could tell Matt and Katie that at least there were no marks or bruises on Annie's face, but Harlan's looked like he'd gone head to head with a mountain goat. He turned the gray's head toward the fort.

"Hold on a minute, Moran," Harlan suddenly called out. Clay held the gray back and Harlan walked up beside him. "I think I owe you and your brother some thanks for what you did last night. I'm ashamed of myself for the trouble I've caused you"— he turned to look back at Annie—"and my wife. And I hope there ain't no hard feelings between us because of it. I'm gonna do my damnedest not to cause trouble like that again."

Clay was dumbfounded, unable to think of the proper response. He was so taken by surprise he just sat there speechless for a long moment. He glanced over at Annie, hoping she would help, but she just stood there beaming at him. "Well, no, there ain't no hard feelings" was all he could come up with right away. Then he grinned back at Annie. "I'm just tickled for both of ya. Yes, sir, tickled to death. Good for you, Harlan." He sat there on his horse then, not knowing what else to say to get out of the awkward situation.

Annie laughed and came to his rescue. "Don't let us keep you, Clay. Harlan just wanted to tell you that. Go get your horses shoed."

"Yes, ma'am, I guess I better." He wheeled the gray and started out toward the other side of the fort. He walked the gray past the doctor's office next to the sutler's store and the blacksmith shop and the farrier's shop beyond.

Bill Anderson, the blacksmith, recognized him when he rode past and he stopped what he was doing and walked over to talk to him. "Mornin'," Anderson said. "Did you ever find the feller that left his wagon at my place yesterday?"

"I did," Clay answered. "And he's back at the wagon train now, a little worse for wear, but he's all right. I think he mighta got hold of some bad whiskey from somebody, but he's all right this mornin',"

"Well, I'm glad to hear that, and I 'preciate you takin' care of that wagon for me," Anderson said. "I got a customer waitin'. I just wanted to know if that feller was all right." He turned around and went back to his shop just as the farrier walked out to meet Clay.

"Yes, sir, can I help you? Looks like you've got a couple of horses that need some work."

"Yes, I do," Clay replied. "I just bought the shoes they're wearin' at Fort Kearny and they look like they ain't wearin' evenly. So I thought I'd see if you can do a decent job with some new ones."

"I'm pretty sure I can give you a first-class job. My name's Philip Denson and you came at a pretty good time because I'm going to be shoeing horses at the army stable after dinner today."

"Clay Moran," he introduced himself. "I'm glad I didn't wait till this afternoon to come see you."

"I'll get right on it," Denson said. "I'll take the gray first, then you can take him for a little ride to see how he takes to the new shoes while I'm workin' on the dun. Then if you don't like the way they fit, you can stop me before I ruin your packhorse. Fair enough?"

Clay laughed. "Fair enough," he said.

"How much you want for that little bit of work?" his surly patient asked.

"Those seven stitches I put on the side of your head are gonna cost you three-fifty," Doc Taylor told him. "Two of the bones in your right hand are fractured. The only thing that I could do was to wrap it in a padded bandage and wait to see if the swelling goes down and you have adequate blood flow for that hand to recover. If it doesn't, we'll have to amputate that hand."

"The hell we will!" Ace Wilson declared.

"Of course, that will be your decision," Doc Taylor said. "But that'll be three dollars for cleaning and bandaging the hand, one dollar for the laudanum for the pain. So that'll be seven-fifty total."

"Seven-fifty!" Ace exclaimed. "That's a helluva lotta money for no more work than you did. I'd say, more like five dollars." He reached into his vest pocket with his left hand and fished around until he came up with five dollars. "There you go. I'll give you the rest next payday, and that looks like it ain't gonna be for a while if this hand don't heal up." He labored to get his gun belt back around his hips, and by holding one side of the belt up with his right thumb, he managed to buckle it with his left hand. "Damn!" he exclaimed, wiggling the fingers on his injured hand, while Doc Taylor waited patiently for him to leave. When finally he walked to the door and opened it, it was to see what he thought was a vision at first. Then he realized it was no vision. It was the devil who sent him to the doctor's office, riding by just as casually as you please. Ace automatically reached for his Colt handgun only to curse the pain when his swollen hand tried to grasp the handle. He had often practiced with his left hand, so he pulled the weapon out of his holster with that hand, but he was too late. By that time, Clay had already passed by. "Damn the luck!" He walked out onto the boardwalk in front of the doctor's office to see where Clay was going. *Dead man*, he thought when he saw him turn in at the farrier's, knowing he was going to kill him. Then an idea occurred to him, and he stopped and pulled his six-gun up from his holster and turned it around so the handle faced forward. Then he dropped it back down into the holster to set it for a cross-body draw. He tried a couple of quick draws with the weapon sitting in the holster backward. *Pretty fast*, he thought. *Not as lightning fast as my right hand but quicker than a rifle.* With his six-gun turned around backward, it didn't fit all the way down in the holster like it would have had it been holstered correctly, but that made the draw even faster. Instead of outright murder, he could call him out to face him in a duel and there would be no trouble from the army or the law. It occurred to him also that it would add to his reputation to have won the face-off with his left hand. *It couldn't be better*, he thought, and headed for the farrier's.

Clay saw him coming, but he was unarmed. Denson had his horse inside his shed and his rifle was in the saddle sling. To make matters even worse, he hadn't even bothered to strap his six-gun on this morning. It was rolled up in his gun belt and stuffed in the saddlebag. He was sitting on a stool about ten yards away from the shed, and he felt sure that if he jumped up and ran to the shed, Wilson would more than likely shoot at him. He didn't like his odds if he just sat there, either, but they might be a shade better than if he tried to get his gun.

"Well, now, lookee here," Wilson said as he walked up, "if it ain't the yellow dog that put this bandage on my hand, and another one on the side of my head. It sure is lucky runnin' into you 'cause we've got some real important business to get settled, ain't we?"

"I thought that was pretty much settled last night," Clay answered. He noticed the bulky bandage on Wilson's right hand and the pistol turned around in his holster for a cross draw with his left hand. "At least, it's settled as far as I'm concerned."

"It's a helluva long way from bein' settled," Wilson declared. "There ain't but one way to settle it. I'm callin' you out, man to man, right here, right now. So get your weapon in hand." By this time both Philip Denson and Bill Anderson next door were aware of what was going on. So work in both shops came to a halt.

"I don't fight duels as a rule," Clay said. "And besides, your hand is injured. You're obviously gonna try a cross draw with your left hand. That don't hardly seem like a fair fight. So why don't I just apologize for causing your injuries and let that be the end of it?"

"All right," Wilson said with a smirk, "you can apologize for bustin' up my hand and knockin' me beside the head with your rifle. And the way I want you to do it is to get down on your hands and knees and crawl over here and lick the dust off my boots with your tongue. Then tell me how sorry you are for what you did."

"Well, Ace"—Clay paused—"ain't that what they call you? You know I'm not gonna do that."

"Then get your damn weapon and face me 'cause I'm gonna shoot your cowardly behind whether you do or not."

"All right, if you won't have it any other way, I'll get my gun," Clay said. He walked into the shed to meet Denson standing there staring at him as if confused. Clay smiled and asked, "You want me to pay you now?"

Denson hesitated, reluctant to seem pessimistic but not certain of Clay's possibilities while quite certain about Ace Wilson's. "It's up to you," he said. "Of course, I'm always glad to accept payment in advance."

His hesitation was enough to make Clay think Ace Wilson must be really fast, even with his left hand on a cross draw. He immediately tried to think of an advantage in this shoot-out he was going to participate in, even if only a mental one. He decided it would be best to use his pistol and he decided the best way to use it would be to reverse the way it was sitting in the holster, just like Wilson did. So with his back to Wilson, he took his six-gun from his saddlebag and quickly turned the pistol around backward in the holster. He walked out from under the shed then, carrying his rolled-up gun belt to stand about twenty paces in front of the waiting Wilson. As he buckled on his belt, he said, "It sure suits me to accommodate you like this, but I swear, I don't know if I can live with myself if I ain't honest about this shoot-out."

"What the hell are you talkin' about?" Wilson demanded. "You ain't wigglin' your way outta this. I'm gonna count to three."

"Fine with me, it's just that it ain't fair to you. So you just try to remember wherever you wind up after this is over, I tried to tell you that you didn't get a fair fight."

"What the hell are you talkin' about?" Wilson demanded again.

"I swear, Wilson, it's a wonder you've made it this far," Clay said. "If you had any brains a-tall, you'd notice that we're both set up for a cross draw, using our left hands. I know why you're set up that way because I jammed your right hand. What you don't know is that I'm set up that way because I'm left-handed, natural born. If it was a fair fight, we'd both have to use our weak hand. But, hell, if you wanna do it this way, I'm more than happy to go along with it. You ready?"

"Hold on!" Wilson exclaimed. "This is supposed to be a fair fight. You're right. If you're left-handed, you oughta turn that pistol around and draw with your right hand." He liked that arrangement even better. *And the dumb cluck even confessed that he was left-handed,* he said to himself. "You're right. We might as well make this a fair fight."

"Well, I liked it better the other way," Clay said as he turned his six-gun around in the correct position, "but you might as well go out as a gentleman. Whenever you're ready..." Wilson reached for his gun and Clay shot him in the chest before he got the weapon halfway out of the holster.

The small crowd of spectators that had gathered closed in around Ace Wilson's body while Clay walked into the shed where his horse was. Philip Denson walked in behind him and asked, "You ain't left-handed, are you?"

"No, I'm not," Clay said. "Is there anybody who takes care of the body?"

"Joe Porter acts as an undertaker. He's the barber. He'll most likely be here directly, if he heard the shot. The soldiers don't like to deal with the civilian deaths. If you're worried about your part in the shootin', I wouldn't. There's enough people who saw that Wilson didn't give you no choice. And I'll certainly tell 'em how it happened. Now, I'd best get back to work on your horses."

Denson finished Clay's horses and Clay was back to the wagons in time for dinner. "Somebody got shot over that way," Matt said as they were sitting around the campfire, finishing the coffee. The children had already eaten and disappeared. "We heard the shot," Matt went on. "I told Katie it was probably you havin' another go-round with your friend from Shorty's. Were you anywhere around whoever did the shootin'?"

"Yep," Clay answered, "it was over near the blacksmith's and the farrier's."

"What happened? Somebody shoot a firearm off accidentally?" Matt asked.

"No, it was done on purpose."

"Did you see it?"

"Yeah, I saw it."

"Who got shot, anybody we know?"

"That fellow, Ace Wilson, that was holdin' Harlan Rice at Shorty's Saloon."

"Well, I'll be . . . Who shot him? Was it you?"

"Yep."

"I swear, Clay . . ." Matt started in frustration, and tried to kick some dirt at him with his boot, but most of it flew in Katie's direction. She reacted by threatening to throw the contents of her coffee cup at him. "See what you cause, Clay? Actin' like a jackass. Why didn't you tell us you got into a mess of trouble over there?"

"I figured you'd ask about it, if you really wanted to know," Clay said, "and you did. And I told you what happened, so what are you complaining about?"

"Is this the way you two were when you were little boys growing up?" Katie asked. "It's no wonder why your poor mother answered her call to heaven earlier than expected."

Later on, Clay told Matt all the details of his duel with Ace Wilson, just as Matt knew he would. "I was mighty lucky he just took my word for it that I was left-handed," Clay confessed. "The man was damn fast on the draw. I was lucky to beat him using my good hand."

Chapter 17

The wagon train pulled away from Fort Bridger at seven o'clock the next morning, following a trail to the northwest that would take them to the mountains of Utah and the Bear River Valley. They saw very little difference in the desolate land they traveled through in the next few days than that which they had traveled before reaching Fort Bridger. The exception to this was the seemingly continuous wall of mountain ridges to the west of their line of travel. After seven days of this monotonous routine, the emigrants were faced with a troublesome crossing of the Thomas Fork of the Bear River. It was not a large body of water and would have been a simple crossing were it not for the steep, slippery banks on each side, making it very difficult for a wagon to manage. There was a way to drive the wagons around the crossing, but it was eight miles of extra travel to do it and Grissom admitted that it was a rough eight miles. Sometime in the past, some emigrants had built two bridges across the river which made the crossing quick and easy. But the bridges had been taken over by some enterprising opportunists who saw the potential to make money off the poor emigrants. The toll charge for using the bridges was one dollar per wagon.

At the social hour on the night before reaching the Thomas Fork crossing, Grissom had discussed the toll bridges with his people. There were many who did not want to pay a high fee to cross such an insignificant body of water. They were already aware of fees they would have to pay when they reached Oregon. But there were just as many who did not want to add eight rough miles to their travel. Whatever they decided, Grissom was hoping for a unanimous decision. If not, he would have to lead those who chose not to pay on the detour. Those who paid to cross the bridges would have to wait for him to catch up, consequently losing the time they saved for their dollar toll.

Foremost among those who voted to pay the dollar toll was Henry Corbett. He argued that the trail they had followed from Fort Bridger was rough enough on his wagon. So he balked at taking a detour that Grissom said was rougher still. "I'm hopin' my wagon makes it to the Willamette Valley, so it's worth a measly dollar to save a little bit of that wear and tear," he said. Corbett was a large man who had sold his hardware store in Independence. He and his wife, Maurine, had no children. He talked with the confidence of a man who had been successful in his prior business and was planning to build a bigger business in the Willamette Valley. "We were all taking a helluva gamble when we decided to make this trip. We've already seen good luck and bad luck after coming this far. I'm a gamblin' man, just like the rest of you. And I trust your word, Mr. Grissom. So when you say that eight miles of road is rougher than what we've been riding on, I believe you. And I'm thinking that piece of road might be the place where I break an axle or turn my wagon over. So to me, I think a dollar is a cheap investment to make sure that doesn't happen." His testimony was enough to persuade ten of the others to pay the toll as well.

At seven the next morning, the wagon train continued on toward Thomas Fork crossing. Just short of reaching it, Grissom called for a halt when they came to a two-rutted road that led to the detour around the crossing. Since Corbett had unofficially taken leadership of the toll payers, Grissom told him to just follow the trail they were on and it would take him to the crossing.

He told him to wait for him and the rest of the train, after the crossing, at a creek halfway between Thomas Fork and Big Hill. "We'll get there as quick as we can," Grissom told him, "but that creek is a good place to water and rest your horses. We'll take the extra horses with us, so you won't have to pay for them to cross." "We appreciate that," Corbett said. "I hadn't thought about that."

Grissom signaled Ike and Ike started his horses up the road that led to the detour and the other twelve wagons fell in line behind Ike. Corbett signaled for the ten wagons behind his to close up the gaps left by the penny pinchers and he started out again toward the toll bridges. Grissom, Clay, and Worley, on horseback, herded the extra horses to follow Ike.

Corbett and the other ten wagons reached the crossing a short time after splitting off from Grissom, and they could see at once why the bridges were necessary to cross. The banks of the creek-sized river fork were dangerously steep on both sides. Grissom had been right, they were charged a dollar to cross, and Corbett was satisfied that they had done the right thing. They were across and on their way toward Big Hill which was less than ten miles away. Within a few of miles after leaving the crossing, Corbett recognized the creek Grissom had described to him, so he led the other wagons off the road.

"Whaddaya think, Henry?" Frank Bowen asked when he walked up to Corbett's wagon. "Think we oughta go ahead and do the noonin'?"

Corbett took his watch out and looked at it. "I don't see why not, it's five minutes to twelve." He thought about the distance Grissom said the detour was and added, "It's gonna be a long time before the rest of 'em get here. They'll probably stop somewhere on that road and do the noonin'." So they watered the horses while the women built their fires to cook the noon meal.

At one o'clock, several of the men came up to talk with Corbett. "Reckon what happened to Grissom and the rest of 'em?" Vernon Tatum asked.

"They're just takin' a little longer on some bad road," Corbett said, "eight miles of it, as a matter of fact. And, like us, I expect they had their noonin'." He could see that Tatum and the others were impatient to get moving. "You know, we could move on up to Big Hill, instead of just sitting here. I mean, the road is pretty obvious to follow. I'd kinda like to get a look at this Big Hill. He's talked so much about it and I don't see any reason why we can't wait for the rest of the train there, if we want to." He chuckled and joked, "I don't suppose you need to be a wagon master to follow a road as plain as this one."

"You're our wagon master," Bowen said. "Lead us to Big Hill."

Everyone was in favor, so they rolled away from the creek at a little after one o'clock, following a clearly marked trail that ran along the base of a continuous ridge of mountains that stood like a great wall between them and the Bear River. When finally Corbett reached the point where the trail no longer ran along the base of the mountains but turned toward them, he pulled his wagon to a stop and climbed down. The other drivers stopped and came up to see what the halt was for.

"The trail just stopped," Corbett told them. "It was plain as can be till I got to this point, then it just quit."

There was some head scratching for only a brief moment, then Tatum said, "The hell it did. You just ain't lookin' in the right direction." When they all looked at him, he pointed to the mountain they were parked beside. The side of the mountain wore the clear impressions of wagon wheels. "This is Big Hill. This is where we cross over to the Bear River Valley."

They all turned at once to see what was now obvious, scores of wagon tracks on the steep face of the mountain. Frank Bowen said, "That's almost straight up. You can't drive a wagon up a grade like that, not loaded like we've got 'em loaded."

"Looks like they did, though," Quincy Lewis remarked. "So I expect we're gonna have to try. If Grissom ever catches up with us, I reckon he'll send Ike up that little ol' hill in his wagon to show us how it's done."

Henry Corbett studied the steep face of the hill while the other men were concentrating on the many wagon tracks that ended in skid marks that indicated sliding. After a while, he began to see a pattern develop that showed a definite proportion of wagon tracks forming a winding trail. He realized he was looking at the road up the hill. "I see it," he blurted aloud.

"You see what?" Bowen, who was standing next to him, asked.

"The road up that mountain," Corbett replied, "that's what I see."

"You're the only one that sees it," Tatum said. "We just have to wait till Grissom gets here to find it."

"I'm pretty sure I can drive my wagon up that hill right now," Corbett claimed. "I might just drive on over this hill and camp tonight on the Bear River."

"Well, I'd like to see that," Bowen said. "If you make it, I might follow you."

"I hope you're just japing," Vernon Tatum said. "You'd best wait for Grissom. I expect we should have waited for him back at that creek where we stopped first. He's most likely figurin' on tacklin' Big Hill first thing in the mornin'. The least we oughta do is go back to that little stream we passed about half a mile back 'cause we might have to camp there tonight."

"You know," Corbett told Tatum, "we're burning a lot of daylight sittin' here waiting for Grissom and the others to show up. And now you're sayin' we oughta go back to camp on a little stream, when there's a river on the other side of this hill. He's talked so much about how much nicer we're gonna like it on the other side of these mountains, that I'm gettin' kinda anxious to see it. I see the road up this hill and I think I'll show it to the rest of you."

"Hell, if you make it, I'll come up after you," Frank Bowen declared. A couple of the other men said they would follow as well.

That was enough to make Corbett's mind up. He climbed back up in his wagon. "Watch closely and follow exactly where I go, boys." He popped the reins on his horses and started up the hill.

Maurine, who was in the back of the wagon while Henry was having the discussion with the other men, climbed over into the driver's seat beside him. "Do you think it's really a good idea to do this, Henry? Grissom might not take this very well at all."

"It's pretty damn obvious that all the folks who traveled this trail before us drove their wagons over this hill. So there ain't any reason why we can't drive over it, too. I think Grissom gets to thinking he's Moses sometimes. Maybe he needs to see we ain't helpless without him to tell us everything to do."

She looked at her husband and shrugged. "Well, all right, if you're sure you know what you're doing," she said.

"Don't I always?" he answered with a smug grin, and encouraged his horses with a slap of the reins to start them up the steep incline. His horses responded with a willing effort and started moving slowly up the mountain.

The other men stood watching Corbett's ascent, carefully making note of the exact route he took as he advanced up the hill. "It's a helluva strain on his horses, but it looks like he's gonna make it," Bowen declared.

"If he can keep it up," Quincy remarked. "It looks like it gets a little steeper when he gets closer to the top of the hill."

"I wonder if it mighta been a good idea to walk up that hill first to take a look at what we've gotta deal with goin' down the other side," Vernon Tatum said. "What if it's like Windlass Hill, back at Ash Hollow?"

"That would have been a smart thing to do, wouldn't it?" Bowen said. "Corbett might have to spend the night by himself on the top of that hill."

"I don't think so," Quincy said, still watching Corbett's progress. "He's stopped and he's still got a good ways to go to get to the top." That brought everyone's attention back to the wagon stopped some thirty yards short of the summit of the mountain. "Maybe he's just restin' 'em a little before they go up that last part," Bowen speculated.

That was not the case, however, for Corbett was beseeching his exhausted horses to make the final thirty yards, but they could not answer. He was almost in a panic when the climb ground slowly to a halt. And once they came to a complete stop, the horses could not get the heavy wagon in motion again. Stopped thirty yards below the top of the hill, he stood up to look back the way he had come with the thought in mind of possibly turning back. It appeared steeper looking down the hill than it had seemed when coming up. "Henry, what are we going to do?" Maurine asked, already in total panic.

"I don't know," Corbett answered frantically. "We'll just sit here for a little while and see if the horses rest up enough to take us on up to the top." He had no idea if that was a possibility or not, but it was all he could think of to tell her. He realized more than ever that he was a hardware store manager and not a teamster as he thought about the prospect of turning the wagon around and going back down the hill safely. *I can't just sit here*, he realized. His exhausted horses were the only things holding his wagon from careening back down the hill. What was going to happen when they gave out completely? He made the only decision he was sure of at that point. "Maurine, climb out of the wagon, honey, over here on the uphill side."

"What are you gonna do?" Maurine asked. "I don't want to get out and leave you alone. You might need me."

"I need to make sure you're out of the way. If this wagon goes over, I want you on the uphill side of it."

Down below, at the foot of the hill, the group of spectators were unaware of the two men approaching on horseback until Quincy looked back and saw them. "Riders comin'," he alerted the others. "It's Grissom and Ike," he said when they were close enough to identify.

"You fellows decide to go on to Oregon without the rest of us?" Grissom asked when he pulled his horse up to a stop. "Who's that goin' up the mountain?"

"It's Corbett," Bowen answered, "and he's stuck right there. Looks like his horses gave out and they can't pull him on up."

"What the hell was he plannin' to do," Ike asked, "camp on top of the hill tonight?"

"I think he said he might camp by the river on the other side of the hill," Bowen answered. He didn't mention the fact that he had said he would go up after him.

"Did anybody bother to walk up that hill and take a look at the trip down the other side?" Grissom asked, making an effort to hold his temper, for he was genuinely peeved at the group for ignoring his instructions. It was more important to him, however, to keep from losing two lives and maybe a wagon. A bad feeling was the reason he had Ike saddle a horse and the two of them rode hard to catch up with the rest of his wagon train. He figured there was a good chance somebody might be in trouble and that's why he brought Ike with him. "All right," he told them, "we need to get him some help pretty quick before he tries to turn around and come back down. Whose wagon is this?" He pointed to the first wagon in the line. Bowen said it was his. "We're gonna need to borrow your team of horses."

"Right!" Bowen responded and Ike went with him to unhitch them from his wagon. When they were unhitched, Ike took the reins and started walking the horses up the hill. Grissom took a coil of rope off his saddle and one off Ike's saddle. Then with a coil on each shoulder, he followed Ike and the team of horses up the steep face of the hill.

"Corbett!" Grissom shouted. "We're gonna give you some help to get this wagon on up the hill. So you just hang on to the reins and wait for my signal." When Ike got Bowen's horses in position, he and Grissom quickly tied the ropes on them. Then while Ike held those horses still, Grissom tied the ropes to Corbett's wagon.

"Should I get back in the wagon?" Maurine asked Grissom while he was tying the two teams together. She had left the wagon when her husband told her to.

"Probably a good idea to just stay with me," Grissom told her, "and we'll walk up to the top of the hill. If that wagon goes sideways, it might be a wild ride down to the bottom of the hill and you wouldn't wanna be on it." He looked at Ike then and asked, "You ready?" Ike said he was. "How 'bout you, Corbett—you ready?" Corbett said he was. "All right, tell 'em to giddy-up!" The four horses dug in and the wagon slowly started to move and continued to roll at that pace until reaching the top. They pulled to a stop at a fairly level spot and Grissom told Corbett that was where the wagon would pass the night.

"You mean just our wagon will stay here tonight?" Corbett asked. "Where will you and the rest of the wagon train be camped?"

"We'll camp at that stream a little ways back," Grissom replied while untying the ropes. "I was planning to camp at the creek where you were supposed to wait for us and come here in the mornin'. It'll eat up most of the day to get all twenty-four wagons over this hill. If you take a little walk over to the other side and look at the drop down into the valley, you'll see why it'll take so long. You can drive your wagon down this hill, but we'll tie the wheels, so they can't roll and we'll have a bunch of us hangin' on ropes to try to slow you down. And it's still gonna be a dangerous ride."

"Just my wife and I, though?" Corbett asked, unable to leave that issue. "You don't mean we should stay up here all night by ourselves. I don't know if we're safe up here alone. We don't know if this is Indian country or anything else about it."

"Of course, that's up to you," Grissom replied. "You don't have to stay up here tonight. You and your wife can go back down with us and camp at the stream with everybody else. It's just the wagon that has to stay here all night because we ain't got any way to get it down without bustin' it to pieces."

"Can't we just take those ropes you've got and slowly lower the wagon back down the way I came up?" Corbett asked.

Grissom laughed and shook his head. "Not just the four of us, we can't. It ain't as steep as the other side, but it's steep enough to get your wagon rollin' out of control."

"I've got to water my horses," Corbett complained, "and there's no water up here on this mountaintop."

"Well, that is a fact. You could try to walk your horses down to the river, but I wouldn't recommend it. Ike is fixin' to take Frank Bowen's horses back. It ain't as steep going back down with Bowen's horses as it is going down to the river, but it's not easy, and Ike's had a lotta years handlin' a team of horses. So my advice to you is to water your horses outta your water barrel and tomorrow you'll be the first wagon to be lowered to the valley. Then you can water 'em good and fill your barrels back up." Grissom watched Corbett sweat out the consequences of his bold move to tackle Big Hill on his own. He wanted him to realize that there was good reason to pay him for leading the wagons to Oregon.

Ike offered no suggestions. He knew he could unhitch Corbett's horses and walk them down to the river to water them. But he figured Grissom was giving Corbett an example of the trouble he could get into if he acted without his okay. So his punishment was to spend the night on top of Big Hill while the rest of the wagon train was camped back at the stream. Ike knew that there was little fear of Indian trouble because this was generally Shoshone country and they were friendly with the white man at this time.

"I expect Ike and I had better take Bowen's horses back to him and get the rest of the wagons back to the camp. It'll be time to cook supper by the time we get back," Grissom said. "Are you and your wife stayin' up here with your wagon, or you wanna go back with us?"

"I can't leave my wagon and horses," Corbett said. "I've got to stay here, but take Maurine back with you."

"I'm not leaving you by yourself, Henry," Maurine replied at once. "We'll just make do the best we can."

"Are you sure you wanna stay?" Grissom asked her. "'Cause we can find you a place to sleep."

"I'm sure," she said. "Henry and I will see you in the morning."

"All right, then," Grissom said, "might as well leave these ropes right here. We'll need 'em in the mornin' to lower your wagon. It'll take us a little while to get here. Let's go, Ike." He started back down the hill.

Ike went over to pick up the reins on Bowen's horses. When he passed by Maurine he spoke softly so Grissom couldn't hear. "This is Shoshone land. They're friends with us white folks. He wouldn'ta left you here if he thought you was in any danger."

"Thank you," she whispered.

Chapter 18

There was a great deal of discussion at the foot of Big Hill when Grissom and Ike came back down without Henry and Maurine. Grissom told them they chose to stay with their wagon when they realized there was no way to get it back down. He said they would better understand that tomorrow when they saw what had to be done to cross over this hill. He also told them that there was little chance of any danger from Indians. Naturally the discussion took new life when they turned their wagons around and followed Grissom back to join the other wagons already encamped at the small stream. There was genuine concern for Henry and Maurine trapped up on top of that mountain, all alone in this wild land. This, even in light of the fact that they would not have been in that predicament if Henry hadn't decided to tackle Big Hill ahead of the rest of the wagons.

At supper, Katie Moran felt so bad for Maurine that she could not stop talking about how frightened the poor woman must be. Finally, to ease Katie's mind, Clay asked her if she would feel better if he rode up that mountain and made his bed up there. "Oh, Clay," Katie responded, "would you do that? That would be such a nice thing for you to do."

"That'd be a dumb thing for you to do," Matt remarked. "They're just spendin' one night by themselves. Grissom said there wasn't much danger anybody would bother them."

"It doesn't make that much difference to me," Clay said. "We've got to go there first thing in the mornin', anyway. And I can spread my bedroll under their wagon just like I do under yours."

"I still say you're crazy to go up there tonight," Matt said.

"Well, you know I always value your advice," Clay japed. "So, I reckon we oughta decide on it the American way and put it to a vote. You vote no, and Katie and I vote go. So, I reckon I'll go on up there."

"I hope you get jumped by a war party of Indians," Matt said.

"Matt!" Katie exclaimed. "Don't even joke about that."

"Who said I was jokin'?"

"He's just complainin' because he's gotta stay here and drive the wagon in the mornin'. Ain't that right, Matt?" Clay asked. "I think I'll get goin' before it gets dark."

"Better let Grissom know what you're gonna do," Matt said.

"Good idea," Clay said as he picked up his bedroll and tied it to his saddle. Then he walked up to Grissom's wagon, saddle on one shoulder, saddlebags on the other, and rifle in hand.

Grissom and Ike were still eating supper. They both watched with a show of curiosity as he approached. "You goin' somewhere?" Grissom asked.

"Yep," Clay responded. "Katie's worried about Henry and Maurine, sittin' on top of that hill by themselves, so I told her I'd go up there and keep company with 'em tonight."

Grissom smiled. "I expect Corbett will appreciate that. I know Maurine will. They didn't seem too comfortable about campin' alone up there tonight. Ike thinks I was a little too hard on 'em for gettin' theirselves hung up on that mountain. But we'da spent half the night tryin' to ease his wagon back down, so he could come back here to camp. It didn't seem fair to the rest of the wagons he had with him." He paused and grinned sheepishly while he stroked his chin with his hand. "Tell you the truth, I'm glad you're gonna give 'em some company."

"I just thought I'd check with you first," Clay said.

"You gonna stay up there all night?" Grissom asked and when Clay said he was, Grissom said, "Good, then nobody will take a shot at you in the middle of the night if they see you come ridin' in."

He went to get his horse then. The gray was by the side of the stream with the other horses and he stopped dead still when Clay whistled. "Doggone horse ain't ever gonna learn to come to me," he muttered.

"Where you goin'?" He looked behind him to see Worley Branch walking after him. He told him what he had in mind and Worley asked, "Can I go with you?"

"If you want to," Clay answered. "The more the merrier, I reckon."

"You wanna try to get somebody else to go with us?" Worley asked.

"No, that's just an expression," Clay replied. "Just means I'm glad to have the company." Worley smiled. "You have to take your packhorse," Clay reminded him. "We won't be comin' back here."

"Right," Worley responded, and hurried away to get his horses.

When they were saddled up, they rode out the gap beside Grissom's wagon and told him and Ike that they'd see them in the morning. After they disappeared up the trail toward Big Hill, Ike asked a question. "I wonder what Clay's gonna do with Worley when we get to Oregon City?"

The light was rapidly fading along the base of the ridge of mountains by the time Clay and Worley reached Big Hill. "I reckon this is it," Clay said. He was judging by all the recent tracks left by the wagons that turned around there and the fact that the road seemed to end there.

"Here's where the wagon went up," Worley said, pointing to an extra-large clump of sagebrush with a recent print of a wagon wheel cutting into the dirt close beside it.

"I think you're right," Clay said, and started the gray up the steep slope. The horse labored under the slope right away. Clay could imagine what hard work it was for two horses trying to pull a heavily loaded wagon up that incline. He decided that if it started to put too much strain on his horse, he'd have to dismount. Since it was getting darker down below them, he also decided to make Corbett aware that he had company. So he yelled, "Corbett! Henry Corbett!"

Up on top of the mountain, Henry Corbett froze and stared at his wife. "Did you hear that?" She said nothing in return, stunned as well as he. But then she nodded her head vigorously. "Thank God," Henry said. "I was afraid I was the only one who heard it." Then they heard the call again. "It came from the trail we came up!" They both hurried back to the edge of the hill to look down to see the two men coming up the hill on horseback and leading a packhorse. "Hello!" Henry shouted. Then to Maurine, he said, "It's Clay Moran and that Worley character's with him!" They both stood transfixed, staring at the two riders as they approached the steepest part of the hill where their wagon was stopped, wondering if their horses would be stopped as well.

When Clay reached the steepest part near the top of the hill, his horse had to labor twice as hard but did not falter. Worley's two horses made it safely, too. They dismounted as soon as their horses gained the top of the ridge. "You folks mind a little company tonight?" Clay asked the two beaming faces focused on him.

"You can't imagine how welcome you are," Maurine answered him.

"Are you going to spend the night up here?" Henry asked.

"If you don't mind sharin' your hilltop with us," Clay replied. "We thought we'd make a little camp close to your wagon."

"You can just share our fire if you want to," Henry said. "No sense in having two fires, and firewood ain't that plentiful up here, anyway."

"Have you had anything to eat?" Maurine asked.

"Yes, ma'am," Clay answered. "Had supper before we left the wagons." Then he paused when it occurred to him, then asked, "Have you had any supper, Worley?"

"Yes, I've et," Worley replied.

"So, I reckon we're fine," Clay continued. "How 'bout you folks? How are you gettin' along up here? Grissom said you might be worried that you can't water your horses."

"Well, I'm afraid that's a fact," Henry said. "There's a whole river down at the bottom of this hill we're stuck on. But I'll be honest with you, I'm afraid to try to take my horses down that steep face. I'm afraid I might lose 'em. And we don't have that much left in our water barrel."

"Let's go take a look at that other side and see if we can walk up it," Clay said. "If we can walk up it, a horse can walk up it. So maybe we could lead the horses down to the river and back up again. Whaddaya think, Worley?"

"I think you're right," Worley said.

They walked over to the other side of the hill and looked down at what at first was a pretty steep drop. The longer they stared at it, however, the more possible routes they discovered that might make for a possible safe trip, up or down. "Worth a try," Clay said to Henry. "We'll take two horses at a time, Worley will take one and I'll take one. We'll lead 'em with the bridle. Walk 'em down to the river, water 'em, and lead 'em back up."

Before they started the watering, they relieved their horses of their saddles and packsaddle. Then with Henry and Maurine watching anxiously, Clay and Worley started down a path they agreed on as the best possible risk. Clay remembered Grissom telling them about Big Hill after they had left Fort Bridger, and the fact that the real danger was on the way down into the valley. Grissom had not exaggerated the danger going down. They found that there was very little sure footing. The horses, being heavy animals, had a tendency to slip on the patches of bare ground on the steepest part of the slope. Leading the horse down the hill, Clay could not lose the picture of one little slip of the hoof and a thousand to fifteen hundred pounds landing on him for a piggy-back ride down the slope. He wondered if Worley ever considered the same thing, because he never showed emotion of any kind, other than a childish beam of appreciation in his eyes for a simple favor. In spite of the potential for disaster, they were able to successfully water all five horses with no loss of life or maiming of limb. The Corbetts were eternally grateful, but there was confirmation enough to prove Grissom right in his estimate that going down Big Hill might be more hair-raising than descending Windlass Hill.

When all the dangerous work of watering the horses was done, Maurine insisted on using some of the precious water left in the water barrel to make a pot of coffee, now that they were not going to give it to their horses. So they spent a pleasant evening getting to know each other better than they had before. Even Worley talked some about his years with the old trapper before the grizzly bear got him. Corbett wanted to know more about Clay's time in the army, which Clay talked about reluctantly and sparingly. To him, that was a time of senseless mass killing, which never seemed to make anything better. Before they turned in, Clay and Worley scouted the general area around their camp just to make sure there was no obvious threat of any unwanted visitors. And the Corbetts enjoyed a peaceful night, one they had not anticipated before the arrival of their guests.

Shortly after seven o'clock the next morning, the wagon train arrived at the foot of Big Hill with the intention of crossing over it to reach the Bear River Valley. After a breakfast of fresh rabbit meat, the three men on top of the hill were ready for the day. The two rabbits were provided by Worley, who had slipped out of his blanket before daybreak and went back down to the river with his bow. They went down the hill to hear Grissom's instructions for the accomplishment of the task before them. In spite of what Grissom had told them of the procedure before, most of the emigrants expected the crossing to be like the descent of Windlass Hill, where their wagons were lowered on ropes and the horses were herded down separately. Now they understood. Windlass Hill was more like a cliff that they drove their wagons right up to the brink of. This was because they had been traveling on a higher plain and they dropped down Windlass Hill to the Platte River Valley below that plain. Now, at Big Hill, they had to first drive their wagons up the hill, then deal with a long and steep ride down the hill. It was so steep in places that the wagons would have to be held back with ropes.

"For safety reasons as well as extra weight, it's best for everybody who can to walk over this mountain," Grissom said. "We're gonna take a team of horses up first to be used to help the wagons that can't make it all the way, like we did with Bowen's horses yesterday." He went on to explain how they were going to try to slow the wagons down when they descended the other side, emphasizing what a wild and dangerous ride it might be. He ended by saying that they would all be helping each other get by this obstacle in their path. "All right then, we might as well get started." He then took the reins of the team Ike had hitched up for him and started up the hill while Ike started up in the wagon. John Henry Hyde picked a different path from the one Ike took and started up the hill next. Other wagons followed behind them, some trying different routes, some just following Ike or John Henry.

On top of the hill, Henry Corbett had his horses hitched up to his wagon and Clay was helping him tie his wheels to keep them from rolling when Grissom arrived with the extra team of horses. "Good mornin'," Grissom greeted him and Maurine. "I see you made it through the night all right. You ready to drive your wagon down to the valley?"

"As I'll ever be, I reckon," Corbett answered him honestly.

"Looking down that slope, though, it doesn't look like you can drive a wagon down it."

"That's why Clay is lockin' your front wheels down now, too, so that wagon don't have a tendency to roll over you," Grissom said. "You're really gonna slide down that slope and there are some places where we'll have to help hold you back. But don't untie those wheels until you get all the way down in the valley, because there's enough slope to give you some problems." He paused then and sniffed a couple of times. Then he looked at the remains of the fire and the few pieces of gristle lying in the ashes. "I swear, it smells like you've been cookin' some meat."

"Oh, that," Corbett said, unable to resist, "that's probably that fresh rabbit we had for breakfast. Worley got two early this morning. It was kinda lucky we had to stay here. It was kind of peaceful here on top of this ridge."

Grissom couldn't suppress the grin that crept upon his face. He knew Corbett was getting even with him for leaving him stranded all night. "Yep, that was lucky," he said. "And if you get down from here without turnin' your wagon over, you'll be the only one that'll remember Big Hill as something you enjoyed. So get goin' and good luck." Grissom walked away to turn his attention to the wagons approaching the top of the hill.

Worley pulled up beside Corbett on his paint pony. "Clay has to wait here to help his brother," he told Henry. "He told me to ride ahead of you, in case you need help." They started down the hill with the wagon wheels sliding like a sled. Behind them, other wagons were approaching the top of the hill where the extra team of horses would be needed to help six of them make it up the final portion. The crossing moved along slowly but steadily until the wagons behind Corbett caught up with him, halfway down the long descent. He was stopped before a section of the slope so steep that he could not risk driving down it without some ropes and as many men as could hold on to them to slow the descent. A few confident souls tried other paths and drove down the incline without the aid of men on the ropes. They were lucky in making it down with the wagon right side up and neither horse injured after a wild ride that forced the horses to run in order to keep a bouncing, nerve-shattering wagon off their backs.

The whole endeavor took a little more than five hours before all twenty-four wagons were safely down in the Bear River Valley. Grissom led the wagon train a short distance to a favorite camping ground on Clover Creek where they went into camp for the night. After an exhausting day crossing Big Hill, spirits were generally lifted by the valley they now found themselves in. After traveling so many days in the dry and windy sagebrush plains they had traveled since South Pass, it was almost unreal to find green grass, flowers, berry bushes, and trees. The social hour that evening was a joyous affair with many stories about the crossing just completed, the frightening climb up the hill, and the hair-raising ride back down the other side. "At least you men got some thrills on your ride," Eleanor Hyde complained. "It wasn't very thrilling for the women and children who walked the whole way." Her remark received a hearty cheer from the other women.

"It sure wasn't an easy walk either," Molly Tatum added. "I ain't sure you men coulda made it."

"I heard somebody had a big banquet last night with fresh rabbit," Julie Batson said. "I sure woulda liked some of that."

"It wasn't last night," Maurine Corbett responded, "it was for breakfast this morning. Everyone was invited, but nobody showed up. Our feelings were kinda hurt, to tell you the truth."

Annie Rice was tempted to announce that their wagon was one of those that made it up the hill without help from the extra team of horses. She thought it might help Harlan's self-respect a little, but she decided it might embarrass him. Grissom was aware of it and had made it a point to tell Harlan he did a good job of driving his horses. Grissom was as pleased as anyone there with the success of the crossing of Big Hill, with no casualties and no real damage. He could look forward to a much easier drive for the next few days, until reaching Fort Hall. He was glad to see the emigrants in a happy mood. He expected to keep them in that frame of mind for a while. They would leave this camp in the morning and follow the Bear River northwest for two and a half days to Soda Springs, where they should get a kick out of the springs filled with soda water.

At seven o'clock the next morning, the wagons rolled out of the camp at Clover Creek and began a journey following a trail that ran right beside the Bear River, which offered cool, pure water for their animals and themselves. There was grass for their horses and wood for their fires. An extra feature of the valley was the abundance of deer sign. Clay and Worley had become the unofficial hunters for the wagon train under an arrangement with Grissom that he would pay them for any ammunition they used to kill deer for everybody on the train to share. Since the hunters would generally leave the camp right after the four o'clock wake-up bugle, they would be far out in front of the wagon train. So, Grissom also benefitted from their use as advance scouts. On the lucky days when they found deer coming down to the river, it was a happy sight for the emigrants when they came to a likely camping spot at the end of the day. They usually found Clay and Worley with two or sometimes three deer hanging from tree limbs in the process of being butchered. Things were not to be this easy after they reached Soda Springs, however, for that was where they left the river and headed in a more westerly direction. There might still be deer but not as often.

Grissom was accurate in his prediction of reaching Soda Springs in two and a half days. They reached the springs just at the time for nooning. Having stopped there before with earlier trains, he knew how the folks would act once they tested the hot soda water. They would want to sample it. They would want to wash their clothes in the hot water. And when he told them they could bake bread with it and it would rise just like yeast, they would all have to cook with it. Knowing all that, he announced that they would remain there after the nooning and not move on until the next morning. That would give everyone an opportunity to sample the waters.

When the wagon train arrived at Soda Springs, they discovered it to be an area of many different springs, all of them bubbling up with this strange soda water. Grissom told them that in the early years, before the wagon trains, the trappers called the area Beer Springs, because of the taste. "You don't have to taste it," Matt Moran remarked. "You can smell it before you even get there."

"I guess you'd be the one to know if it tastes like beer," Katie replied.

"Maybe," he responded to her remark, "but you could ask Harlan Rice to be sure."

"Matt!" She gave him a deep frown. "Don't make jokes about that. Annie's standing right over there."

"Heck, she can't hear that from where she is," Matt said. He was right. She was standing beside a pool where hot water was bubbling up from the bottom, watching her daughters playing in the water with some of the other youngsters. Like most of the other women, she was already planning to wash all their clothes in that hot water. The springs were a phenomenon that not one of them could explain, but they would all remember it as one of their most interesting memories of the journey.

After the half-day holiday at the springs, it was business as usual the next morning and the wagons were rolling again. With some reluctance, they said goodbye to the Bear River after a short ride when the river made a sharp turn to the south and headed toward Salt Lake. The emigrants, on the other hand, turned to the northwest on the trail up the Portneuf River Valley to Fort Hall. They arrived at the fort after a problem-free journey of five days. At the end of the Civil War, the volunteer Union troops that had manned the fort left it and moved to Camp Lander, which was three miles southeast of the original fort. However, there were still traders and craftsmen at Fort Hall to deal with for needed supplies and services. Grissom did not plan to make it a long stop.

After the wagons were circled up and the normal routine of caring for the horses and preparing for supper was underway, Matt Moran was struck by an almost forgotten thought. Curious about it, now that it had returned, he mentioned it to Clay. "If I remember correctly, ain't this where your shadow said he wanted to go when he hooked onto us back at Independence Rock?"

Knowing his brother was talking about Worley Branch, Clay answered, "Come to think of it, he did say he thought he'd go to Fort Hall. I forgot about that."

"He ain't said anything about us being here?" Matt questioned.

"Not a word to me, anyway," Clay answered. He gazed around them, looking for him. "You reckon he just took off as soon as we got here? You know, Worley doesn't do things like most folks."

"Brother, you can say that again," Matt remarked.

"You know, Worley doesn't—" Clay started before Matt punched him on the shoulder. "Ow, whatchu do that for?"

"Bright boy," Matt said. "I can't believe Worley would leave without tellin' you he was goin'." He thought for a second, then added, "Or begged you to let him stay with you." He paused again, then said, "Speak of the devil . . ." He nodded in the direction behind Clay. Clay turned and saw Worley coming from Grissom's wagon, leading his horse and packhorse.

"Where you been, Worley?" Clay asked, noticing the grin on the face that was usually expressionless.

"I been talkin' to Mr. Grissom," Worley answered. "He said I could stay with the wagon train all the way to Oregon City."

Clay and Matt both laughed. "Is that a fact?" Matt responded. "I thought you wanted to leave us when we got to Fort Hall."

"I just couldn't think of nowhere else at the time," he stated, speaking softly. "I ain't never knowed as many people as I know on this wagon train right now."

"You have any idea what you're gonna do when you get out to Oregon?" Clay asked.

Worley shrugged, never thinking that far in advance. "What I've always done, I reckon, look for somethin' to eat when I get hungry, and shelter when it's rainin'."

Chapter 19

Grissom urged everyone who needed work at the blacksmith, or new shoes for their horses, to go see Ned Blanchard early in the morning. "Ned does both," he told them. "He's the blacksmith and farrier, too. I don't want to spend more than one day here at Fort Hall. It's gonna take us three and a half to four days to get to the Raft River from here, and we need to get that crossin' behind us. There's a reason they named it the Raft River, because if you don't strike it when the conditions are right, you have to build a raft to cross it."

"And that would slow us down plenty," Vernon Tatum finished the sentence for him, punctuating his remark with the sharp slap of a mosquito on the back of his neck. "I swear, am I the only one gettin' eat up by these damn things?"

"No, I thought I was," Elmo Steptoe said.

"Mosquitoes are bad here every year I've been through Fort Hall," Grissom said. "Ike can back me up on that. But I don't believe they're as bad as they were last year. Do you, Ike?" Ike just shrugged. Grissom didn't bother to go into his real interest in the mosquito population. His main concern was the crossing of the Raft River. If there were not as many mosquitoes as usual, maybe it meant the weather had not been as damp as it usually was. That would mean they had not had much rain, and less rain meant less water in the Raft River. Of course, rain was not the only cause of high water in that river. A good part of the blame could be attributed to the many beaver dams along the creeks and streams of that river. But it was the potential for heavy summertime thunderstorms on the Snake River that Grissom concerned himself with. And right now conditions looked favorable for crossing the Raft River. He wished he was there, instead of waiting out the day at Fort Hall. *Ain't no sense fretting about it,* he told himself. *I'll worry about it when we get there.* "I need a drink of likker," he said to Ike. "How 'bout you? You wanna go get a drink of likker?"

His question surprised Ike because it was not typical. Like a lot of men, Grissom enjoyed a drink of whiskey now and then, but he had never heard Grissom say he *needed* one. "Well, sure, I reckon I could use a drink. Where you thinkin' about gittin' one?"

"The only place I know is that hog ranch about a mile up behind the fort on the bank of the river," Grissom said. "You oughta remember it. You went with me to buy a bottle of whiskey to take with us to give that judge for his birthday. Lucky's, I think was the name of it. I don't know if it's still there or not, since the soldiers moved outta the fort and went down to Camp Lander. We can ask Ned Blanchard if that fellow that owns it is still there. I remember his first name's the same as yours, Ike Somebody. I just can't remember his last name, never had any reason to."

"Ennis," Ike Yocum said. "Ike Ennis is his name. I remember it. I can't remember the judge's name."

"Welker," Grissom said, "Judge Welker. I'm gonna walk over to the blacksmith shop before it gets any later to let Ned know he needs to be ready for a busy day tomorrow. I'll ask him if Ennis still has his place up on the river."

"Want me to walk over to Ned's with you?" Ike asked.

"Only if you want to," Grissom said. "Like I said, I just wanna make sure he's gonna be ready to take care of our people in the mornin'."

"I'll just stay here and clean up the supper dishes," Ike decided. "And I'll be ready to go get a drink, if there's still a place to get one."

"Good idea," Grissom said, and got up and started walking toward the fort.

"I'll ask Harlan Rice if he wants to go with us," Ike called after him.

"Don't even joke about that," Grissom answered. "I don't wanna light that fuse."

As he predicted, Grissom wasn't gone long and when he got back, he said, "Lucky's is still there, but that Ennis fellow that owned it ain't."

"He move with the soldiers?" Ike asked.

"No, he was shot by an unhappy customer," Grissom replied. "You ready to run up there and get a couple of shots?" Ike said he was. "I'm gonna throw my saddle on my horse. I ain't gonna walk a mile up there just for a drink or two," Grissom said. "You want me to put your saddle on a horse, too?"

"Nah," Ike replied. "I'll just take my bridle and ride bareback for that little distance."

"I'm gonna take a minute to tell Clay Moran where we're goin'," Grissom said, "since both of us will be gone. Couldn't hurt to let somebody know where we are."

"I reckon that's a good idea," Ike said. Then he gave him a serious look and added, "I notice that you're goin' to Clay a lot when you're lookin' to get something done."

Grissom hesitated before responding. Then he said, "That's right, I do. He's a damn capable young man and seems dependable. He's a good scout and he ain't hampered with a wife and children. But I wouldn't tell him anything if you were gonna be here while I'm gone."

Ike chuckled and said, "Don't get me wrong. I ain't jealous. I agree with you, and I'd do the same thing. He's a good man. Wish we'd had him on every one of these trips we took. Let's go get the horses."

Grissom threw his saddle on his buckskin gelding while Ike selected a bay horse to ride. He didn't have a favorite riding horse because he very seldom had a use for one, but he had a saddle in the wagon just in case he did need one. This was not the case tonight. They rode their mounts back in the circle of wagons to find Clay helping his brother seal some newly developed cracks in his wagon box. With the prospect of some big river crossings facing them in the weeks ahead, Matt wasn't sparing the wax. "Gettin' it ready for the Raft River, are ya?" Grissom called out when he and Ike rode up to the wagon.

"That's right," Clay responded, "and when we get through here, we're gonna seal up any cracks we find on my horse."

"Ike and I are takin' a little ride about a mile up the river," Grissom said. "We won't be gone long, but I wonder if you would kinda keep an eye on things, if you don't mind?"

Clay was a little surprised, but he said, "No, I wouldn't mind. Is there anything in particular you're concerned about?"

"No, nothing at all," Grissom answered. "If I was goin' by myself, Ike would watch things. But he's goin' with me tonight." When he saw that Clay was concerned that something was really wrong, he said, "Oh, hell, there's a saloon a mile from here on a little road right out the back of the fort. Me and Ike ain't had a drink of likker in a coon's age and we decided we wanted one tonight. We'll be back before Vernon and the boys get their instruments tuned up good. I just don't want to advertise it."

Clay had to chuckle. "No problem, if there's any trouble, I'll send somebody to get you. Hope you enjoy your whiskey."

"Thank you, Clay, I knew I could count on you." Grissom turned to Ike then and said, "Come on, I don't wanna be gone too long."

"What was that all about?" Matt asked when Clay walked back to the wagon.

"Nothing, really, he and Ike wanna go get a drink of whiskey and he doesn't want the folks on the train to know about it. And he asked me to keep an eye on things while he's gone."

"That's crazy as hell," Matt replied. "Nobody cares if he takes a drink of whiskey."

"I think what was botherin' him was this place he's goin' to is a mile away from here. And Ike's goin' with him, so there ain't anybody in charge here."

"Nobody but you, right?" Matt couldn't pass it up. "So whaddaya say we give the order to move out of here and we'll take this wagon train to California?"

"Doggone it, Matt, don't say anything about this to anybody. There's some folks on this train that wouldn't appreciate it."

"I'll think about it," Matt said. "Depends on how much you help me make this wagon act more like a boat."

Grissom and Ike found the little road behind the fort in rather run-down condition compared to what it was the year before. They chose to attribute that to the fact that there was not as much traffic on it since the soldiers moved away. When they reached the end of the road they came to the two-story log house with the weathered old sign on the porch that said *Lucky's River House.* There were three horses tied at the hitching rail in front of the porch. Grissom and Ike tied theirs up beside them. Then they chose the front door, instead of a side door that led directly into the saloon, thinking to see the working ladies. A little bell attached to the top of the door announced their arrival. The front room was originally a parlor where the doves would lounge while waiting to greet their customers. But the room was empty now of doves, only the lonely sofas and chairs remained. Grissom and Ike walked on through the parlor to a door that led to the saloon. Inside the saloon, they paused for a few moments. The room was quiet, seeming more like a morgue than a saloon. There were three men seated at a table, the riders of the horses at the hitching rail no doubt. All three stared at them with appraising eyes. They looked to be of a rugged breed, maybe cowhands, maybe stagecoach robbers, they could be either.

A large man with bushy sideburns but bald on top stood behind the bar. Both Grissom and Ike recognized him as the bartender and now owner, according to Ned Blanchard. They walked over to the bar, their boots producing a thudding sound on the wood floor, emphasizing the empty quiet of the room. "Benny Thatcher, right?" Grissom asked.

"That's right," Benny replied. "Whatchu gents gonna have?"

"We need a shot of whiskey," Grissom answered. "What's that you're pourin'?" He pointed to the bottle on the bar.

"That's corn whiskey," Benny said.

"That'll do fine for me," Grissom said. "Pour me a shot of that." Ike said he'd have the same, so Benny produced two shot glasses and filled them. "This is the quietest saloon I've ever been in. Did somebody die?" He tossed his shot back.

"Funny you should ask that," Benny said. "That'll be two bits."

"Fill it up again," Grissom said.

Benny poured two more and promptly said, "Four bits."

"Damn, Benny," Ike remarked, "you act like you're tryin' to get rid of us."

"I am, damn it," Benny said, almost in a whisper. "Do yourself a favor and turn around and get outta here!"

The sad look in Benny's eyes told them it was too late. They turned around to see the three men get up from the table, one of them already walking to the door to the parlor. Grissom and Ike turned then toward the outside door. One of the three men quickly produced a double-barreled shotgun and demanded, "You think you can make it to that door before this scattergun splatters your hide? And don't give me no pitiful story about how you ain't got but enough money for them four drinks. The last feller that tried that is floatin' in the river behind us." He nodded toward the younger man beside him. "Go relieve them of them handguns they're wearin', Billy." He walked over a little closer. "Now, I hope like hell you two are carryin' more money than that last feller 'cause this has been a slow night. You ain't with that wagon train that pulled in today, are you? I bet you are, and you oughta be carryin' money to pay for all them tolls and things, and maybe money to buy land. Let's get them outta their clothes and see where they're hidin' all their money."

"If we were who you think we are, do you think we'd be totin' all our money around everywhere we went?" Grissom asked. "Especially if we went to a saloon, we wouldn't. Use some common sense, man." He felt his holster lighten as Billy Crowder lifted his pistol.

"Are you callin' me stupid?" the man holding the shotgun and obviously the boss of the three responded. "That's your second mistake tonight. Your first one was walkin' into this place. What's he packin', Billy?"

Billy took a step back and examined the weapon. "It looks like a Colt Army model .44 in pretty good shape, Merle."

"Well, that'll be worth a few dollars," Merle said, "but you better come up with some cash money if you don't wanna end up in the Snake River. Better make it easy on yourself."

Grissom was at once concerned with the rather casual way the three bandits dropped their names. It told him they didn't plan to leave any witnesses. He made an attempt to talk his way out of the situation. "Listen, Merle . . ." He paused. "Is that your name?"

Merle gave him a wide grin, obviously amused by the man's attempt to save his money and his life. "Yeah, that's my name, Merle Bacon."

"Well, Merle, looks like you got the jump on me and my friend, here." Merle's smile grew even wider as Grissom continued. "We are with that wagon train, but we ain't emigrants lookin' to buy land out in Oregon. We're just workin' hands that keep the wagons rollin'. I've got a couple of dollars in my pocket and you're welcome to 'em. I don't know if my friend has any money or not, but I doubt he does, since I had to pay for our two shots of whiskey. So what I'm saying is, take what little bit of money we've got and let us go on our way. We'll be pullin' outta here first thing in the mornin' and that'll be the last you see of us. And if you let us keep our pistols, we won't have to explain to anybody why they're gone. Whaddaya say, Merle? We'll go on our way and no hard feelin's."

Merle continued to grin, saying nothing for a moment or two before responding. "I swear, boys, this feller's a regular speechifying son of a gun, ain't he? If we don't shut him up pretty quick, he's liable to talk Junior into shootin' me." His smile faded away then as he turned back to Grissom and Ike. "Now, you two, I want you to start shuckin' them clothes, right down to your long johns. I wanna see all your secret little hidin' places."

"That last feller had that little pocket sewed right on his long johns," Junior Bacon remarked. "That was the slickest thing I ever saw."

"Hurry it up!" Merle barked when Grissom and Ike both hesitated to start undressing. "Maybe you druther one of us do it when you got a hole in your head."

Grissom and Ike started taking their clothes off. As soon as they pulled their boots off, either Junior or Billy would grab them and search inside them for money. And through it all, Benny continued to stand in the same place behind the bar, watching. When the two bandits were engrossed with the searching of their boots, Grissom took a chance and whispered to Benny, "Shotgun under the bar?"

"That's it he's holdin' on you right now," Benny whispered back.

Grissom shook his head, frustrated, and unbuckled his belt and dropped his trousers to the floor. Billy grabbed them immediately and started searching the pockets when he stepped out of them. "Four dollars and a half," Billy exclaimed triumphantly. "He said he didn't have but two dollars. And a pocket watch," he added a few seconds later. "Ain't nothin' in his shirt pockets, nothin' in his hat. I reckon he weren't lying when he said he didn't have much."

I wonder who's going to be the lucky one to find out those three .44 car-

tridges in the back of my gun belt are empty shells with a twenty-dollar bill rolled up in each one of 'em? Grissom thought. Junior and Billy conducted a similar search of Ike which netted seventy-five cents and a pack of cigarette rolling papers and half a dozen matches. "All right if we put our clothes back on now?" Grissom asked. Before he got an answer, they heard the bell on the front door ring.

"Uh-oh," Merle responded. "Catch 'em at the door, Junior!" Junior hurried to the parlor door and stood ready to greet the unlucky customer. "The rest of you jaspers just stand right where you are, unless you want the shootin' to start early," Merle said, the double-barreled shotgun still leveled at the two victims standing in front of the bar in their underwear. The bartender remained behind the bar, never having moved from that position since Grissom and Ike walked in.

The parlor door opened to reveal a short little gray-haired man, wearing what appeared to be new clothes and holding a little bouquet of flowers. Junior grabbed a handful of his new shirt, pulled him inside the saloon, and closed the door behind him to leave him standing pop-eyed in confusion. "That's Hootie Beamer," Benny spoke out at once. "He's harmless. He just comes to see Sally Switch."

"Is that right?" Junior asked the dumbfounded little man. Hootie nodded his chin rapidly and held the little bunch of flowers up for him to see. Seeing that Hootie was not wearing a gun, Junior said, "She's right over yonder in the corner behind the piano." And he gave him a little shove in that direction to get him started. "She oughta like them posies."

Hootie looked from left to right, at the two men standing in their underwear, to the man holding a shotgun on them, to Billy standing there grinning at him. Unable to think of anything he should do, he went straight to the piano in the corner of the room where he found Sally Switch behind it, a bullet hole in her forehead. He recoiled in shock and turned to find Merle looking at him. "She wouldn't sit down and shut up," Merle told him. "And now I'm telling you the same thing. You understand?" Hootie nodded again, backed up, and sat down on the piano bench. After a minute, he reached over behind him and laid the bouquet on Sally's breast.

Grissom looked over and met Ike's look of surprise in return. They had not even known there was a dead woman behind the piano. That was evidence enough to convince them that the three bandits were not bluffing when they threatened to kill them. Grissom had been halfway suspicious of their claims to have killed one man and thrown his body in the river. They had been so casual in their talk about it that he was led to believe they were making up the story. The bartender might have given some signal to indicate it was all made up in an effort to scare them into cooperating with their demands. But he made no such attempt, so Grissom had to accept the fact that he and Ike were going to be subject to the same fate as Sally Switch and most likely poor Hootie Beamer. As if to prove Grissom's assumption, Hootie got up from the piano bench to address Merle. "Sir, I just wanted to bring Sally some flowers. Can I just leave them with her and get outta your way?"

"Now, Hootie, I told you to sit down and shut up, didn't I?" Merle answered. Then he chuckled and said, "Hootie, how'd they happen to name you that? Did your daddy get it on with an owl or something?"

"No, sir," Hootie replied. "My daddy named me Horton, but my baby sister had a hard time sayin' Horton. It always sounded more like Hootie when she said it. After a while, everybody started callin' me Hootie."

"I swear, that's a tender story, ain't it, boys?" Merle asked. "Makes me want some cornbread and a glass of buttermilk." Junior and Billy chuckled with him. "But you remember what I told you, Hootie. Maybe ol' Sally Switch is waitin' out on the front porch for you." He gave Hootie one barrel in the face at point-blank range. The force of the shot knocked Hootie backward to land on top of Sally. "Look at that, boys, that's what I call a real shotgun weddin'." Junior and Billy found it hilarious, knee-slapping humor. "Now, we need to do something with these two jaspers," Merle said.

Grissom could hold his tongue no longer. "You three are damn-near the very definition of evil, ain't you? I'd like to see how tough you are when you ain't killin' women and helpless old men. I'm an old man compared to you, but I'd like to take you on in a fair fight with any weapon you choose—guns, knives, fists. I don't reckon you'd be interested in that, would ya?"

"Well, ain't he somethin', boys? He's callin' me out with any weapons I choose. Well, old man, I accept your challenge. I'll fight you fair and square. You say I can pick the weapons, so I pick fists." He paused for a few seconds, then continued. "Fists for you and this shotgun for me. To be really fair about it, I'll just use one barrel, since I spent one on ol' Hootie over there. So I'm ready. You ready? Let's get on with it."

"Virgil! No!" Ike cried out at once. "That ain't no better'n murder. I'll take him on, you've got folks dependin' on you."

"It don't make any difference, Ike," Grissom said. "This scum is gonna kill both of us either way."

"He's right, Ike, we're gonna kill both of you, but if you wanna make it more fun, you can both take me on with your fists. 'Course, for both of you, I'll have to put another shell in the shotgun. And who knows, one of ya might still be standin' after I empty both barrels."

"And then get a shot in the back from Junior or Billy," Grissom said.

Merle chuckled outright. "You're pretty smart, so you probably figured it out, we're cleanin' this place out and we can't leave no witnesses, includin' ol' big'un standin' behind the bar. It's just your tough luck you decided to come to this place for a drink tonight. If it'll make you feel any better, we won't throw you in the river. It takes too much time and we've wasted too much time here already. Back up against the bar. Make your choice, front or back, it don't make no difference to us."

"Hold it, Merle," Junior stopped him. "I heard that blame bell on the front door."

"Always room for one more," Merle said. "Go let 'em in. Maybe this time it'll be somebody who's got some money."

Junior took his place at the door and waited. He stuck his ear to the door and listened. "It sounds like just one person."

"Run!" Grissom suddenly yelled as loud as he could, which earned him a blow on the back of the head from Billy's pistol.

When Grissom yelled, Junior didn't wait, he pulled the door open only to get the butt of Clay's rifle right between his eyes, dropping him to the floor, stunned. Clay didn't wait for any explanations. The picture he saw told him all he needed to know. When Merle turned toward him with the shotgun, Clay cut him down with a shot to his chest, cranked in another round and dropped Billy, who was too slow to react. Without pausing, Clay took a quick look around him to see if there were any more threats. With a new round already chambered, he shifted his aim to Benny, standing behind the counter. Benny immediately stuck both hands up in the air, so Clay returned his attention to Junior, who was up on his hands and knees by then. "Don't shoot!" Junior cried. "I'm done. I think you broke my head."

"Can you get up?" Clay asked, with his rifle still aimed at him.

"I think so," Junior groaned, and slowly climbed to his feet until he started to straighten up, then he suddenly reached for his pistol. Clay calmly pulled the trigger and the Henry rifle spoke one last fatal time.

"Is that it?" Clay barked, looking all around him, his rifle ready to fire another shot. "Are there any more of 'em?"

"That's all of 'em!" Ike blurted excitedly. "I can't believe we're still standin'. I'd already said my prayers!" They both looked at Grissom then, who had gotten up on one knee. Ike hurried over to him. "How bad is it?" he asked. "Throw me that bar towel," he said to Benny, who was still standing in the same spot behind the bar. Benny threw the towel and Clay caught it before it landed on the floor and handed it to Ike, who was examining the back of Grissom's head.

"It feels like he knocked something loose in my head," Grissom complained.

"You got a cut on the back of your head, but it don't look too bad," Ike said. "It's bleedin' pretty much. Take a look, Clay." Clay looked at it and agreed with Ike that it didn't look serious. "All right," Ike continued, "me and Doc Moran think you're gonna live. I'm gonna tie this towel around your head and that oughta stop the bleedin'."

"It still feels like he knocked my brain loose in there," Grissom said.

"Well, maybe we better check," Ike said, and held three fingers up behind Grissom's head. "How many fingers do you see?"

"What are you talkin' about?" Grissom replied. "I don't see no fingers."

"Good," Ike said. "You can't see behind your head, so you ain't crazy. You just have a headache."

Clay looked around him then and asked, "What in the hell happened here?" Then he turned to stare at Benny, standing behind the bar, and waited for an answer.

Grissom, on his feet now, with the towel tied around his head, looked at Benny, too, thinking the bartender and owner of the place hadn't offered much help in the situation. He decided to tell him as much. "I can't say as you helped out a lot to stop those three from killin' innocent people." He said to Clay then, "He was standing in that same spot when me and Ike walked in here. Wasn't he, Ike?" Ike said he was, so Grissom went on. "And with everything that went on in here, shootin' that poor old fellow over there, and strippin' the clothes off me and Ike, and you comin' in blazin' away with that Henry, he never moved from that spot. Did he, Ike?"

"No, he never did," Ike agreed. "And we don't know about

when they shot the woman, or the fellow they threw in the river. He mighta been standin' in the same spot then. How 'bout it, Benny? How come you never made a move to help?"

"I couldn't," Benny answered. "My feet are tied to the back of the bar. Billy was outside gettin' something outta his saddlebags and he saw you two comin' up the road. So he ran back in here and they tied me to the bar, then they sat down at the table, so you fellers would walk on in. And that was when you saved my life 'cause they was fixin' to shoot me just before you came."

"So, I reckon that's worth a free drink right there," Ike was quick to suggest.

"I reckon so," Benny said. "I'd be even more grateful if one of you would untie my feet. I'd set down and untie 'em, myself, but they tied me up so tight to the bar that I can't bend my legs to set down."

Chapter 20

Grissom and Ike, as well as Benny, were well aware that Clay Moran wore the wings of an angel on this night. And Grissom was especially interested to know why he happened to come at all when he had asked him to keep an eye on the wagon train for him. What prompted him to leave the wagons and come to the saloon? So he had to ask.

"I don't know for sure," Clay answered honestly. "When you left, you said you and Ike were just gonna be gone long enough to get a couple of shots of whiskey and you'd be right back. What was it you said? The musicians wouldn't even be warmed up good by the time you got back. Well, they were about ready to take a break and you weren't back yet. I just had a feelin' something might be wrong and I decided I'd better see if you were all right. I knew you wanted me to stay here till you got back, so I told Matt and John Henry about it and they said they'd keep an eye out. So I just rode on up here to see if you two were all right."

Grissom nodded in response when Clay said he just had a feeling. He may have come like an angel sent from heaven, but thinking back about his arrival, he looked more like a death-dealing warrior from hell. That thought brought him another question. "There ain't a window in this barroom. How did you know what you were walkin' into?"

Clay grinned and said, "There is one." And he turned and

pointed to a small, two-foot square window right up against the ceiling behind the bar.

"That's right," Benny said, "that little window has a tilt sash. I open it up sometimes when it gets too hot in here, open up a door and it draws the air outta here. But how'd you know about that little window?"

"I didn't," Clay replied. "But when I rode up in the yard, I heard a shot from inside the saloon."

"That would be when Merle shot Hootie Beamer," Benny said.

"I reckon," Clay went on. "Anyway, I thought I'd best take a look inside before I went in, but there weren't any windows that I could see. There was a door that looked like it might lead into the saloon part, but there was no glass in it. So I rode around the side of the buildin' and I saw that little window way up high. I pulled the gray up under it and stood up on the saddle to look in. I could see the bar and you and Ike standin' there in your underwear, and a fellow behind you holdin' a gun on you. I couldn't see much more than that, but that was enough to keep me from walkin' into an ambush. I was plannin' on sneakin' in the front door and tryin' to catch those three by surprise, but I didn't notice that the door had that little bell on it."

"Well, you sure spoiled their little welcome they had planned for you," Grissom said. He turned to face Benny then while he buttoned up his shirt and prepared to pull on his trousers. "I reckon we could give you a hand gettin' these bodies out of your saloon. That's a helluva lot of grave diggin', if you're gonna bury 'em." He was inclined to simply carry them outside and leave them on the ground for the buzzards to take care of, since he had no investment in them, and he would be on his way the day after tomorrow. But it seemed like the wrong thing to leave Benny with it all on himself.

"I ain't plannin' to dig all them graves," Benny said. "To tell you the truth, I ain't plannin' to try to run this business no more. Since the soldiers left, there ain't any business but people like them three, just saddle trash and outlaws, and their business don't amount to much. I'd already decided I couldn't make enough to make it worthwhile. I'm tempted to leave the bodies lay and set the place on fire. But it's a good buildin' somebody might have some use for. So I'll dig one grave for Sally and Hootie and send the three of them down the river."

"That still sounds like a lotta work," Clay said. "I'll give you a hand."

"I 'preciate it," Benny replied. "And I'll take you up on that, but it ain't gonna be as much work as you think. You ain't ever been here before, so I'll show you what I mean. Take hold of his boots and we'll take care of Junior first." He reached down and took him by the shoulders.

"Wait a minute," Ike asked, "don't you wanna see if he's got anything on him worth keepin'?"

"That would be a good idea, wouldn't it?" Benny responded. "I still ain't got my wits about me." So they unbuckled Junior's gun belt and searched his pockets while Ike and Grissom did the same with Merle and Billy. Then Clay and Benny picked Junior up and carried him out the back door of the saloon to a large porch on the back of the building. Clay could hear the river far below, making its way through a rocky area. He was surprised to realize the slope behind the building was so steep that the porch was about fifteen feet above the ground. "Lift him up on the railing," Benny said, and they did. "Now let him go and he'll bury himself." They let him go and he dropped the eighteen feet or so, counting the three-foot railing. He landed hard on the slope to bounce once before rolling and bouncing toward the river, some fifty feet below. "One down, two to go," Benny said. "That's the way Ike Ennis, the fellow who used to own this business, handled anybody who came up on the short end of a gunfight in the saloon. Matter of fact, he ended up takin' that same roll to the river. It kinda seemed the right thing to do after he got shot down."

"Yeah, I can see where that would be the sentimental thing to do," Clay said, facetiously. They went back inside and met Ike and Grissom coming out with Billy's body. Evidently they knew the funeral rituals practiced at Lucky's. "I see you picked up the smallest one," he said to Ike in passing.

"We figured you'd want to tote the boss out," Ike responded.

Clay and Benny brought Merle's body out and dropped it for the river roll, then Clay asked Benny if he wanted to bury the old man and the woman that night, or if he was going to wait until the next day. "I can help you either way," Clay said. "We ain't leavin' till day after tomorrow."

"I declare, that's mighty neighborly of you, Clay, after all you've done tonight, it don't seem right to expect you to dig a grave, too. I'm gonna bury 'em tonight because I'm leavin' this cussed place in the mornin'. I expect the three of you are ready to get back to your wagons after the kinda evenin' you've had."

"I imagine Grissom and Ike probably do want to get back, but I ain't got any big reason to get back there in a hurry. Let's get some shovels and a pickaxe if you've got one and put those two folks in the ground."

"I swear, Clay, I can't tell you how much I appreciate your help. I've got the tools in the shed beside the house. I feel like I owe it to Sally to give her a decent grave and I reckon Hootie deserves one, too. He ain't never done any harm to anyone that I know of. And all he ever wanted was to come and set with Sally for a little while. So we'll dig one grave and let him spend the rest of eternity with her. I don't think Sally would mind."

They went back inside and told Grissom and Ike what they were going to do, and they promptly offered to stay and help, gambling on the certainty that Clay would tell them they weren't necessary. When he did, they didn't linger, and when they all walked outside together, Grissom commented that Benny had gained three horses with saddles. "I hadn't even thought about that," Benny confessed. "I reckon I'll put them in the barn tonight."

"Doggoned if you ain't gonna have a busy night," Grissom

said. "Come on, Ike, let's get out of the way. Sorry for all your trouble tonight, Benny, and I hope you find something better down the road. And thanks again for the bottle of likker." Clay almost laughed at their hasty departure. They got on their horses and headed back down the narrow road to the fort. After a few dozen yards, Ike pulled up even with Grissom and said, "Next time you feel like you need a drink of likker, ask somebody else to go with you."

Clay and Benny wasted very little time in digging a grave on the other side of the toolshed where the ground was fairly level and not too hard. They dug it big enough and deep enough to accommodate the two fairly small bodies. When it was to their satisfaction, they went back inside the building. Benny got a couple of blankets from Sally's room and they wrapped each body in a blanket. Then Benny carried Sally in his arms and Clay carried Hootie on his shoulder and they transported them to the grave. They lowered each body into the ground as gently as they could, then covered them with dirt. "Well, I reckon that just about does it," Clay said when he handed Benny his shovel. "I saw the three horses for the three we threw in the river, but I didn't see one for Hootie."

"Hootie didn't own a horse," Benny said. "He walked. He didn't live that far from here."

"Is that so? Is there somebody who oughta be notified of his death?"

"Hootie didn't have anybody. He lived by hisself in a little tent by a stream about half a mile from here. I doubt there'll be two or three people that even know he's gone."

Clay didn't comment further on the subject. He didn't even know the man, but he couldn't help feeling grief for a poor soul like Hootie who might be a lot better off where he was now. Maybe Merle Bacon did him a favor. He shook hands with Benny and wished him luck, climbed on the gray and rode back to the wagon train. The social hour had already ended, even though it probably lasted a little longer than it normally would have, since there wouldn't be any four o'clock bugle in the morning. He went through the narrow "gate" between Grissom's wagon and the last wagon in the train, then dismounted and closed the gate by putting Grissom's wagon tongue back where it was acting as the gate. After he took the gray where the other horses were, he took his bridle and saddle and walked back to his brother's wagon where he found Matt sitting on a blanket with his back against the rear wagon wheel. "You waitin' up for me?" Clay greeted him.

"Katie would raise hell with me if I went to bed before all the kids were home," Matt cracked.

"Sorry I'm so late then. I know how you old men need to get your sleep," Clay came back.

"I saw Grissom when him and Ike came back. He had a towel wrapped around his head, so he couldn't put his hat on straight," Matt said. "He told me what you walked into over at that old hog ranch. He said if you hadn't come when you did, both him and Ike would be dead now."

Clay shrugged and replied, "Mighta been, I reckon. Didn't look like they intended to leave any witnesses. I'm tired, I've been digging a grave. I'm goin' to bed." He knew Matt would like a blow by blow recounting of the confrontation with the three outlaws, but he didn't feel like talking about it. He was tired and he wanted to go to sleep and forget about the pitiful couple he and Benny had buried that night. "I'll tell you all about it in the mornin'. Tell Katie all the kids are safe in bed."

"Yeah, I'll tell her," Matt said. "I was just fixin' to turn in, myself." He preferred not to tell Clay that he was waiting for him to show up. And if he hadn't shown up after another half hour or so, he was going to saddle a horse and go look for him, even if Grissom said all the trouble was over.

The following day was a busy day for some of the wagons that needed the services of Ned Blanchard for wagon repairs as well as horseshoeing. Neither Matt nor Clay were among those in need of Ned's services, so it was a casual day for them. Clay used up part of the day cleaning his weapons and trying to teach the gray gelding to come to him when he whistled. It didn't take Clay long to clean his Henry rifle and his 1860 Army Colt .44, and the gray never figured out what Clay wanted when he made the whistling noise. So he paid a visit to Grissom's wagon to see how he and Ike were recovering from the evening just past. Grissom was wearing a new bandage around his head. It was the same type as the towel he came back from Lucky's with, but it was a piece of sheet and looked much neater. Molly Tatum took over the doctoring of his injury when she saw him last night wrapped with the bar towel. Grissom said it wasn't a bad cut on the back of his head and it ought to heal up pretty quick. Ike was busy with a needle and thread, attempting to sew a flap of canvas to his long johns with the idea of making a secret pocket. It was an idea he had heard mentioned the night before. "You must notta got back here till pretty late," Grissom said. "I never heard you come in. Did you bury them two people?"

"Yep, we dug 'em a nice grave, wrapped 'em in blankets and covered 'em up."

Grissom nodded slowly as he thought about that. Then he said, "Damn, I'll be glad to leave this place in the mornin'." The image of himself and Ike standing barefoot in their long johns, facing an execution, lingered long in his mind's eye.

"I reckon I'll go on back to Matt's wagon to see if there's anything they need my help with to get ready to pull outta here in the mornin'," Clay said, and turned to leave.

"We're goin' over to Lucky's tonight to get a drink," Ike called after him, joking. "You wanna go with us?"

"I think I'll pass this one up," Clay called back without turning around.

They both watched him until he reached his brother's wagon. "Have you really thought about what he did last night?" Grissom asked Ike. "He walked into that dad-blamed ambush and took down three gunmen, head-on, right by himself, with a rifle at that. I ain't never seen anything like that before. And I'll bet you ain't either."

"You'd win that bet," Ike said with a chuckle. "Yessir, we got us a real mountain lion on this trip west. He'll be real handy if we run into any hostile Indians."

Clay didn't go to the social hour that evening because he didn't know if word had gotten around about last night's incident, and he didn't care to discuss it. Ike didn't attend because Ike seldom did, and besides, he had a bottle of whiskey that required his attention. Grissom appeared at the end of the evening to remind everyone to be ready to roll the next morning, and the bugle would sound at four o'clock.

At seven sharp the next morning, Ike led the column of wagons out of Fort Hall to start what would be a segment of their journey that would take them to the Three Mile Crossing of the Snake River. It would be a trek on the south side of the Snake through a dry and barren-looking land of about one hundred and seventy miles. With the river running almost entirely the whole distance in deep gorges and canyons, Three Island Crossing was the first place they would be able to cross over to the north side where there was better grass and camping. The first major obstacle was the Raft River, so named because it was deep and often required a raft to be built to ferry the wagons across. This was a concern ever present in Grissom's mind until the river was behind them. If they were unlucky enough to cross the river when the water was high, it would cost them precious time to build and then use the raft to cross over.

They journeyed along the path of the river, past American Falls, where the river dropped fifty feet to go crashing onto the rocks below with such force that the angry roar of the Snake could be heard for miles. They passed through Massacre Rocks, a narrow passage so named because of an Indian attack on a wagon train that killed eight of the emigrants. Grissom called the narrow passage Devil's Gate, like the one on the Sweetwater. They passed Register Rock a little way beyond that, another place emigrants wrote their names and the date they passed. At nooning time of the fourth day, they struck the Raft River and another Parting of the Ways. For this was where the California Trail left the Oregon Trail. When they approached the river, Grissom and Clay, two of only three on horses, rode up to the bank to gauge the depth of the water. The third rider, Worley Branch, followed at a respectful distance behind them. "I've seen it higher," Grissom exclaimed joyfully. "I think we caught the river with her pants down. You wanna help me find the path?" he asked Clay, since Clay had done it before.

"I figured I might," Clay answered. "No sense in botherin' Mr. Yocum to go saddle a horse."

Grissom walked his horse along the bank until he found the place he liked best to enter the wagons into the water. Then he looked directly across at the bank on the other side where the wagons would exit the water. "I think this'll do for goin' in and pullin' out. Let's see what the bottom's like between here and there. You be the left wheels and I'll be the right wheels," he said to Clay. Clay nodded in agreement and they entered the water, trying to maintain a distance between them that would approximate the width of a wagon. The water crept up gradually on the legs of the horses for only a few yards before it suddenly rose up to touch their bellies, causing immediate concern for both riders. But the water stayed at that depth until almost halfway across, when it rose to the riders' knees. Still, the horses seemed to have firm footing on the bottom. "Here comes the test," Grissom announced when they could tell by the current that they were approaching the channel and the deepest part of the river.

They walked the horses a few yards farther before they began to swim. Both riders were clinging to their horses, trying to feel every movement of their limbs, when suddenly Clay yelled, "Bottom!" Grissom echoed the same call a split second after Clay. The horses were walking on the bottom again and continued on to climb out on the other bank. "That looked good to me," Clay said. "I don't believe the wagon will have much time to float before the horses are walkin' on the bottom again."

"I agree with you," Grissom said. "Let's check it on the way back to make sure this ol' river ain't messin' with us." The return trip confirmed what they had found, so Grissom was in a hurry to get the wagons on their way across. He and Clay rode back along the column telling the people to ready their wagons and what to expect.

"Ain't we gonna have the noonin'?" Elmo Steptoe asked when Grissom got to his wagon. "It's already after twelve noon."

"We'll have it on the other side," Grissom told him. "This river's got a fancy for devilment. You've got to take advantage of her when she's in a good mood."

Clay came to Harlan Rice's wagon and Annie was sitting on the driver's seat beside her husband. So Clay told them what to expect from the crossing and ended by saying, "Right now, it's just like any other crossing. It's about like all those Sweetwater crossings you've made."

"We're ready to go, aren't we, Harlan?" Annie sang out at once, suspecting that Grissom and Clay were still concerned about Harlan's panic way back at the Kansas River crossing.

"That's right," Harlan answered, "ain't no problem here."

"I didn't think there would be," Clay said. "Just remember, the bottom drops off kinda sudden right after you enter the water, but it's just a gentle slope after that till you reach the channel." He rode on then, down the line of wagons. By the time he rode back to the riverbank, Ike was already approaching the deepest part of the river, so Clay pulled his horse to a stop and watched as John Henry Hyde followed right behind Ike and Dick Batson followed John Henry. Clay glanced over at Grissom, watching intensely from the other side of the column of wagons. He knew Grissom didn't trust this river, he was convinced it had a soul, and when he suddenly flinched, Clay quickly looked back in the river and saw that Ike's horses were swimming. He started counting the seconds to himself, *One tomato, two tomato, three to-mato, four*... all the way to sixty-seven before the horses stopped swimming. He wasn't aware of the smile on his face as he watched the wagon drift slightly with the current before its front wheels found the bottom again and the horses pulled it up onto the opposite side of the river. He glanced back at Grissom and saw the tension drop out of his body. *Maybe the river's got a benevolent soul today*, he thought.

The crossing continued without incident, but Grissom did not celebrate until Vernon Tatum, who drove the last wagon in line that day, successfully pulled up on the other side. The Raft River, with a reputation as one of the worst river crossings, and the cause of much concern in the days leading up to it, turned out to be one of the easiest crossings they had encountered. They immediately picked a spot to circle the wagons and set up for the nooning. They could now look forward to the Three Island Crossing, another one that could be difficult, but it was about one hundred and twenty miles away. Grissom's concerns about that critical crossing were lessened somewhat by the success of the Raft River crossing. The water was definitely low in the Raft River. That had to mean the water was low in the Snake as well, which meant a crossing attempt was justified. When the water was high in the Snake River, the crossing was too risky and the alternate route along the south bank of the Snake had to be taken. That meant a longer route to Fort Boise over a dry, rocky road with little feed and water for the horses.

Chapter 21

After leaving the Raft River three days behind them, each day a monotonous repeat of the day before, Grissom told the people at social hour the scenery would soon be changing. "So hang on a little while and things will change. We should camp tomorrow night at Rock Creek Crossing. A fellow named Ben Holladay built a place there last year for the home station for the Overland Stage Line. When we came through here last year, they said somebody was planning to build a store there, too. I don't know exactly when, but maybe they've already built it. Anyway, we'll find out tomorrow."

Nearing the end of another day on the hot, dusty road through a countryside that didn't look suitable for any useful purpose, the buildings of Rock Creek Crossing popped up on the horizon. "Thar she blows," Grissom declared. "I was just about to say she oughta pop up pretty soon." He squinted his eyes in an effort to see better. "I believe there's some more buildings there than there was last year. Don't you think so, Ike?"

"Hell, don't ask me," Ike replied, "I can't see any buildin's a-tall till we get a helluva lot closer."

Grissom looked back a few wagons and signaled Clay, who was on his horse, riding along beside Matt on the wagon. Clay gave the gray a little nudge with his heels and loped up to the front of the column. Worley, who had been riding on the other side of the wagon, wheeled his horse around and came up beside Matt. "Looks like Mr. Grissom needs Clay for somethin'," Worley said.

Matt smiled and said, "Yeah, looks that way, all right." He looked at Katie, who happened to be sitting in the wagon beside him, and winked.

She smiled back at him and said, "I'm right proud of you for holding your tongue." When Worley dropped back to the rear of the wagon, she said, "Worley can't help it. He's not stupid, he's just innocent."

"I know that," Matt said. "I think Clay oughta keep him. It'd be like havin' a dog that feeds himself."

She punched him on the shoulder. "That's a terrible thing to say about poor Worley."

Up ahead of them, Clay caught up beside Grissom. "You got young eyes," Grissom said. "How many buildings do you see up ahead of us? I don't mean outhouses or barns, but how many just regular-sized buildings?"

Clay peered up ahead of them. "Is that Rock Creek Crossing?" Grissom said it was. "Well, parts of a couple of 'em are hid by the trees, but I'd say three plus a barn."

"That's what I thought," Grissom declared. "I'll bet that fellow built that store Holladay was talkin' about. I hope he did because I forgot to buy some chewin' tobacca before we left Fort Hall."

It was not quite five o'clock when the wagons pulled into the Rock Creek Crossing, and Grissom was pleased to see a building that looked as if it had just been built. He recognized Ben Holladay when he walked out to greet them, and another man came out of the new building to join Holladay. Grissom got off his horse and walked over to shake hands with Holladay. "Virgil Grissom," he said. "I see you got your business up and running."

"Yes, sir," Holladay said, "I remember you, Mr. Grissom. Glad to see you again. This is James Bascom. He's the owner of the new store just completed this spring."

"Welcome to Rock Creek Crossing, Mr. Grissom," Bascom

said. "Like Mr. Holladay said, I just built this store and I'm stocked and open for business, should any of your people need anything."

"Have you got any chewin' tobacca?" Grissom asked.

"Yes, I do, as a matter of fact," Bascom said.

"Then you've got one customer for sure," Grissom said with a chuckle. "We're gonna stop here for the night, so I'm sure you'll get some business. I'm gonna circle these wagons up down the creek a ways first. How late is the store open?"

"Since your wagon train is a onetime opportunity, I'll stay open late to accommodate your folks," Bascom assured him.

"Good," Grissom said. "That's mighty neighborly of you. All right then, let me get these wagons outta the way." He climbed back into the saddle.

The wagon train forded the creek and circled up in a scrawny patch of grass beside the creek downstream from the station. The segment of their journey from Fort Hall to Three Island Crossing offered very little grazing for the horses anywhere they stopped. All the better grazing was on the north side of the Snake River and there was no way to cross the river until they reached Three Island Crossing. The horses were beginning to show the effects of the poor grazing, with five days still to go before reaching the crossing. To make matters worse, the crossing was a difficult and dangerous one, even for horses that were well fed and watered.

As soon as the wagons were circled and the horses unhitched, they were released to go to the creek for water and to feed on any grass or small plants growing there. Grissom told them to take care of their horses first because the owner said he would keep his store open late. "For your convenience, and because he's only gonna get one chance to take your money," he added.

The usual camp routine was altered only a little as the folks who needed basic supplies managed to get back to the store at their convenience. Mr. Bascom seemed reasonable in his pricing, although it was not as reasonable as the prices set at Fort Kearny and Fort Laramie. There was little complaining on the part of the emigrants, however, for they considered the lack of local customers and the fact that the man had to make a profit. And it was likely to be quite some time before the next opportunity for them to replenish supplies. The social hour was celebrated as usual although it started a little late. Mr. Bascom was invited to join the gathering and he thanked them for the invitation but said he was content to sit in his rocking chair at home and listen to the music. He no doubt heard Grissom's bugle at four o'clock the next morning as well. As to whether or not he enjoyed it would be debatable.

The wagons rolled away from Rock Creek at seven o'clock and the next couple of days would take them past Kanaka Rapids and Thousand Springs on their way to Upper Salmon Falls. Grissom had promised them all the fresh and smoked salmon they could trade for when they reached the falls. He had told them the day before that they would be swarmed by maybe a hundred or more Shoshone and Bannock Indians trying to trade salmon for anything of value the emigrants could come up with. He implored them to look through their trunks and search their wagons for any item of clothing or trinkets or furniture, anything they didn't mind giving away.

The wagon train reached Upper Salmon Falls shortly after the nooning and were immediately set upon by swarms of Indians, holding up huge fresh salmon to trade for anything. The emigrants looked toward the falls and saw fifty or more Indians perched on ledges and rocky spurs, anywhere there was safe footing, spearing the salmon as the big fish challenged the massive waterfalls. The water seemed so thick with the crazed salmon that it appeared the fishermen had to take no aim, that any cast of the spear would catch a salmon. Some of the more enterprising Indians were even smoking salmon to trade, knowing the fresh salmon would only stay fresh for so long. Needless to say, every wagon acquired as much salmon as they could find discardable items to trade for. It was an experience that surely would be reminisced over many a campfire weeks from that day.

When all the possible trading was done, the wagon train pulled away from Upper Salmon Falls to escape the Indians still selling their salmon. But the train only went as far as the first sizable creek that had something for the horses to eat and was far enough away from the falls for peace and quiet. It was a little early to make camp, but everyone had salmon to clean and cook. It was a happy camp that night with a feast of something that wasn't sliced off a pig. Even Worley had something to trade for salmon, and when he ate that one, he was offered more than he wanted at Matt and Katie's wagon. It was still a day and a half to Three Island Crossing, but nobody worried about that tonight.

Clay Moran got his first look at Three Island Crossing at nooning time when he and Worley rode forward of the wagons with Grissom to check on the condition of the crossing. Grissom's first concern was if the river was high or low and he was relieved to see the level of the water looked low enough to warrant a successful crossing. At the social hour the night before, he had told the emigrants how dangerous that crossing could be if the river was high. And if they found it too high to risk a crossing, the alternate route would be a longer, dry, rocky trek along the south bank of the river, all the way to Fort Boise. He had told them he would give them his opinion of the risk of a crossing, but he thought it only fair to let them vote on whether they would rather take the alternate route than risk the crossing. After all, he had stressed, you will actually be making four crossings of water.

After his first inspection of the conditions, he was going to recommend the crossing. Since it was already noon and time to rest the horses, it would be best to camp on this side of the river tonight, instead of just a nooning. He preferred to have a whole day to make the crossing and he was afraid if they started after a nooning, he would end up with part of his wagons on one side and the rest on the other. And he didn't care for that situation. There was the natural urge to cross while the river was low, but he looked up at the cloudless sky. There was no indication of rain. Unless there was a major storm north of here right away, the water level was not likely to change overnight.

When he told Clay what he had been weighing in his mind, he said that he had decided to camp on the south side tonight and cross in the morning. "I don't think it'll rain tonight," he said.

"It ain't gonna rain tonight, or tomorrow neither," Worley announced.

Clay looked at Grissom and grinned. "There you go. That oughta make you feel easier about it. That's the straight word from wherever he's hooked up to. Ain't it, Worley?"

Worley blushed. "I don't know . . . I reckon," he answered.

Grissom grinned back at Clay and said, "That's good enough for me. I'll tell 'em we're gonna spend the night on this side of the river. And this afternoon we'll try to find the best route across to the first island, so we can start right away in the morning." He wheeled his horse around and rode a little way back toward the approaching wagon train and signaled Ike to follow him. Then he rode over to a clearing he had used before to wait for the wagons.

"How's it look?" Ike asked when he pulled up even with Grissom's horse.

"Like it wants us to cross," Grissom answered. "So we'll camp right here tonight and start the crossin' first thing in the mornin'. After we get 'em in place, I'll go pick us a place to cross." He stayed there in the clearing and directed the wagons as they formed up the usual circle. And once they were all in place, he rode out in the middle of the circle and waited for the men to gather around him. When most of them were there, he told them that he had found conditions more favorable for crossing than he had ever seen them before. "So unless a majority of you would rather take the long way, we'll stay here for the night and start the crossin' in the mornin'." There were no objections, so he said, "Well, you might as well go on with the noonin', then."

"Hell, Grissom," Quincy Lewis called out, "I've et so much salmon in the last day and a half, I might just swim across and let Mildred drive the wagon."

Grissom laughed with everybody else. He was glad to see them all in a carefree mood about the crossing. He hoped they would be in the same frame of mind tomorrow as he returned to the riverbank where Clay and Worley were still searching for the best-looking spot to go into the river. "There's supposed to be some wide gravel bars runnin' almost all the way across the river," Grissom said when he joined them. "That's what most people try to locate, but I think those beds shift around, depending on the weather and the season. So I'm fixin' to ride across to that first island yonder, like we do at every river, and see what kind of bottom we've got."

"Well, we ain't been in the water yet," Clay said. "Every time I pick a spot to cross to that island, I look at Worley and he shakes his head no."

Grissom chuckled. "Where do you say, Worley?"

Worley turned his horse and rode about five yards and stopped just short of a clump of willows. Then he went into the water there and went straight across to the island and the water never got deeper than the bottom of his horse's belly.

"Well, I'll be . . ." Grissom started. "He makes a good case, don't he? How'd he know that? 'Cause I'd like for him to teach me that."

"I don't think he knows how he knows. He just knows," Clay said. "I reckon it's maybe because he grew up in the woods like a wild animal and he just knows things."

Grissom just stared at him for a long moment before asking, "You're serious, ain't you?"

Clay shrugged. "I can't say one way or the other. A wolf has instincts. A coyote has instincts. Why can't a kid raised in the woods have instincts? It ain't for me to question."

Grissom thought about it for another long moment, while he stared at Worley sitting on his horse on the first island, watching them. "Me, neither," he said. "Let's go test that bottom to see if it's wide enough for a wagon to pass over."

They rode over to the clump of willows and saw Worley's horse's tracks where it entered the river. Grissom paused to decide how he wanted to measure the width. He decided to make Worley's tracks the center of the wagon trail. So he and Clay started across keeping the distance of a wagon's wheels between them, like they had done at the Raft River. They experienced the same results that Worley had with no evidence of a mushy bottom.

When they rode up on the island to join Worley, Grissom didn't waste any time before asking him, "Where would you go across for that next island?"

"I hadn't thought about that," Worley said. He started his horse walking along the edge of the little island. When he came to a place he liked, he turned his horse into the water and rode him across to the second island with similar results as those he got with the first crossing.

"Damn," Grissom swore, amazed. He looked back to see if the wagon would have a clear path across the island. Then he looked at Clay and said, "Same as the first one," and they entered the water with Worley's tracks the center line. Their results were good again and when they came up out of the water this time, Worley was already on the other side of the island choosing the place he would enter the river this time. Like before, it didn't take him long before he went into the water again. This time, Grissom and Clay didn't wait to see him across but went in the water behind him when he was only halfway. Their results were good again, with the water maybe two inches deeper than the first two crossings but the bottom solid and no problem for a wagon.

As before, Worley started looking for his next crossing as soon as he rode up onto the third island. But this time, he hesitated to select an entry point. He stopped and considered one place, then moved on to study another. *Uh-oh*, Grissom thought. "What's the matter, Worley?"

"Gonna have to swim here," Worley said. Grissom wasn't surprised. The last crossing was always the hardest one because the river's channel ran between the third island and the north bank. And the deepest part of the river was very close to the north bank, making it difficult for the team of horses to pull the wagon up the steep bank.

"How far?" Grissom asked before he thought.

"I don't know," Worley answered, "till they touch bottom again."

"Right," Grissom replied, realizing Worley couldn't possibly know how wide the deep water was.

"There ain't but one way to find out," Clay said. "What spot you like best, Worley?"

"Where you wanna come outta the river?" Worley asked. Clay turned and looked at Grissom. Grissom pointed to a spot on the bank that was not so steep. Worley turned his horse upriver and rode about five yards before going into the water and starting straight across. About three quarters of the way across, his horse started swimming, straight across at first until the strong current caught him and swept him downstream. The horse kept struggling to get across, but it finally made it to shallow water and came out of the river at the spot Grissom had pointed to. Clay and Grissom turned to look at each other, amazed. Clay grinned and Grissom swore.

Knowing they were going to have to test it, they started their usual exercise and rode into the water at the same place Worley went in. Right away, they confirmed that the bottom was solid, so they continued on straight across as the water grew deeper and deeper until they reached the place where the bottom dropped away and their horses started swimming. Like Worley's horse, their horses remained on a straight line across until they reached the strongest current. Then, no matter how hard the horses swam, the current swept them downstream and they found footing again at the same place Worley did.

The question now was how would a team of horses pulling a

wagon respond to that same situation? They had to assume that the same conditions of water depth and strength of current would prevail in the morning. Once the horses found footing again, would they be able to pull the wagon out of the current's grip? "I'm afraid there ain't but one way to answer that question," Grissom said. He didn't have to say more. Would the wagon drift peacefully until the horses pulled it up the bank? Or would it tumble in the current and end up drowning the horses? "Well, hell," Grissom declared, "it's my decision that the river is fordable, so it's up to me to demonstrate that it's not such a dangerous thing." He interrupted himself when a thought struck him and he turned to face Worley. "Do you think the wagons can make it across like we just made it across?"

"Yes, sir." He was afraid to tell him anything else.

Grissom continued then. "My wagon will go across before we start any other wagons. Dad blame it, I'd like to try it this afternoon, but I don't want to leave my wagon over here on this side of the river tonight when the rest of the whole train is over on that side."

"Besides," Clay couldn't resist japing, "you might wanna spend one last night with your wagon, in case things go wrong in the crossin'."

"I know you're japin'," Grissom replied, "but don't think I ain't considered that. I ain't ever run into this problem at this damn devilish crossin' before. It was always a problem if the river was high, but it looks like more of the bottom close to the bank has caved in or washed away. 'Cause if the water wasn't too high to make the crossin', you could always drive straight across without the current turnin' your wagon downstream. It might be comin' to the point where you just forget about crossin' here and take the long, dry route to Old Fort Boise." He paused but Clay had no response. "We might as well go on back for something to eat. I wanna mark those crossin' places on each one of the islands on the way back."

They returned to the wagons where the nooning was already

well underway. Following orders from Katie, Clay brought Worley back to Matt's wagon with him. She wanted to cook the last of the smoked salmon they had traded for and there was plenty for Worley, too. It bothered Katie to see Worley over near the horse herd in his own little camp alone. Consequently, more often than not, Worley ended up sharing the noon meal with the Morans. Matt didn't object to Katie's tendency to mother a man he was sure was older than he, because Worley always compensated for the attention with fresh game.

When Grissom returned to his wagon, Ike wanted to know right away what he had found the conditions to be in the crossing. "Did you pick a crossin'?" Ike asked. Grissom said that they had. "Hell, that didn't take you no time at all," Ike commented. Then Grissom told him about the last crossing from the third island and how it was to be accomplished. "Hell, Grissom," Ike responded, "these folks ain't gonna be able to make that final crossin' like that, when their wagon starts floatin' downstream. Hell, Harlan Rice'll go completely loco."

"It might not be that bad," Grissom said. "We don't know how bad it'll be until we send one wagon across to test it. And Harlan was drunk when we crossed the Kansas River. Anyway, I'll drive my wagon across to test it, if you don't want to."

"Hell, I'll drive the blame wagon!" Ike declared stubbornly. "I ain't afraid to drive the wagon."

"Well, we're gonna wait till mornin' to try it because I don't wanna have you and me and that one wagon across the river by ourselves tonight, while everybody else is over here." Grissom then told Ike about Worley picking every place where the wagons would enter the water and how every place he chose was the right one. "Everybody thinks Worley's simpleminded, but he ain't, really. He just ain't had no time bein' a young'un. He had to start livin' like a man right after he was weaned. I'm tellin' you, Worley knows some things that have to come from animal instincts." Ike chose not to respond to that, other than to look at Grissom and shake his head slowly.

Grissom spent the rest of the afternoon talking to all the wagon owners and reminding them to get their wagons ready for an extensive crossing in the morning. He also impressed upon them the importance of crossing to the north side of the river where they would enjoy plenty of potable water and ample feed for the horses, all the way to Old Fort Boise. The social hour was held as usual that evening and much of the casual conversation was focused on how much Grissom had prepared them for the morning's crossing. It may have influenced the song selections made by the musicians that night. Katie Moran commented that there seemed to be a definite leaning toward songs of sad farewells and missing loved ones.

Chapter 22

The four o'clock bugle announced the start of a day that held nervous anticipation for their wagon master, although he was careful not to show it to his charges. The normal routine was followed with the animals being watered and grazed while the women fixed breakfast. The only difference was that at seven o'clock, only one wagon rolled away from the camp. It was accompanied by Grissom, Clay, and Worley on horseback as it proceeded toward a small clump of willows on the bank of the river. It was followed by a large crowd of observers on foot who stopped on the bank to watch the crossing.

The three men on horses acted as guides as they entered the water and started across, and Ike followed them in the wagon. When they reached the first island and the wagon came up out of the water, Vernon Tatum remarked, "Well, that looked like it weren't no trouble a-tall."

"Yeah, but I expect that first leg is the easiest leg," Elmo Steptoe replied. "Like he said, the deeper water's over yonder next to the other bank." The three guides led the wagon across that island to enter the water again, again with the same results, and so on until reaching the final crossing. Especially interested now, John Henry Hyde stared unblinking, for his wagon was the first to follow after Ike. It was some distance now, but he could still see well enough to know what was happening. The guides led the wagon to the point of entry, but they didn't enter the water. Grissom signaled Ike to drive the wagon up to the bank where he had placed the branch of a tree the day before. "This is the fun part where you're gonna have to do a little bit of work to keep those horses drivin'. You ready?"

"Hell, I was born ready," Ike replied.

"You just drive 'em straight across," Grissom told him.

"Hell, you coulda picked a better spot on the other bank to pull this wagon out," Ike complained. "It'd be a helluva lot easier on these horses if we could come outta the water down yonder a ways where it ain't so steep."

"You just drive 'em straight across," Grissom repeated. "The river'll take care of the rest. Just make sure you keep those horses workin' hard."

"What are we gonna do if those horses can't pull that wagon up the bank, once they get their footing?" Clay asked as they watched Ike drive the wagon into the water.

Grissom gave him a sober look and said. "I ain't got an answer for that question, so let's just hope it don't happen." He turned his full attention back to the wagon that was approaching the middle of the channel and still driving straight toward the steep bank ahead of it. "They're swimmin'!" Grissom suddenly barked as the horses veered slightly from their original path and Ike flogged them with the reins and yelled encouragement. The wagon remained on the original path until the front wheels came off the bottom. Then the wagon turned slightly as the horses struggled against the current's pull on them. When the back wheels came away from the bottom, the rear of the wagon was swept around, causing a slight downstream turn as the horses found solid footing again. Ike stayed hard on them and they pulled the wagon out of the river. He drove them up the bank a little way before pulling them to a halt. Then he jumped down from the wagon, ran back to the edge of the bank and shouted, "Is that what you want, Mr. Grissom?"

"That's what I want, Mr. Yocum," Grissom said softly. Clay and Worley were not in a position to see his eyes raised toward the heavens when he said it. Reluctant to waste any more time, he turned around and said, "I'd appreciate it if you two could help me with this crossin'."

"Glad to help," Clay said.

"Me, too," Worley said, delighted to be asked to help.

"They know where to go into the river by the willows," Grissom said. "So one of us can stand on each of the islands and tell 'em where to go in the water to the next island. I'm gonna take the third island, so I can give 'em the same instructions I gave Ike. Clay, why don't you go back to the first island? Then Worley, you'll go back to the one in between. All right?" He figured Clay would get all the questions when the wagons made the first crossing and Clay would be better at answering the questions than Worley. They had no objections, so they crossed back over to the second island where Clay paused long enough to ask Worley if he had any questions. He didn't, so Clay went back to the first island.

"All right, John Henry!" Clay yelled when he got in position. "Start the parade!"

John Henry climbed up on the wagon seat and started toward the clump of willows, and all the other drivers scrambled to their wagons as well. Clay stood by on his horse, and when John Henry's wagon climbed up the bank of the first island, Clay walked him over to the second crossing. "What's the problem at the last crossin'?" John Henry asked. "From where I was standin' back on the bank, it looked like the wagon got turned sideways or something."

"There's no problem," Clay told him. "It's just that the current there will turn your wagon a little bit when you get in the deep water. But you don't stay in it long enough to cause you any trouble. That's why Grissom is over there, to explain the whole thing and tell you what to do." He turned the gray and went back to guide Batson's wagon, which was approaching the bank already. He looked back toward the south bank and saw the steady line of wagons, with no long gaps in between. It appeared that everyone was anxious to get on the north side of the Snake River after the long dusty dry journey from Fort Hall. The promise of green grass and plenty of good water was enough to ensure these weary travelers would take the risks of this crossing even if Grissom told them how dangerous it could be.

After Batson, Vernon Tatum's wagon arrived, and Bowen was close behind. Clay answered their questions as best he could, at the same time keeping an eye on the progress of the first wagon. To Clay, as it was to Grissom, John Henry's experience on that last crossing was critical. It could make or break the success of the entire crossing. Finally John Henry drove his wagon off island number three. Clay guided Paul Courtland to the second crossing as fast as he could while trying to keep one eye on John Henry's progress. Paul's wife, Evelyn, asked Clay playfully if he was Grissom's official scout now, distracting him for a few seconds. He told her, "No, I'm just helpin' out." When he looked back, it was to see John Henry's wagon pulling up the bank on the other side. *Hallelujah!* he thought. *Worley, you're a genius!*

The wagon train continued to cross over the three islands in the middle of the Snake River without mishap. When Matt's wagon climbed out of the water onto the first island, Katie and the kids all gave him a big hello. He had told Matt about the little sideways move with the river current's help the night before after a promise of secrecy. So Matt wanted to know how that was going. "Well, you can see how well the column is moving across the river. So I think he's convinced everybody that it's a standard maneuver that wagon masters employ every day when they're crossing rivers."

"You may be right," Matt said, "but the real test is comin' up pretty soon. That's Harlan Rice drivin' the wagon behind me."

Poor Harlan, Clay thought, *still wearing that reputation ever since the first river crossing and he hasn't had any real trouble since.* "Just be sure you ain't the one that makes a mess of the crossin'," he said to Matt. "Keep your eye on him, Katie."

"I will," Katie returned. "If he starts looking shaky, I'll let Jim take the reins."

"Good idea," Clay said as the wagon approached the next entry point. "I'll turn you over to Worley now and I'll see you later." He turned the gray around and rode back in time to meet Harlan and Annie and the girls. "Good mornin'," he said.

They all returned his greeting cheerfully. "If they're all as easy as this one, there ought not be a bit of trouble," Harlan remarked.

Clay thought he should give him a little warning. "The next two oughta be just like the one you just made. The last one's a little different because of the deeper water and the current will turn you a little, but it actually helps you. Grissom will tell you what to do when you get there."

"Right," Harlan responded, "we'd best keep movin'. See ya later, Clay." He whipped the reins to keep his horses moving. Annie looked at Clay and smiled proudly. He nodded to acknowledge her signal. Things were looking better for the Rice family. Clay was glad to see it, for the sake of Annie and the two girls.

The crossing continued flawlessly, much to Grissom's delight, as twenty wagons climbed to safety on the north bank of the river. It was beginning to look like they would complete the crossing in time for the nooning when he had expected it to take most of the day. Wagon number twenty-one, however, was not to be so lucky as the twenty before it. To add to the irony of the situation, it was the wagon belonging to Henry Corbett. Although no blame could reasonably be laid at Corbett's feet, it was hard to forget the problem he had caused at Big Hill. It was determined that a corner of the gravel bar the wagons were crossing on gave way and crumbled beneath the downstream rear wheel of Corbett's wagon, causing the back of the wagon to sag to the downstream side and turning the wagon before the other three wheels were off the bottom. This resulted in a situation where the wagon was swept in a turn too sharp for the horses to straighten it out. Thanks to Corbett's relentless pressure on the horses, they managed to gain footing on the north bank to hold the wagon against it, but they could not pull the wagon up onto the bank. As in times before, Ike unhitched his team of horses and brought the ropes down to the water's edge.

Since the last three wagons were already on the second and third island, Clay and Worley rode on over to the north bank and Clay volunteered to go in the water to tie the ropes onto Corbett's wagon. He pulled off his boots, hat, and shirt. Worley at once did the same. Ike thought he might, handed him the end of one of the ropes, and told him where to tie it on the wagon. Clay took the other rope and the two of them went into the water. They found that the front wheels were resting on the bottom and the back of the wagon was hung up against a steep part of the bank. Clay told Worley to tie his rope and then meet him at the back of the wagon. When Clay started swimming to the back of the wagon, Henry Corbett leaned over and said, "Looks like you show up every time I get in trouble."

"Looks that way, doesn't it?" Clay answered. He met Worley at the back of the wagon and explained what they would try to do. "You ready, Mr. Corbett?" Corbett yelled back that he was ready, so Clay yelled to Ike. Ike started his horses and Corbett whipped his horses, and when the wagon started to move, Clay and Worley pushed the back of the wagon against the current in an effort to straighten it out of the sharp turn it had gotten in. The wagon resisted for a few seconds, then finally straightened out enough for the horses to pull it on up on the bank amid a chorus of cheers from the crowd of spectators.

Clay called out to Grissom, who was still on the third island. "As long as I'm already wet, I'll swim over there and take a look at that bottom before you send those other three across." He started swimming across to the island, so Worley started swimming after him. When Clay reached the spot where the bottom dropped off, he went under to take a look at the gravel bar the wagons had been rolling on. He confirmed what Grissom suspected. The edge had crumbled under Corbett's rear wheel. When he came back up, he told Grissom he was right. "The good news is that the wagons have been running right along the front edge of that bar. There's plenty of room to move 'em over that way four or five feet." He pointed upstream. Grissom took his word for it, moved the next wagon over three or four feet and sent it across. It performed just as the first twenty wagons had with the last two right behind it. Three Island Crossing was behind them and with no casualties or loss of possessions. This was a good day and the crossing was completed at half past one o'clock. It was late for the normal nooning time, but the horses would do best if rested after their struggle with the river. So they let the horses rest and graze, and the camp set up for a delayed nooning.

After he turned the gray out to graze with the other horses, Clay's next priority was to get out of his wet britches and underwear. He had spares for both items so he went into his packs to get them. The only clothes he had were army issue except for the two shirts he bought in Fort Kearny to keep from looking like a soldier. And he had thought to take that off before he went into the river, along with his hat and boots. He wondered then if Worley had a change of clothes. He always wore the same clothes, buckskins, and they always looked the same. With the women and the older girls fixing dinner and all the younger children running around the wagons, there was no place for a man to get out of his wet clothes. So he got his dry pants and underwear along with his boots and his towel. Then he took a walk down the river. As soon as he figured he had a screen of trees thick enough between him and the wagons, he peeled off his wet clothes and put on the dry ones. Then he found a spot to sit down at the edge of the water and rinsed his feet as best he could before drying them and getting his socks and boots back on.

When he walked back to the wagon, Katie saw him and called to him. "We're gonna be ready to eat in a few minutes. We were wondering where in the world you were." She paused then to give him another look. "You don't look very wet." Then she saw what he was holding. "Is that your wet clothes? Here, give 'em to me and I'll hang 'em up to dry. You go on around on the other side of the wagon and we'll eat pretty soon."

"Yes, ma'am," he said, like a child might. He walked around the wagon to find they had a larger than usual fire going a little farther away from the wagon. Matt and Jim and the two girls were sitting around three sides of the fire, gathered around Worley Branch, who had a blanket wrapped around him. The fourth side of the fire was occupied by Worley's buckskins draped on a drying frame of willow branches.

"Hey, Clay," Worley greeted him, "I tried to find you, but I didn't see you anywhere. Where were you?"

"Oh, I just took a walk in the woods," Clay answered. "I always feel like a nice long walk in the woods after I go swimmin'."

"Katie invited me to eat with you," Worley said. "She said I was a hero for jumpin' in the river to help you, so I deserved to get fed. And Matt said it was okay."

Clay looked at Matt, who was grinning at his obvious surprise. "Well, I agree, Worley, you do deserve to be fed. I ain't sure I coulda moved that wagon by myself. I mighta drowned trying. So you mighta saved my life." The glow of acceptance in Worley's face might have rivaled that coming from the fire. Eight-year-old Sarah asked her mother what she should call Worley, since he was obviously older than Uncle Clay. Katie was impressed that the child was concerned with respect for a grown-up, so she said she and Jim and Hannah could call him Uncle Worley. Somehow, Mr. Branch seemed a bit stiff and awkward for Worley.

Although the nooning was later than usual, Grissom gave the signal to move out after one hour, and the wagon train left Three Island Crossing at half past two. It was the start of a trek up the Boise

River Valley of around one hundred and thirty miles to the original Fort Boise and the next crossing of the Snake River. The old fort had been abandoned for years due to trouble with the Indians at that time. It was now referred to as Old Fort Boise. New Fort Boise was built in 1863, but it was built fifty miles east, up the Boise River. For that reason, it would not be a stop for the wagon train. They would continue straight up the valley to Old Fort Boise.

Compared to the dry dusty journey from Fort Hall, the valley on the north side of the Snake was lush with good drinking water and grass for the horses. With nothing to impede their progress, the drive to Old Fort Boise took nine days. During this time, there were several sightings of Indians—Shoshone, Grissom presumed. They were always at a distance, small hunting parties usually, and they never made any attempt to make contact. At the creeks and streams when they stopped for nooning or for the night, Clay and Worley would always find plenty of deer sign. Sometimes the two of them would hunt together, but almost every night *Uncle* Worley would hunt for some kind of game, whether it was deer, antelope, rabbit, or raccoon. More often than not, he would take Jim with him, which worried Katie somewhat but Matt was all in favor of. Clay was in favor of it as well. He figured Worley was hunting and teaching Jim how to hunt as a way to pay for his adoption by them. Young Jim was an eager student for Worley's teaching and he was especially keen on learning to hunt with a bow.

The wagon train reached Old Fort Boise late in the afternoon, so they circled the wagons and went into camp, planning to cross the river in the morning. It was apparent that they were expected, no doubt the result of the occasional hunting parties they had sighted along the way. Since the Snake had been receptive at the Three Island Crossing, Grissom expected it to be the same at this crossing. And when he went to the riverbank to verify it, he was met by several of the local Shoshone who operated bullboats, built specifically for the purpose of ferrying wagons across the river. They quoted a reasonable fee to ferry the wagons, and Grissom told them that he would present their proposition to his people and he was sure some of them would use their services. "But the river looks fordable to me, so we will be drivin' the wagons across in the mornin'." He knew from experience that there would also be Indian boys there who would swim in the river to guide the herd of loose horses across for a small fee.

That evening after supper, Grissom called everybody together before the social hour started. He told them that he would be fording the river in the morning, but anyone who preferred was free to pay the fee to have their wagon ferried across on a bullboat. Since there had been several people concerned about camping here right in the middle of a village of Indians, he told them they had nothing to fear. "These are just like the Shoshone and the Bannock that sold you the salmon. They're friendly toward the white man now. And there's a good chance you're liable to collect a crowd of 'em when Vernon and the boys crank up their instruments tonight. So if that's gonna make you nervous, you might decide not to have any music tonight. It's up to you, but I think it'd be mighty entertainin' to the Indians." He paused to let them discuss it for a while. Then he looked at his roster to see who was on schedule for guard duty that night. He called out the names to be sure they remembered. "Since we're right in the middle of so many Indians, I'll be stayin' awake as well. Just as a matter of principle," he hastened to add.

There was a lot of discussion on the matter, but when it was over, there was a vast majority of the folks who thought it might keep the Indians in a peaceful state of mind if they got to hear some good music. "Who decided it was good music?" Dick Batson japed.

"That's right," Paul Courtland answered him. "The jury's still out on that one. We might cause a whole new Injun uprisin'."

The playful debate continued for a little while until it was time to break out the instruments and it was obvious most everyone saw no danger in having their regular social hour. So Vernon

Tatum announced, "We're playin' as usual and anybody got a complaint with that can discuss it with John Henry Hyde."

When the meeting was over, Clay came over to talk to Grissom. "Elmo Steptoe wants me to trade off with him on the guard roster. He's got the twelve midnight to four in the mornin' shift tonight, and I've got the seven to midnight tomorrow. I said I would if it's okay with you."

"Tonight, I'm more than okay with it," Grissom said. "I'll make the change right now."

"Who's got the first shift tonight?" Clay asked.

Grissom looked at his roster and said, "Frank Bowen and Bryan Roland."

"I'll tell one of them to wake me up if I'm asleep at midnight," Clay said, and went to find them. He saw Steptoe first and told him he'd made the change, and he was now on the early shift tomorrow. Steptoe was greatly appreciative. He said he didn't mind the late shift, it was just that he had been having trouble lately staying awake after seven or eight.

Whatever, Clay thought. *I think they call that Shoshone fever. I'll admit I've got a touch of it, myself, and I'd rather have me on watch late tonight than Elmo Steptoe.* He saw Frank Bowen talking to Bryan Roland on the other side of the group that had gathered for Grissom's meeting, so he went over to check with them.

"Grissom gave you the midnight shift?" Bowen asked. "I thought Steptoe had it."

"He did," Clay said, "but Grissom changed it and now I've got it and I wanted to tell you in case I oversleep or something and don't show up on time."

"Right," Roland remarked. "Don't worry, one of us will wake you up. And it might not be good news to you, but it's sure as hell good news to me."

Clay knew what he meant, but he let it pass as if he didn't. He didn't blame Steptoe all that much. Some men were born to do other things. "Okay, then, I'll see you at midnight," he said, and walked back to the wagon. He could hear the musicians tuning up their instruments behind him. He told himself that he would try to get a couple of hours' sleep, but it might be in vain.

When he got to the wagon, he found Worley there, which he expected, but Matt was still there, too, which he didn't. It occurred to him then that he hadn't seen him at the meeting. So he told him and Worley what the meeting was about. "Why didn't you go to the meeting?" he asked then.

Matt looked at him as if he couldn't understand why he would ask the question. "I didn't go because we're settin' here surrounded by I don't know how many Indians. And damn-near every man in this wagon train is out there in the middle of the circle with no protection but a banjo, a fiddle, and a couple of guitars. In my mind, that don't add up to the white man having any sense a-tall. All I've got in this world is right here in this wagon and I aim to protect it. If those Indians start thinkin' about the opportunity they've got right now, they're gonna catch hell when they hit this wagon."

Clay didn't know what to say. When he looked at Worley, Worley said, "I'm gonna help him protect it."

When he looked back at his brother, Matt continued. "I know we all think Grissom knows his business, but why the hell didn't we stop and camp tonight somewhere short of here?"

"I understand why you think that way, Matt, but I don't think we're in any real danger from these friendly Indians. And I'll admit, I had a kinda funny feelin' about it myself, but I reckon I don't think we're in danger of a massacre like you're thinkin' about for a couple of reasons. In the first place, these Shoshone right here have been doing a regular business with their bullboat ferries for quite a few years now. We'd have to be awful unlucky to be the one wagon train they decided to go crazy on. And we've been at peace with the Shoshone and the Bannock for a long time now. I think they know, if they turn on us, it'll mean a reservation for them. Like I said, I was a little worried, myself, but it wasn't because of the possibility of an Indian attack. It was because of the possibility of a few young bucks thinkin' this a golden opportunity to steal a few horses. That's what I'll be lookin' for tonight when I'm on guard duty after midnight. And Grissom said he wasn't plannin' on goin' to bed tonight, either."

"You got the midnight watch tonight?" Matt asked. "I didn't think you were on the schedule till tomorrow."

"I traded with Elmo Steptoe," Clay said.

Matt grinned. "Whose idea was that?"

Clay grinned as well. "His."

"Well, it was a good one. I feel better already, knowin' you're gonna be watchin' this camp tonight. You need me to help you?"

"No, I don't think so," Clay replied. "Like I said, Grissom's gonna be there, too."

They were interrupted then when Katie came from inside the wagon. "All the supper mess is cleaned up," she said. "The girls and I are going to the social hour. Are you coming?"

"No," Matt said. "I'm stayin' here. You and the girls go ahead. The Indians ain't gonna attack until after midnight when there ain't nobody but Clay watchin'."

"What?" Katie asked. "What are you talking about?"

"Nothin', I'm just ramblin'. Clay's gotta get some sleep. He's got the midnight watch tonight."

"Oh, that's too bad," Katie said. "I'll tell the girls to be quiet when we come back."

Chapter 23

Much to Clay's surprise, he managed to fall asleep for a couple of hours before he had to rouse himself for guard duty. In the hours before that, however, he was very much aware of the music coming from the center of the circle of wagons. He was also aware of the people gathering outside the wagons to listen to the strange music. After a while, he could hear humming and even singing but not in tune with the instruments. It did not stop until Vernon and the other musicians quit for the night. Then he heard their whispering as they withdrew from the circle. Then, content there was to be no all-out attack, he finally drifted off to sleep.

When he woke up, he rolled out of his bedroll and pulled his watch out of his pocket. With nothing but the light of a three-quarter moon, he could barely make out the time as a quarter to twelve, so he checked his boots for uninvited guests, then pulled them on his feet. All was quiet around him as he rolled his bedding up. Sarah and Hannah were asleep in their tent, Jim was asleep in his blanket and there was no sound from the wagon. So he strapped his gun belt on, picked up his rifle, and went out to the middle of the circle to the fire and the pot of coffee that Grissom provided for the guards every night. There was no one at the fire, so he picked up one of the tin cups, looked to make sure there were no living occupants in it, then poured himself a cup.

One sip and he dumped the cup on the ground, then dumped the coffeepot and filled it with fresh water from the small water barrel left there by Ike, along with the coffee, the pot, and the cups. Frank Bowen walked up to the fire as he was putting the pot in the fire to boil. "I was gonna do that for ya," Bowen said. "Then I was gonna go wake you up."

"Anything goin' on?" Clay asked.

"Nope," Bowen answered. "There were a helluva lot of Indians hangin' around right outside the wagons, some of 'em singin' and dancin'. I watched 'em for a little while. The singin' sounded like the same thing, no matter what tune the boys were playin'. And the dancin' was, you know, like Indians dance, more like they're walkin' on hot coals. I think they had a good time. And as soon as Vernon and them quit playin', the Indians went on back to where they came from. The rest of the night has been pretty quiet. Here comes Bryan. I expect he'll tell you the same thing."

"Evenin', Clay, or I reckon I mean good mornin'."

"Right," Clay replied, "Good mornin', Bryan. Frank was tellin' me there ain't nothin' goin' on, that I might as well go on back to bed. But I just put on a fresh pot of coffee, so I reckon I'll have to stay up and drink it. If you two want a cup of fresh coffee feel free to have one when this pot's ready 'cause I doubt I'll drink more than a couple of cups. As long as we save one for Grissom, who said he was gonna be up," he added.

Bowen waited for the coffee to boil, but Roland retired to his wagon right away. After Bowen had a cup of coffee with him, Clay situated the pot in the coals to keep the coffee warm. Then when Bowen left, he took his first tour around the circle of wagons. As both Bowen and Roland had said, all seemed quiet as he walked around the south end of the circle. And when he passed near the herd of horses, they were quiet as well. When he walked around the north end of the circle, approaching Grissom's wagon, he was met by the wagon master. "Good mornin'," Clay said. "There's some fresh coffee on the fire out there, if you need some."

"I could definitely use a cup," Grissom replied. So Clay walked back to the fire with him and they paused there to talk while Grissom drank his coffee. "I intend to stay up until time to wake everybody up," Grissom said. "Like I said earlier this evenin', I don't expect one bit of trouble out of these people here. But I don't want to take the chance on some freak thing happening and get caught with my pants down. You know what I mean?"

"I understand what you're sayin'," Clay assured him. "It doesn't pay to be careless."

"That's right, so why don't we split this thing up and you won't have to cover the whole circle. Let the fire, here, be the dividing point and I'll keep an eye on everything north of it. And you take care of everything south of it, all right?"

"That's fine with me," Clay responded, frankly relieved, for he was afraid that Grissom was going to suggest that the two of them patrol the whole circle together. He wasn't sure he could stand four straight hours of one-on-one conversation with Grissom. So when Grissom finished his coffee, they split up and started to patrol their half of the circle.

After approximately two hours into his patrol, with everything typically peaceful and quiet, Clay's thoughts were tending to run more toward the crossing of the river in the morning. From what he had seen when they first arrived, it appeared to be no more than a typical river crossing and he wondered why a fair number of the men were planning on paying for the bullboats. His thoughts were interrupted then when he heard a dog barking. It caused a second dog to bark. Granted, the dogs weren't barking very loud, but it was a nuisance, so he decided to see if he could quiet them down. Tomorrow was going to be a busy day, everybody needed their sleep. So he paused to listen, so he could try to see where it came from. There it was again! It sounded like they were moving, for this time, one dog barked like it was closer to the herd of horses. It occurred to him then why the barking bothered him. No one on the wagon train had a dog. So how could there be dogs barking unless they came into the circle from outside? He moved quickly toward the last barking sounds, his rifle ready to fire if necessary. As he approached the horses, he noticed some movement on the other side of the herd. Half of the herd seemed to be moving toward the wagons near the east side of the circle. So he bent over as he ran, trying not to be taller than the horses. Then he stopped suddenly and dropped to one knee, for inside the circle of wagons, he saw an Indian kneeling as well. He brought his rifle up to his shoulder but did not fire because the Indian had not seen him. He decided to see if he could check for any others before he showed his hand. A few seconds passed and then the Indian made the sound of a dog barking. It was answered almost immediately by a barking sound from inside the herd of horses.

Clay moved up to the horses, so he could use them for cover while he attempted to get closer to the Indian kneeling between the herd and the wagons. He knew he could probably end this attempt to steal horses by simply shooting the Indian kneeling helplessly in the open, then waiting to get a shot at whoever else was in the middle of the herd. But he couldn't help wondering what effect it might have on the rest of the village if one or more of their young men were killed. It might bring the whole village down on the wagon train. With that in mind, it might be better for everyone if he could just keep them from stealing any horses and chase them out of the circle. He couldn't even guess what the barking signal meant. It could mean anything. Then he looked behind the Indian and realized he was in line with a wider gap than the gaps between the other wagons. *So maybe he's telling someone to drive the horses through this gap*, he thought. He stared hard at the gap then and realized the wagon tongue was sticking straight up in the air. The gate was open, in effect!

The kneeling Indian got up and backed quickly away toward the gap between the wagons, making barking sounds as he did. Clay started to run, thinking to get between the horses and the wagons, but he was too late, for he saw another Indian brave in the middle of the herd jump on a gray horse. He obviously planned to ride the horse toward the gap, driving all the horses in front of him out the gap. Then in a moment of shock, he realized it wasn't any ol' gray horse. It was *his* gray gelding! And he knew he couldn't get in front of the horses before they reached the gap. Desperate, he knew of only one thing to try. He stood up so his horse could see him and he whistled as loud as he could. As he always did, the gray stood dead still, ignoring the frantic kicking and urging the frustrated Indian applied. "You, there!" Clay demanded. "Get the hell off my horse!"

The would-be horse thief looked then and saw Clay for the first time, his rifle ready to fire. And beyond him, rumbling across the middle of the circle like a crazed buffalo, Grissom came charging to help, having heard Clay's demand. Since the horse refused to move, the Indian had no choice but to save himself, so he slid off the gray's back and with no other horse handy, he ran for the gap. Clay tried to head him off, but the Indian was faster and beat him to the gap. Grissom arrived at the gap in time to see the two young bucks fade away in the darkness.

"I swear, I ain't in no kinda shape to run like that," Grissom complained between gasps for breath.

"I coulda saved your breath, I reckon," Clay said. "I had a can't-miss shot at one of 'em, but I didn't take it." He went on to explain why he decided not to kill the horse thief.

"You did the right thing," Grissom said at once. "That coulda made for a messy piece of business if you'da killed two of their young men, and us tryin' to make a river crossin' in the mornin'. I'm damn glad you had enough sense to think about the results if you had taken that shot. And why'd you say your horse wouldn't move for that Injun?"

Clay explained again about his lack of success in getting the gray to come to him when he whistled. "He just stops dead still till I come to him. He ain't got enough sense to think that he could come to me."

"I'm glad he stands still," Grissom said. "If he hadn't, if he'd run through that gap, would you have shot that Indian off his back?"

"I don't know," Clay said. "I'd have to think about that. He's a pretty good horse."

"I don't expect we'll see any more from those two tonight," Grissom said. "Looks like the only thing we had to worry about was horse thieves. We've got less than two hours before I'll blow the bugle to get everybody up. So maybe we'll make it through the night now."

"I think you're right," Clay said. "So for the rest of the night, I'll mostly just keep my eye on the horses, in case those two are crazy enough to try it again." He walked over to the wagon and pulled the wagon tongue back down to the ground.

"I reckon I'll go on back to my half of the circle," Grissom said. "But I gotta tell you again how I appreciate you using your brains tonight. That coulda turned out real ugly." He paused when he thought of one more thing. "You gonna feel sharp enough to test that river bottom tomorrow mornin'?"

"Yeah, I'll be all right. How 'bout you? You ain't gonna have no more sleep than I do."

Grissom chuckled. "I'd be okay, too, but to tell you the truth, I'm thinkin' about havin' you and Worley find our path across that river tomorrow. After that business with him at the Three Island Crossin', I'm plannin' to use him a lot more."

"That's smart thinkin' in my opinion," Clay agreed. "And he'll be tickled to think you want him to help." He didn't say anything to Grissom about it, but his comments regarding Worley caused him to recall thoughts that had occurred earlier when he encountered the two Shoshone braves. Where was Worley during this time? As a rule, Worley usually made his camp near the horse herd and he would surely have been aware of the two horse thieves had he been anywhere near the horses. *At least he should have heard me whistle for the gray*, Clay thought.

They parted then and Clay walked back into the horse herd

where the gray was still standing in the same spot he was when he whistled. Clay shook his head, amazed. "How long would you stand here, boy, if I didn't come get you?" He scratched the gray's head and neck. "You know you're a hero, don't you? If you hadn't stood your ground, we'da lost a bunch of horses, includin' you. Go on and sleep now. We're gonna have to work in the river again in the mornin'." He gave him a friendly slap on the rump to make him trot a few yards away just to make sure he wasn't going to continue to stand on that spot.

Grissom's bugle actually took him by surprise. The time left before four o'clock passed much more quickly than he expected. He rinsed out the coffeepot with a little water left in the water barrel and put it with the cups inside the barrel so he could carry it all in one hand while he carried his rifle in the other. After he left the barrel at Grissom's wagon for Ike to take care of, he went back and helped the other men let the horses out to get water and graze. Then he went back to the wagon to eat breakfast. "Well, good morning, Clay," Katie welcomed him. "I'll bet you're ready for some breakfast."

"You've got that right," Clay said as he watched Katie pour him a cup of coffee. "And I need this pretty badly right now."

"Well, at least there wasn't any Indian attack on the train last night," Matt said. "We did a lotta worrying for nothin'. You coulda just left ol' Steptoe on the midnight till four stretch."

"Yeah," Clay responded, "I expect he mighta handled those two horse thieves better than I did."

"Say what?" Matt replied.

"Those two Shoshone fellows who came into the horse herd and were fixin' to drive a bunch of our horses out through the big gap between two of the wagons on the other side of the circle."

"Are you japin' me?" Matt asked. "I didn't hear anything last night."

"Of course you didn't. I had to take care of it real quietly, so I wouldn't disturb your sleep."

"Right," Matt replied, certain he was being japed then, "well, I'm glad you've got your priorities straight."

Clay glanced at Worley, who was enjoying his cup of coffee, a ritual recently encouraged by Katie, who felt sorry for the innocent soul. Worley's gaze was concentrated upon him and the seriousness of his expression told him that Worley believed him. Consequently, he was concerned. Instead of answering Worley's unasked question, Clay asked him, "Where were you last night?"

"I camped outside the wagons last night," Worley said. "I went huntin' to see if I could find something to pay for the coffee Miz Katie gives me."

Clay had to chuckle then. "Well, that sure explains why you missed the whole thing last night. But weren't you takin' a chance campin' outside the wagons, right in the middle of all these Indians?"

"No, Shoshones are friendly Injuns," Worley said.

"Yeah, I reckon they must be," Clay replied. "Are you gonna be ready to find our path across that river with me this mornin'? Grissom told me last night he wanted you and me to do it."

Worley's eyes lit up, as Clay expected, and he immediately replied, "Yes, sir, I'm ready."

Impatient with the idle banter between Clay and Worley, Matt interrupted. "Good, you're gonna test the river. Explain to me what you were talking about when you said we had horse thieves last night." Clay went on then to tell them about the visit that night and the part his horse played in the outcome.

Grissom rode down to the river with Clay and Worley to look for the best place to cross over. The wagon train was divided, with roughly the same wagons whose owners paid the toll to cross the bridges at the Thomas Fork Crossing now choosing to pay the Indians who operated the bullboats to ferry them across. Those who decided to pay to be ferried across were already lining up and waiting to be loaded aboard a bullboat while Clay and Worley rode across the river, deciding the best line to travel. When they agreed on the path, Grissom started across. The crossing went better than expected with none of the wagons in trouble. After they were reunited with their bullboat wagons, the train moved on through Keeney Pass to cross another river after a day and a half's drive. This one, the Malheur River, offered no challenge and another day and a half brought them to the Burnt River at a place called Farewell Bend. It was so named because it was the point where they saw the last of the Snake River, as it turned on a more northward course. It was at this point in their long journey that Grissom felt the obligation to prepare the emigrants for one of the roughest segments they would face.

At the end of the day just before the social hour got underway, Grissom told them that for the next five or six days they were going to have to follow the Burnt River up the canyon on the worst roads they had faced so far. "The Burnt River Valley ain't nothin' but a steep canyon where there ain't really many places to build a road. That smoke you been smellin' for the last day or so comes from the hills and mountains all around the Burnt River. They're mostly covered with tall bunch grass and the Indians that live in this area set it on fire."

"Why in the world do they do that?" Henry Corbett asked.

"I don't know for sure," Grissom answered him. "But I've heard some people say it's because they found out that every time they burn a clump of that bunch grass, a little growth of green grass comes up. I've also heard that they've been burnin' it for years to discourage people like us from wanting to settle here."

"That don't make any sense," Paul Courtland commented.

"No, I reckon not," Grissom said, "but that's the way it's gonna be for the next week till we get up that valley to Flagstaff Hill. Then you'll see some pretty country again and you'll get your first look at the Blue Mountains in the distance. But till we get to Flagstaff Hill, everything's gonna be black and smoky. I just wanted to prepare you for it ahead of time."

"I swear, that don't sound like it's gonna be a very happy week comin' up, does it?" John Henry Hyde commented. "We better play something cheerful."

The days that followed proved Grissom to be accurate in his prediction for the trail ahead of them. They entered a valley of black charred earth, as far as they could see, in any direction. The road was narrow and winding, often following a winding branch of a spring or creek. Then it became steep as it climbed up the valley. Most of the road had been cut out of the side of a mountain because there was no other place for it. And the resulting road was narrow, just barely wide enough to accommodate a wagon. And sometimes it was cut on a slant, so it was not level. In that case, they found that it required two or three good-sized men hanging on the high side of the wagon to keep it from turning over. There was no grass for the horses, except an occasional bank of the river that escaped the fire. Other than that, horse feed was whatever the river could provide in the form of grass and plants of any kind. At least they had the river. Without it, their task would have been impossible.

It was the deathlike feel of the entire valley that did the most damage to the human spirit. The smell of smoke was constantly in the air, because something was always burning somewhere. The ground, the steep sides of the mountains and hills, everything was burnt black. There was no circling of the wagons at the end of the day, for there was no place to circle them. There was no social hour because no one felt very sociable and there was no place to gather, anyway. The only thing that sustained life was the river. And then, with over twenty miles to Flagstaff Hill, they lost the river. It took a sharp turn to the southwest. They filled their water barrels and every other container they had that would hold water before they left the river for two and a half days of constant searching for streams or branches of creeks.

Then when many on the wagon train had given up hope, a little before noon one day, they could see the road starting to level up ahead of them. And they suddenly noticed the black fading away to green and brown, and the road circled around a hill that Grissom said was Flagstaff Hill. He halted the train there, so everyone could get out of their wagons and enjoy the clear fresh air. From where they now stood, they could see the verdant Powder River Valley far below them, green with grass and water. "If you want to get your first look at the Blue Mountains, you can see them in the distance if you climb up Flagstaff Hill," Grissom told them.

Some of the emigrants walked up the hill to enjoy the view, most of them children. But Clay and Worley went up the hill to take a look out over the valley they would next be crossing. Quincy Lewis spoke for a lot of them when he said to Grissom, "I'll just take your word for it. I'm too damn tired to climb up that hill."

Grissom waited a while for those who wanted to climb the hill, but a few lingered up on top after most of the others had come back down. So he sent Jim Moran and Skeeter Tatum back up to tell them it was time for the nooning and the wagon train was going to go down into the valley where there was fresh water and green grass. In a very few minutes, everyone was back, and Ike started his horses down into the flat, treeless valley. Although treeless, the valley floor was covered with grass and Grissom led them to the bank of the Powder River where there were plenty of woody shrubs to make a fire.

Chapter 24

After a nooning that seemed more a celebration than just the noontime meal, the emigrants started across the flat, green valley on their way toward the Blue Mountains. Clay and Worley moved up to ride beside Grissom. In the distance ahead, a single object sitting on the flat plain caught Clay's eye. "There's something sitting on the ground way the hell up there," he said, "and it ain't moved since I've been watchin' it."

"It ain't likely to, either," Grissom remarked.

"Why is that?" Clay asked. "You know what it is?"

"It's a big ol' pine stump," Grissom answered. "It used to be one great big pine tree, the only tree for miles around this valley. Everybody who used this road remembers it. Indians and traders and trappers all used to guide on it. You could see it for miles, standin' tall. They called it the Lone Pine. Then some ignorant son of a buzzard came along and sawed it down. So now, it's just the Lone Stump."

Able to make good time on the flat Powder River Valley, the wagon train required only five and a half days to reach the east slopes of the mountains they had gazed at in the distance every day since descending Flagstaff Hill. Following a rough and winding trail, they came to a popular resting place for travelers on the Oregon Trail. It was called Emigrant Springs and was known for the excellence and abundance of the spring located in the forest of tall trees. They made their camp there that night and took advantage of the opportunity to refill their water barrels. Grissom had advised them that this spot would be the best camping place they would find for a while, until reaching the Umatilla River. "When we leave here in the mornin', we're gonna go over Crawford Hill to get to Emigrant Hill," he told Clay. "That's about a seven-mile climb over some pretty rough road. Only, they don't call it Crawford Hill no more. They call it Deadman's Pass now because some renegade Bannock Indians jumped a lone teamster there and killed him. That was some time back. What kinda time we make gettin' over Crawford Hill will depend a lot on what kinda weather they've had up here this summer. If they've had a lot of storms this summer, there'll likely be some trees down or limbs layin' in the road and we might have to clear us a road to get by. Maybe we'll be lucky, like we were on the Snake River."

When Clay went back to the wagon for supper, he told Matt what Grissom had said about the next few days of travel. "Sounds like it could be another stretch of tough trails before we get by these mountains." When young Jim brought his plate and sat down beside Clay to eat, Clay playfully took his hand and ruffled the boy's hair. "Grissom said we've gotta ride through Dead Man's Pass!" He teased, "Where the Injuns will be lookin' for some ten-year-old boys to snatch."

"Ha!" Jim came right back at him. "They most likely would rather have old worn-out uncles. Wouldn't they, Pa?"

"I don't expect they'd want either one of you two," Matt japed, then asked Clay a serious question. "Did Grissom say anything about puttin' extra guards on duty tonight?"

"Not to me, he didn't," Clay replied. "Why? You think there's some reason we should?"

"I don't know," Matt answered with a shrug, "no reason, really. It just seems like we've been mighty lucky when it comes to Indian trouble. We've pretty much avoided trouble with 'em except for those two you chased out of our horse herd at Old Fort Boise. But I look at us camped here by this spring and everybody ready to take a rest." He snorted a chuckle and asked, "And what did you say they call that hill we're gonna go up tomorrow? Dead Man's Pass? Did he tell you why they call it that?"

Clay had to chuckle then. "Because a fellow was killed by some renegade Indians there," he said.

"Uh-huh, right," Matt responded. "I think we'd better watch our horses tonight."

Clay shrugged then. "I don't know. Maybe you're right." It was a different setup from their usual camp with the wagons circled and the horses inside. Here by the springs, the forest of ancient trees was so thick that there was not really any open space to circle the wagons. The horses were between the wagons and the spring, with the wagons in one long line, like a fence open at both ends. The guards tonight were going to be posted at each end of that fence. "I reckon it's the way Grissom parked the wagons the last time he was here. I don't see how he could do much different, do you?"

"I reckon not, but I'm still gonna worry about it," Matt decided. "I reckon I'd better, since I've got guard duty tonight."

"You didn't tell me that," Katie said. "Early or late?"

"Midnight till four," Matt answered, "me and Dick Batson. I reckon I'll be standin' at one end of the wagons and he'll be at the other end." He looked around him then when it occurred to him someone was missing. "Where's Worley? He ain't here for his cup of coffee."

"He said there's bound to be something to eat in all these woods, so he went huntin' tonight," Clay said, just as they heard the first notes of the banjo turning up. "Are we eatin' late or are they startin' early?"

"I think they're starting early," Katie answered him. "I guess they can't wait to get going since they didn't play at all coming up the Burnt River Valley."

"I reckon," Matt said. "That oughta scare any Indians away. Doggone! It is good to have that valley behind us." John Henry frailed a half dozen chords solo, then Vernon and the guitars jumped in to rescue him.

Running Man and White Elk turned to look at each other, startled when the strange weapon the big man was holding suddenly made such a strange and unexpected noise. What was he shooting at? Then the other three men joined him with noisemakers of their own, and they realized they were making white man music. It was not totally unpleasant but was without the steady beat that a song must have. There was no discipline to the music. The two Bannock warriors relaxed their sudden feelings of alarm when they at first thought their presence had been discovered. On the opposite side of the spring from the horses and the wagons, they were hidden in a patch of ferns, waiting for the darkness that set in heavily in this forest. The white men had many horses. It was only right that they should pay for passing through Bannock country. If all the people who had come out of their wagons to hear the music would go back to their wagons, then the two warriors would have only to wade across the spring and drive the horses back down the hill. If the white men would go to bed, Running Man and White Elk could stampede the whole herd of horses away from the camp. The only thing better would be if they could steal some guns from the white men along with the horses. Neither Running Man nor White Elk owned a gun. They both had patience, however, and by exercising that talent, they would wait until all of the white men went to their beds. And then they would drive all their horses away.

"How long will they make this noise?" White Elk wondered aloud after half an hour had passed and more people were coming from their wagons to join those already there.

"Maybe they don't go to sleep at night," Running Man suggested.

"Everyone has to go to sleep at night. Why would they not go to sleep?" White Elk asked.

"Because they are white men," Running Man answered. "White men do crazy things."

White Elk realized then that Running Man had been joking. "Surely they will not go on with this noise for much longer. When they finally go to their beds, then surely they will have some guards to watch their horses." There was always the concern for the white man's guns. If things worked out as they planned, the white men would leave one, or hopefully two, men to guard their horses. If they did, a couple of arrows in the backs of those guards might reward them with two guns as well as the horses. "We must be patient," White Elk reminded Running Man. "The longer we wait, the deeper they will be in sleep and the easier our job will be. We can chase all the horses back down to the valley and the white men will be on foot and cannot chase us. When we drive all those horses across the valley to our village, everyone will see how strong our medicine is, especially when they see our guns and the scalps of the guards we took them from." Running Man nodded and smiled his satisfaction when he created that image in his mind.

"Clay, wake up," he heard someone talking softly. "Wake up," it came again.

Fully awake then, Clay raised up on his elbow to see who was urging him to wake up. "Worley?" Clay asked. "What is it? What's the matter?"

"Injuns," Worley said, "they're after the horses."

That brought Clay out of his blanket immediately. He grabbed his rifle and crawled out from under the wagon, looking all around him for signs of horse thieves. But all he saw was Worley standing beside the wagon holding the reins for three horses. The horses between the wagons and the spring were all standing quiet. "Talk to me, Worley! What are you talkin' about?"

"I found these two Injun ponies down the hill on the other

side of the spring," Worley said. "They was tied to a tree limb, so I figure whoever's ridin' 'em is fixin' to try to steal the horses."

"I think you're right," Clay said, and sat down to pull his boots on. "First thing, we need to tell Grissom and Matt. You go tell Matt. He's on guard duty at that end of the wagons." He pointed to show him. "Just tell him to keep a sharp eye on the horses. I'll go wake Grissom up and he can tell Batson. But you meet me at Grissom's wagon as soon as you tell Matt. Most likely the two Indians who were ridin' these horses are still waiting before they make a try for our horses. Can you show me where you found their horses?" Worley nodded vigorously. "Okay, then be sure you tell Matt that we're goin' down below the spring to see if we can be there when they go to get their horses. We don't want him shootin' at us, right?"

"Right!" Worley agreed at once. "I'll tell him." They hustled off in different directions.

"What? Who is it?" Grissom barked when Clay shook him awake. When Clay identified himself, Grissom was awake immediately. "What is it, Clay?" Clay hurriedly told him what was going on and what he and Worley were going to do, that Matt knew but Batson didn't.

"Maybe I can find the two of 'em before they find out their horses are gone," Clay said, "and try to stop 'em before they cross that spring and get our horses stirred up. Hard to say what they'll do if they go back and find their horses ain't there anymore. Don't know if they'll run for it, or go back to our herd, jump on a horse and try to run however many other horses off down the hill."

Grissom pulled his boots on and grabbed his rifle as Ike crawled out of his blankets. "What's all the chatter about?" Ike asked.

"Get your rifle," Grissom told him, "we might have some Indians tryin' to steal our horses."

"All right, let's go, Worley," Clay said. "Take me to where you found their horses. We'll go on foot." He made a last request to

Grissom and Ike. "If you shoot, please identify your target before you pull the trigger. It might be me or Worley."

Clay realized how useless his request was as soon as he and Worley went above the camp and crossed over to the other side of the spring. It was so dark in the thick forest, identifying a target at any distance would border on impossible. "I reckon we're just gonna have to keep our heads down," he told Worley. As dark as it was, however, Worley led him down the slope, through the darkness, that he had climbed before when leading three horses. *Maybe this wasn't such a good idea after all*, Clay thought to himself. *I can't see a damn thing.*

"This is where they were tied," Worley said when they reached a tiny patch of grass between two big trees.

"Are you sure?" Clay asked, "'cause it's so dark in these trees, it's too dark to—" He paused, then said, "Yeah, this is where they tied 'em." He bent over then. When he did, he heard the swish and the thud as the arrow passed over his back and embedded in the tree behind him. With no time to think, he reacted strictly by instinct. Dropping to his knee, he fired at a moving shadow some fifty feet away, cranked another round in the Henry and squeezed off a second shot and the shadow crumpled to the ground. Knowing his muzzle flash had just created a target for the other Indian, he dived to the ground and rolled over next to a tree. He searched the darkness desperately for the second Indian. Then he realized he couldn't see Worley. There was no sound of any movement in the bushes between the trees, and after what seemed a long pause, he asked softly, "Worley, can you see where the other one is?"

"Yes," Worley answered, "he's dead."

"Dead? Are you sure?"

"Yes, I'm sure," Worley said, and proceeded to wipe the blood off his knife blade using the second Indian's shirt.

"Where did he come from?" Clay asked. "Wasn't he with the one I shot?"

"He was behind you," Worley said.

Clay couldn't understand how that could have happened and Worley seemed uninterested in how it played out in their favor. He realized then that he and Worley had walked into an ambush. The Indians must have heard them coming down through the trees, so they planned to use surprise to overcome the white man's advantage of having guns. One of them hid and let them pass by him while the other one waited ahead of them behind a tree. The one behind the tree would use the tree as cover, knowing it was so dark the white man would not see him draw his bow and take aim. Then when the white man fell, the other white man would rush to his side, only to get the second Indian's arrow in his back.

When Clay tried to paint that complicated picture for Worley he seemed interested in asking only two questions. "Did you see him aiming at you? How did you know to bend over so the arrow would miss you?"

"Oh, that?" Clay responded as if just remembering. "No, I never saw him aiming his bow at me. I reckon I could tell you it was instinct. But I'll be honest with you—it was another kind of stink. You remember? Just before that happened I asked you if you were sure this was the place where they left their horses."

"Yeah, and I said that it was," Worley remembered.

"Well, I knew you were right because one of their horses left a little something behind and I stepped on it. I bent over to see how hard it was gonna be to get it off my boot."

Worley didn't react for a long moment while his sometimes slow mind processed the picture described. When it registered, he laughed delightedly, so hard in fact, that his laughter was heard up above at the spring where Matt and Grissom had taken a defensive position to meet the rustlers after they heard the shots. Never having heard Worley in a laughing fit before, they could not be sure it was not one of the Indians, which made no sense. Finally Matt yelled, "Clay! Are you all right?"

"Yeah," Clay yelled back. "The situation's under control. The two Indians are dead." He looked back at Worley then and said to him, "And we're still alive because I stepped on some horse dung." That triggered another laughing fit for Worley.

"What the hell's so funny?" Grissom yelled.

"Nothing," Clay yelled back. "Worley's just laughin' at a close call we had. We're comin' back up now." He waited a few moments while Worley searched for anything useful on the two bodies. Finding nothing but two knives, Worley compared their bows to his and decided he liked his bow better but settled for some extra arrows. Clay decided that was as good a place as any to leave the bodies, far below the springs, so they climbed back up to the wagons and a camp awake, thanks to Clay's two shots.

Grissom was anxious to hear what Clay had to say about the encounter with the two Indians, which he presumed to be Bannock. "You sure there was just the two Indians?" He asked again, "And not part of a bigger party of horse thieves."

"Well, that's what I think," Clay answered. "I can't say for sure, but it was just the two of 'em for quite a while by themselves. So I don't think there's any more out there." He knew Grissom was concerned about the possibility of a raid by a bigger raiding party. And he guessed that Grissom was also worried about the killing of the two would-be horse thieves. If the two were members of a larger raiding party, their deaths would likely demand vengeance beyond the theft of horses. "I would have preferred to have been able to just chase those two away, but we didn't have a choice in the matter. The one I shot almost got me with an arrow, so I had to shoot before he notched another arrow. The other one was comin' after me with a knife, so Worley had to stop him."

"I reckon you're right," Grissom said, "you didn't have much choice. I always like to avoid killin' if I can, but sometimes you can't." He pulled his watch out of his pocket and squinted to see the time in the darkness. "It ain't but twenty minutes before time to blow my bugle. Camp's awake, anyway, might as well go ahead and make it official." He went to his wagon and got his bugle, walked back away from the wagon and promptly blew the morning wake-up call. The two Indian ponies jumped back in fear and Worley's paint was startled as well.

"Damn," Matt swore, "that thing is loud up close, ain't it?"

Worley went over and calmed the horses down, which prompted Clay to remember his absence at supper. "That's right," Clay said, "you went huntin' last night. And you didn't come back with anything."

"Two Indian ponies," Worley said in defense.

Chapter 25

The normal morning routine started with no one but Henry Corbett complaining that the bugle went off twenty minutes early. The word explaining the two rifle shots was passed around so that everyone knew about the two dead Indians below the springs by the time breakfast was ready. At seven o'clock, Ike started the wagon train out of Emigrant Springs for the beginning of a rugged seven-mile climb up Deadman's Pass to the summit that had been named Emigrant Hill. Grissom's plan was to complete the seven miles to Emigrant Hill in time to observe the nooning on top of the hill. He used Clay and Worley as advance scouts, riding out before the train to check the trail for anything that might cause a delay. Their main concern was fallen trees that were large enough to block a narrow passage, a sure sign of an ambush. Much to Grissom's relief, however, there was to be no ambush in Deadman's Pass this year. The trail was free of any obstructions, by nature or man-made. The difficulty of the trail, however, was still taxing on man and beast. As planned, they arrived at the summit of Emigrant Hill shortly before twelve noon, ready for the nooning respite.

The emigrants were rewarded for their torturous climb over Dead Man's Pass with a magnificent view of the broad Umatilla Valley some two thousand feet below them. Looking westward, far in the distance, a dark green wall of the tree-covered Cascade Mountains ran across the broad valley, with two great white-capped cones protruding up from it. According to Grissom, the cones were Mount Hood and Mount Adams.

While the view from the summit of Emigrant Hill was breath-taking, Grissom had to inform the people that the descent from this hill could be equally breathtaking but not in a good way. "To descend this hill, we've got about seven miles of narrow, windin' road, with some curves so sharp you're gonna have to be careful you don't turn your wagon on its side. The road goin' down is like the road we just rode up here on, with rocks and shale in the roadbed to try to tear your wheels up. There's been a lot of accidents comin' down this hill."

"I swear, Grissom," John Henry Hyde said, "you sure know how to spoil a pleasant noonin'."

Grissom chuckled. "I just don't want anything to jump up and hit you when you ain't ready for it."

"How far is it to that river I see, way down yonder?" Vernon Tatum asked. "Least, I think it's a river. Looks like one."

"That's the Umatilla River," Grissom said. "I expect it's about twenty-five miles. It looks like it's closer than that, but we've got seven miles of a road like a snake to get offa this hill."

"And we've already come seven miles from where we camped last night," Vernon said. "So I don't reckon we'll be campin' by that river tonight, will we?"

"That's right, Vernon, I'm just hopin' we get every one of these wagons down offa this hill today," Grissom answered. "There's a nice little creek near the bottom of the hill and I expect we'll be ready to camp when we reach that." He took a look at his pocket watch then and added, "I expect we'd best get started, folks. And remember, some of those sections of road are pretty steep, so slow and easy will get you down faster. Anybody who don't have to ride, might be better off if they walk down. Everybody remember the number twelve. If you start with the first curve you come to and count every one after that till you hit curve number twelve, that's when you need to take it really slow goin' around that one."

"What if you can't count that high, Grissom?" Henry Corbett asked.

"You can let your missus handle that for you, Henry," Grissom replied.

The descent from Emigrant Hill began at a few minutes after one o'clock as Ike started his horses down the narrow road toward the first turn. It was a road that Ike had driven before, so he gave it the respect he knew it demanded. It was because of his respect for the road that the wagons following behind him were able to proceed without serious problems. Soon, as more of the wagons followed, they took on the appearance of a great serpent winding its way down the hill in the eye of a hawk circling high overhead. So many of the sharp bends in the road were not level, causing the wagon to lean away from the hill as it went around the turn. Consequently, the great serpent would slow down even more at some points, then pick up the pace a little at others.

Overall, Grissom couldn't be more pleased with the progress, again thanks to Ike's experience. He remained at the top of the hill until the last wagon started down. Then he rode his buckskin down the road to be at the bottom when Ike arrived. With barely enough room to pass on the narrow road, he encouraged each driver as he went past each wagon. When he passed Elmo Steptoe, he couldn't help but notice that Elmo was sweating profusely. "You doin' all right, Steptoe?" Grissom asked. Steptoe didn't answer but nodded, his eyes glued to Bowen's wagon ahead of him. Grissom decided he was making him nervous, so he said, "You're doin' fine, just don't let your horses get up too close to Bowen." He rode on then until he finally caught up with Ike.

"How we doin'?" Ike called out to him when he came up beside him.

"Everything looks good," Grissom replied. "Just keep that

pace you've set and we might make it down without losin' anybody." As soon as he said it, he wished he hadn't. Ike still had a
long way to go and he was afraid he might have skunked himself,
saying something like that.

Still, everything continued smoothly, even though the wagons
tended to lean away from the hill on some of the curves, instead
of leaning into the curve. Then the hawk circling high overhead
noticed a gap in the body of the serpent. It was between Bowen's
and Steptoe's wagons. Remembering Grissom's caution not to run
up on Bowen's wagon, Elmo reined his horses back a little more
than before. It gave him a safer feeling as his wagon bumped and
bounced over the rocky trail, so he reined them back a little
more. In the wagon behind him, Quincy Lewis noticed they
were beginning to really slow down. At first, he just figured the
whole column was slowing down. Then, coming out of a double
curve, he saw the wagons up ahead and the large gap that now
existed between Steptoe and Bowen. He stood up then and
shouted, "Hey, Steptoe! Wake up! You're gettin' behind!"

Steptoe heard Quincy and reacted right away, whipping his
horses to catch up, which was the wrong thing to do when entering curve number twelve. A nasty curve that turned a sharp
angle, coupled with the bed of the road that slanted away from
the hill. There was no way Steptoe's bouncing wagon could stay
on it. His three girls started out in the wagon but had soon gotten
out and begun walking down the hill when they decided the ride
in the wagon was too uncomfortable. Elmo's wife, Cora, was in
the wagon seat beside him when they entered the curve and the
two wheels close to the side of the hill came off the road. Leaning severely, the wagon continued around the curve on two
wheels as Cora scrambled to the high side in an attempt to hold
the wagon down with her ninety-eight-pound body. Elmo managed to stop the horses before the wagon toppled over, but it was
still balanced on two wheels and showing a tendency to want to
go on over on its side. When Irene, the Steptoes' fifteen-year-old

daughter, saw her mother clinging to the side of the wagon, she yelled to her two younger sisters, "Come on!" And she ran to the wagon to hang on the side. Her sisters, Millie, twelve, and Cassie, ten, understood, so they followed her, grabbing any handhold they could find. The wagon was still balanced on two wheels until Quincy jumped down from his wagon and ran to help. His weight was enough to bring the wagon back down on all four wheels.

Up ahead of Steptoe's wagon, Frank Bowen was unaware of Steptoe's trouble until he happened to take a look back and saw the gap between them and the wagon up on two wheels. He immediately yelled to a man named Claude Varner ahead of him that Steptoe's wagon was about to go over. Then he stopped his wagon to see if he could help Steptoe. Varner yelled the news about Steptoe's problem ahead to the wagon in front of him, and the incident was passed down the whole line of wagons until it reached Grissom, who was riding beside Ike in the first wagon. By the time the news reached Grissom, however, the report was that Steptoe's wagon had turned over but it was not known if anyone was killed. So Grissom immediately turned his buckskin around and hurried back up the line of wagons.

The only people who were unaware of Steptoe's problem were Clay and Worley and that was because they had volunteered to take care of the herd of extra horses. They drove them down the hill before the wagons started down, all the way to the creek Grissom wanted to camp beside that night. Even had they known, they would not have left the horses unguarded while they rode back up the hill. Grissom's fears were dissolved when he climbed the hill again to find Elmo Steptoe on the driver's seat of his wagon and the wagon riding right side up down the narrow trail. "You're too late, Grissom!" Quincy yelled at him. "The Steptoe girls saved the wagon!"

The last wagon rolled up to complete the circle by the creek at a few minutes before five o'clock with the driver fully ready to call it a day. This in spite of having done no more in half a day than to come down a hill. Grissom was quick to applaud them and remind them they drove seven miles of twisted hell to come down that hill. "Tomorrow, we'll strike the Umatilla River in about ten or twelve miles and we'll follow it for the rest of the day." He told them that the next eight and a half to nine days would be the time it would take them to cross the northern part of the Columbia Plateau. "I ain't gonna lie to ya, a good part of it is little more than a desert, dry and dusty with only a tree here and there on our drive to the Columbia River. Once we get there and cross the Deschutes River, you're gonna be done with the desert."

"That don't sound like we're gonna be enjoyin' ourselves for the next eight or nine days, does it?" Vernon asked John Henry when they were getting their instruments tuned up for the social hour.

"It kinda reminds me of the first look we got of the Platte River Valley," John Henry answered. "Flat and dry, with no grass and no trees, but Lordy, I hope the water's better than the Platte."

They followed the Umatilla River for the next three days until it took a turn due north and they continued in a more westerly direction on their way to a later rendezvous with the mighty Columbia River. After passing through an area of thick, high grass, they spent the next few days crossing the high tableland above the Columbia. It was a dead land, desertlike with little water and no grass, and morale was rapidly sinking to a new low. Morale improved just a little when they crossed the John Day River and made their camp on the west bank. Grissom told them they were only a little over twenty miles from their first look at the Columbia River. The social hour that night was a great deal more cheerful than recent nights and lasted a little longer.

Anxious to get started the next morning, since there were only twenty miles to the Columbia, they started a little before seven, with many of the emigrants in favor of pushing the horses this one time to make that twenty miles in one day. There were a smaller number who opposed the idea, including the wagon master. "With the scarcity of water and grass for the past week, your horses are not in any shape to go twenty miles today," Grissom told them.

In support of Grissom, Matt Moran spoke up. "When we had water and grass, how many days did we make twenty miles?" He waited for an answer but there was none. "That's right," he said, "not a damn one."

"Matt's right," John Henry Hyde said. "I'm as anxious to get to Oregon City as the rest of you. But I want my horses to get there, too."

"Hell," Ike announced, "there's a right nice little creek about fourteen miles from here. We camped there last year. I'm hopin' my horses can make it there by quittin' time. I expect that's where I'll be campin' tonight." He wasn't being entirely truthful. Like Matt and Grissom, he didn't want to push tired horses to go twenty miles, even though they could do it, unless it was absolutely necessary. He was against it because he knew twenty miles would take them to the high plateau overlooking the Columbia River. And he didn't want to camp up there where there was no water or firewood.

Clay looked at Ike and said, "I'll keep you company tonight, partner." Even as he said it he was thinking, with the shape those horses are in, they look more like a fourteen-mile day.

They left the John Day crossing following a road that headed in a more northerly direction. The road was not difficult and the women and children who normally walked gave no indication that the wagons were moving any slower or faster than they normally did. When it was time for the nooning, they continued for almost two miles more before finding a stream big enough to water the horses. After the midday nooning, they pushed on once again, and when five o'clock found them still short of Ike's choice of camping sites, they pushed on for the additional mile to reach the creek. It was obvious to everyone that the horses had voted for Ike's choice of camping sites. And with a journey in the neighborhood of only six miles or so in the morning before their first glimpse of the Columbia River, the level of excitement was elevated once again.

Grissom and Ike were not surprised by the emigrants' feelings of accomplishment. Back in the spring, when they left Independence, Missouri, the Columbia River was a goal eighteen hundred miles distant. In fact, the point at which they would strike the Columbia was only about twenty miles east of The Dalles, which at one time was thought to be the end of the Oregon Trail. That, however, was no longer the case. The goal of this wagon train was Oregon City, an additional one hundred-plus miles beyond The Dalles on a trail around Mount Hood which was both rugged and dangerous. "But why spoil their feelings of accomplishment by tellin' 'em how hard it's gonna be on the Barlow Road?" Grissom thought aloud.

"That's right," Ike agreed. "Hell, they're gonna be disappointed enough when they get their first look at the Columbia River tomorrow."

"They always are," Grissom agreed.

The conversation that night at the social hour was again more of a positive nature with the anticipation of reaching the Columbia River literally only hours away. It would signal the end of the long crossing of the barren tableland and day after day of dry, dusty roads with seldom a tree in sight. It had been hard on the horses and hard on the people as well. Grissom had told them that the land they saw after the Columbia would be more like the land they longed to see. The visiting broke up a little earlier that night than usual, as it typically did when there was something to look forward to the next day.

The wagons rolled away from the little creek right on schedule at seven o'clock the next morning, following a road that looked little different from the roads they had followed since leaving

Emigrant Hill. Even after a couple of hours, there was no sign of a river up ahead of them. Then, after another half an hour, Grissom pulled his horse to a stop while Ike continued on, following a trail that appeared to go down into a ravine. Driving half a dozen wagons behind Ike, Matt Moran said to Clay, who was riding the gray beside the wagon, "Looks like he's tellin' everybody something." All the people walking seemed to stop to gawk at something Matt nor Clay could see.

"I'll go see what's goin' on," Clay decided, and rode on up ahead. When he rode up beside Grissom, he saw the cause of all the discussion. They were looking at the river several hundred feet below the tableland they had been traveling for days. Flowing deep in a gorge was the Columbia River.

Julie Batson, who was one of the walkers, looked up at Clay and commented, "It sure isn't what I had pictured paradise to look like."

"I guess I had a different picture in my mind, too," Clay replied.

"Come on, girls," Julie said to her daughters, "Daddy's getting ahead of us." She hurried them along to follow the wagon, already dropping out of sight.

"Kinda disappointin', ain't it?" Grissom said.

"I reckon," Clay answered.

"It's always the same. Folks think they're gonna see the land of plenty they've been pinnin' their hopes on. And first sight of the river being squeezed out of a gorge a couple of hundred feet below 'em ain't what they came all this way to see. It'll look better when they get down there beside it."

"I reckon," Clay said again, not really having formed a picture of it beforehand, himself. Instead of riding back to tell Matt, he decided to wait for him there.

"What is it, Clay?" Katie asked when she walked up with Sarah and Hannah. When Clay said it was the Columbia River, she stood gazing at it for a long time before turning to Matt in the wagon and saying, "Well, that sure is disappointing, isn't it?" Matt shrugged, indifferently. Katie picked up Hannah and handed her to Matt. "She's tired of walking. Come on, Sarah, looks like we're going down to the river."

"Where's Jim?" Matt asked.

"He and Skeeter Tatum went down to the river with Ike's wagon," Katie told him.

Matt started his horses again and turned to ask Clay when he came up beside him, "Where's Worley this mornin'? I ain't seen him all mornin'."

"Probably down by the river," Clay replied. "He left right after breakfast. Said he was gonna go on ahead of us."

Grissom had not deceived them. It was quite different when they descended to the river below the high tableland they had been traveling. The road now ran along the bank of the powerful river and there were trees and green grass. Ike kept going for a couple of miles before coming to a wide pasture-like area that looked as if it had been used as a campground before, with plenty of wood for fires and grass for the horses. The wagons were formed up in the circle there for the nooning. Clay helped Matt unhitch the horses and get the wagon in place. While they were doing that, Worley rode up. Hanging from his saddle horn was a string of sizable fish. "Well," Clay said, "I reckon I don't have to ask you how your mornin's been goin' so far. Those are some nice-lookin' fish. You look like you've got enough to eat and some to share."

"I already gave some to Grissom and Ike," Worley said. "I told 'em they have to clean 'em. I ain't gonna clean 'em." Seeing the string of fish, Katie walked over then to get a closer look. "I'll clean ours, though," he said to her.

"Bless your heart," Katie said. "Don't you worry, Worley, we'll help you clean the fish. I can hardly wait to taste one. Thank you, Worley."

"We better get movin', then," Matt said, "if we're gonna cook 'em for nooning. Clay, if you'll cut some wood and get a fire started, I'll help Worley clean the fish." The typical time for nooning was one hour, so everybody hustled to try to get all the fish cooked. The only regret was that Worley hadn't waited until suppertime to catch the fish.

But then Grissom came around to each wagon to tell them they would be staying there all night due to how difficult it would be to cross the Deschutes River. "I want to have the whole day to make this crossin'," he told them. "It might not take that long, and I hope it don't, but I want the day in case we have trouble. So we might as well stay right here. We're less than three miles from the river. Now, you can pay these Indians that live near here to ferry your wagon across, just like you did at Old Fort Boise. But these Indians here are gonna charge you five bucks to take you across. What makes this crossin' so hard is the fact that it's right at the place where the Deschutes comes off the Columbia and it's about a hundred and fifty yards across where the road is. There's an island in the middle, but the dangerous part is the rocks on the bottom of the river. You see, the Columbia is so strong that it forces its way through these rocky gorges, breakin' off pieces of rocks. And it forces a lot of these big hunks of rock into the mouth of the Deschutes, so they're movin' around on the bottom. I'm gonna ford this river just like I've done with any river, but I can pay one of these Indians to show me a path across where there ain't no rocks. That's what these Indians do. They swim across the river and see where any big rocks are. They go underwater and see if any big rocks have been moved by storms and high water. But like I said, if you'd rather pay to have them take your wagon across on a bullboat, that's up to you." He started to move on to the next wagon but paused when he thought to say, "There is one more option. If you'd like to make the money I'm gonna pay an Indian, you can swim across that river and spot the rocks. But that water is mighty chilly this time of year." Then he laughed at his humor and went on to the next wagon.

"Good news and bad news," Matt said. "The river might be a dangerous crossing, but we've got all night to cook the fish. And I suspect the real reason we're stayin' right here is because Grissom wants time to clean and cook the fish Worley gave him."

After Clay cut enough wood for their fire, he went down to the water's edge where Matt and Worley were cleaning the fish. "I came to help," he said, "but it looks like you're almost done."

"I was savin' this last one for you, just to see if you knew how to clean a fish," Matt said.

"Is that a fact?" Clay responded. "Well, you ain't gonna find out whether I can or not 'cause I ain't gonna mess up my knife for one fish."

When all the fish were cleaned, it was obvious that they had more than they could eat, for the fish were sizable as well as many. So Katie kept one fish for each of them and gave the rest to the wagons on either side of theirs.

The next morning, they hitched up and drove the wagons the short distance to the Deschutes. As Grissom had predicted, there were at least forty or fifty Indians waiting there for them. There were a few of the emigrants who joined Henry Corbett and paid the five dollar fee to be ferried across the river, but not as many as had joined him at the Snake and the Thomas Fork Crossing. Grissom told Corbett to drive his wagon up on the high bluff when they reached the other side and the rest of the wagons would join them there.

Then Grissom took his business to the young men and the boys. He looked over the crowd of faces eager to earn the money for providing a safe passage, trying to see if he could recognize the face of the young man who guided him the year before. He was about to flip a coin when one young man smiled and said, "Mr. Grissom, I am Lame Bear. I guide you good?"

"Lame Bear!" Grissom exclaimed. "You've grown a foot or more. I didn't recognize you. Yes, you guided me good. You want to guide me again?"

"Yes, I guide."

"Same price as last year? Or have you gone up in price?"

"For you, same price."

"That's more than fair," Grissom said. "Have you been in the water to find the rocks?"

"Yesterday," Lame Bear answered. "I will go in the river now, make sure nothing move."

"Good man," Grissom said. "I'll tell you what I'll do. If all my wagons get safely across the river, I'll pay you the money and I'll make you a present of a bay horse." Lame Bear's surprised reaction told Grissom that he was overjoyed. The young man had worked so hard to make sure his path was clear last year that Grissom wanted to reward him. He decided to give him one of the Shoshone ponies, the bay, that belonged to one of the two would-be horse thieves at Emigrant Springs.

"I will search every foot of the river bottom," Lame Bear declared. "If a rock has moved, I will know it." Then he hesitated when he thought of something. "What if wagon falls off ferryboat?"

Grissom laughed. "That's not your fault. You just worry about the wagons that drive across the river. Now I need to hire two or three boys who wanna guide the herd of horses across the river."

After Grissom engaged several young boys who looked to be in their teens to swim the horses across, he and Ike, and several of the other men, including Clay and Worley, stood on the bank and watched Lame Bear as he tested the river bottom for rocks or other impediments that might damage a wagon's wheels. He would disappear under the water to look around, then reappear and usually stand up straight to show Grissom how deep the water was at that point. The men watched attentively as the water level began to creep up on Lame Bear's body until he reached the point in the middle of the river where he pretended to stand straight up but sank beneath the water. Anxious to see how far it was before he could stand up again, they then tried to guess about where and about how far the horses might be swimming and the wagons having to float. At about seventy-five yards distant, it was difficult to determine exactly, but Grissom and Ike agreed that it was doable. So, when Lame Bear started back, the men went to their wagons where many of their wives were trading with the Indians for fish.

"You ready, I lead?" Lame Bear asked Grissom when he climbed out of the water. Grissom said that he was, so Lame Bear went to get his horse that was tied to a tree nearby and returned to the riverbank.

Ike pulled his wagon down to the entry point and waited for Grissom to give the signal. Grissom, on his buckskin, rode back to the second wagon and told Vernon Tatum to follow Ike's wagon exactly. "'Cause it ain't a straight path across. It's a little bit crooked because of the rocks on the bottom." Then he gave the signal and Lame Bear started across the river on his horse, and Ike followed, and the column of wagons began the crossing.

Watching from his wagon behind Vernon's, Matt said, "Why didn't the Indian do that in the first place and just lead us across?"

"Because he had to check to make sure none of the big rocks had been moved," Katie answered.

"I knew that," Matt quickly replied, "that's what makes this crossin' so dangerous, the damn rocks rollin' around."

The column of wagons, led by Lame Bear, made the crossing with no difficulties other than some of the wagon boxes taking in a little water during the short time the wagon was floating. They proceeded to climb up from the river to the high bluff on the other side where they waited for the wagons that were being ferried across. Grissom, Clay, and Worley herded the extra horses up on the bluff after they had been guided across the river. Grissom picked the bay gelding out of the herd and presented it to Lame

Bear, along with the regular fee. He appreciated the young man's honest attempt to do a good job, two years in a row for him. And he wasn't sure he would make this trip again.

The nooning was held to rest the horses after their swim and nearly everyone in the wagon train had fish for dinner. Afterward, they started out again to drive the ten-plus miles to reach The Dalles, where they would camp that night.

Chapter 26

In spite of what Grissom and Ike Yocum had told the emigrants about The Dalles, they were all surprised to find a thriving town with many shops and stores, a hotel, several saloons, even a courthouse. It was the only town in this untamed land of the northwest and a town where emigrants, trappers, and gold miners crossed paths. The end of the Oregon Trail for many years, this was the place where the emigrant paid a big price to risk his wagon on a raft to take the perilous journey down the Columbia River, if he desired to go past Mount Hood to the Willamette Valley. The steep, rocky mountain was impassable for horse and wagon. The only land route to Oregon City and the Willamette Valley was a treacherous one hundred-plus mile trail around Mount Hood called the Barlow Road.

So close now to the end of their journey, the town was a welcome sight to many on the wagon train as a place to resupply themselves with exhausted basic items. They circled the wagons in a vacant field beyond the courthouse, primarily to keep their horses from wandering through the town. Grissom said they would stay there for an extra day, so they could do what restocking they had to do. "And don't forget to save some money to pay the toll on the Barlow Road," he said. "And maybe a few dollars to buy a piece of land in the Willamette Valley," he added as a humorous afterthought.

He received a few exaggerated horse laughs for his attempt at humor, and Dick Batson said, "Don't tell Julie, but I was thinkin' about spendin' that money for whiskey tonight at one of those saloons."

"Damn right," Frank Bowen declared. "We sure as hell deserve the right to celebrate what we done, makin' it to The Dalles. I think a little drink of likker would make it official." All the men standing in that little group agreed wholeheartedly, all except one. Harlan Rice didn't disagree with the other men. In fact, he agreed one hundred percent. But he'd made a promise to Annie and he had been sober since Fort Bridger. Listening to the men talking, he remembered how much he used to enjoy a drink of liquor to celebrate an occasion—like the sun coming up, he had to confess. But it had been some time now since he had even thought about taking a drink of whiskey. Of course, there wasn't any whiskey available and that made it a hell of a lot easier. He couldn't help wondering now, however, if he might not be cured of that craving he used to have for whiskey. He might be like most other men now and could take a couple of drinks and be satisfied with that.

"Well, I've made up my mind," Bowen said. "After supper tonight, I'm goin' to have me a drink of whiskey. Anybody wanna join me, I'm gonna go to that first little saloon on the other side of the courthouse, the Rooster or something."

"Red Rooster," Paul Courtland spoke up. "It's called the Red Rooster. I'll join you for a drink and we'll drink a toast to the Barlow Road while we're at it."

"Hell, count me in," Ike Yocum said to everybody's surprise. "I could use a drink tonight."

"All right," Bowen remarked, "we're gonna have the number one wagon with us. Now, don't nobody go sayin' anything about this to the women. Just tell 'em you're goin' to get some smokin' tobacco."

"I reckon we'd better go to supper now," Paul Courtland said and the group dispersed. As they walked away, he asked Dick Batson, "You reckon we shouldn't have said any of this with Harlan Rice standing there?"

Batson thought about it for a moment before answering. "I don't know. You know, I thought about his problem with the bottle, but he's give it up, ain't he?"

"He said he has," Courtland replied.

"Well, he just won't show up then. It's up to him whether he wants a drink or not. It ain't up to the rest of us to butt in, anyway. If he shows up, ain't none of us gonna try to make him take a drink."

"And we ain't gonna tell him not to take a drink," Courtland added. "He can do what he wants."

Batson had to laugh then. "Well, I'm glad we got that all straightened out. Now we'd best get the word to the rest of the fellows not to complain about Grissom, since we're gonna have Ike Yocum join us."

"Maybe we shoulda told Ike this party's for customers only," Courtland said.

With supper finished and the pots and pans all cleaned up, Annie Rice walked out in the middle of the circle of wagons and sat down next to Molly Tatum. "Where's Vernon and the boys? Aren't they gonna play any music tonight?"

"Oh, they'll be here in a little bit," Molly said. "Some of 'em wanted to go have a drink to celebrate us getting to The Dalles. Having a boys-night-out affair, I guess." She laughed and added, "Vernon won't have more than one or two. He can't play the fiddle if he has more than that. Where's Harlan? Did he go with 'em?"

"No," Annie said. "Harlan went to buy some smoking tobacco. He'll probably be back any minute now." She tried to keep the frown from her face as she silently prayed he would show up with nothing but tobacco on his breath.

"Oh, there's John Henry," Molly said when she saw the big strapping banjo player coming from his wagon, banjo in one hand, a stool in the other.

"Evenin', ladies," John Henry greeted them when he walked up and positioned his stool, then propped his banjo on it while he put some more wood on the fire. "These nights are gettin' a touch cold," he remarked. "I believe Old Man Winter is anxious to visit."

"You might have to give a solo performance tonight, if Vernon and the other boys don't show up pretty soon," Molly commented.

John Henry laughed. "I don't know if you'd like that or not. I need Vernon and the guitars to cover up my mistakes."

"I don't believe that," Molly said. "I've heard you playin' solo many a time."

"Where the hell are they?" Annie suddenly blurted. Silently coming to a boil listening to Molly and John Henry babbling silly talk, she wanted to see Harlan and she wanted to see him stone sober. She was afraid that what she feared was coming true the first time he came into contact with temptation. Then she suddenly realized that Molly and John Henry were staring at her. "I'm sorry," she said. "I didn't mean to burst out like that."

"Are you all right, honey?" Molly asked.

"Yes, please forgive me. My mind was just somewhere else and my mouth flew open, I guess," Annie pleaded. "I think I'd best go back to the wagon."

"Are you sure?" Molly asked. "Is there something I can do for you?"

"No, really, I'm fine," she insisted. "Must have been something I ate. That fish probably."

"Are you worried about Harlan?" Molly finally decided to pull the problem out in the light of day.

"Harlan?" Annie reacted. "No. Why would I be worried about Harlan?" She paused when she saw her two daughters coming from the wagon to join her.

"Aren't they gonna play any music tonight?" Alice, her thirteen-year-old, asked when she and her sister came up to the fire. "Yes, they're just a little late getting started tonight," Annie told her. "See, Mr. Hyde is here with his banjo already." She hesitated then as if afraid to ask but then came out with it. "Is your daddy at the wagon?"

"No, ma'am, he ain't back from the store yet," Alice answered. Annie's face immediately reflected her concern, but it was not noticed right away due to the arrival of Vernon Tatum and Bryan Roland with fiddle and guitar. When the three musicians started tuning up their instruments, Molly glanced at Annie and saw the troubled expression still in place. She wondered if she should ask Vernon if Harlan was at the saloon when they were there. And if he was, should she tell Annie. She decided she didn't want to know if he was there or not. It was none of her business.

Like the men he walked into the Red Rooster with, Ike paid for his first drink. He was about to order another one when Harlan Rice walked into the saloon. "Uh-oh," Ike muttered, mostly to himself. "Clay and Matt ain't gonna be too happy to hear about this." He watched to see what Harlan was going to do. Ike knew that he had sworn to his wife that he was giving up drinking after Clay and Matt sobered him up.

Harlan said howdy to Ike and the men he came in with, then promptly ordered a drink of whiskey. The bartender poured one and Harlan paid for it, but he didn't drink it right away. It was still sitting in front of him on the bar when Henry Corbett walked in and ordered a bottle. "Come on, boys, and have a drink on me," he said. "Bring your glasses and we'll drink to celebrate our arrival in The Dalles." He picked up the bottle and a glass and walked over to sit down at a table. The men at the bar were happy to join him. Harlan picked up his shot glass, still filled with whiskey, and went to the table with the others. Only Ike remained at the bar, feeling as if it should be a celebration for the emigrants only.

"Come on, Ike," Corbett called to him, "you're invited, too."

"'Preciate it, Mr. Corbett," Ike responded, "but I told Grissom I'd just be gone long enough to get one drink of likker. He's got somethin' he wants me to do. You fellers enjoy your drinks." He ordered one more shot, tossed it back and left the saloon. Outside, he hurried past the courthouse to the field where the wagons were parked. He wasn't sure there was any cause for alarm, but he thought the situation held the makings of a collapse for Harlan and heartache for poor Annie and the girls. So when he got back to the field, he went straight to Matt Moran's wagon where he found Clay and Worley, too.

"What's up, Ike?" Clay asked.

"Hell, maybe nothin'. I ain't sure," Ike said, "but I thought I oughta tell you and Matt that there might be a good chance that Harlan Rice is gonna get hisself in trouble again." He went on to explain that Harlan hadn't taken a drink by the time he left the saloon to come here, but he had bought one. "Hell, he's got that shot of likker just settin' there on the table in front of him like they's havin' a contest to see who's the strongest, him or the shot of whiskey."

Clay and Matt looked at each other, each one giving the other the chance to speak first. Finally, Clay said, "I'll go and see what he's gotten himself into. But, damn it, it ain't none of my business. If it wasn't for Annie and the two girls . . ." He started but couldn't finish. "How many of our people are there with him?"

"There were five when I left," Ike said.

"You'd think one of 'em . . ." He started again. "Doggone it, I'll go see if there's anything I can do to talk him into going back to his wagon."

"Good man, Clay," Matt japed, "I knew we could count on you. I woulda volunteered to go, but Katie don't like for me to go in saloons."

"You've got it backwards," Clay came back. "Katie doesn't

care if you go to a saloon. You comin' home is the part she doesn't like." He looked at Ike again. "Red Rooster?"

"Red Rooster," Ike echoed as Clay went out the door.

"You fellers on that wagon train that came in today?" Dan Bogart asked Frank Bowen when he walked by the table where Bogart and his friend were sitting.

"That's a fact," Bowen answered, "crossed the Deschutes this mornin' and pulled into The Dalles this evening."

"You gonna be raftin' them wagons down the Columbia?" Bogart asked.

"Shoot no," Bowen replied. "After drivin' those wagons the best part of two thousand miles with everything I own loaded on it, I sure as hell ain't gonna watch it all sink to the bottom of the Columbia River."

"Well, you're gonna play hell tryin' to drive them wagons over that mountain settin' right in front of ya," Bogart said. "Best way is the river and I can give you a good price to raft them wagons, and we ain't never lost a wagon, neither."

"I expect we'll be takin' the Barlow Road around that mountain," Bowen said.

"You'll be makin' a big mistake doin' that," Bogart said. "That's a hundred and fifty miles around that way and the road's so rough that you don't never hear about folks again who try to go that way. Most of 'em perishes because of the dangerous roads or the Injuns."

"I reckon that's the chance we're gonna take," Bowen said, and walked over to join the others who had put two tables together.

"You're makin' a mistake," Bogart called after him, then turned back to talk to his partner. "It was worth a try, I reckon. You know dang well they've got some money if they're fixin' to buy land out here. We need to get our hands on some of it, since we ain't done squat minin' for gold."

"What were you gonna tell him, if he'da started askin' you a bunch of questions about how we was gonna float their wagons down the river?" Jeb Smith asked. A brute of a man, who was not burdened with a great amount of intelligence, Jeb had once killed a man with a single blow of his fist. "I don't know nothin' about raftin' wagons and you don't know as much I do."

"We weren't gonna tell 'em how we were gonna float 'em. We was just gonna take their money in advance and tell 'em when to bring their wagons." Bogart was distracted then. "What the hell is he doin'?" He pointed to Harlan Rice, sitting at one side of the two tables, staring at a shot glass filled with whiskey. The rest of the five men were tossing back shots one of them was pouring from a bottle, until the bottle was empty. But the one man staring at the drink in front of him seemed unaware of the drinking going on around him. "He's tetched in the head," Bogart said.

"Anybody that needs another drink is gonna have to pay for it, himself," Corbett announced. "I'm not buyin' but one bottle, and now I'm goin' back to the wagon."

"Me, too," Bowen said. "That's all I wanted and I thank you again for your generosity," he said to Corbett. All the others followed suit with the exception of Harlan Rice and he remained seated, still staring at the one shot of whiskey left to be consumed. "You comin', Harlan?" Bowen asked as they all filed out toward the door.

"I'll be along directly," Harlan answered. Then when Bowen started to walk away, Harlan stopped him. "Frank, did anybody at this table see me take a drink?"

"Why, no," Bowen said. "I don't know how they could have. There's your one glass of whiskey still settin' right there."

"I want to sit here a little bit longer." Harlan said. "I'll see you back at the social hour."

"Right," Bowen said, and hurried along then to catch up with the others.

Interested spectators to the unusual conversation and especially the weird individual seemingly hypnotized by the shot of whiskey, Bogart and Jeb went over to Harlan's table. "Howdy, pilgrim," Bogart said. "I couldn't help noticin' you was havin' trouble knowin' what to do with that shot of whiskey, so I'm gonna help you." He reached down, picked up the glass and tossed it back. "See, there weren't nothin' to it." He looked at Jeb and the two of them chuckled over it. When Harlan was obviously distressed by his uninvited gesture, it seemed to please the two strangers. "What's the matter, pilgrim? Ain't you got no money to buy you another drink to look at?"

"Yes, I've got money to buy another drink," Harlan responded. "That ain't the point."

Bogart looked at Jeb and grinned when he said, "That's where you're wrong, pilgrim. That is the point. Come on, we'll go outside and get some fresh air." He grabbed one of Harlan's arms and Jeb grabbed the other one. They lifted him up out of the chair, then walked him toward the door, his feet barely touching the floor. They almost ran into someone coming in the front door.

"Why, thank you very much, gentlemen, I'll take him from here," Clay told the two puzzled abductors. "You ready to go home, Harlan?"

"I damn sure am, now that I see you," Harlan's sober voice confirmed.

Bogart and Jeb were confused for a brief moment, still holding on to Harlan. "It's all right," Clay said. "You can let him go. I'll take him from here."

"Who the hell are you?" Bogart demanded.

"I told you, I'm the man who came to get Harlan, so how 'bout lettin' go of him."

Bogart and Jeb looked at each other, amazed that the brash young man was challenging the two of them. So Bogart turned back to Clay and said. "Us and Harlan's got some business to talk over, and if you don't want your back broke, I expect you'd best turn around and make some tracks."

"He ain't got any business with you two. Ain't that right, Harlan?" Clay asked.

"Damn right that's right," Harlan said at once, and tried to pull himself free but was unable to.

"All right, mister, you had your chance," Bogart said. "Jeb, you wanna move him outta our way? I've got hold of ol' Harlan."

"I'd love to," Jeb replied, grinning with the anticipation of demonstrating his brutal strength. Thinking to take Clay out with one punch, he stepped toward him and threw his haymaker right cross. But Clay ducked under it and came up with his knee between the brute's legs, causing Jeb to double up with pain and crash to the floor. He was quick enough to avoid the knockout punch, but not quite quick enough to keep from having his leg pinned by the massive body.

Stunned for a moment by Jeb's disastrous attempt to crush Clay's skull, Bogart didn't act. But when he saw Clay struggling to get his leg out from under Jeb, he pushed Harlan aside and drew his pistol and aimed it at Clay. Before he could pull the trigger, however, he was hit flush in the face by Harlan's fist, causing him to stagger backward a couple of steps. That was enough time for Clay to free himself and charge into him, taking him to the floor where he dropped the gun. "Pick it up!" Clay yelled to Harlan. Then he hustled over and pulled Jeb's gun from the suffering brute's holster. "Let's go," he said to Harlan. Then to Bogart, who was still sitting on the floor in a daze, he said, "We'll leave your guns out in front."

They hurried out of the Red Rooster and dropped the two guns in the watering trough in front of the building, then hustled up the street past the courthouse. Clay glanced at Harlan, who was grinning like a schoolboy playing hooky. "You know, you probably saved my life when you punched that fellow. I was hung up under that big ox and his partner was fixin' to shoot me till you hit him."

Harlan fairly beamed when Clay said it, but he tried to act as if it was not an unusual thing for him to do. "I reckon I couldn't let him shoot you after you came to help me," he said. "Those two were pretty rough-lookin' characters."

"Yes they were, but we took care of 'em, didn't we?" Clay responded, continuing to feed Harlan's ego, since it was obvious that Harlan needed it.

They walked on for a few minutes longer before Harlan asked, "Did you come to the Red Rooster looking for me?" Clay admitted that he did. "Why?" Harlan asked.

"Ike was worried about you," Clay answered. "He said everybody else was drinkin' whiskey, but you just sat there and stared at a glass of it, like you were in a trance or something. So I decided I'd just make sure you were all right."

Harlan considered that for a few moments then said, "That's the second time you've come to get me when I got myself in trouble. You're the best friend I've ever had, and I want you to know that this time when I got in trouble, it wasn't because I did anything wrong. The only thing is, I shoulda got up and left that saloon with everybody else. But Clay, for the first time since I can remember, I was feelin' good about myself. I was settin' there, starin' at that glass of whiskey, knowin' that I didn't want it and I could set there for the rest of the night if I wanted to. And I'd never drink it. And I never did. You can smell my breath, if you want to."

"I druther not," Clay said, "but I'll take your word for it. I expect Annie is sure gonna be proud of you. When we get back to the wagons, you need to give her a great big kiss and let her find out that way that you didn't take a drink."

"That's what I'll do," Harlan said, thinking about her reaction.

Clay realized that he was experiencing some good feelings over Harlan's change also, and he planned to help him upgrade his image with the rest of the emigrants on the train. The social hour was underway by the time Clay and Harlan returned to the wagons. They stopped by Harlan's wagon first and found that Annie and the girls were out by the fire, so they went to find them. They found Annie sitting with Molly Tatum, and Alice and Jenny were close by. Annie spotted the two men when they were halfway across the circle of wagons, and even at that distance,

Clay could see her body suddenly tense and her expression go blank. He slowed his pace a little then to let Harlan arrive ahead of him, afraid that Annie would look to him first to get a clue for how bad the news was going to be.

Harlan walked up before Annie and extended his hand. She hesitated to take it, not sure how drunk he was. But he insisted silently, motioning with his extended hand until finally she took it. He gently pulled her to her feet, then pulled her close up against his body and before she could avoid it, planted a passionate kiss on her lips. She jerked her head back, unsure, and looked at his smiling face, and realized there was no evidence of alcohol. She threw her arms around his neck and returned his kiss with joyful passion, fully aware of what this meant. Vernon Tatum realized he was playing solo when the other instruments suddenly stopped in the middle of the tune and everyone started to applaud. When he looked around and discovered what the applause was for, he pulled his fiddle from under his chin and clapped as well.

"Now, that's how I wanna be welcomed when I come home," Frank Bowen called out.

"I reckon you do," Doris Bowen sang out, "but I doubt you can talk Annie into it."

After a while, the musicians took a break and the social hour turned into a general visiting time. Bowen, Courtland, Corbett, and the others who were at the Red Rooster all approached Clay to find out how he happened to be with Harlan and if he met up with him in the saloon. Clay was happy to give them the complete story of the trouble with the two men who had been sitting at a table near theirs. "I just happened by and thought I'd go in and see what the Red Rooster looked like. You'd think I'd learned by now from this wagon train that saloons are one of the most dangerous parts of the journey. Well, these two fellows took a notion to rob Harlan, so they jumped him when he was just sittin' at the table doin' some thinkin'. When I got there, it evened things up, two against two. Although that one fellow was so big you had to count him as two. Well the whole story boils down to the fact that Harlan and I got the best of them, but the one fellow pulled his gun and was fixin' to shoot me. And he woulda killed me but Harlan gave him a punch right on the nose and sat him down. So Harlan saved my life tonight. Oh, and he never did take that drink of likker. He said he's found out that stuff affects your reflexes."

The little group of men were impressed to hear about the incident. "You think you know a man," Frank Bowen said. Clay decided he would let Annie know about Harlan's bravery when he got the chance.

Chapter 27

The next day was spent resupplying basic needs and doing any repairs needed on the wagons. Both Clay and Harlan were especially alert for any sighting of Dan Bogart or Jeb Smith, but there was none. The day passed without incident, followed by a peaceful night, and the wagon train pulled out of The Dalles the next morning on their way to the Barlow Road. The road was said to be eighty miles, but Grissom figured it was more like one hundred and twenty by the time all the extra miles were added just to reach the real road. They started south on a hilly trail that led to a small but fertile valley called the Tygh Valley where the trail turned sharply to the west at Gate Creek. After a short ten miles they reached what was the original toll gate to use the road, but the toll gate had long since been moved high up in the mountains. Another twenty miles or so would signal the start of the ordeal that defined the Barlow Road as the emigrants challenged Barlow Pass. At the pass, the difficult part of the Barlow Road began, with steep climbs up rugged, rocky trails that sometimes required doubling the teams on some of the wagons. Before reaching Barlow Pass, however, the emigrants would make reasonable progress on roads that were not difficult to travel, so Grissom pushed to get an extra mile or two each day. With that in mind, he also had to allow for the fact that there was no good forage along the rocky trails the horses would be traveling.

The days that followed were unlike any they had experienced to this point in their journey. They had conquered the crossing of the Hill and the smoky climb up the Burnt River Valley, the lowering of their wagons down Windlass Hill, as well as the hair-raising drive down Emigrant Hill. But the steep, rocky trails they were following now had the added peril of a light dusting of snow, enough to add a slippery effect to the road. As a consequence, the use of a double team of the horses was necessary a lot more often than would have been the case had the road been dry. But it was even more dangerous when descending a steep section of the trail.

Painfully slow was the daily progress of the wagons as they struggled to climb the rugged mountains around the south side of Mount Hood. There was no circling of the wagons for men and horses at the end of each exhausting day. The wagon train simply stopped in place on the narrow trail. And the nightly social hour was a forgotten pleasure. The only enthusiasm was for crawling into the blankets and going to sleep. This was the state of their minds when they went into camp on the summit of Laurel Hill with plans to descend the infamous hill in the morning. "This is the place that makes me ask myself why I keep making this trip every year," Grissom remarked to Ike as they stood looking down the steep decline.

"Hell," Ike replied, "every time I see it again, I wonder if we ain't both crazy. I swear it looks steeper than it did last year."

"I see about five chutes this year," Grissom said, referring to the deep tracks carved out of the earth by the wagons sliding down the two thousand feet to the base of the hill. "I don't think there were but about three last time."

"Please tell me we took a wrong turn back there and we ain't supposed to drop off this cliff in the mornin'," Henry Corbett cracked when he walked up to join the small group of men gathered there.

"That's a fact, Henry," Paul Courtland said. "Right now, we're tryin' to figure out how to turn the wagons around on this little trail."

"The only trouble with that is I don't think I'd wanna try to go down some of the trail we just came up," John Henry Hyde declared.

Starting early in the morning, the wagons, with all four wheels tied so they couldn't roll, were lowered over the brow of the hill with ropes wrapped around a sturdy tree. Other methods were tried as well. John Henry felled a forty-foot fir tree and tied it to his wagon as an extra brake when his wagon dragged it down one of the chutes. Elmo Steptoe, afraid his horses would be injured, wanted to unhitch them and lower his wagon backward on ropes. Grissom talked him out of it. He told him that some folks had done it that way, but there were more cases of runaway wagons crashing down the mountain than of horses. Guessing Elmo's real reason for his suggestion was his fear of driving the horses on that descent, Ike volunteered to drive them down. The descent of the hill took the entire day and daylight was fading when the last wagon was safely lowered to the bottom.

About five miles from Laurel Hill, they came to the Barlow Road tollgate, where they were charged five dollars per wagon and ten cents for livestock. From there they continued on to cross the Sandy River and on to the Devil's Backbone, a long steep ridge that took them back across the Sandy River, past Eagle Creek and one more river to cross, the Clackamas. From there, it was an easy road to Oregon City.

It was a little before two o'clock in the afternoon when Clay rode up beside Grissom at the head of the wagon train. "How much farther is it to Oregon City?" Clay asked.

"'Bout three miles," Grissom said. He looked over at Ike. "Wouldn't you say, Ike?"

"Hell, if it's that far," Ike said.

"Much obliged," Clay said, and wheeled his horse around and rode back to his brother's wagon. Pulling up beside Matt, he said,

"Switch over with me. Let me drive the wagon. You take my horse and ride on into Oregon City. It ain't but three miles." When Matt acted as if he didn't understand, Clay explained. "When this train rolls into town, there's gonna be twenty-four folks hurryin' to the land office. If you ride on ahead you'll be first in line."

"Damn, I hadn't thought of that," Matt said, then hesitated. "Why me? You want land, too. Why don't you ride on in and maybe you can get mine, too, if they'll let you."

"I'd rather you get to see what's available and get what you think is best for you. You've got a family. You're the farmer. You'd know more about what you need. I can get by with anything. So let's swap and I'll drive your wagon on in." He could see Matt trying to decide. "Don't forget to take the money with you. If they'll let you get a parcel for me, too, then get the one next to yours. But take the best one available for you and Katie and the kids."

"Katie!" Matt called out to her. She was walking on the other side of the wagon and when she came up beside the wagon, he told her to hop on. "Get that wallet with the land money in it," he said. "Clay's gonna drive you on in." She sensed his urgency, so she didn't question his purpose and went immediately to fetch it.

Then without stopping, Clay and Matt switched places and Clay stood on the side of the wagon, holding the gray's reins until Matt stepped over into the saddle. "Good luck," Clay said as he handed him the reins. Then he settled himself in the driver's seat and took the reins from Katie.

"It's a wonder both of you didn't break your necks," Katie said. "Now, what was all that about?" He told her what the plan was then and she said, "Good idea. It was worth the risk. I hope today ain't Sunday."

"I do, too," Clay said. "I didn't think about that."

Matt passed Grissom and Ike at a comfortable lope. He called out as he loped past, "I'll tell 'em you're comin'."

"Hell," Ike swore, "that's Clay's horse. What you reckon he's doin'?"

Grissom chuckled and answered, "Goin' to the land office, I'd bet."

Robert Campbell was happy to show Matt the property still available along the Willamette River from the giant plat on the wall of the land office. When Matt told him about the wagon train on its way into town, Campbell knew he might be late going home for supper that night, but he seemed good-natured about it, knowing Matt and the others had just survived the Barlow Road. He even accommodated Matt on his request for the parcel next to the one he was buying. "I'll fix the deeds for both properties, but your brother's won't be any good until he signs it." He chuckled and extended his hand. "But you are a bona fide Oregon landowner. Welcome to Oregon." He even walked outside with Matt and pointed toward the road he would take to find his acreage and told him how far it was from town.

When the wagons arrived, Matt was waiting for them in a large pasture area at the edge of town that Campbell said was the usual camping place for wagon trains. There was water from a creek and trees nearby for firewood. So after they formed a circle for the last time, they took care of the horses before the rush to the land office. Matt and Clay joined the others, but while the others lined up in front of Robert Campbell's desk, Matt signaled him and Campbell waved them up. "Glad to meet you, Mr. Moran," Campbell said. "If you'll just sign this paper here, I'll give you this deed and you're all set. Good luck to you both." They ignored the hissing and booing from the men in line as they walked out.

"We'll just stay here tonight," Matt said when they went outside. "Our land is about eight miles from town. But thanks to Mr. Campbell, we can buy what supplies we need this afternoon and go home in the mornin'."

They made it a point to have one last social hour that night in celebration of a successful arrival in their new land. Most everyone planned to leave in the morning to start their new lives and there were quite a few solid friendships that had formed. Some of them made it a point to buy land near each other. Henry Corbett picked a vacant lot there in town where he planned to build his hardware store and said that he expected to see all of them when he opened it. Harlan and Annie Rice walked over to say goodbye and good luck to Clay. "I wanna thank you, Clay, for everything you've done for me and Annie," Harlan said. "I hope you don't mind, but I consider you my best friend."

"I consider you my friend as well," Clay responded. "I wish you and Annie and the girls the very best of luck." He extended his hand and Harlan shook it. Annie, beaming happily, placed her hand on their two hands.

"Now, let's go before I start bawling," Annie said.

Everyone seemed to be enjoying the last performance by the musicians, with the exception of one person. Worley Branch had been quite content with his journey from Independence Rock, but now the journey had reached its end. He sat off by himself, listening to the music and the noisy chatter of the emigrants talking about their land and what they were going to do with it. His thoughts were interrupted by a voice from behind him. "What are you sittin' over here away from the fire for?"

"Hey, Clay," Worley said. "I was just thinkin' 'bout where I'm gonna go now that we got where we was goin'."

"Oh? Is that so?" Clay asked. "Where were you thinkin' about goin'?"

"I don't know. Just somewhere far away, I reckon, somewhere there ain't nobody else."

"I'm kind of sorry to hear that," Clay said. "I was hopin' you'd wanna come along with me and help me build a cabin on my piece of land. And maybe help Matt get his farm started. But if you've got somewhere you want to go, I can understand."

Worley didn't say anything for a long time, but his eyes grew wider and wider. Finally, he found his voice. "You're japin' me, ain'tcha, Clay?"

"Hell, no, I ain't japin' you," Clay blurted. "I was countin' on you all along. How 'bout it? Can I count on you?"

"You can count on me, Clay," a totally happy Worley answered. "I'd die for you."

"Whoa! We won't take it that far. Just help me build a place where we can both get outta the rain. All right?"

"All right!" Worley responded.

Later that evening, Clay told Matt he'd invited Worley to come along with them in the morning. "I hope that's all right with you. I told him he could stay on my land and help us both, if you want it."

"It don't bother me," Matt said. "I figured he was gonna go with you." He shrugged and added, "I figured if you didn't take him, Katie would."

With morning came the farewells as the Morans and Worley Branch headed down a road that ran south along the Willamette River. They were just one of almost two dozen wagons heading down the road, but they were no longer traveling as a train. And after eight miles Matt Moran's wagon was the first to leave the road when they came to the post bearing his parcel number. Matt's land was divided from Clay's by a nice deepwater creek. There was land in the valley for farming and timber in the hills beyond for building. They all looked at the land waiting to be developed and they were all smiles. Clay looked at his brother and they nodded to each other. They both looked at Katie then and she was beaming with anticipation, and they knew it was good. To confirm it, she declared, "We've finally reached the Promised Land!" Matt drove the wagon to a spot Katie pointed out before getting down and unhitching the horses. They went at once to the creek, so Clay rode the gray to the creek and let him drink with the other horses. He looked around to see what Worley was doing and saw him riding toward the hills. Young Jim was riding behind the saddle.

"They've gone to look for signs of game for supper tonight," Matt told him. "Katie made me park the wagon here because she said this was where the house was gonna be." Clay nodded his understanding.

When the gray finished drinking, Clay forded the creek, thinking to take a better look at his land. He rode all the way across it until he came to a small stream, which, when he recalled the plat he was given, should be the property line. He rode along the stream, following it back into the tree-covered hills. Then he suddenly pulled the gray to a stop when he caught glimpses of a house or barn back in the trees. *My neighbors*, he thought. Not ready to meet his neighbors yet, he wheeled the gray around, then stopped him suddenly again. Standing directly behind him now, holding a shotgun in a threatening position, was a striking young lady with long black hair. "Was there something you were looking for?" she asked. "Maybe I can help you."

"No, ma'am," he said. "I was just looking."

"Do you know this is private property?" the young lady asked.

"Yes, ma'am, I do. As a matter of fact, it belongs to me. If you live in that house in the woods, then I guess I'm your neighbor. I'm sorry if I startled you, but to tell you the truth, Mr. Robert Campbell didn't tell me there was a house built next door. Will you blow a hole in me if I step down from my horse?"

She lowered the shotgun, flustered by his calm demeanor. "Of course not," she stammered. "I'm sorry I threatened you."

He dismounted and said, "My name is Clay Moran and I hope I'll be a good neighbor. Maybe if I call on you again, I will have found the road up to your house, so I could properly introduce myself to your husband and your family."

"Well, I'm sure you would be welcome, Mr. Moran. But you should know that the house belongs to Jack and Elaine Townsend. She's my sister. I'm not married."

Startled for a moment, he fairly blurted, "I'm not, either, which is neither here nor there. But I hope when I do call on your sister and her husband, you'll be there."

She smiled sweetly. "I'm always here. I live here. My name is Penny and I'm pleased to meet you. I hope you find you like it here in the valley."

"Oh, I think I will," he quickly said. *Oh, Lord, maybe this really is the Promised Land.*

Visit our website at
KensingtonBooks.com
to sign up for our newsletters, read
more from your favorite authors, see
books by series, view reading group
guides, and more!

Become a Part of Our
Between the Chapters Book Club
Community and Join the Conversation

Betweenthechapters.net

Submit your book review for a chance to win exclusive
Between the Chapters swag you can't get anywhere else!
https://www.kensingtonbooks.com/pages/review/